Iris of Avalon
By Katrina Rasbold

Book Four of the
SEVEN SISTERS OF AVALON
Series

Text Copyright © 2017 Katrina Rasbold
All Rights Reserved
Published by Rasbold Ink
www.rasboldink.com

ISBN-13: 978-1542370639

ISBN-10: 1542370639

Cover artwork source material by Marina Avila on Deviant Art, spring 2016

Many thanks to William Thomas for his editing

TABLE OF CONTENTS

CHAPTER 1	1
CHAPTER 2	12
CHAPTER 3	24
CHAPTER 4	38
CHAPTER 5	51
CHAPTER 6	62
CHAPTER 7	75
CHAPTER 8	87
CHAPTER 9	102
CHAPTER 10	117
CHAPTER 11	133
CHAPTER 12	145
CHAPTER 13	157
CHAPTER 14	168
CHAPTER 15	180
CHAPTER 16	194
CHAPTER 17	205
CHAPTER 18	215
CHAPTER 19	228
CHAPTER 20	242
CHAPTER 21	257
CHAPTER 22	268
CHAPTER 23	281
CHAPTER 24	294

CHAPTER 25	304
CHAPTER 26	315
CHAPTER 27	328
CHAPTER 28	341
CHAPTER 29	356
CHAPTER 30	368
CHAPTER 31	380
CHAPTER 32	391
CHAPTER 33	403
CHAPTER 34	414
CHAPTER 35	427
CHAPTER 36	438
CHAPTER 37	451
CHAPTER 38	463
CHAPTER 39	474
CHAPTER 40	484

CHAPTER 1

"One, two, three, four..." the crash of thunder that followed the lightning strike caused me to gasp and even to shudder a bit. The storm was drawing closer and what started out as a spring shower was now a deluge. I pulled my heavy cloak tighter, not that the wet fabric offered any true protection from the downpour, but somehow its weight was comforting.

"How long do we wait, Iris?" Laoghaire asked, pulling her pony up alongside mine. I recognized my foolishness in forcing Laoghaire and the horses, not to mention myself, to remain here on the hill overlooking the narrow road into Tintagel. We still had more than an hour's ride before we gained entry and the narrow stone bridge that led to the true ascent to the castle's entrance looked treacherous and foreboding, especially in the rain and dense fog. Naught but my own cowardice and hesitancy to embrace this new and unexpected chapter in my life held me back. I did not want this and could not see the gain in it, yet I was compelled to follow the orders of my parents and the wise ones of Avalon. I was not Aster, who would fight to the death for what she believed in, nor was I Rose, who would argue anyone into the ground who tried to make her do what she did not wish to do. Of all my sisters, I was not the most reticent by far, but I was the one with the greatest capacity for the festering feelings our priestess training intended to train out of us. By the time we took the oath and our mother, as Lady of the Lake, tattooed the blue crescent moon onto the top of our brow, we should above such petty emotions and yet it was my secret embarrassment that there were times when the awful, fetid flower of resentment bloomed fully in my heart.

"Are you afraid?" Laoghaire asked, her eyes seeking out mine and her hands clasped white-knuckled and tense on the reins. "Because I am. I was excited to go see something new, but that place looks more than a scant frightening and we are so very far away from everything. What if it all goes wrong? And there are so awfully many ways it could go wrong."

A wave of irritation came over me, even though she voiced the very thoughts that plagued my own mind.

"Trust in the Goddess and where She leads, Laoghaire." I said, curtly. "The elders would not send us here were it not our destinies, for good or for ill."

"They sent *you* here," she qualified "Not me."

"And where in this process was your free will violated?" I snapped, bothered by the implication almost as much as by weather and my own fears. "As I recall, you jumped at the invitation."

She sighed. "'tis true." Her voice reflected aptly the supreme lack of enthusiasm I felt myself and I felt my cheeks flush with the shame of it, even in the chilly rain. "It is but apprehension that drives me to say such things. This is just so different from home."

She was younger than I by a good three years and one of my finest apprentices. It was rare that I saw her exhibit any sign of insecurity or fear, which was one of the reasons I valued her so in my practice. No matter how challenging a birth might be, I could depend on Laoghaire more than my other two students, to keep a calm head and to never trouble the laboring mother with her own fears and apprehension.

"Why *did* you choose me?" she asked. "I realize I was not your first choice, but why me at all?"

Why indeed. While it was true that she had not been my first choice as a companion on this quest, she was the most reasonable by far.

"No," I admitted, "You were my fourth, but you did make the list, at least. I would take my mother but she must remain on the island to attend to the governing and rulership of the Priestesses. She cannot take indefinite leave of the island and appoint another as Lady of the Lake in her absence and who knows how long we will be gone? Aunt Maia committed to accompany Violet."

"That makes sense," she said. "They have been close for as long as I can remember."

"Since we were born," I agreed.

"What about Belen? I know you are close with her."

I shook my head.

"Belen is far too old, but to be fair, I did ask her." I smiled. "Her eyes twinkled and I know the idea intrigued her, but she could not manage the trip at her age."

Her brow furrowed and I could tell that she tried to imagine who else might have come before her, so I offered her assurances.

"The next and obvious choice was you. You are a clever apprentice and we work well together. Who else for my lady in waiting?"

She laughed at this.

"Is that what I am to be?"

"Unfortunately, in the structure of court, that is what you must be. Even relatives of the Queen may not elevate beyond that position, although they can make a good marriage with men of means and status, if that sort of thing interests you."

Her horse whickered nervously and she patted the side of its neck.

"I think not, but should my mind change, I will let you know."

"Out here," I said, "Girls as young as twelve and thirteen are promised into marriage, so you are quite old to be first wed."

"Ha!" she scoffed. "You are older even than I! An old maid, practically."

"But I am marrying a man previously wed," I pointed out.

"...and who seems to be unmarriageable," she added.

"It is not he who is unmarriageble," I said, "but his daughter who is the problem and that is where you come in."

"Me?" she asked, her eyes widened in surprise. "What have I to do with this beyond helping you get dressed and putting hot bricks at your royal feet at night?"

"You know my patience with young people," I said.

"You mean your lack of patience?" she smiled, eyebrows arched. She shivered in the chilly air and I wondered if her encouragement of the conversation delayed our passage for my benefit or for hers.

"Indeed."

"I remember what you used to tell me that how you could not bear their gooey fingers and dirty feet. That your affinity for them left as soon as they no longer suckled."

"It is true," I said. "My sisters were the opposite. They loved the little ones and said babies all looked the same until they toddled about and took on personalities of their own. It was I who forever skirted duties in the House of Mothers to avoid their neediness and their never-ending stream of questions."

"But the Princess is not a little child. She is nearly a woman grown."

"And that is my plan," I smiled. "She is your age. Perhaps a young woman who is isolated up there," I nodded toward the foreboding castle, "in the far reaches of Britain will appreciate having a young woman her own age around. Perhaps you can even make inroads for me to connect with her."

"Ohhhh," she laughed. "So that is your plan. Well, your mother or Maia or Belen could hardly do that for you."

"No," I agreed, "But they would have their own value. My mother has past-life memories of Cornwall and Tintagel, which would guide me well. Belen and Maia are my mentors and Goddess knows I will need all of the wisdom I can get to navigate this path successfully."

"So memories, wisdom, or child-minding, is it?" she smiled. "And how can you imagine that you do not connect well with young adults? You and I got on well and I have worked with you since my twelfth summer!"

I frowned. "Older children perplex me with their defiance and their odd form of logic, which seems to me like no logic at all. This Princess Eselde has already sent several prospective stepmothers fleeing from their betrothal to her father. I do not wish to be yet another, cannot *afford* to be yet another, so I need your help."

"Ah, so you are spooked by the tales of Lady Lucia from the Summerlands, are you not?"

During the first days of our travel, we stayed the night in the court of Lady Lucia's father, Lord Faraway. Although we never actually saw Lady Lucia herself, she having been whisked away to a convent after her refusal to marry King Marcus, the ladies of the court were all aflutter and eager to regale us with gossip of her adventures while in Cornwall.

"Would you not be?" I asked. "The stories she told were more suited to the highwaymen of the roads than to a young princess raised in court. She fled in the dark of night for fear of her very life!"

"And over that very bridge in the dark, no less." Laoghaire shuddered, likely from the cold as well as from the thought. The bridge looked treacherous as it loomed between us and the castle.

"She must have wanted away very badly," I said, "and she was but the latest in several," I continued. "To my mind, that does not bode well."

"I have heard the King is very handsome," she said, obviously trying to lighten the mood. "And he has ruled for many years, since he was a young man, so he must be quite wise and beloved to keep the throne through these troubled times."

"Or fearsome enough to do so," I groused.

"Well," she smiled, "as long as you are a proper wife who spins a fine thread, embroiders the neatest stitch, throws the best fetes, and squeezes out a litter of royal heirs on schedule, I am sure you will win his favor. You are certainly beautiful enough."

Her sarcastic tone earned a disdainful look from me and she laughed again despite our physical and emotional discomfort. We saw the noble women of the Britain Beyond Avalon as greedy and lazy, expecting the finest accommodations by birthright rather than earning the distinction through any sort of hard work. In contrast, those of us trained on Avalon, as were I and my six sisters as well as Laoghaire, lived our lives immersed in hard work and servitude throughout our priestess training and into our adult lives. From the time we were aged twelve or thirteen years, we faced grueling demands and managed experiences that played hard upon the nerves. Princesses or not, my sisters and I worked and served alongside our non-royal priestess sisters with no luxury afforded to us that was not also offered to them.

None of us could imagine a life with no greater aspirations than to marry well and produce a noble line of children. Nor did we wish to. We were healers, bards, stewards of the land, and even warriors. It was not that we did not crave love and family as did most young women, but we sought life beyond that as well and the idea of limiting our focus to running a household and living subservient to a man was abhorrent to us. On Avalon, men and women were valued equally and there was no gender hierarchy. Here in the Britain Beyond, however, such was not the case.

"Then there is the other task," she said, more serious now. "It is folly for us to attempt to imagine how *that* will unfold."

"Indeed," I nodded. The underlying mission was not only more complicated, but also more secretive and yet it was one laid upon my shoulders and those of each of my sisters regarding our individually assigned kingdoms. I was to find some means to influence King Marcus of Cornwall to end the persecution and forced conversation to Christianity of those people in his lands who still worshiped the Goddess in all Her forms. That would be a bit dicier than reining in his notably rapscallion daughter, especially since he was known to be a devoutly Christian man fully committed to the High Throne's immersion in the Church of Rome.

Could I in fact convince him that tolerance was the higher path? After many years on the throne of

Cornwall, I could not think he would seek to push over the royal apple cart simply in deference to the wishes of his Queen.

"Laoghaire," I said, getting lost in my own thoughts. "How do people back home think of me?"

"Think of you?" she asked, obviously confused by the question.

"What do they say of me? How would they describe me?"

She thought for a moment, whether because she feared to offend me or was genuinely looking for the right words, I could not say.

"Shrewd, I think. Calculating. They know you can aptly size up a situation quickly and quite well, not just as a midwife, but as a strategist."

"I supposed it could be worse," I grumbled.

"Had you hoped for different?"

"Clever, maybe. Wise. Strong. I suppose I will settle for shrewd and calculating. It is better than not being thought of at all."

"I would think those qualities would serve a queen well," she said gently.

I considered her words. "I suspect it depends on the king."

"I think most of this depends on the king," she said. "And we shan't know more about that while shivering on a hill in a thunderstorm." She pulled her cloak around her for what little good it did as water pelted into her face. To punctuate her words, another thunder clap sounded from above us.

"Off we go then," I said, urging the horse on with my heels. The rocky path, for one could hardly call it a road, to Tintagel was almost too narrow for the passage of the wagon's great wheels. Less than a leg's length of clearance on either side had my nerves jumping and the horses shying and fussing, especially with the flowing rainwater sluicing so strong that the stones were nearly obscured. The ledges offered nothing but certain death on each side, either onto rocky crags or into the sea that swept in, bashing against the shore. Thick, foggy mists rose up from the turbulent waves and wrapped around the stone bridge that separated us from the path that led up the steep hill to the courtyard and entrance. I tried to imagine how such a structure could be built, but had to bring my mind back to focus on the task at hand lest I misstep.

    I sent Laoghaire ahead of me since my horse pulled the wagon and under the finest Roman roads, hers got skittish walking behind it rather than side by side or ahead of me. She was less than thrilled with the idea of leading the way, but it was the only reasonable choice. The horses were ill at ease from the storm and I had no mind to agitate them further. Avalon was by truth an island within the embrace of the greater island of Britain and as such, we rarely got thunder and lightning storms. I had seen maybe five or six in my entire life and I was significantly older than the horses, so I could only imagine what the strange energy of the weather oddity did to them. I tried not to take it as an unfavorable omen, but more of an acknowledgment of the gravity of our quest.

    Up and up and up we went. I could see the muscled shoulders of my horse straining to pull even our small wagon up the hill and felt grateful for the many trunks Laoghaire and I chose to leave behind in favor of lighter travel. The beast's feet found uneven, faithless stones on its path and although it trudged forward, its complaints and irritated head shakes increased, almost as if the animal refused its given task and told me "No. No. No."

Ahead of me and through the sheets of rain, I could barely make out Laoghaire's form. Now and then as our individual paces changed, she would come into view and then melt away into the gray mists once more, those so different from the mists that separated Avalon from the rest of the world. These were cold and menacing. The wind whipped hard around our bodies without the cliffs to break its force and it took our full concentration to maintain balance in the gusty gales.

I had no clue of the time of day. It could have been late morning or late afternoon. The clouds and rain stripped away any sense of time and left me feeling as one does when in the Faerie country. That nauseating sense of timelessness and placelessness. If I could not have seen the towers of the fortress of Tintagel ahead, reaching up out of the downpour and eerie waves of fog, I would have no sense of where I was at all.

At some point along the way, I could not say where, I stopped my horse and dismounted, needing a stronger sense of footing and clearance. I led the horse that pulled the wagon and even he seemed to calm a bit with me at the helm. Step by step, we inched our way along the great stone bridge with the wagon creaking in protest behind us. It was not heavily weighted, but the rain had the joints swollen and the wheels fussed as we moved along. I expected at any moment to feel the reins ripped from my hand as a back wheel slipped off the side, taking all of our belongings and the horse with it.

Eventually, the pitch of the hill steepened further, but the reach widened and as the fog momentarily wafted away, I could see that we were now on solid ground rather than bridge. The path was rockier by far and the sea water in the air made the stones slippery under our feet. Although I was in good health and could walk long distances without issue, my calves began to ache from the incline and from so carefully choosing my steps. The wagon behind us pitched and rolled as the poor horse struggled even harder to drag it behind him while his footfalls slipped and shifted.

    At last, the mud under our feet turned to smaller cobblestones and then we were protected from the rain and wind by the overhang of a long entrance way. Looking back, I glanced around the wagon to see just how narrow the stone bridge was that we had just navigated and I shuddered, both inwardly and outwardly, grateful that the passage was over.

CHAPTER 2

I expected we would encounter some form of resistance, yet it was not until we were well into the entryway that two burly looking King's Guard knights stopped us. They were kind enough once I showed them my papers guaranteeing us safe passage through the Summer Country and into Cornwall.

"My Lady," the two knights deferred, bowing slightly. "The King is expecting you."

One of the men took our horses, saddle bags, and wagon, promising to have our belongings sent to our rooms. The other escorted us through the long courtyard and into the castle itself. So few people moved through the courtyard that I was surprised and again, wondered aloud at the time of day as we slodged through the mud and muck.

"Just before the evening meal, My Lady," our escort said. "Our chamberlain will receive you and show you and your woman to your rooms, then bring you right down to be presented if that is not too much of a rush for you."

I looked at back Laoghaire, who now trailed behind me, and she mouthed, "Your woman," and smiled. On Avalon, even though I was of the island's royal blood, she and I were equals as priestesses.

"That is most welcome," I said. "We look forward to a good meal and pleasing company." He led us through a series of winding turns and hallways as he conversed.

"Your trip must have been most taxing with only the two of you," he said. "We thought you would have an entourage."

I shook my head. "We are of strong stock, sir. We have no need for luxuries, but thank you for your concern. Our trip was blessedly uneventful and we are eager to settle in."

"Ah," he said, gesturing to a middle-aged woman who stepped out of the shadows as ascended a large spiral staircase. She looked at me strangely and covered a gasp with her short fingers, then dropped into a deep curtsy.

"This is Bersaba," the knight said, "the wife of our chamberlain, Herschel. Bersaba, this is Lady Iris from Avalon and her woman…"

"Laoghaire," I provided. "And she is not my woman, but my dear friend and traveling companion. I do not require staff. And please rise. I do not stand on such formalities."

The older woman was round and gentle-faced and her eyes crinkled warmly as they met mine and she smiled, slowly returning to a standing position. "I suspect My Lady must adjust her expectations around here," she said. "King Marcus appreciates a well-staffed and formal household and a respectful one as well. Here, allow me to show you your rooms." Her voice was accented, but not with the blunted Cornish dialect I expected. From the countries to the Far East, I wondered?

She led us into a large suite of rooms, easily bigger than the entire cottage my father and mother shared back on Avalon. Elegant furnishing glowed with the luster of polished wood. Silk and damask decorated the chairs and even a fainting couch. We passed through a receiving room and on to a larger sleeping area.

"My Lady Iris's quarters are here and there is a separate set of rooms adjoining for the Lady Laoghaire and any other attendants you may have."

"I have none but she," I repeated.

"We have many here who will gladly serve you," she smiled, "some of whom, like myself, even served the previous Queen."

"I will take my leave of you now," the knight said, bowing. "My Ladies," he nodded in our general direction and we nodded back.

"On a personal aside," Bersaba continued, "I am told these rooms belonged to the Lady Ygraine when she housed here, and I understand she is an ancestor of yours."

"Indeed," I said, both pleased and surprised that my lineage was known, but who would not investigate the birth line of the future Queen of Cornwall? Of course, they would know. They may even have, in fact, chosen from my family to avoid a potential usurping of the throne simply because of my own Cornish heritage. Sometimes the things I never considered seem so plentiful and so important.

"Then it is said that your many greats grandfather was conceived in this very room when King Uther claimed the Queen of Cornwall as his High Queen by virtue of the spoils of war. It is good we may now make our choices for better reasons, is it not?"

I smiled at the woman and glanced around the room, which was dimly lit due to the rain and gloom. As if reading my mind, Bersaba said, "Oh, dear me, let me light the lamps. How can you expect to see anything in this dreariness?"

"It is good," I said, "but from the writings of the Lady Morgan, her mother loved Uther well, to the point that it was thought she was not so much under the illusion of glamor that he was Gorlois as was everyone else."

She laughed.

"I have heard the same spoken, but wished not to take liberties with the memory of your ancestors."

Soon, the room was ablaze in warm lamp light. Laoghaire ignored my room and slipped into the smaller anteroom that joined near the small dining area.

"Well," she proclaimed, returning almost immediately. "It is small, but I will make do. I do trust someone will bring in a bed?"

"Oh no, dear, no," Bersaba corrected her. "This set of rooms is an apartment, really, and you are now in the Queen's changing room. Your own room is beyond that even. Keep on walking to the next door across from this one."

"Ah," Laoghaire said with surprise as she disappeared into the fourth adjoining room, and when she did not return right away, I followed where she had gone.

The dressing room itself held four armoires, a dressing table, and three chests of drawers. A wash stand stood between the two largest armoires and I knew exactly what would replace it once my belongings arrived: my mother's mirror, the magical token I brought with me from Avalon.

Through the dressing room was another door and it opened onto quarters almost as large as mine. Three beds lined the walls, as well as wardrobes, a dressing table, and a large chest of drawers.

"We expected several ladies in waiting for the Lady Iris, so we prepared this room for three and the next for three more. Since there is only the one of you, I can have the other beds removed if you wish. Will this suffice for you?"

Laoghaire twirled around like a young child and then flopped herself onto the nearest bed. "It is splendid," she cooed. "Thank you."

Bersaba nodded. "You will want to freshen up from your ride and to dress formally for the evening meal. Can you dress yourself or shall I send up one of the girls from the Lady Zelda's staff?"

I exchanged a glance with Laoghaire, who quickly hid her smile behind her hand and turned away.

"I can dress myself," I said, momentarily confused. I paused, then felt compelled to ask, "Do ladies of nobility often have difficulty dressing themselves? I never myself found it to be a struggle."

Once again, her smile lit up her face in a delighted array of laugh lines and she chuckled merrily

"I am certain you know, Lady Iris, that most ladies of nobility are far different than are you. I presume not to know the style of dress to which you are accustomed on Avalon, but the ladies of court tend toward the modern frivolities of the day and some of them are cumbersome."

I felt a stab of unaccustomed insecurity as I realized that I knew so little of the latest fashions of court. Even my finest garb from Avalon might be inappropriate for formal wear at the King's table.

Seeing my expression, Bersaba correctly interpreted my thoughts.

"Some of the other ladies who have come to court have, from time to time, left items behind. The Queen, upon her death, also left behind a full wardrobe of clothing and although that was ten and five years ago, Her Majesty had impeccable taste and many of her gowns are, as one would say, timeless. The carriage men may take some time in getting your bags to the room. Would you care to try on some of the dresses that are here? Either of you? I am certain there are some no one would recognize."

"Thank you," I said, silently conferring with Laoghaire over the woman's shoulder. The younger girl nodded excitedly. "But tell me, why did you startle so when you saw me? I know I am quite worn from our travels. Are we so bedraggled as that?"

She lowered her eyes. "Oh no My Lady, not at all. 'tis only that… well… you look so like her."

"Like who?" I asked.

"Like the Queen," she said. "You resemble her strongly and it took me aback."

I found this to be an interesting development. On Avalon, my sisters and I resembled few but our parents. I envied Rose and Dahlia their beautiful red locks. Aster had my black hair coupled with Father's dark skin which gave her a fierce and exotic look. Lily and Jasmine were both fair and ethereal in their own way. Violet was the closet to looking like me with her dark hair, but where my face was round and pale, hers was heart-shaped, tanned, and regal. I favored my mother and she was always so beautiful to me, but I could not see the magical allure she possessed in my own reflection. Most of the women on Avalon were variations of blond or brunette and most wore their hair in the same simple plait down their back. I also favored the long plait, but I wound mine around my head to keep it well out of my way during births. To hear I looked anything at all like the former queen took my breath away since I was unaccustomed to looking like anyone except my own mother.

"Truly?" I asked.

"Oh yes," she nodded. "She too was very fair skinned with pink cheeks and beautiful black hair that she wore pinned up on her head. You are of similar body structure as well."

"Did you server her yourself? What was she like?" My curiosity was in full power and now that I had a river of information flowing, I intended to mine it.

Bersaba thought for a moment as though lost in memory. "She was kind, thoughtful, quiet, often sad until she was pregnant with Zelda. I never saw a woman so happy in pregnancy as her. She and the King were very much in love."

"I see."

"He was inconsolable after her death and despite the advice of his ministers, it was many years before he thought to take another wife. Since then…" she shrugged, "…they come and they go."

Thinking the direct approach might be best, I said, "I have heard they go because of Princess Zelda."

Her look was pained. "I do not speak ill of the family I have supported for so many years but yes, the Princess can be a challenge. Many who sought the King's favor were looking for no more than to be Queen and had little interest in also being a mother. For King Marcus, the two are inseparable."

"As they should be," I agreed.

"Come," she said, leading me back into the hallway as she dug a heavy metal key from her pocket and slipped it into the lock on a door several rooms down from my own. "Let us see what we can find."

Laoghaire followed her into the room which was as large and elegantly furnished as mine, but covered with such a thick layer of dust and cobwebs that it was hard to identify the furnishings. Bersaba went to one of the wardrobes and opened it, revealing an array of beautiful jewel toned fabric.

"This one for you, I think," she said, handing me a wine-colored satin gown with a low cut bodice and fine gold strands wound through the material.

"It is lovely," I said.

She opened a drawer and handed me small clothes and a clean, white linen shift.

"This will compliment it nicely," she said as she opened a drawer in the dressing table and pulled out an elaborate comb with emeralds and rubies encrusted in the shape of a peacock.

"Oh my," I gasped. "I cannot."

"Pshaw," she said, "The Queen has no use for it now."

"But what about Lady Zelda? Will she not want her mother's jewels?"

"Ha. When you see Zelda, you will understand. She has no interest in jewels and her mother died giving birth to her, so she has no memory of what she did or did not wear."

"And now for you," she said, "and your name was… Lowry? I am saying it wrong…"

"It sounds like Le-airy," Laoghaire said. "I will not try to spell it for you. It will only make matters worse."

Bersaba laughed merrily. "The Cornish. The Welsh. Always making spelling so complicated. And your name is what? Gaelic?"

Laoghaire nodded.

"La-airy," Bersaba attempted. "L'airy."

"Close enough," my friend smiled.

"Well, L'airy, we will look for something for you in this room. I believe the former Queen was tall enough that her dresses would trip you up if you try to wear them, but perhaps Lady Number Four will be a good choice. She was slight and small as you are."

She opened the door to the room that joined onto Laoghaire's opposite mine. It was arranged the same as Laoghaire's room with three beds, wardrobes, chests of drawers, and a dressing table. She opened one of the wardrobes, clucked her tongue in great consternation, closed it, and then opened another. Truly, this potential bride had fled with great haste, leaving behind more clothing and adornments than I had owned in all my years combined.

"Ah, here," she said with great satisfaction. She pulled out a fine gold gown with ivory embellishments, including satin ribbons and tiny seed pearls sewn into the pattern of a perfect rose on the bodice. We both gasped aloud.

"Now I cannot say that I ever saw either of the ladies wear these dresses, so I do not imagine anyone would think ill of you using them. Evening meal is coming up quickly and Cook serves quite punctually, so we should get the two of you washed and dressed quickly. Are you able to sit a full meal after such a long ride?"

We nodded and my stomach growled in avid agreement.

"We have not eaten since we broke our fast at dawn," Laoghaire said, "and then 'twas only a bit of fruit and cheese. We are grateful for a hearty meal."

"Good," Bersaba smiled. "It will be quite appropriate for the King and the rest of the court to meet you at evening meal, then I am sure the King will want to speak with you tomorrow."

"Very well," I said.

Her expression grew serious and she looked away from me. "His Majesty is a good man, My Lady, who has faced disappointments and grieved over many losses in his life. I have long prayed a happy and compassionate marriage into his life."

"I am eager to meet him, as well as the Princess Zelda, and I do pray that ours is a good match."

"I have a feeling," she said, "that I did not have with the others and it is most hopeful."

Once we were washed and dressed and our hair reset, all at unbelievable speed despite our fumbling with the unfamiliar style of dress, Bersaba led us to the royal ballroom. I now completely understood why the ladies of nobility needed an extra pair of hands simply to dress. Our simple deerskin tunics and robes of Avalon were quite primitive compared to the hooks, ties, buckles, laces, and fasteners of the clothing Bersaba provided to us. I needed an extra person just to see that I had not missed some vital connection and wandered out half-dressed. For reasons other than the comfort of the familiar, I looked forward to the arrival of my mother's mirror.

The dresses pulled our torsos in so tightly that I wondered if perhaps the keen eye of Bersaba was off in the sizing, but she assured me that the style was intended to be constrictive. I could not contemplate how women dressed this way day in and day out, but I could not imagine that my simple clothing would do for court. Mother sent several fashionable dresses with me, but I had scarcely taken time to look at them, never imagining they would be so different.

"Don't you worry now," she said, again reading my thoughts. "In no time, the seamstresses will have you in beautiful gowns all your own should you choose to stay with the King."

I felt my brow furrow. "Is that truly in question?" I asked. "Have so many fled the allure of marrying a king?"

"Oh, so many as that, yes," she confirmed. "At least…" she seemed to count in her mind and then settle upon a number, "…seven come quickly to my old mind, but I know there were more. The King, as I said, is a good man, but he comes with certain…concessions that are difficult for some women to make."

"Well," I said, "I was not raised to be a pampered weakling. I understand it will not be easy, but if the King will have me, I am ready to serve His Majesty and this court to the best of my ability."

She looked pleased and I felt a shine of pride at making her smile.

"Oh," I continued, "I am also a trained midwife with some healing experience as well. I would like to meet with whoever is tending your pregnant women and see if my skills can be of use."

"Oh, think of that," she said, "we have not had a skilled midwife here in several years. We must call a woman in from town if someone is set to deliver and then she must stay within our walls until the lady gives birth. If the King sees fit to allow you to practice, this will be quite a boon."

"Allow me to practice?" I said before catching myself. "Is it such a way that he bids me come and go and how to spend my time?"

She gazed at me intently.

"Yes," she said, "I believe you will do nicely, but I caution you, he is King and is of the old ways, so yes, he is accustomed to having his way in all matters. He is amiable enough, but still, he is King."

"Of course," I smiled. "And about that evening meal of which you spoke…"

"Indeed, My Lady," she said with a nod of her head. "I suspect we are just in time to make a grand entrance."

CHAPTER 3

"Presenting the Ladies Iris and Laoghaire of Glastonbury."

I shot the herald who presented us a scathing look since I had clearly identified my origin as Avalon and certainly, it was known as such. He looked back at me, half cowed and half indignant, then led us into an opulent dining hall with the largest table I had ever seen, surrounded by several smaller tables. Even the smaller tables were bigger than the ones we used at our communal meals at home. Easily twenty people sat around each one, all richly dressed and finely combed. The men rose from their seats and the women nodded in polite deference.

The herald led us to the head of the largest table, he holding my fingertips between his upwardly turned palm and thumb with Laoghaire trailing behind us. A servant behind the King pulled back his chair as he stood.

"Your Majesty," I said, dropping into a curtsy as we approached him.

"My Lady," he replied, holding out his right hand to me. I kissed the ring on his index finger, a large, multi-faceted ruby with odd strands of dark through it. He bid me to rise and indicated two chairs to his left.

The men in the room took their seats again and resumed conversations already in progress when we arrived while all at the table stole not-so-secreted looks at the two of us.

The King was, as Laoghaire had speculated, starkly handsome, clearly a man in his fifties, but distinguished and quite polished. His hair was greyed and short cut, as was his beard. I was glad he was not clean-shaven for as much as the style suited my father, my own preference was toward a strong beard. It framed his face most attractively.

He was strong and fit, thankfully taller than I and broad of shoulder. His face was lined, but attractively so, and his eyes were dark and mysterious. I felt an unaccustomed quiver in my core as our eyes met. I have never been one given to ideas of romance and love and like each of my sisters, at least as so they would admit, I came to this quest a virgin. In my case, it was in both body and mind. My work was always my first love and it never failed that the passionate energy of the Beltane season sent any woman near her term into labor. Inevitably, I spent the night of the Beltane fires rubbing backs, wiping brows, and holding women up as they walked around and around the birthing hut. No time for passion and celebrating the Goddess through physical expression for me. I celebrated Her through coaxing women through their own rite of passage into motherhood.

Now, however, I felt a stirring I could not deny. What little interests I had before were always toward older men and it was the senior Druids who pulled my eye more than the young warriors or scholars. I came here to perform a duty for Avalon, but when first I met the King who would become my husband, I confess to a fluttering in my stomach that was beyond the ravishing hunger for food that was now in full command.

To my relief, he stared at me for longer than a proper moment, his lips separating without words. I could only hope that he too felt a twinge of interest.

Servants came into the room with steaming trays of savory meats, rich broth soups, honeyed breads, and fresh, delicious vegetables. As hungry as I was, I forced myself to eat lighter than my cravings demanding, know if I overfilled my belly, it would rebel later in the night and I would feel bloated and uncomfortable for hours. I sampled everything, however, and that was quite an accomplishment given the extravagance of the spread. Laoghaire showed no such restraint and ate like a warrior woman, making audible sounds of pleasure and appreciation that caught the King's ear and caused him to smile.

No introductions were made of the people around me, which I found odd, but I suspected either I had a long time to get to know other people in the court or they thought me as disposable as the others and no longer bothered with personal presentations. As I ate and my belly found its fill, I felt the weariness of the trip come upon me.

I wondered if I should attempt to engage my betrothed in some way, but an unaccustomed shyness fell over me and I determined that quiet repose could cause me no humiliation, but ill-placed words certainly could, so I limited myself to polite smiles and murmured appreciation of the food. Several times, I caught his gaze as he stared at me intention, no doubt as curious about his future marriage partner as I was about mine.

Conversation around the table again ceased when the food arrived and all focused on the splendid feast. I marveled that perhaps they ate like this every night. I was pleased that even though he ate with tremendous enthusiasm, the King continued to periodically glance in my direction, even smiling now and then.

As the main courses were taken away and wine glasses were refilled, the herald again entered the room.

"The Princess Eselde," he announced in a robust voice that caused me to jump.

Again, all the men at the table rose, including the King, who held out his arms to his daughter.

She was slight and lovely with the fairest skin I have ever seen, like the sweetest cream. Her cheeks were pink and her hair the color of purest ebony. She melted into her father's arms as he swept her into a warm embrace.

"Dear Zelda," he smiled, "Allow me to present to you the Lady Iris, to whom I am contracted to wed, and her companion, the Lady Laoghaire."

Zelda curtsied to each of us and we nodded to her. Laoghaire tilted her head in the girl's direction.

"Oh," she said with true remorse in her voice. "I am too late for the evening meal. Father, I am so very sorry. I was in my room studying for my session with Father Francisco and time got away from me."

The King motioned to a servant who hurried to his side.

"Please bring out a filled plate for the Princess." The servant nodded as though this were a normal occurrence and slipped away.

Zelda smiled demurely at her father and slipped into an empty chair halfway down the table. She tapped her glass and a servant filled it with wine.

"To my father and Lady Iris," she said with an unmistakable and well-trained regal tone to her voice. "May they reign happily forever more."

Everyone at the table lifted their glass and joined in her toast, which was the first mention of our proposed and impending marriage. Before this moment, I had started to think perhaps I and my elders had mistaken his intention.

The servant brought out a rounded plate for the Princess and she ate heartily as others around her conversed amongst themselves in low tones. Still, the King barely acknowledged my presence or theirs except for those occasional intense glances. By this time, the lack of interaction was starting to unnerve me. On the other hand, after his initial warm greeting, he also did not engage the Princess either, nor anyone else at the table. Perhaps this was some Cornish custom of which I was unfamiliar. On Avalon, our meal times were lively, interactive occasions full of laughter and sharing.

Finally, able to bear it no longer, I leaned toward him slightly and whispered, "Are all these people your friends?"

He looked confused. "My friends?" He looked around the table as though seeing the people seated there for the first time.

"Those two down at the end of the table," he waved his hand toward two distinguished looking men involved in an animated conversation with a busty, well-dressed woman of middle age, "are Sir Charles, the Duke of Sherborne, and Sir John, the Duke of Devon. I have known them since we were boys and I value their advice more than anyone in court. You can trust them implicitly. The older man at the middle of your side of the table who looks like he just ate something bitter is Father Francisco, our court priest. Beside him is Father Damian, who is his assistant."

He picked up his wine glass and gestured to the other side of the table with it.

"The woman to the right of Sir Charles is Lady Charlotte, my daughter's nanny. That stalwart soul has cared for Zelda since she was born and has the patience of Job. I would wager she is one more midnight escape away from utter lunacy."

"You don't say," I laughed.

"My daughter is a challenge and Lady Charlotte has borne the worst of it. To her left is, of course, Zelda, who is putting on her best airs and pretending butter would not melt in her mouth when she has less likely come from prayers, as she claims, as from stealing my horse from the stables and riding into the forests outside the courtyard to cavort with the thieves and miscreants that live in the thickest parts."

He eased his fork and knife into the meat on his plate as though this concerned him not at all. Not knowing him well enough, I chose not to react to this admission.

"On the other side of Zelda is Nimien, who is Zelda's governess, responsible for her training as a lady. If anyone is closest behind Lady Charlotte in terms of an untimely trip to madness, it would be Nimien.

"This ruddy looking man to the left of your woman is the court physician, Lord Gawen, who is called Colin. He holds lands in South Wales and is the best healer I have ever met. He is not much for conversation, but he does know his business. These other people," he gestured to the smaller tables, "are members of the King's Guard and their wives, who take the evening meal with us each night."

"Why do they not talk to you?" I asked.

He shrugged. "I am the King. It has always been this way. I never thought to question it. They certainly address me plenty when there is work to do."

The desserts arrived and although I knew I could eat not even so much as another bite, I forced myself to pick at a blueberry tart just to be polite. At last, he King stood and as he did so, the rest of the guests at the table did as well, so Laoghaire and I followed suit. The only one who remained seated was Princess Zelda, and she continued to eat without regard to the King's rising.

"I am prepared now to retire," he said to the assembled group. "I hope you will all remain as you wish to enjoy more wine and fellowship among yourselves."

"Your Majesty," they all said, bowing or curtsying as was appropriate. Not knowing what to do, I stood and held out my hand to him. He smiled as though amused and bent to kiss it, then nodded to me and left the room. Some of the guests returned to their places and others readied to depart. I looked at Laoghaire and she moved her head in the direction of the door. I could not more heartily agree.

We stood to take our leave and no one acknowledged our exit. Such an odd set of manners in this edge of the world.

"Ugh," Laoghaire moaned once we were in the hallway. "That food was delicious, but I should not have stuffed myself so. I fear I will sleep uneasy the entire night."

"At least we will be abed instead of on the ground," I offered. "And such a bed it is."

"Do you wish me to lie with you this first night, Iris? Neither of us is used to sleeping alone."

In Avalon, we slept in the Hall of Maidens, a bunker of many beds, with many of us two to a bed, not only for space, but for companionship.

"You may if you wish," I said, "but I will be fine on my own should you wish to acclimate to your new quarters. I suspect we must both get used to different sleeping arrangements after the wedding."

"How does that work?" she asked. "The chamberlain's wife said that your quarters used to belong to Queen Ygraine and surely those are not the King's quarters. Does he not bed with his wife?"

"I cannot imagine," I replied, having wondered the same thing at the moment she voiced the question. "I suppose these quarters are temporary until the wedding night or perhaps he visits the Queen in her chambers. I know Ygraine's husband was away on campaign for much of their marriage, so who knows how it shall be with this king? Surely there are those who will guide us in what is to come."

"When *is* the wedding, do you know?"

"I have no idea," I admitted. "The King seemed none too eager to speak of it. I hope I have not already given offense."

"The way he kept looking at you, I cannot fathom he was offended."

So she had seen it too. I thought I had imagined his interest as well as the marriage.

"Still, he was very distant, did you not think? To be meeting his future bride for the first time?"

"Well," she speculated. "It is an arranged marriage and not as though you met and fell madly in love. He also has been married before and Bersaba said he loved his wife dearly. Perhaps this is difficult for him."

"Perhaps," I agreed. "I supposed I shall know soon."

"Indeed." We had reached our rooms and she tiptoed and kissed my cheek warmly. I was not accustomed to acts of affection from her and in this foreign environment, I found it sweet and was grateful.

"Sleep well," she smiled. I will be just the two doors over if you need me. I am sure tomorrow brings many revelations.

I wished her goodnight and slipped into my room.

The bed covers were pulled back and hot bricks wrapped in cloth were waiting at the foot of my bed to warm my feet. On the pillow was a paper with a wax seal. I eased open the seal and held the paper to the lamp on the night stand.

"The King wishes to break his fast with you in the atrium tomorrow morning."

Revelations, most assuredly.

I crawled into the bed and thinking that perhaps I should have taken Laoghaire up on her offer of company lest I never get to sleep in this strange place, I sank almost immediately into the deepest, darkest slumber ever, completely undisturbed by dreams or any stirring.

Although I am given to rising very early, usually before the sun, the following morning, I awoke to a gentle shaking of my shoulder.

"My Lady," Bersaba whispered. "My Lady, you must rise so that we may ready you to meet with the King."

I blinked and tried to force my eyes open, surprised to see sunlight peeking through the wooden shutters.

"My room faces the East, then?" I murmured.

"Blessings for new beginnings and the winds of change," she smiled.

"Are you certain you are not from Avalon?" I said as I eased myself up and then onto the edge of the bed.

"Would that I were," she said, pushing open the shutters and allowing the full light of the early sun to flood the room. "I always had the greatest respect for those ladies who were so dedicated to service of their spirits and of the Great Goddess and let me say that Father Francisco would have me whipped for speaking such heresy."

"Has it gone such then that even speaking of the Goddess and her followers is heresy?"

"Aye," she said. "Within His Majesty's walls, he will hear nothing of it. Father Francisco governs with a strong hand, he does, and there is naught for him but the word of the Church."

"How then does the King seek to marry within an Avalon family?" This truly had me baffled and I had sudden fear for my own safety and for Laoghaire, wondering what into what madness I had dragged her. I forced myself up out of the bed, but first, sat with my feet dangling off the edge and sought to right my mind after sleeping so hard.

"Believe me, My Lady," she answered frankly, "he exhausted all other resources first. Then there is the matter of your lineage itself. Father Francisco counseled him most urgently against it and still carries a brooding mind over the decision. You would do well to steer as far clear of him as you can."

"Thank you for telling me that," I said, my mind turning. I had wondered over the intensity of the Court Chaplain's fervor for his religion and now I knew.

I saw that the bags and trunks from our wagon had not only arrived, but were now unpacked in the dressing room that joined my room with Laoghaire's.

"My Lady," Bersaba said with slight hesitation in her voice, "I took the liberty of bringing in a few more dresses that I thought would fit you and be appropriate for you to wear until the seamstresses measure you and finish your wardrobe, if that is acceptable to you."

"That is lovely, Bersaba, thank you."

I could not help but feel like a charity case, but the truth was that we never wore fine gowns of any kind on Avalon, so my supply of them was remarkably short. I thought of the other prospective queens arriving with trunk after trunk filled with satin, velvet, and other costly fabrics, embellished with beads and jewels. I never felt impoverished before, but now, a blush of shame touched my cheeks. I felt a quick rush of anger at the Avalon elders for sending me here so disadvantaged and unprepared, then felt even deeper remorse at even formulating the thought when I was here safe within walls while some of my sisters were still on the road and no doubt moving into true mortal danger.

As if reading my thoughts, Bersaba laid a hand on my arm.

"It will be well, My Lady. Please, do not despair."

I placed my hand over hers, grateful for her kind words.

"You do not know me," I said. "Why are you so good to me? I would be lost here without you."

"It is selfish, truly," she smiled. "Whoever becomes Lady of this house takes me under her charge. Some who have come," she suddenly looked pained, "well, they were less than kind, even as guests here. I sense that you are a good and fair person. If I help you to successfully navigate these waters, then I am blessed with a better mistress than what could have been."

"Well, when first you brought me to my room, you asked if I needed help dressing and offered to send up one of Princess Zelda's women if I did so. This tells me that what you are doing to help me is not within the purview of your usual household tasks."

"No," she said. "But you leave that to me. For now, let us get you spruced up to meet your future husband."

When she used those words, I felt a bit of a shock go through me. Husband. I was seriously to be married.

At eighteen, I was already far older than when other girls were usually wed. Most already had a child or two by my age. My sisters and I were all of one birth, so for there to be seven of us who were all unmarried and virgin was a miracle, especially on Avalon where the patriarchal and pious views the rest of Britain held against healthy sexuality were neither honored nor appreciated. To us, the sexual act between two or more people or even on one's own was a celebration of life and of the sun tides that ran through us all. We did not modestly hide our bodies, nor did we hide our sexuality.

And yet, when we were but fifteen, our mother and Danu, one of the Crone priestesses, informed us that the Goddess commanded we keep our maidenheads sacred, and so we had done as nearly as I knew.

For myself, I never expected to marry. I had little interest in men or women in the act of pleasure, although all of us were taught the fundamentals of how to share the lovemaking experience. I knew various methods of self-pleasure, as well as how to please either a man or a woman. Such things were unimportant to me, as were the romantic heart flutters that so many girls in the House of Maidens spoke of feeling when they were with the object of their affections. I had never felt smitten with anyone and if I had any passion at all, it was for my work.

Now, however, I was to have a husband, likely before any of the rest of my sisters, depending on how their own quests unfolded. What a strange old world! My mind flashed back to the glances King Marcus sent my way at the evening meal the night before and I felt my insides quicken and a jolt of excitement run through me. Was this attraction? Or merely a reaction to experiencing something new and different?

Bersaba helped me into the layers of clothing, although I begged her not to lace me so tightly into the outer contraption that shoved my breasts up nearly to my chin and forced my ribs to feel as though they would bend and break. Truly, this style of dressing could not be healthy for women, compressing the internal organs as it did. The night before, I felt awkward and almost unable to sit due to the constriction on my body. Was it so that no matter how healthy or lean a woman might be, she must appear even tinier?

She carefully brushed my hair and swept it into an elaborate style, different from my usual wound braid and held snugly in place by combs and pins. She then touched certain creams to my face and lips that she said would more bring out the color. A floral tincture dabbed behind my ears and between my breasts was the finishing touch.

"You look perfectly beautiful and regal," she beamed.

"Bersaba," I said, suddenly feeling nervous. "Do I look enough myself? I do not wish to garner his favor by merely looking like the first queen. Is there enough distinction that he will recognize me for myself?"

She patted my arm. "Don't you worry any, My Lady. Answer his questions honestly and fairly. Be yourself. He is charming and kind, he is. Be not afraid to smile, to laugh, and to enjoy his company. With luck, you will be married to him for a very long time and I can think of far worse fates. As I told you last night, he is a good man with a fine heart. It just needs some care and mending."

I nodded briskly and as much as I looked forward to knowing more about my future husband, I knew that in the short term, I would be fully pleased to have crossed this first hurdle and have the morning meal over.

CHAPTER 4

The formality of the evening meal the night before was a stark contrast to the morning breaking of our fast. The King wore a fine tunic of beautifully woven linen with his crest embroidered on over the heart. His crown was simpler, a narrow coronet, and was not on his head, but was instead on the table in front of a chair to his left.

He rose when I entered the atrium and bowed slightly. "My Lady," he said in greeting.

"Your Majesty," I returned, dropping into a curtsy. He extended his hand has he had done the night before, but when I went to kiss his ring, he instead gripped my hand and pulled me into a standing position, quite close to him. Close enough, in fact, that I could feel the warmth of his body and smell a spicy, fresh scent on his skin.

My lips parted in surprise and he smiled down at me.

"I do know that many kings, even the lesser ones, stand on such formalities, even so with their families. I prefer that my servants maintain the dignities afforded to royalty, but when we are in private, as we are now, there is no need for you to stoop and bow in my presence, nor, I hope, for me to in yours."

"No," I said. "Of course, you mustn't, Your Majesty."

"My name is Marc," he smiled, "and I ask that you call me that, unless, of course, we do not wed, then King Marcus is fine."

I could not help but show my surprise and I felt my eyebrows shoot up. "Already you presume failure, Your Majesty?"

He chuckled. "It is no secret that I am apparently not as marriageable as one would think, given the number of women who have fled from betrothal to me."

"And why so, do you think?"

He gestured for me to sit across from him at the lovely iron table and pulled my chair out for me most graciously.

"I could pretend otherwise," he said, "and tell you it was that they were disinterested in living at the end of the world here at Tintagel. Cornwall is richly beautiful in the spring and summer, but most inhospitable in the late fall and winter. I could say that they wanted a man of greater wealth and means or that they desired someone closer to their own age."

He began to butter a piece of bread as he spoke and then stopped and looked at me intently.

"The truth of it is that being raised by only her father and servants without the influence of a mother, my daughter, Zelda is… challenging."

I took a sip of the glass of wine by my plate and listened intently, knowing that how he viewed his history of engagement would tell me much about how aware of himself he might be. So many men were blinded by ego and ambition that they did not see the reality of their circumstances. His ready admission of Zelda's exceptional behavior impressed me.

"She seemed amenable and biddable enough at the evening meal last night. She was perfectly lovely."

"Yes," he said, placing his knife neatly across the edge of his plate. "That is the trouble of it. With me, she is always so. Never in the fifteen years since she was born has the child spoken a cross word or acted inappropriately in my presence. She is well-mannered, loving, and thoughtful, and yet…there is something about her. What it is, I cannot say. At first…no, what am I saying? For the first three and perhaps four times that a woman contracted to marry me and then left abruptly, each time with reports that my daughter was intolerable, I told myself they simply had no experience tending children, that they were pampered peahens who ran at the first sign of adversity.

"Then, her behavior was witnessed by trusted servants and I had more than the word of my fleeing intended brides. Oh, she denied it to me most heatedly, but as much as I wanted to believe her, the unease I felt in my gut caused me to question my own daughter. She takes her lessons from Father Francisco without fault or complaint. Servants have taught her graces as her mother would have done. Now, she refuses to spin, to sew, or to even attend our royal functions as Lady of the House, despite being fifteen and of a marriageable age even. I no longer know what to do and yet, my advisers insist that I marry as I have no male heir to take the throne when I am gone. I believe they are all terrified of the crown passing to Zelda. The whispers about her are no longer behind the backs of hands, but now openly known and spoken and yet she makes no effort to hide her miscreant behavior from anyone other than myself."

I started to reply, but he held up one hand to stop me just as a servant entered with plates of fresh fruit, bowls of porridge with honey and quail's eggs nicely cooked. The girl had entered so quietly I had not even heard her do so.

"Will there be anything else, Sire?" the maiden asked, bowing.

He waved his hand and she discretely left.

"I apologize for being so abrupt. Even though they all know this, I do not discuss the problem of Zelda in front of them, for the sake of decorum."

"Of course not," I agreed.

"Do you know, by way of gossip or rumor, how many times I have contracted to wed since my wife died giving birth to Zelda?"

"I do not," I admitted. Even Bersaba had only given an approximate number.

"Nine," he said. "Nine women of varying ages, station, and temperaments. You are number ten."

"That many?" I tried to refrain from reaction, but felt my eyebrows raise.

"Indeed. To be frank, since your cousin, Philip, was deposed from the High Throne earlier this year, those who are in power at Cameliard have come to fear an uprising from Avalon and from those who still support what it represents. Knowing that through your father's line, you hold a legitimate claim to the throne of Cornwall, I was strongly advised to marry into your family. Admittedly, your mother and father provided quite a few selections from which to choose. Just over a month ago, we received unsolicited an offer of marriage for you from your father and it seemed, well… ordained somehow that it should be so."

"I understand," I said. I wondered if I would have been his choice had he seen my other sisters, all of whom I judged to be more beautiful than me.

"Thereby, even greater weight is added to the burden this betrothal already carries. The High Throne wishes me to keep Avalon under control through a marriage alliance, my advisers wish me to marry a woman young enough to produce an heir, and my daughter seems to send everyone else fleeing for their very sanity. So, before we get far into this, I have to ask, do you feel you have the strength to endure such hardships? And I pray you know yourself sufficiently to compose an objective evaluation."

He revealed so much of himself and his situation that I did not quite know where to begin, but I did hide a smile at how closely his words mirrored my own thoughts about him. I remembered one of our elders on Avalon telling us, "It is better to wait and choose your words than to speak with haste and regret it."

I took another sip of wine and thought carefully before I responded. I chose my words carefully and used a firm tone when I spoke.

"Your Majes... *Marc*, I have no intention of leaving. I came here to fulfill my own sacred and political duty and I intend to see it through. You have no cause to know anything about me, but I tell you now, I am tenacious and I do not cower easily. I do not suffer fools lightly and I am not easily dissuaded from a task once I take it on. If you are willing to accept a rather willful wife who undoubtedly shall struggle from time to time in learning the ways of being in court and what all is expected of her, I am here for as long as the Goddess wills."

He frowned slightly and I cringed inwardly, recalling that I was now in a land divorced from the Goddess and often hostile to any mention of Her.

"That must cease," he said, simply.

"What must cease?" I asked.

"In my court, you will have no mention of your teachings on Avalon or of this Goddess you serve. We are in all ways a Christian court and I will confess that I have no patience for whatever witchcraft or devil's work you employ in your home. You are now in my kingdom and I say these with respect of you personally, but none for the place from whence you came. All that talk must be put behind you, left on the shores of your home. I worship the one true God and demand that my family, nay, my entire household, also be as the faithful. If this you cannot do, then you should take your leave now."

His voice was demanding, but not unkind, and yet, I felt a sting of mortification come into my cheeks and my breath caught in my throat. Deny the Goddess in favor of his Christian God? How so? I studied the stem of my wine goblet, awash in thought. This coming after he had just clearly laid out that he needed me far more than I needed him…as far as he knew.

If I abandoned my task now, how then would I complete my underlying mission? Only then would I truly deny Her and would failed in my quest before even it began. Yet here he was, staring at me intently and demanding an accord on this. I drew in a breath and let it out slowly, regulating the beat of my heart and the flow of my blood as I did so.

"My Lady?" he prompted.

"Sir, I am who I am and when you accepted me from Avalon, you no doubt learned of my training, *all* of my training, and knew well from whence I came and from whom I came. My parents are holy people and royalty in their own right or I would not now be here with a proposal of marriage between us. Know ye right now in this moment that I am no witch, but a holy woman trained in matters of the spirit. I will not be referred to as such when that is not what I am. In fact, I would confidently wager that through my training, I am at least as knowledgeable about matters of faith, if not more so than your Father Francisco as I was taught from the moment of birth. I congress with no devil and refuse to be accused otherwise."

I saw his face redden slightly and he himself drew in a breath, but I held up my hand as he had done to me.

"Already I have told you that I am willful and I ask that you hear me out."

He nodded, but to his obvious displeasure.

"As you say, I am now in your home and I am to be the lady of your home. In that capacity, I will serve you in every way, including this one. Despite what you may think, I am well versed in your Christian religion, as well as the writings and practices of many other faiths, and I will honor it in all ways as far as in the eyes of your court and your people. My heart and my spirit shall always belong to the Goddess and it is She I shall serve, but not so that any could see or tell. You will have no cause for shame from me and if that means we are parted when it is our time to go into the afterlife, then I shall bear that burden."

He mulled my words for a few minutes before replying.

"Any children you bear me must be raised in the Christian faith," he said.

"Of course."

"And for the love of all that is holy, Zelda must never know of your… whatever it is."

"*Religion*," I said, not trying to hide the terseness in my voice.

"…your religion."

"And if I am to in all behavior and deed adhere to your *religion*, I insist that you do not denigrate mine or me as you have just done."

His mouth twitched and worked as if he had words that would not fit well through it.

"Agreed," he said at last.

I cut into my eggs and began to eat them as he watched me intently.

"You are so like her," he said at last.

I decided that the best approach was to act as if I did not know to whom he referred.

"Oh? Now who is that?"

"My wife," he said. "She too had the dark hair, the fair skin, the same build, but it is beyond that. She was stubborn, wiser far than I, and had such a biting wit. The woman could be scathing in one minute and delightful in the next."

I took another drink of wine.

"I fear you give me too much credit. Unfortunately, I am neither witty nor delightful, although stubborn I have most assuredly heard mentioned in my own regard."

"She was so beautiful," he said wistfully.

"You loved her?"

"Oh yes. From the time I can first remember loving anyone, I adored her. We were pledged at birth, so I grew up around her and we married when we were both only seventeen. Now, here I am at five and forty, the same age my father was when he died, and I am taking a wife nearly thirty years younger than I and speaking of heirs. Are you sure you can bear the attentions of an old man and the responsibilities of a household? I hold you to no fault if you wish it not."

He could certainly change his tune on a moment, snapping from condescending and demanding to concerned and gentle.

"If you married her at seventeen and your daughter with her is but fifteen, how long were you without children?" I asked

"Fourteen years," he answered. "We had a son three years in. He died when he was but three weeks old."

"And yet you did not set her aside for barrenness?"

"I could not imagine my life without her, so no, I did not. Despite the number of times that I have attempted to wed since her death, this must tell you how serious of a matter marriage is to me. So no, I did not put her aside, even though some of my advisers encouraged me to do so for the good of the kingdom."

"And yet she conceived."

"We gave up on having children and then suddenly, after those years, she was with child. We thought her courses had stopped because she had grown too old to have children, but then she felt the baby quicken and her belly began to grow. I admit I did not wish to feel close to the child as it grew inside of her because I feared it would die as our son had. Instead, it was she I lost to the child bed fever."

"Who attended her?" I asked.

"I am sorry, what did you ask?"

"Who attended her in birth? Who was with her?"

He looked confused. "A midwife from the town, as well as the court physician and her ladies."

"I see."

"I am to understand that you are a midwife trained?"

"Yes, both myself and Laoghaire are skilled midwives."

"So when your time for birthing comes, you will have competent assistance."

"I shall. I also hope that you will allow us to attend to the births of your women in court and even into the town if need should arise."

"I do not wish a Queen who does no more than stitch and gossip. My first wife was not so and I do not think it would please me much to have a wife of such simple means. If that sort of life appealed do you, I would concede; however, I am grateful that you have a needful profession that pleases you. I ask only, for the obvious reasons, that should your womb quicken, that you do nothing to endanger yourself or the child and that your dedication to the women and their birthing not interfere with your duties as queen."

"Of course," I agreed quickly.

"You do understand that one of the purposes of this marriage is to produce an heir. I hope that was made clear to you."

"It was," I said.

"And yet I must ask, are you confident that you can also serve as a parent to my daughter? As I said, I understand that she is a handful, but I cannot help but believe that had her mother lived, she might have turned out different than she did. Do you think it too late to guide her in a different, more refined direction?"

"That depends on what you mean by 'refined,'" I answered. "It is my experience that young people have within them a certain core personality and that the only way to bring some into full submission is to break their spirit. I would have no interest in doing such a thing with Zelda. On Avalon as part of my training, it was incumbent upon us to spend time caring for children and young people of all ages, so I have a degree of experience with many different types of youth. Some are simply more adventurous and daring that others, requiring a certain amount of stimulation to feel alive and engaged. Forcing such a child into a mold of total obedience and subservience can damage their spirit beyond repair. I prefer instead to harness that drive for life and point it in a positive direction. That by no means she should be defiant and incorrigible, but more that it is the adult's role, not the child's to find a way to best utilize their strengths."

"An interesting philosophy. How is this sort of thing managed on your Avalon?"

I was grateful he showed a less hostile interest in how I was raised, but still chose my words carefully.

"On Avalon, from an early age a child is monitored to see what talents they possess and where their interest lies. If they are inclined toward music, then a lyre, a flute, a harp, or a drum is offered to them early on. If they love animals, they are quickly taught the appropriate care of many. Mostly, we observe and we listen to see what will stimulate their spirits best. When a child knows that they are seen, heard, and understood, it is easier for them to trust the adults around them to make good choices for them. When they are punished for what they do not know and for not fitting into a standardized mold for what each child should be and how they should act, then they ultimately rebel."

I chose *not* to share with him at that time my avoidance of child care in my training. I justified this omission by imagining that despite his blatant honesty about some things, there were no doubt parts of his own life that would remain shrouded in secrecy. Besides, if he did ask me directly, I would not lie. I simply declined to tell the entire truth.

"Yours is most certainly an unconventional perspective, however, I cannot say that I disagree. I have always felt that the reason Zelda is so amiable and obedient around me is that I do not pressure her as do her governess and Father Francisco. How is your morning meal? Does it suit you?"

"It is delightful," I said, popping a grape into my mouth. "I thank you. And as to your earlier question, the age of my intended husband is of no consequence to me so long as he treats me well and is an honorable man."

"I shall strive for no less, My Lady."

"I must ask, given the fervor of your earlier rejection of my religious beliefs, do we have an accord and are we well met?"

"I am grateful for the opportunity to know you better and I appreciate your candor and your honesty. You are," he chuckled, "quite direct and I am admittedly unaccustomed to that. Most people are so eager to please me, they hesitate to speak their minds. Yes, I would say that we are well met and we have an accord."

"I am pleased. I will also tell you, if it eases your mind at all, that my interests in the male form have always tended toward the older rather than the younger."

I thought this would please him, but he looked uncomfortable and shifted in his chair.

"Marc? I fear I have offended you with my candor on so early a meeting."

"No," he said, "Not at all, but there is one more thing that I must discuss with you and I ask that you accept what I say knowing it comes from a position of honesty and disclosure."

"Of course." I nodded.

"I am not a soldier. I came to my throne by inheritance, not by any act of conquest or valor. It is my shame that I send my troops into battle and yet I allow my generals to leave and do not go myself and yet, that is why I am still alive to rule in Cornwall. Because of this, I am here in court very nearly at all times. You will find that I do not go on campaign to leave you or my household to its own devices."

"I understand."

"This means we must be compatible to effectively lead this court."

"Yes."

"On first assessment, I do believe that we are so, more even than I expected or hoped. That being the case, I must confide in you."

"Go on," I said, considering that few conversations that went this direction ended up anywhere favorable.

"This I must tell you in absolute confidence and ask that you repeat it to no one as none in my employ nor even my closet friends know this of me."

"You have my vow of silence, Sire."

He nodded and attempted to continue, breathing in and out heavily as though the very words labored him.

"Since my last attempt at marriage…" he looked at me as though he feared I would bolt at whatever he was to tell me. "…I met a woman for whom I have… developed an affection."

CHAPTER 5

Truly, that was the last thing I expected to hear. My heart fell and I exhaled heavily. Clearly, he was warranted in his hesitancy to present this to me and yet, a part of me took note of his forthrightness in doing so. If he was honest and up front in revealing this, it stood to reason that I could trust him in other issues as well to be equally as honorable.

"I realize this is not appropriate to reveal to a woman to whom I am pledged to wed and the last thing a young woman wants to hear from her betrothed, but I have no interest in secrets or duplicity."

"Then why you do you not wed her?" The question seemed obvious to me.

"Would that I could," he said, throwing up his hands, and I felt truly sorry for the anguish that slipped through his expression. "There are many reasons, both personal and political. She is my age, so well beyond her childbearing years and I must produce an heir. The High Throne would never sanction our union due to some unfortunate political obstacles. Also, as of late…" he looked away and then back at me as if weighing how much he should confide. "As of late, she often does not seem to be of her right mind. She suffers from some type of dementia that is recurring. Sometimes, when I am with her, she is vibrant, lively, clever, loving, engaging… other times, she does not recognize me and hardly knows where she is, thinking herself in a different time with others who are now dead. You can see why under these circumstances, it would be impossible for me to make her my Queen."

"Yes," I agreed. "So, what do you propose?"

"I do not know," he admitted. "There is no fairness to the situation. Either I must forsake her and cleave only to you or I must ask you to endure knowing that I have a mistress, and certainly plenty of queens have done so, my mother included."

"Does your religion not forbid such adultery?" I asked, feeling wicked for doing so.

"Yes," he said, pain evident in his voice. "Does yours not?"

I shook my head. "May I speak freely, Marc, since you asked?"

"Yes, please do."

"Our Goddess says that all acts of love and pleasure are Hers and as such, are sacred. We do not attach to the act of lovemaking the shame and restriction that does the Christian church. On Avalon, those who are married, or handfasted as we call the act, do so for life, or for only a year and a day, or for all eternity, life after life. They then decide between themselves how and if fidelity shall exist. Some bed who they choose even though married, often sharing one to another among many. Some, like my parents, choose to share their bodies only with one another. We hold no word such as 'adultery,' only honor or dishonor to the vows between those who wed. The point is that each couple decides what is proper for them within the bounds of their union. Government or religion does not play a part in it. The community simply honors what they choose."

Again, his cheeks reddened.

"And should you wonder why many think those on Avalon to be hedons?"

I startled at his words and peered at him with great intention.

"And yet," I chose my words carefully, "You would judge my people as hedons because they do in the daylight without shame what kings and their lessers have done in the shadows since the dawn of time?"

He drew in a breath and let it out again.

I pushed further. "What does your Father Francisco say of your affection for this woman?"

He cleared his throat nervously. "As I said, no one knows, including the Father. He would no doubt reprimand me harshly and likely force me to do atonement. Certainly, he would forbid me to ever see her again."

"You see," I said, "this is what vexes me. Are you not the King? Whereby did these priests and bishops get so much power that they command kings? How so?"

"Britain is by all measure now a Christian land and as such, we must allow the representatives of the Church to guide us in the behavior suiting to good Christians. As humans, we are fallible and despicable in our base needs. These men of God are above such things and can clearly identify where we err and help us to see and correct our mistakes and atone for them. That is why they must direct even kings to be good men and true to the word of God in both deed and in thought."

"Do you see these men as more than mere humans? As ambassadors of God who dictate not only your actions, but your very thoughts?"

"To some degree, yes."

"And yet accepting and knowing this, you slip around behind his back and see this woman, knowing he would forbid it?"

"...yes." His jaw began to clench in unclench and I felt instinctively that it was from shame rather than anger over being questioned.

"And to feel what you feel as a human, as a man, makes you despicable in the eyes of God? Is this what he tells you?"

He turned his head from me.

"We must all work to overcome our sinful desires. They are a ploy of the fiend to draw us further away from God. God detests the sin, not the sinner"

"But what if," I ventured, "God does not detest what brings us joy and pleasure. What if it is men who interpreted God's words as those of judgment and condemnation when God created us to bring love and pleasure to one another?"

When he did not reply or turn to face me, I pushed back my chair and rose to stand. "May I approach you?"

He continued to look away from me, but said, "You may."

Dearest Goddess, but he was handsome. As I walked to him, it was only a few steps, but it felt like miles. Closer now to him, I could see that the elegant crow's feet at the corners of his eyes and the grey of his hair were all that belied his age. He was tanned and strong, but so conflicted between honor and faith. In that moment, he reminded me of my father, who worked so hard to marry the two at all times.

I reached out and touched his cheek, letting my fingers trail down his jawbone.

"When we are wed, presuming you still wish to have a hedon such as myself, I will not ask you to put aside this woman you love for I do not subscribe to the dictates of a faith that detests joy and pleasure. In this, we will follow what my faith says and choose our own rules. I ask only that you honor me and not make a fool of me to others who do believe us to be exclusive in our affections."

He placed his hand over mine and pressed it to his face, closing his eyes.

"My Lady, I do not imagine you could ever play the fool, even if someone tried to make you one."

"You flatter me, Your Majesty."

He brought my hand to his lips and kissed it.

"I will honor you in all things and in all ways. On my word, shall I fall upon my own sword should you ever have cause to feel shame from my words or actions. And as you have given me leave to cleave not only to you, but to her as well, I swear to you that I will not pass judgment upon you nor allow anyone else to do so should you choose to take others to your own affection. Any child you bring to our marriage should your womb quicken I would raise as my own and be damned any who take umbrage to it."

"Thank you," I said, forcing him to meet my eyes by sheer will. "But I shall not now require your generosity in that respect. Should matters change, I will tell you."

"Your discretion is all I require since like you, I wish not to be made a public cuckold or a fool," he said, moving even closer to me. "Although I must admit, I am a jealous man by nature, my better sense will override and know it is neither just nor fitting for me to think less of you for what I do myself"

I could feel the heat of his body as he stood so close to me and my own body, suddenly awake to feelings it had long denied, aching to draw closer to him. I studied his face carefully, memorizing every line, every nuance. He still held my hand, so with my other hand, I reached to touch his strong jaw. He was, after all, soon to be my husband and I would spend many hours of my life even closer to him than this. Or was he mine? Certainly, not in all ways. What arrangement would he want? He spoke of heirs, but would we be intimate at all? My heart constricted at this thought and I imagined it was best to be forthright and get all into the open before we wed. Who knew how often we would have pause to talk like this before we came to one another as man and wife?

"Should you wish not to come to my bed since you love another," I said softly, "I will make certain no one knows of what we do not do and I will do all within my power to perpetuate the belief that ours is a conventional marriage."

He slipped his hand on the nape of my neck and stroked the skin there with his thumb, sending shivers of delight through me.

"You, magical Priestess of Avalon, woman of mysteries and secrets, can you not tell?" he asked, looking deeply into my eyes. He ran his hand along my neck and pressed gently against the back of my head, pulling me close to him until his mouth was right at my ear. His breath was warm and soft as he spoke and despite the heat coursing through me, the intimacy he showed froze me in place.

"Iris," he whispered. "Oh Iris. I was prepared to feel nothing for you and to treat this marriage as a contract of law and court. I could not know how you would react to the many complications I bring to our marriage and even to our bed and yes, I do say 'our bed.'"

I felt my eyes widen as he spoke, realizing he likely could not say these things and continue to look me in the eye.

"Although I bear love for this woman in my life who is so dear to me, you awaken something in me that I cannot deny. Even now, standing close to you like this,

I find I want to rend your clothing off you and take you here on this table like a common street thug takes a whore. That is why I thought you witch because surely, you have cast a spell over me that I think of little but you since first I laid eyes on you last night. You were in my dreams, Iris. My every other thought is of you."

   I swallowed hard and of all that he had said, of every secret the King of Cornwall had revealed to me upon only the second time he had met me, this was the most unbelievable.

   "I can only pray," he continued, "that my wife will someday feel the same for me that I feel for her and that it will grow into a passionate and loving pairing. Truly, if you wish your own sleeping quarters, they are yours, and if you wish you keep yourself from me, I will honor your wishes, but my preference is that you share my bed and I swear to you that if you will allow it, barring crisis, I will come to our bed each night for you and I will make pleasuring you my concerted task."

   "You say these things to me while you love another?" I whispered back to him, confused and feeling my cheeks alight with sudden flush. Somehow, whispering with him this way made our words just surreal enough that I could speak more freely.

   "It puzzles me just as it does you," he breathed into my ear, "but I cannot deny what is there and what holy man of the highest order would deny me to feel arousal for my wife? True we barely know one another, but with every word and motion, you intrigue and excite me more. I wish in no way to frighten or overwhelm you, but I cannot have you leave here thinking that I would not gladly and eagerly go to your bed. Holy God, woman, I would worship at your sacred altar and drink of your blessed cup as a man dying of thirst at the Sacred Well of Avalon itself if you allow it."

My knees all but buckled at his words, pushing me further into his arms, this man who had minutes before shamefully proclaimed his love for another woman and denounced me as a hedon.

"You tease me, Marcus. Why do you tease me so with these sweet words and promises?"

He held me even tighter, so close that I could feel the truth of his claims pressing firmly against my thigh. It was certainly a majestic truth, hard and large and jerking with intention.

"Ask any who know me and they will tell you that I am a man who keeps his promises. My word is my bond."

To my surprise, he pressed his fingers through the tightly bound strands of my hair and his lips dropped to my neck, trailing the lightest of butterfly kisses down my collarbone and toward my breasts, the tops of which the bodice of my dress dared expose.

My insides leapt and churned and pleasure ricocheted through my body like an erotic lightning bolt. How had I gone from feeling sexually dormant to this ignited inferno of desire? What I knew was that a holy compulsion that felt separate and apart from myself, yet wholly within my own design, wanted him *in me*, filling me and driving his passion home. My breathing was harsh and ragged as he moved his head back to look at me again, holding my face in his hands.

After those moments of sweet candor and intimacy, it felt a strange shift to now look him in the eyes, as though he had caught me in fantasy about him and knew my desires.

"May I kiss you?" he asked, roughly and without the refinement so natural to his voice. "God, Iris, let me kiss you."

"If you do not, I shall perish right here," I breathed and then without a moment's hesitation, his mouth claimed mine, powerfully and proudly, as the first man I ever kissed in full desire. I opened my lips to him and his tongue was warm and seeking, dancing with my own in a way that caused my inner core to tremble and clench into a heat that leaked wetness onto my small clothes, even slipping down my thighs. He kissed me on and on, moaning deeply in his throat and clutching the back of my head so that our mouths met tightly and perfectly.

Never had I felt so invigorated and alive. No wonder why priestesses claimed that this feeling fueled their magic so intensely. This was raw, primitive, and more powerful than anything I ever felt before. The Goddess was alive inside me and demanding Her due.

He pulled away from me at last, his breath heaving and his eyes glazed. I knew I looked none the better than did he.

"This, I assure you," he gasped. "This I have not felt, not ever, for any woman. Do you swear you have put no enchantment on me?"

I smiled, "No more than you have on me. No, I never thought to do so. What good is a love charm when one would then never be sure the one you charmed wants to be with you for reasons other than magic? No. If you come to me, it is from your own loins and heart. Not from any spell or potion."

"Good," he said, kissing me again, deeply, but more gently.

"But I could," I said, when he broke away again.

He smiled and pointed at me with his index finger, shaking it as if at a naughty child. "This I shall remember."

"And this I shall remember," I said, touching my fingers to my lips and feeling the slight bruising there that left a delicious tingle on my mouth.

Had I truly not even yet reached Cornwall this time yesterday? How could this be such in less than a day? Slowly, I realized he was saying something to me and I forced myself into focus.

"I am sorry, what were you saying?"

He smiled.

"I said, I will send a full staff to you to prepare you for the wedding. Many details are already arranged, but you will forgive my people if they fail to take very seriously my intentions to wed." I laughed despite myself. "You will be very busy until the wedding, which I intend to have in three days' time."

"Three days?" I said, amazed.

"I wait that long only out of decorum. If my staff cannot make all the wedding arrangements in that due course, then we shall go without what they cannot manage. I would marry you today if I could but know that for your own honor, hedon or not, I will not take you before we are married. Should you decide to flee like the others, I wish not to have compromised your maidenhood."

"You are very kind, Marc, and were I not a hedon, I would thank you for your consideration." Since my insides still ached for him, it was hard to appreciate his restraint.

"Trust me," he said, "I will work with great haste toward this wedding." He brought my fingers to his lips and kissed them, keeping his eyes locked on mine.

"And you are certain you are at peace with marrying an old man like myself?"

I did not drop my gaze from his as I said, "Sire, from what I have experienced today, this 'old man' can rouse in me what an island of young men never once did."

His expression went serious and he said in a low voice, "My Lady, it is best you take your leave before I forget my promises to your honor."

I thought to push my advantage, for surely, I did know that not only was there pleasure in the intensity of this emotion, but also power. Instead, I remembered one of the basic tenets we were taught in the act of seduction: *Always leave your lover wanting more of you.* If I gave all to him now, yes, he would know the pleasures I could bring to him and yes, I could learn what he could do for me, but a playful part of me that hours before, I did not know existed, wanted to keep him on tender hooks for a while. If indeed, I had competition for his affection and if indeed, he desired me as he proclaimed and as was evident through his trousers, then let him burn with longing for a while, Anticipation would make the culmination even more intense, I was certain.

I would share my husband if must be, but if this be a contest for his attention, I fully intended to win.

CHAPTER 6

I saw little of my future husband in the days after our breakfast and before the wedding. As early as that afternoon, the castle began to buzz with excitement about our upcoming wedding, so I knew he was making arrangements. I could not get through an hour even without thinking of how it felt to be in his arms, his mouth burning into mine.

Each day, a servant brought a tray to me and Laoghaire upon our rising and we would break our fasts with a hearty meal. In those first few days, I met with so many different people it was hard to keep my thoughts straight and remember who was who. The cook came to me personally to discuss the arrangements for food, treating me already as though the household were mine to manage. I was flattered and pleased to be included so in the planning of the courses. It seemed that seamstresses were forever in my room measuring, pining, and planning as they clucked and tisked tisked their way through the creation of the gowns Laoghaire and I would wear, as well as several attendants who I did not even know. Most were Marcus's nieces and grandnieces, as well as, of course, Lady Zelda. A young woman named Ursa was assigned as my primary lady in waiting, which pleased Laoghaire since she had no design on waiting on my every whim where it seemed to be Ursa's only ambition.

The Princess and I had shared only a moment or two since I first saw her at the evening meal the night of my arrival and always with others around us. She made obvious efforts to avoid my gaze and while I knew it was within my rights to summon her and spend time to get to know her better, as well as weed out any attempts she might have at subterfuge. I tamped down that urge to dig into her nefarious little mind and decided instead to wait until the ink was dried on our marriage document and her recourse was minimized.

She stood ambivalently to the side of the activity, sighing heavily as she endured measurements and questions about what colors she favored for her gown. When she was not an active recipient of the seamstresses' attention, she looked sullen and lost. At last, I could bear no more of her resentment flowing through the room and made my way to where she stood. She pulled away from my mere presence, pretending to gaze out the window with grave indifference.

"Lady Zelda," I said, quietly enough that only she could hear me. "You must hate all of this fuss and bother. You are welcome to stay if that is your wish, but if anyone has told you that you must be here, refer them to me. I do not want you to be here if you wish to be elsewhere."

She turned and looked at me as one would eye a wild animal that circled them, wondering if they would flee or attack.

"You truly do not mind if I leave?" she asked.

I smiled. "Do you know from where I come, Zelda?"

"Avalon," she answered. "That makes you different from the others, doesn't it? You could cast spells on me or turn me into a toad or a fish."

I chuckled despite myself.

"Well, I *could*," I said, "but I have no intention of doing so. What I hope to do is turn you into a happy young woman who has a life she loves. I am not seeing that here in this room."

She chewed on her thumbnail and looked around.

"If there is a hell, as Father Francisco says," she said, trying to shock me, I felt, "then it is filled with seamstresses and ladies in waiting. Not fire and brimstone."

"They have measured you and I will order them to make your gown with no further trouble to you. You do not have to remain here, dear, if you wish not to. Just be at the wedding wearing the dress and smiling pretty to please your father. That is all I ask."

"You are serious, aren't you?" she said, cocking an eyebrow at me. "I can go?"

"If you wish," I answered.

"Is this some kind of test? If I stay, I win favor and if I go I lose?"

I shook my head. "I play no games such as that. Stay or go as is your choosing. I cast no judgment on you either way and will allow no other to do so. You are a young woman who knows her mind and if others cannot see the value in that, I do."

She eyed me suspiciously, but I met her gaze with confidence and compassion. I would not allow her the opportunity to manipulate or intimidate me as she had the others. By taking the offensive position, I hoped to ward off any interference from her.

"If this comes back to haunt me later," she said, her voice determined and strong. "I am blaming you, true?"

"I welcome it," I said, refusing to back down. "I have your back, Zelda. Never doubt that."

Without further discussion, she eased from the room unnoticed and did not look back. I exhaled heavily, hoping the trust I showed in her would not backfire. To my mind and as the strategist I was rumored to be, the only hope of success I had lived in the fact that as she had noted, I *was* different from the others and if she feared me a little because I could turn her into a toad, all the better.

Bersaba and Ursa gently guided me to the appointments I had to meet and walked me carefully through the processes toward becoming queen, which I quickly found was more than the measuring of garments and the setting of jewels in a tiara.

~*~

Each night at the evening meal, things were much as they were on the first night. The people from the court who joined us for the meal talked among themselves and Laoghaire and I sat at the head of the table with the King. The food was expertly cooked and very delicious, served in several courses, each more delightful than the one before it.

Marcus often held my hand as we sat there, gently stroking my fingers and catching my glance from time to time with heat smoldering in his eyes. My desire for him grew with every course of the meal.

"So how is it," he asked at the evening meal after we breakfasted together, "that your family has not stepped forward to claim the High Throne?"

I thought at such a direct and poignant question, surely the conversation at the table would stop and all eyes would focus on me to hear my answer. In fact, I choked on the bit of lamb I was eating and yet, people continued talking as if he had not spoken.

He passed me a water glass and I drank from it gratefully, nearly choking again from the brackish taste that was so unlike the sweet water from the Sacred Well.

"Are you well, Iris?" he asked, his eyes narrowed with concern.

"I am," I said, still gasping a bit. "Your direct launch into heavy subjects makes me laugh, which causes me to choke if food or drink get in the way."

He smiled.

"I am not a man given to small talk. If I want to know something, I ask. If I want something known, I tell."

"I admire such candor in anyone," I said. "Too often we are given to dancing around the subject and hoping to find our nugget of truth rather than simply asking. This is by far my preferred type of conversation. It is only that I have found it sadly lacking with most people I have met."

"You have a legitimate claim, as does your father and all of your sisters. Before I agreed to our marriage, I ordered careful investigations. Your father claims to be the great writer and philosopher, Taliesin, reborn and many reputable scholars have validated his claim, even those who knew Taliesin himself. Your father was born directly from King Arthur's line as well as King Gorlois, the greatest warlord Cornwall ever knew and yet no one from Avalon has stepped forward to claim either the High Throne or mine through lineage or conquest."

"My father has no aspirations to be king anywhere but on Avalon," I said. "As you have pointed out, our beliefs are not welcome here and our beliefs are central to who we are and what we do."

"Your claim to the throne of Cornwall is greater even than mine since I come through a distant cousin and yours is direct. Prince John was set on the throne by the Church, not by any legitimate claim. Surely your father's lineage would ultimately prevail. There are many who are against Prince John's reign and would fight for a descendant of Arthur's to sit on the throne."

I shrugged. "Perhaps. Or perhaps if we made a bid for the throne, those who are the true machinations behind Prince John's reign would have us killed before ever we stepped foot in Cameliard. Phillip had a legitimate claim and look where it got him."

"Phillip had a legitimate claim through a father who was a weak and frivolous king. Constantine abandoned his kingdom to perish to the Saxon sword and torch for far too long while he chased the Sons of Mordred long after anyone else cared if they lived or died. It is his fault and his alone that Britain stood unprepared for the attacks after using so many of our resources on his quest for vengeance. Your father, however, has a claim as descendant of quite possibly the last true and just king who was also a warrior who defended and united our country. That holds tremendous power in the minds of Britons who still think of him as the consummate ruler."

"We are not an army, Marcus," I said. "We have skillful warriors on our island, certainly, but not enough to take the High Throne. Sure, we could likely harvest supporters from within the villages, especially those taxed beyond their means by the High Throne, but anyone strong enough to swing a sword is off fighting at The Wall. We would stand little to no chance of winning in an outright war against the anointed King and his High Court and do you truly believe anyone who wields the true power at Cameliard would honor even a legitimate claim to the throne without war?"

He thought about this for a moment.

"Perhaps not," he said. "But even if your father does not have these aspirations, do you nor any of your sisters?"

I felt as though he tested me, to merit the veracity of our marriage as genuine or merely an easy way to achieve power. I sensed on a visceral level that how I answered was important in the future dynamic of our life together.

"I cannot speak for my sisters," I said carefully, "but I have no aspiration other than to be a good wife to you and an honorable queen to Cornwall."

"And your claim here is even stronger? Why marry me when you could easily depose me?"

I smiled and stroked the palm of his hand with my middle finger.

"Because marriage brings with it greater spoils than does war, does it not?" His hand trembled under my touch, so I pushed my advantage further.

"Your people love you, Marcus, and your kingdom runs with great efficient. It is prosperous and your subjects do not know the oppression that other kingdoms suffer. Why ever would I wish to upset that balance? A true queen must care more for her kingdom than she does for power and what is best for Cornwall is that the king who has protected them for decades stay on his throne and continue to do so."

I took a drink of my wine, preferring it by far to the water, and met his gaze.

"Truly," he said, "You are a wise and amazing woman, Iris."

He tapped his fork on the side of his goblet and all silenced to attention.

Holding his goblet in one hand and my hand in the other, he stood and said, "I propose a toast to my lovely bride who has not only agreed to marry me, but is, miraculously, still here." There was nervous laughter at the table. "To Iris," he said, lifting his glass.

"To Iris," they all joined in, clicking their glasses one to another. It was, I realized, the first time the honor of a toast had been paid to me and I smiled my thanks to him.

~*~

Two of the meetings in the intervening days before the wedding were particularly awkward. One was with Father Francisco, who the day after my morning meal with Marcus, bid me to meet him in the Tintagel abbey. Ursa led Laoghaire and I to the far back of the courtyard well behind the castle to an ornate building with carved pillars and colored windows the likes I had never seen before. It was no larger than our Temple of the Moon on Avalon, but was elaborately embellished, showing me that their Christian God demanded far more in terms of adornment than did our Goddess.

The dark wooden doors opened onto two rows of wooden benches that stood on either side of the aisle, leading down to an elaborate and heavily polished wooden altar with a huge, carved stone crucifix hanging on the back wall, showing their dying savior gazing mournfully onto the empty pews as if begging for help. I could not imagine connecting with my spirit with such a gruesome and pitiful display in front of me and had to avert my eyes from the visage.

"Do you indeed cringe away from the presence of our Lord and Savior, Lady Iris?" the priest asked me as he stepped out of the church's shadows. He lit a candle on a fine display of dipped tapers and continued to the next one once the first one caught. It was dark inside the building, even though it was only midday. The lack of windows and the dark wood interior made the abbey much like a cave, despite its opulence.

"Your Christ and I get along quite well, in fact," I said, refusing to be cowed. "It is his followers who give me pause, not the Lord himself."

He seemed to think on that for a moment as he continued lighting candles around the single room of the church.

"You wanted to see me?" I asked.

"You may dismiss your women," he said. "You have no need for an infantry here."

Laoghaire and Ursa turned to leave, but I stopped them.

"I believe I will have them stay," I smiled. "I cannot imagine either of us has anything to say that cannot bear the light of others hearing. It is those things said in the dark that create misunderstanding and fear."

He tilted his head. "Wise words for such a young girl."

"Not so young as all that," I countered.

"Lady Iris," he said, "You must know that when the offer of marriage came from your father, I counseled the King against it."

"I see." Not that this surprised me in the least. "And whatever did I do to garner your disdain before ever we met?"

He sat on a pew in the first row and patted the bench seat beside me, bidding me to sit. I did and gestured for the women to sit a few rows back, but within earshot.

"We have no room in this court for the likes of witches, of sorceresses, of those who conjure demons and worship them."

"Then Father, I am much relieved for I much prefer to live in a land free of make believe villains such as those."

"Oh, make no mistake, child. Evil is not make believe."

"No, evil is not, but I find evil to reside in the hearts of men more so than in fairy tale creatures such as sorceresses and demons. It is the fallibility of man that I fear, not the conjuring of magic, as you suggest."

"You are well taught to bend the words of good and Godly people," he observed.

"Again, no, I merely refuse to engage in the persecution of others for a subject that is so, well, subjective."

"And you find the word of God to be subjective?"

"I find the opinion of men to be subjective and it is they who interpret the scripture. If I speak to four different bishops from four different parishes, they will each one give me a different meaning of the same passage. And yet upon those mutable passages, lives are lost and laws are created."

He studied me carefully for a moment. "Do you mock me in front of the Lord himself?"

I feigned a look of shock. "Most certainly not. In fact, I believe you would find your theologies not so different from mine once the agendas of paradigm and prince are removed. For instance, does the scripture not forbid that you make unto you any graven image? And yet within your church's walls there hangs an image of your suffering savior. It is the subjective interpretation of your book's passages such as this that leaves me convinced of the fallibility of the men who convey it to the rest of us and as I said before, it is the fallibility of man I see as the damage, not the book or the Christ."

"Make no mistake, Lady Iris," his eyes flamed with rage, but his voice was controlled and calm. "I will have none of your spells, your godless witchcraft, your heathen beliefs, nor your talk of Goddesses or 'all gods are one god.' Perhaps all Pagan gods are one false god, but there is only one true God who rules over all."

"My," I said, "That escalated quite quickly. And here I thought we were having an intelligent theological discourse, Father. Do you really feel sufficiently threatened to resort to demands and attacks?"

"There is nothing about you that threatens me, young lady. What you are is an affront to God."

"I am an affront to God? To the Christ who came to this earth to teach love and acceptance? 'Thou shalt love thy neighbor as thyself; greater than these there is no other command.' It seems to me that you and I are to be neighbors, Father. Should we not love and revere one another as Christ commanded and as brothers and sisters of the sacred?"

"Oh, do have a care, My Lady, for if you read on in that scripture, it says clearly, 'There is one God, and there is none other but He.'"

"Which does bring us back to my philosophy which you just openly maligned, 'All gods are the one God,' does it not?"

He studied me for a moment, his eyes laced with fury.

"You are as I suspected, a witch out of that devil island sent to usurp God's hand over this kingdom."

"Heavens!" I smiled. "How much power you give to me! In your faith, are women not to defer to their husbands in matters of the spirit? Why do you fear me so? I have done nothing to warrant your hatred and if you tend your flock with half the passion you put into your attack on me, surely there would be no reason to worry for their souls, with or without my influence."

"You ask why I fear you? You have been here for less than two days and already you have the King's ear and he wanders around court in a daze like a besotted puppy. Your witchcraft is already at work here in my homeland. I smell its stench and it sickens me."

I laughed. "Father, it is not the King's ear that interests me, I can assure you that, but other parts of his anatomy. It may be hard to imagine, but the truth is that if the King desires me, I did nothing to make it so. He is a man who knows his own mind and I have no will to change that in him."

"You brazen, low-born mongrel…"

"And when you are finished name-calling like a common street cur, you can research my lineage and see that it goes back to a Cornish claim from long before and much higher than King Marcus's, so if you want to get specific, he is more low-born than am I. Imagine if I enacted my own claim and took back the throne that is rightfully mine! You would be out of this court so fast your pious head would spin."

His face fell and I had to wonder if he, of all people, had not known of my lineage.

"You…"

"…have to go speak to the cook about the banquet courses, I believe you were about to say. Now that you have taken your time to fully insult the future Queen of Cornwall and Lady of your court, I will tell you that I mean no affront to your faith or to your church. You stay on your side of the altar, Priest, and I will stay on mine. I will honor the faith of my husband and this kingdom and you will find no cause to rebuke me save your objection to where I was born and raised. If you have any other complaints about me, you will bring them up in the presence of my husband and your king so there is never cause to doubt what is said. Do you understand?"

"As you say, My Lady."

"And if you ever again attempt to take a heavy hand to me when I am alone, I swear by all that is holy to both you and to me, I will give you much and more to fear."

He stared at me, grinding his back teeth as if biting back words.

"If, on the other hand," I continued, "we both work for the greater good of Cornwall and our king, I see no reason we must be enemies at all when we have such a powerful common goal. Do you?"

"No, My Lady. Not at all."

"Ah. Your lips say yes, but your eyes say no. What am I to believe? Ah well, even the Christ sat with the wretched and the hated amongst him, so why would I not wish to sit with you? I bear you no malice, Priest, even after seeing how you have behaved here today. Christ also even on the cross forgave those who wronged him. That I can also do."

I stood and smoothed my skirt.

"But not today. Perhaps tomorrow, but today, I will remember and reflect upon all you have said to me and how sorely you have treated me."

We left him sitting there and as we walked away from the abbey, Ursa said, "I fear you have made a formidable enemy there, My Lady. I would not turn my back on him if I were you."

"I intend not to," I assured her. "I have my eye on that one."

CHAPTER 7

The second uncomfortable meeting was with the court physician who was sent to confirm my virginity. Bersaba assured me it was necessary to the process of royal marriage and I again puzzled at the remarkable value these Roman-bred Christians placed on chastity. Would a man not prefer a woman who knew how to pleasure him and had experience doing so? No. For them, it was more about the claiming and conquering of a woman than reaching the heights of pleasure with her. No matter how many women he had bedded, I must come to him pure and wholly unpenetrated.

It struck me that as a midwife who had performed countless internal examinations on women, I had never had one myself, much less by a man. Bersaba stayed with me while the physician laid drapes over me and then poked and gawked at my quim with a lamp to light it up like a sunny day. I feared as he juggled the lamp and the drapes, he would set us all on fire, not the least of which, my lady parts.

To his credit, he seemed uncomfortable with what he had to do, so I began conversing with him in hopes of allaying his discomfiture. The last thing I wanted someone nervously shuffling around my lower body if they must shuffle at all.

"Do you do this often?" I asked. "I know the King has had many future brides. Did they all submit to the examination?"

"None made it this far," he said, reaching over the drape to push on my womb, bringing it further down to his exploring fingers.

"Good Lord, man, you can see an intact hymen with good light and a wide view, what exactly are you doing down there?"

I heard him chuckle, which was reassuring. At least he did not take himself too seriously and was not wrapped in self-importance like so many other doctors I had met in occasional passing. Because our island was renowned for low infant and maternal mortality rates, many physicians came to us to train in obstetrical practice, fewer as of late. It was always a struggle to get them past the interfering processes of the ego and convince them to allow the births to guide them rather than them guiding the births. Their godlike personae must inevitably be stripped away if they were to learn anything from us and that was one of the greatest surgeries we could perform, according to Belen, our senior midwife.

"I not only examine you for virginity, Lady Iris, but also to look for any obstacles to your fertility. Surely you know that one of your primary functions as Queen is to successfully produce a living heir."

"My mother birthed seven daughters in one birth," I said, "so my family legacy is supportive of fertility."

"Fecundity even," he said from under the drapes. "But that is testimony of your mother's ability, not your own. Your reproductive abilities are inherited from both your father and your mother, so if your paternal grandmother struggled with birth, so could you."

The progressive views he expressed impressed me.

"She gave birth to twins in a barn," I said, "but I am told it was by a roughly hewn surgical birth, so perhaps birth did not come easily to her."

I had never felt a moment of concern about my ability to conceive, but now that he mentioned it, I had to wonder.

"Your pelvis is wonderfully wide and I feel no capses in the womb that would prevent a pregnancy from catching on. Are your courses regular?"

I was delighted to hear the report of my wonderfully wide pelvis. Since I had never, in fact, examined myself in such a way and knew the challenges of a narrow pelvic inlet to birth, it was a relief.

"They are," I said, "I have never suffered irregularities there."

"You mention the inherited physical composite of a woman regarding births. Do you then subscribe to the notions of Sister Singer from Glastonbury who posits that we are not a summation of the physical attributes of our same gendered parent, but of both parents?"

"I believe," he said thoughtfully, still from under drapes, "that just as we are as likely to have the coloring or stature of our opposite gendered parent and thusly could we have the internal composition of either parent or both. I have read Sister Singer's work and tend to agree. You have read her then?"

I smiled. "Read her and met her."

"You have met her?" he asked, now looking around the drapes to see me.

"Indeed. She apprenticed on Avalon for many months."

"I am envious," he said, gently lowering my knees by extending my feet and offering me his hand to pull me into a sitting position. "Although obstetrics is not my primary field of study, I do find it fascinating."

"Another hurdle leapt," he said to Bersaba, then smiled at me. "I will report to the King that you should have no difficulty in presenting him with as many heirs as he wishes to father."

"I would enjoy having some say so in that decision," I said as Bersaba helped me to adjust my clothing. "And you will him that I come to him a pure and sacred vessel, unclaimed by any other?"

He laughed. "I will tell him that your maidenhood is indeed intact."

I found that I liked him and the idea of an intelligent and open-minded colleague in the court pleased me.

"I enjoy having conversation with you under circumstances not quite so intimate," I said as I adjusted my bodice over the skirt that had dislodged from my waist in the exam.

"I welcome the opportunity, Lady Iris," he said, bowing slightly. He impressed me by going to the wash basin and thoroughly washing his hands, a practice that many doctors seemed to shun and which I was convinced as instrumental in the spread of child bed fever. This was why I had asked Marcus who attended the Queen in Zelda's birth. A midwife will typically take great precautions in personal hygiene, especially when moving between patients, but I had heard horrifying tales of doctors examining cadavers and then going directly into the birthing field. I strongly advocated for the advanced learning that dissecting the dead could offer in terms of medicine, but taking those humors into the process of birth was ill done, I was certain. Birth and death were closely related, but should never cross paths by the act of humans, only by the will of the Goddess.

~*~

After having my lower body fully examined and exposed to fire hazards, I thought to enjoy a cup of tea in the atrium and fantasize about the time spent there with my now missing future husband the day before. As I looked for a servant to send to the kitchen, I found myself waylaid by one of the many court staff I still did not recognize by sight.

This was yet another priest, but younger and with a kinder face than Father Francisco.

"Apologies, My Lady?" he said, bowing. "I am Father Damian? I know we have not yet met, but Father Francisco sent me to find you?"

"Did he and I not conclude our business earlier today?" I asked brusquely.

"I... I do not know anything about that, My Lady? This is about your preparation for the wedding?"

"Do you mean a rehearsal?" I asked, "Learning my vows and what to say and when to kneel and when to eat Eucharist and drink wine?"

"Not exactly?" he said, "but I am certain that will come? This is about your baptism?"

When he spoke, his voice lilted and the end of each sentence rose as if forming a question. I found it painfully adorable and struggled in vain to dislike him. And yet...

"My what? I am sorry, my what?"

"Your baptism? You cannot marry into the Church unless you are first baptized into it?"

I blinked. "I am sorry, Father Damian, *my what*?"

"Your baptism? My Lady, are you unwell?" He touched my arm gently, but clearly prepared to catch me should I faint away.

I started to laugh. All the tension of the long ride, of adapting to an inhospitable landscape after growing up in the gentle sands and scents of Avalon, of meeting the man I was contracted to marry, of rousing a sexual inferno with no means to bed it down again, and of sparring with a holy man with tremendous power and knowing how far out of my element I actually was, all of that tension flowed out of me in a gale of manic laughter.

"My Lady?" Father Damian repeated, "Are you unwell? Are you in hysteria? Shall I call the physician?"

Something about this made me laugh even harder and he helped me into an embroidered chair that I was quite sure cost more than all the clothing I had ever worn in my life and had likely never before been sat upon. Even that thought made me laugh.

Tears came into my eyes from the exertion of laughing so hard and I felt strong, warm arms close around me. At first, I thought in his fear, Father Damian had crossed a huge gap in inappropriate familiarity but then I saw that it was Marcus who held me, rocking me back and forth like a child as he pulled me against him. I nestled into his firm, fragrant chest and slowly, the nervous laughter went away.

"Your Majesty?" Father Damian was explaining, "I was telling her about the baptism? And she succumbed to a fit of laughter?"

I pulled away from Marcus's chest with great regret, but I had to free this poor man of his responsibility toward my condition. I wiped my eyes with my fingers and Marcus passed me a kerchief that he pulled from some pocket on his person. I dabbed at my eyes and noticed it smelled of lavender. The spoils of royalty, I supposed.

"Father Damian just told me that I am to be baptized into the Church," I managed to say. "I did not realize."

"Well, yes," he said. "It is a formality for you to be wed to me under Church law, presuming you have not already been baptized."

I shook my head, biting back another gale of choked laughter.

"Father Damian," Marcus barked. "Why is Father Francisco not himself baptizing the future Queen of Cornwall?"

The young man looked aghast.

"He sent me to do it, Your Majesty?" His voice shook and I wondered that Marcus inspired such awe from the people in his court. "He said something about an affront to God?"

"Oh, for the love of God," Marcus barked.

"That same God that is affronted!" I said, and began chuckling again. Marcus looked at me with irritation.

"I will speak with him later," Marcus growled.

"I would be honored for Father Damian to baptize me, if it pleases my dear King," I said, as sweetly as I could. "Shall we not trouble Father Francisco since he is so busy preparing for the ceremony?"

The priest's face was transformed from fear to glowing pride.

"Of course," Marcus said. "Shall I bear witness?"

"If you have the time," I said, truly trying not to appear coy.

"I do, but just barely," he smiled. "Shall we?"

He led me into a room on the lower floor of the castle that was obviously a private chapel from those who dwelt within the actual walls of Tintagel castle itself rather than the entire courtyard, which the larger, freestanding abbey serviced.

Father Damian went to a font in the far corner of the room and Marcus and I followed him. He produced a basin and poured water from a vessel into it.

"Holy water?" he said to me.

"Rain water infused with frankincense and silver, blessed by a holy man of God."

He smiled, "Indeed?"

As he began to speak, his voice lost its insecure lilt and transformed into a mighty oratron that would put the angel Metratron himself to shame.

"IN THE NAME OF THE FATHER, THE SON, AND THE HOLY SPIRIT, I baptize thee now, Iris of Glastonbury…"

"Stop!" I said.

Both he and Marcus looked at me and froze in apprehension.

"Why am I announced as 'Iris of Glastonbury?' even now to God? I have never in my life been to Glastonbury. When I come to the evening meal, the herald announces me as 'Iris of Glastonbury' and now as you enter a holy and binding sacrament in my name, you say 'Iris of Glastonbury.' Why so?"

Father Damian glanced at Marcus, then at me. "Your Majesty?" he said.

Marcus sighed. "My staff have been instructed to say that you are from Glastonbury rather than Avalon due to the…" he paused, searching for words, "…spiritual implications and conflicts that exist between Avalon and the High Throne."

I stared at him. "So, you lie to God in a room where 'tis only us three so that you do not offend the jokers and thieves in Cameliard?"

"Iris!" Marcus snapped.

"Father Damian, if I go into this holy rite under an untruth, am I not then unworthy of the honor of redemption in Christ?"

"Well? By letter of Church law? I suppose?"

"Then use my true name," I insisted. "And from this day forward, the King will proclaim that I am to be known only by my true name…"

"Iris…" Marcus looked at me with a storm of warning brewing in his handsome eyes.

"That I am to be Iris of Cornwall until I become Queen Iris of Cornwall, first of her name."

Marcus exhaled heavily and then waved his hand at Father Damian to continue.

The priest nodded and continued in that masterful voice.

"IN THE NAME OF THE FATHER, THE SON, AND THE HOLY SPIRIT, I baptize thee now, Iris of Cornwall, to be pure, unadulterated, and free of sin, redeemed by the blood of Our Lord and Savior, Jesus Christ, now and forever more. So be it and amen."

I raised my face to him and he cupped his two hands into the basin of holy water and released it over my head and face.

"I give thee now the body of Christ, that you may partake of his flesh in communion and accordance with his Divine Providence as he said, 'This ye do in remembrance of me.'"

He placed the Eucharist on my tongue and I closed my eyes and tried to imagine that the tiny toast had become the sanctified flesh of their Christ.

"And as you said unto us, 'Drink of this that it might be my blood,' I commend this drink unto your daughter, Iris of Cornwall, that she might be whole in your name and for your own sacrifice."

I drank the wine and found it bitter, but pushed aside the obvious correlation of that.

Taking oil from a vial he had in his pocket, he drew the sign of the cross directly under the blue crescent moon that marked me as a Priestess of the Goddess.

Something in that delighted me. I was not certain I would contain myself if the cross, even through the veil of oil, overlaid the crescent moon of the Goddess.

"Go in peace," he said.

Little chance of that around here, I thought, but instead, I smiled and nodded amiably.

"There now, was that so bad?" Marcus asked. His hand cupped my elbow and guided me out of the chapel room.

"I am but your humble servant," I said.

"I have plenty of those," he quipped, "but I swear, woman, you shall be the death of me."

I turned to face him and leaned in so that my lips barely touched his ear.

"I would prefer, Your Majesty, to be the life of you."

He made a noise low in his throat and pushed me against the wall, kissing me deeply as his hand slipped around to my bottom. I pressed against him and felt that same stirring in the pit of my belly.

"When I at last get you to bed…" he said, his voice low and intense.

"I will inform Father Francisco that the baptism is completed?" Father Damian said from behind Marcus.

Marcus pulled back from me and turned to him.

"Do so, Father Damian, and make sure Father Francisco knows that the future Queen has been consecrated in the blood of Christ as witnessed by the King."

"I shall, Your Majesty?" the priest said, turning to leave.

"Oh, and Father Damian," Marcus said, calling him back.

"Your Majesty?"

"Never again interrupt me when I am ravaging my Queen. Am I understood?"

"Indeed?" With that the priest scuttered away.

I smiled under his lips, which again pressed against mine.

"Is it inappropriate to say that I missed you?" I asked, testing the waters of familiarity.

"No," he said, "but it is most dangerous to say so when I feel this way." He pulled back and adjusted the front of his trousers. "I am sorry I have had to leave you alone over much these days. There is much to do in the way of planning a major royal event. Our kingdom has not had a royal wedding in nearly thirty years."

"I understand," I said. "I only hope that at some point, I might have your undivided attention."

"My Dear," he said, kissing my fingers one by one. "I promise that you will have my entire focus very soon. Now, I am late to a session with the royal scribes, who must finalize the invitations and send couriers to as many as can get there within a day and my lawyer, who must tend to some documents for me."

"Thank you for our stolen moment," I whispered, "and for witnessing my baptism."

"And thank you for taking it in good spirit...*Iris of Cornwall*." He kissed my forehead, then grimaced at the taste of oil he encountered and strode away from me.

I leaned against the wall where Marcus had just pressed against me in his rush of passion and appreciated its firmness against my back since my legs were still unsteady under me. I marveled at the effect he could have on me after so short a time, but this had to be the hundredth time since our meeting that I wondered such a thing. Any who knew me on Avalon would laugh at me losing my head over a man so quickly or at all since they knew me not to be so given.

I smiled to myself, thinking how life could take such dramatic turns so quickly and as such, how could we ever truly know ourselves? I was certainly not now the same woman who boarded the barge on the shores of Avalon and watched my mother and father sadly waving goodbye to all of us at once. Now, my spirit soared to know I could give Marcus the heir he needed and wanted and my insides ached to feel his touch again and hear his words of passion whispered in my ear. Who was this woman, so quickly falling in love with a man she barely knew? My only redemption was that for whatever blessed and sacred reason, he seemed to feel the same for me. Anything else, we could work out in time and by all appearances, we had plenty of that ahead of us.

CHAPTER 8

To my surprise, my parents arrived the day before the wedding, riding in on horseback with no more than saddle bags to carry their provisions. I felt as though I had not seen them in months, even though it was barely a fortnight. It did not take the calculations of a genius to figure out that to arrive in time for the wedding, they had to leave Avalon a mere two days after I did, so it was clear they did not wait for an invitation. They had simply known, as was their way.

I was in my final dress fitting when Ursa came to me and bowed low.

"My Lady, your parents have arrived from Avalon."

"My...what? My parents are here?"

Laoghaire put down the leather shoe she was polishing to wear at the ceremony and squealed with delight.

"Iris, they've come! We must go greet them!"

Quickly, I finalized the fitting and hurried to the entry way. News must have traveled fast because they were not yet even inside the castle, so I rushed into the courtyard behind Laoghaire and then even further into the breezeway.

My father held his arms open to Laoghaire and swept her up into a monstrous bear hug, kissing her head.

"Dear girl!" he beamed. "Are you staying out of trouble or at least enjoying yourself if you are not?"

She beamed up at him, reminding me that every female in the twenty years since he had arrived on Avalon had first lost their hearts to my father before any man. He was tall, strong, and strikingly handsome.

Age only made him more distinguished and exotic looking. He stood a head and a half taller than most men and his olive skin and sloe eyes caused him to stand out even more. He kept his skin marked with arcane sigils, which changed depending on the magical work he was doing at the time. He now dressed in the saffron robes of a Senior Druid, which made his skin appear even darker.

My mother fussed over Laoghaire, stroking her hair, and kissing her cheek fondly. She was regal beyond measure, and yet one of the kindest, most affectionate people I have ever known. She saw no threat in the women young and old who fawned over my father, for she was secure in the knowledge of her place in his life. She was also aware more than anyone of his dynamic sexuality and raw male attraction. How could she fault any young priestess for the stirrings he created inside them since he was their representation of the God on earth? He had long ago pledged his fidelity to her, and she to him, even though it was not required of them. On Avalon, she was the Goddess to every man and he was the God to every woman. Every male on Avalon wanted to *be* him and *be with* her and every female on Avalon wanted to *be* her and *be with* him. That was the way of things.

So tall was he and so short was she that her head came up only to his chest. The blue robes of the Lady of Avalon draped her round, curvy body and she carried herself with unimaginable grace. As they walked through the breezeway, everyone stopped what they were doing to turn and stare. I realized quite abruptly that this was the first time I had ever seen my parents outside of Avalon and with the same eyes the rest of the world turned on them. Of course, I had the filters of them being my parents but apart and away from that, to me they were the most beautiful sight anyone could imagine.

When they saw me, my mother's hand went to her mouth and she smiled broadly behind it while my father's eyes shown with great pride. A fierce wave of homesickness crashed into me and I resisted the urge to run to them as Laoghaire had done. If I were to be queen to the people around us, I must establish dignity with them now, not merely after I wore the crown.

I met them halfway through the courtyard and embraced them warmly, each in turn.

"Are you well, dear one?" my mother asked.

"I am…" I struggled to find the words. Lonely? Overwhelmed? Confused? Terrified? Humbled? "I am well," I said at last.

Like the devoted servant she was, Bersaba joined us in the courtyard and I introduced her to them.

"I will prepare a room, My Lady," she said to me. "We do still have some unclaimed."

"It sounds as though you have quite a houseful," my father smiled, looking around at the crowd that assembled to gawk openly at them. "Royal weddings do tend to bring out the dignitaries."

"Some of the ones who wish you jailed or worse," my mother fretted. "I feel no sense of safety here, Bran, I will not lie, but we could not miss our daughter's wedding."

"Have you heard from any of my sisters?" I asked, eager for news of their safety.

My father's forehead furrowed. "Not yet. I am quite sure we will soon. And do not worry, my love," he said to my mother. "If I thought we were in danger, we would not have come. Let us lay aside all grudges and political turmoil and rejoice in our daughter's marriage. We are here but for two nights and a day, so shall we not make the most of it?"

All around us, festival tents, colorful flags, and striking banners covered nearly every space in the courtyard as dignitaries from all over Britain staked out their tiny territories, making encampments all through the enclosed walls. Commoners and lesser aristocrats camped on the grassy lawns before the great sea cliffs and inland to the gardens at the rear of the castle. I recalled that Bersaba had told me earlier that day that many were whispering that the king rushed the marriage so his beautiful betrothed would not have time to flee like the others. I felt a stab of embarrassment for him that they should speak of him so. The idea that such a powerful and honorable king would be the butt of a joke raised my ire.

"So how are things with your future stepdaughter?" my mother asked as we passed through the open doors of Tintagel proper.

"I barely see her," I said. "For all the trouble she caused so many others, I have seen her only at evening meal and then she behaves as a proper lady. I cannot imagine so many were mistaken, especially since they barely knew one another."

"I would keep my eye on that one."

"Certainly," I said, "as well as... Ah, Father Francisco."

I smiled my most insincere smile as we turned a corner and I very nearly collided with the man himself.

"Father, I am honored to introduce my parents, Bran and Lillian, the Lord and Lady of Avalon, first of their names, and each sovereign in their own right."

He stared at them and did not bow, as he should have given his station and theirs.

"Your Holiness," my father smiled and nodded in the father's direction.

"Father Francisco," my mother said, bowing slightly.

The priest's lips were pressed hard into a straight line.

"I cannot allow this," he said, his voice edged with agitation.

"Allow exactly what?" I asked, feeling the steel come into my spine. My patience was running thin with this man, yet I knew he and I had miles yet to walk together.

"I cannot allow these heretics and sorcerers into our court. It simply cannot be."

My father took him by the elbow, not in an aggressive fashion, but more in the style of camaraderie, and steered him away, though still within our hearing.

"Brother in God," he said warmly, his smile broad and engaging, "I look forward to sharing ideologies and philosophies with you. Will you have time to share a glass of wine and ruminate with me this night before such a joyous and auspicious celebration tomorrow?"

Father Francisco jerked his arm away and rubbed his elbow as if he had been burned.

"I will not," he spat. "I do not lie down with dogs lest I get up with fleas or worse. Now take your leave," he waved his hand as if shooing a fly, "before I summon the King's Guard to have you removed." I felt my cheeks go white with rage at his overt disrespect.

"Francisco!" a voice boomed from behind us. I turned to see Marcus, his eyes ablaze with a fury all his own. "You will treat my future in-laws with the respect due not only to visiting dignitaries, but to my own family."

The priest was not to be cowed.

"Your Majesty!" he argued. "These are Pagans and they have no place in a Christian ceremony nor a proper Christian court!"

"Then respectfully, Father Francisco, *you* have no place in my court. Perhaps I have acquiesced to your wisdom on too many occasions and you have forgotten which of us is actually King of Cornwall." His voice was sharp and unyielding and I believe it was in that moment that my lust for my future husband transitioned into love.

Now, it was the priest's turn to pale. "Your Majesty," he said again, this time with undisguised pleading. "I beg that you not force my hand in sending word to Rome of your actions."

Marcus raised one eyebrow.

"Threaten me again, holy man, and you will be on a donkey to Cameliard faster than you can say ten Hail Marys. I am quite confident that Father Damian can perform tomorrow's ceremony even if our vows do sound less like promises and more like questions."

Father Francisco's face twisted in undisguised rage.

"My Lord…" he began, but Marcus cut him off.

"Apologize now to my guests for your insolence and disrespect."

"Truly," my mother cooed. "It is not necessary. We are accustomed to these sorts of behaviors in this time of confusion and unease. There is no need."

"With all respect, Madam, there is every need," Marcus stared at Father Francisco and then raised his eyebrows expectantly.

Father Francisco swallowed hard, as if something distasteful had lodged in his throat.

"My…" he closed his eyes and drew in a heavy breath. "My deepest apologies My Lord," he nodded to my father, "and My Lady," and nodded to my mother.

"Take your leave," Marcus said firmly. "And I will personally accept your apology to me later. Meanwhile, I suggest you contact your cohorts in the High Court, Rome, or whatever higher authority you must to live at peace in your own skin, but know now that you will not usurp my authority within this court or pay insult to my bride or her family. You yourself do not live outside of the charge of treason should it become necessary."

"Your Grace," he bowed elaborately to the King and then quickly took his leave.

Marcus turned toward my parents and dipped his head deferentially.

"Lord Merlin," he said, "I would enjoy taking my chaplain's place for that wine and discourse this night if you will have it so."

"Just Bran," my father said, smiling. "And I would enjoy that very much."

"You will forgive me for not calling you 'Father' as you are younger than I," Marcus joked.

My father laughed aloud.

"I believe that is a formality we may dismiss under the circumstances."

"Speaking of formalities," my mother interjected. "We come with a substantial dowry for our daughter if your servants may bring it in."

"Lady Lillian, you have already presented me with the finest gift for which a man could ever hope." He smiled at me and reached for my hand. "I require nothing from your kingdom in token of our marriage."

"You are most kind," she said, "however, the dowry provides for our daughter should her need ever arise, so if you would be so kind as to store it on her behalf should she ever need it… even we Pagans are not divorced from traditions of the court."

"I never imagined so, Madam. And truly, I do know the reputations that Ladies of the Lake have had for all time of being learned in matters of state and spirit, so should you choose to join myself and your husband tonight, you are most welcome to do so."

"Your kindness is most appreciated," she said, "However what I crave more than anything is to fill my belly, have a hot bath, and get a good night's sleep before my daughter's special day tomorrow."

He bowed at the waist to her.

"Our evening meal is served within the hour. Bersaba will tend to your every need."

"Indeed, I shall," the woman said. "Shall we?"

As we left, Marcus and my father each kissed me, my father on the forehead and Marcus on my cheek. My father also kissed my mother and the men resumed talking in an animated fashion as we took our leave.

"He seems lovely," my mother observed as we walked.

"As nearly as I can tell, he is," I agreed.

"Does he…handle you gently?" she asked, so delicately that I took her meeting immediately.

"He has yet to handle me much at all," I admitted, "but what little handling he has done has been as respectful as I cared for it to be."

My mother laughed. "Iris, you do have a way with words."

She slipped her hand into the crook of my arm and I placed my hand over hers. It felt good to walk with her again, even though I knew that when they left the day after the next, I would likely not see her again for a very long time.

"Are you afraid?" she asked.

"Afraid of what?"

"Anything."

I thought for a moment, then said, "I realize I should be, I suppose, but no. As I was about to say when we were interrupted, Father Francisco has made it clear that he has no love nor tolerance for me. Oh, and I was baptized into the Christian church yesterday."

"Indeed?"

"And Father Francisco said I was, let me get this correct, a 'brazen, low-born mongrel.'"

"All that then?"

"All that."

"It has been a lively week for you, daughter."

"Most assuredly."

Bersaba and I escorted my mother to the room on the opposite side of my quarters from the dressing room.

"I will send for a hot bath, My Lady," the servant said, "and ask for me personally should you have need for aught."

My mother thanked her and looked longingly at the bed.

"Were my belly not full of demands rather than food, I would bathe and slip right off to sleep."

"Madam, if you wish, I am happy to arrange a meal in your room."

Mother exchanged glances with me.

"They are most hospitable here," she said.

"They are," I agreed. "I run a very tight ship."

We three laughed together.

"Truly, it has been this way since I arrived," I said. "Bersaba has quite taken me under her wing."

My mother looked at the woman with true gratitude.

"It pleases me to know my daughter is in such capable and loving hands."

"She is a rare gem, this one," Bersaba smiled.

"She is."

My mother glanced at the bed again.

"As tempting as is your offer, I believe I would prefer to dine at the King's table tonight if that invitation is open. It has been long since I have dined in court and I have little enough time to get to know my future son-in-law as it is."

"His Majesty will no doubt welcome you at his table," Bersaba assured her. "The sea air here at Tintagel makes our guests sleep like stones, but I am sure you know about sleeping in the sea air, being from the Holy Isle."

"I do," my mother said, almost wistfully. "I look forward to returning. As Iris can vouch, the ride feels long and challenging, and especially on my bones that are older than hers."

"Allow me to say, My Lady, that it is a privilege for me to tend on the Lady of the Lake myself. Never in my life did I imagine I would have such an honor."

My mother studied her intently.

"It is rare to hear anyone speak fondly of the Holy Isle in these times," she said.

"There are still those about who honor the old ways, but must do so in the shadows these days for fear of such harsh reprisals. More so even, that is why I am grateful your daughter has come to us as Queen and all."

Mother squeezed the older woman's hand.

"I pray our time will come again, Sister," she said softly.

~*~

To my surprise, when the herald announced my parents, my father greeted very nearly every one of the strangers at the King's tables warmly and by name. Housed for my entire life on Avalon, I had forgotten what a diplomat he was, often traveling from kingdom to kingdom throughout the Britain Beyond, campaigning on behalf of the people of the Goddess, but also acting as an accomplished mediator and adviser. As much as he was admired for his ability to navigate the choppy waters of adversity and bring harmony to difficult situations, there were also those who despised him for his life-long defense of those who worshiped the Goddess. As my mother had reminded me, he had been jailed and suffered many indignities for his beliefs and actions, so she was altogether within rights to have concerns for their safety. Father Francisco was not the only one who held false beliefs of who we were and what we did. Our holy practices on Avalon were much maligned and misunderstood by those who wished to subjugate the people of the Goddess and turn them against their native spiritual practices.

Other dignitaries, within the court for the wedding festivities of the coming day, joined us for the evening meal around the King's larger table and those smaller tables set around the room. There was little time for Marcus and I to speak and unlike our previous meals, the table was lively with conversation and laughter. Wine and ale flowed liberally and soon, many were well within their cups before even the second course of the meal was finished.

I looked for Princess Zelda, but she never appeared for the evening meal. When I asked Marcus, he said she had asked to dine in her room for the night and he had agreed. For a moment, I envied her that freedom.

While I hungered for his attention, even merely in conversation, I realized that this was the life of a queen, to forever share the attention of her husband with an entire kingdom. I thought back to the eros instruction we received on Avalon of "always leave your partner wanting more of you" and smiled wryly that it seemed such would forever be the case in my pending marriage.

"And what has your mirth afloat?" Marcus said, seeing my secret smile.

"Only that my future husband is needed in so many places at once that I fear I will be forever in want of him."

He studied me intently and such a length of time that for a moment, I thought perhaps I misspoke.

"You swear that you are no sorceress," he said in a low voice, leaning closer to me, "and yet when you speak like that, I swear you enchant me beyond reason."

Playing the minx had never been in my feminine bag of tricks, but that did not stop me.

"And did you hope for a wife so pious and cold that you caught frostbite to touch her?"

He looked pensive and broke his gaze from mine.

"I never again dared to hope for any wife who would want aught beyond the station and comforts I could afford her."

"And why so?" I asked, at once surprised and sad for him. "Is it truly so rare beyond the shores of Avalon for a wife to treasure her husband's attention beyond the material?"

He took my hand and squeezed it and the mere sensation of his skin against mine caused my blood to race. For all my banter, I did know how something of how he felt. How could I have imagined that an arranged marriage would quicken my pulse so? When I first heard how much older he was than I, my mental image was of a gnarled old man who smelled of leeks and sweat and elderberries who would heave and gasp and shove his withered cock into me in hopes of planting an heir before his imminent demise. Never had I hoped for such a handsome, virile, and pleasing husband.

"Perhaps not," he answered, "however I have been alone for over fourteen years now and after the parade of empty-headed hens that passed over my threshold during that time, I suspected I would die alone or worse, end up wedded and miserable. That is why… well…" he smiled and patted my hand. "…conversation for another time."

I was not as gifted with The Sight or thought perception as was my sister Lily, but I knew he spoke of her, that other woman who had his heart before me. Without words, he was saying that he grasped onto love when he found it, regardless of the unworkable circumstances it presented. Because he expected always to be alone or in a loveless marriage, he had secured some haven of precious joy for himself. I could not fault him that, but I also could not deny that my heart wept a bit each time I thought of him in the arms of another and giving her the affection that was due me as a wife.

One of the many wisdoms my mother imparted upon me is that all marriages and in fact, all relationships, come with some degree of personal sacrifice. I never expected that sharing my husband with a woman even older than my mother was what my sacrifice would be, but I also had to admit that had he not revealed in stark honesty the condition of his own heart and personal affairs, I never would have known he loved another for all of the desire and graciousness he had shown to me.

Was it for me to play the shrew for what was in play before ever I came to him, demanding that he end his relationship with her and cleave only unto me? Or was it for me to truly be a lady of worth and love him, pleasure him, and allow him to do what he admitted to me in candor and other kings did behind the back of their queen? Were I on Avalon and in love with a man there, none would think twice about him having two women or me having lovers other than my husband. There, the act of love was free and unbridled and knew no societal definitions or restrictions. From where did this possessiveness and neediness arise?

    This bid me to wonder how *she* felt, knowing that the man she loved would tomorrow wed a woman who was suited to be his queen when she could not be, and who could bear him children when she could not. Did she wonder if I would place demands upon his affections or make a scene over his admission when came push to shove? As my mother recognized in my father, how could I fault another woman for loving a man so kind and handsome as my future husband? Granted, my mother never had to imagine that my father shared intimacies with other women, but was it really that different?

    In my heart and mind, I knew the woman I wanted to be and that I would allow him his freedom to love and honor, so long as he offered me the same.

    After the final course as those gathered at the King's table dissolved into loud and drunken revelry, I noticed my mother leaning her head onto my father's shoulder while he engaged in animated conversation with a man who I thought I remembered to be the King's lawyer. Quietly, I bid Marcus goodnight asked his leave to retire for the night. He nodded and I kissed him on the cheek and then gently touched my mother's arm. She startled awake and then smiled at me and nodded.

Knowing my father could converse for hours, I asked her if she would care to share my bed for the night and she eagerly accepted. As we slipped under the covers, she folded herself around me, even though I was easily a head and a half taller than she, and I drifted off to sleep with her absently stroking my hair as she had done when I was a small child, surrounded by her warmth and the smell of lavender and rose from the oils she rubbed into her own locks as she dried them.

CHAPTER 9

My wedding day dawned bright and beautiful in early June without a trace of the rain and fog that plagued us only a week before. Bersaba shook me awake, her smile nearly as bright as the sun coming through my eastern window.

"'tis a beautiful day, My Lady," she said. "What an auspicious sign for a long and happy marriage to have a sunny day in Cornwall!"

Beside her, Ursa squeezed cool, scented water from a linen cloth and patted my face with it to help me wake up. I had slept little the night before, my mind stirring with thoughts both fearsome and glorious over my pending marriage. My stomach churned almost as much as my mind and even the warm presence of my mother did coax me into deep sleep.

"Your dress has arrived," Ursa smiled. I could not imagine that she would be happier even if it were her own wedding day. If my own sisters not surround me with their support, I was at least comforted that the women closest to me in the court were happy for me and fawned over me with loving attention. I was not usually one to need affection or fussing over, but today, I welcomed it.

"We will summon the seamstresses after you break your fast for the final adjustments," Bersaba said.

"Is the King yet awake?" I asked, hoping for a few moments of his time before we entered this ritual that would forever change our lives and bind us together. I wished to ask him so many things, such as whether he was sure he wanted to marry when his heart lay elsewhere or perhaps if he was certain he wished to bind to a Daughter of Avalon. I felt a need to reach out to him and gain reassurance that both his heart and his mind were at peace with what we were about to do.

"Oh yes," Bersaba said. "His Majesty was up before dawn and has spent the early morning riding through the courtyards, personally welcoming the dignitaries who have arrived."

"Oh," I replied, feeling my voice weaken.

"Is something wrong, My Lady?" Ursa asked.

"I had only hoped to see him before the wedding, if only briefly" I sighed.

They looked at one another, aghast.

"No!" they both shouted, nearly in harmony.

"Oh, you mustn't," Bersaba said, her eyes wide. "He cannot see you on the day of the wedding! 'tis bad luck, it is!"

"Bad luck, indeed!" Ursa echoed.

"Bad luck?" I asked. "Do you truly believe in such superstitious nonsense?"

Bersaba clucked. "You from the magical isle and you doubt why I take no chances in this?" she said sternly. "You will have plenty enough time to talk the King's leg off for the rest of your lives if you will it and he allows it. Today, however, you are in our hands and we are keeping you as far from His Majesty as we can until you walk down that abbey aisle on your father's arm."

For the first time since I was a child, I felt like pouting.

"Besides," Bersaba continued, "the kitchen staff has prepared a fine morning meal for you and Miss Laoghaire to share with your mother before the day gets away from you. Won't that be nice, now?"

I smiled, despite my disappointment. She was right. I would have plenty of time to visit with Marcus later and no man could have done more to assure me that he was ready to marry. It was only my personal insecurities that longed for stroking and it would be good to have quiet time with my mother, especially considering that there was little knowing when I would see her again after today. She would ride back to Avalon within a day and I would begin my official tasks of finding a way to protect the Goddess worshiping people of Cornwall, as well as producing heirs to the Cornish throne. If not now, there would be no time.

I dressed hastily, knowing that I had slept well past the dawn rising I had planned and now had a matter of hours before I had to begin preparing for the late afternoon festivities. Because the household ran quite effectively without a Lady of the Castle before me, I had little to do for the feast or hospitality. I knew it would not always be so easy and truth be told, hospitality was not my talent. I left that to my sisters who reveled in parties and socializing. For me, preparation involved meeting in the abbey at noon for a quick rehearsal of the ritual, and then retiring to my suite to primp my dress and hair. I likely had less to do than anyone involved and I quite liked it that way. No one would ever accuse me of shying away from my fair share of work, but I did like to choose what that work would involve and this type of energy investment was not my cup of tea.

We ate in my mother's room and the food was already laid out with servants at the ready when I arrived. Since I first came to the castle, whether it was out of fear that I would get lost in the huge and winding corridors or suspecting I might bolt like the others, I was rarely alone. I had only to step out of my door and some handmaid or courtier appeared at my elbow, asking if I needed anything and bowing and bowing with the endless bowing.

Laoghaire laughed about it at first, but I could tell it was starting to unnerve her as well.

"Do you suppose we are being held prisoner?" she joked, but then looked serious. "Do you?"

"I think they are just trying to be helpful," I said, but I could hear the hopefulness in my voice. "Maybe it will ease up after the wedding when they are more confident that I will not flee in the night."

"I hope so," she grimaced. "I half expect a hand to reach through the door to help me take a piss."

"They do coddle," I agreed.

My mother looked tired, more so than I thought I had ever before seen her and I felt a stab of concern. She smiled pleasingly, but weariness tugged at her features and slowed her usually graceful movements. I loved these times on the rare occasion when they came, when she was simply my mother and not Lady of the Lake, Queen of Avalon. Although Avalon no longer enjoyed the respect and sovereignty that it once held in the Britain Beyond, it was still one of the lesser kingdoms, much to the dismay of the High Court. Once the High Throne of Britain came completely under Christian rule, the priests did their worst to demonize our home, stripping away from it many of the privileges previously bestowed upon it. My father, for instance, the Merlin of Britain, no longer sat in counsel to the High King, who was a boy prince with a regent in place until he came of age. The regent was one of the great Archbishops of the land, and as such, there was now no room in the High Court for any who did not follow the Christ.

My mother too would once have sat in on matters of the court as did the Ladies of the Lake before her, but their holy books taught that a woman did not have a place in determining law, justice, or warfare. Our only condoned tasks were to sew, cook, and make babies without complaint. On Avalon, she ruled decisively and was revered for her wisdom, but the moment she stepped off its shores, she was naught but an arrogant female who stood above her own raising and brought insult upon her station and her husband by daring to expect her own measure equal to a man's place in the world.

She had not spoken out of turn when she voiced to my father her concerns about those who visited our court and might want him in prison or worse. In fact, he had not known that my sisters and I even existed until we were weeks old, missing her entire pregnancy which was fraught with worry as a multiple birth, because he was held prisoner in more than one of the kingdoms for no more than petitioning the court for equal and peaceful rights for the Goddess worshiping people of our land. As an engaging, charming, and convincing diplomat, many would prefer his game piece off the playing table and for him to be permanently silenced. For his entire adult life, he championed for the people of the Goddess to be left in peace to honor their holy connection to the land and to their gods as they saw fit. He alone, by his own merit and efforts, managed to keep the peace, but so tenaciously balanced was it that when his brother-in-law died and our cousin, Phillip, was subsequently dethroned, the Christians at last held their sway. They burned the holy groves and altars and persecuted or even killed those who were caught practicing the old ways.

That was when my sisters and I were sent into each of the seven kingdoms of Britain to find a way to work from within and soothe the waters for those who believed as we did. We were ambassadors for Avalon, whether anyone knew it or not. What I understood that the elders of Avalon did not tell us directly was that this was the last hope, the final effort in a battle in which we were sorely disadvantaged once the momentum of the Church took hold of Britain. We did not wish to overthrow or demand that other worship as did we. We believe all gods are one god, so as they honor their man on the cross, they also honor our god who sacrifices himself each year through the corn that is hewn and through every apple picked, giving his life so that others may live. No, we welcomed those who believed differently and in fact, my ancestors on Avalon, one of whom was my father in a previous yet remembered life, invited the Christians to build a sanctuary on Avalon that Druid and Christian might kneel together in worship.

All we wanted was for those who hold our beliefs sacred to worship unmolested and without persecution. We wanted our people in the Britain Beyond to dance by the Beltane and Samhain fires, to crown their Lady of the May and to light their sacred candles at Imbolc. It was my task to find a way for them to do that safely in Cornwall. Another of my sisters would go to North Wales, one to South Wales, to the Summer Country, and so on. Each of us were tasked to fulfill a sacred duty and each of us would find experiences that would shape or even possibly end our lives while on our missions.

As we ate quietly on the morning of my wedding day, content in one another's company. Mother and Laoghaire engaged in small talk about the wedding and what they would wear. They talked of how people on Avalon responded to our leaving and what simple things had befallen those we knew since we left. I was never one for chit chat, so I happily ate my buttered bread and porridge and nibbled on some fruit while they visited. Masey, one of the girls who found herself with child after the last Beltane celebration, had miscarried. Old Belen, the midwife who delivered us, was troubled by swelling in her feet and fussed because she had to stay seated with them elevated. The apple trees were loaded with tiny green fruits that promised a bountiful harvest.

Hearing of such normal, familiar occurrences put my heart at ease as they passed the time together over scones and jams, fruits, and quail eggs.

"Where is Father?" I asked, knowing he, such a social butterfly, was likely passing time with the people he knew in court.

"He is meeting with your future husband," my mother said. "Did the King not mention it?"

"I have seen nearly nothing of the King. The last time I even spoke with him was when he greeted you."

"I imagine he is busy," Laoghaire offered. "A royal wedding is quite a lot to plan and you have hardly been here long enough to know what to do."

"True," I agreed. "What are they meeting about?"

Mother patted her mouth with a linen napkin. "The exchange of the dowry. Likely some veiled threats about how you are to be treated."

"Mother!"

She shrugged. "It is what men do. No legally binding contract ever happens without a good bit of man bits being exposed and waved about. Your father is far from immune to such traditions and in fact, likely takes pleasure from the process."

"It all seems ridiculous and barbaric to me," I snipped. "As though we are naught but chattel to transfer from one column to the other on the audit books of men."

"Welcome to the Britain Beyond, my dear, and to the world the Romans brought to us."

Before I knew it, the servants were clearing away the dishes and my mother and Laoghaire rose from the table.

"I believe we should start dressing the bride, should we not?" My mother said to Laoghaire. "Will you please summon the handmaidens?"

Laoghaire nodded and slipped away as my mother and I returned to my dressing room.

The seamstresses delivered the dress in our absence and waited patiently outside the door to fit it to me for the final and most important showing. Before long, women with various tasks to their credit surrounded me as they rubbed cream into my skin, pinched and rouged my cheeks, shaped my eyebrows, and pinned my hair into an elaborate upsweep.

My dress was in the traditional colors of the Cornish court, deep red and gold, and made of fine brocade. Again, I felt I could not breathe as I was laced into the corseted contraption of the time which tightened my already trim waist to unreasonable proportions. I argued and complained until they loosened it slightly and vowed never to again wear such a thing. I regret that words certainly unbefitting to the Queen of Cornwall passed my lips during these garment negotiations.

"And where is Bersaba? Is she not attending me on today of all days?"

"She is overseeing the feast," Ursa said, her voice more soothing than I deserved to hear. "That is her responsibility as wife of the Chamberlain. She would be here if she could, My Lady."

I had so much to learn before I could fully consider myself the Lady of Tintagel or Queen of Cornwall or any such lofty title. As if sensing the sudden wave of panic that threatened to choke me, my mother laid a cool hand on my arm and gave it a squeeze. I felt swept along in a current I could not control and I skirted on the edge of panic. Years of priestess training that started very nearly as soon as I could walk and continued nonstop until mere days ago abandoned my mind and my spirit completely. I felt my chest constricting, and not only from the damnable device no less than three women had laced me into just minutes before. My breath left me and the last thing I heard was a voice saying, "We are losing her. She's going down."

I woke to my mother washing my face with a cool, wet cloth and cooing to me softly as she had done when I was very little. I was on the floor with my head in her lap while countless worried faces peered down at me from what seemed miles above. Never had I ever in my life fainted until that moment and even as I tried to rise, I felt the floor threaten to rise to meet me, pitching every bit as if I were on the deck of a ship at storm.

"Get her a cup of water, now!" I heard Laoghaire say.

"Someone call the court physician," I heard a worried voice call out, shrill and impatient.

I waved away the cup because the Cornish water tasted foul to me and I feared I would wretch if I had to swallow it, especially now with my stomach already at odds with the morning meal we had eaten.

My mother said something to Laoghaire and in a few minutes, the girl returned with a drinking horn and put it to my lips. The sweet, clear taste of water from Avalon was a blessed relief as it slipped down my throat. I thought to weep from it, but instead, felt the color coming back to me and my head clearing.

"Get this thing off her," my mother ordered. "Can you not see your Queen can barely breathe in it?"

"But Madam," said one of the seamstresses. "If we take off the corset, the dress will not hang properly on her and the workmanship will be lost."

My mother stared her down with hard eyes. "And pray tell, who will notice if the dress hangs a bit tighter on her body than it would have otherwise? I shall not sacrifice the health of my daughter for your fabric artwork."

"Yes, My Lady,' the seamstress said. As she pulled at the ties at the back of my dress, I felt air, fetid and humid, but air, nonetheless, rush into my grateful lungs. Sure enough, as I breathed it in deeply, I heard the crack of seams rupturing at my sides. I literally would be unable to breathe fully if I wore the dress as it was designed.

I saw the pained look on the seamstress's face and knew she too had heard the seams break open. I thought she might cry.

I reached over and took her hands in mine, still lying recumbent in my own mother's lap like a young girl.

"These hands," I said, "still made the wedding dress of the Queen of Cornwall, whether I breathe or do not breathe. Take pride in that, girl. It is a lovely dress and we shall stitch the sides on the wider edge of the seam and all will be well, but get that contraption far from me and never let me see it again."

She nodded and the women helped me to ease out of the dress. With deft hands, she restitched the seams, so quickly I could barely see her fingers move. Within minutes, they hooked the buttons up the back and channeled me back into the dress without the corset. It fit quite comfortably.

"No one will know there were other pieces," I said. "And if you are questioned, tell them I demanded otherwise and there was naught you could do."

Almost immediately after the dress was on my body once more, we were interrupted by Bersaba, who clasped her hands over her mouth, her eyes wide.

"My Lady," she breathed. "You look ever so splendid."

"It is the first dress I have worn since I arrived that I could call my own," I marveled. "All others were borrowed from previous potential brides."

"Or from the Queen herself," Bersaba added, "and you certainly did them justice. And this as well. Saraba, you and your women have outdone themselves on this dress."

Saraba curtsied to Bersaba and murmured her thanks.

"Come now," Bersaba said to all of us. "We must get you to the abbey lest our good king think that yet another potential bride has abandoned him outright."

The King's Guard, finely turned out in formal uniforms and burgundy capes with white fur trim led me to the breezeway where a gilded carriage waited. The Commander of the Guard help me and my mother into the carriage and the ladies in waiting onto white ponies that stood behind it. I could hardly believe that we would ride the distance from the entry to Tintagel to the rear of the courtyard where the abbey stood, but I knew it was for show and pageantry to allow those who would not fit into the church a chance to see the bride. Within the sway of the carriage, my stomach continued to pitch and roll and I wondered how much of an affront it would be if the bride happened to vomit on the King as she spoke her vows. My face was covered with a finely stitched, long gold veil that held in the heat most uncomfortably and I eagerly threw it over my head until I reached the waiting area for the ceremony.

My mother and I smiled and waved at the crowds of people who pushed onto the small trail leading to the abbey. "God save the Queen," some shouted and "Long Live Queen Iris!" They blew kisses and waved banners as we rode past.

At last, we arrived at a vestibule on the side of the abbey where my mother and my handmaidens, as well as Bersaba and Laoghaire, waited with me. I heard a fanfare of trumpets and knew the King had arrived. Harp music played and I could hear it ever so faintly as it drifted in from the auditorium where the wedding would take place.

Blessed Mother Goddess, I thought, *this is really happening. I am truly to be wed to a man I barely know.*

This was so far outside of our experiences on Avalon, although we were told of such things often happening in the Britain Beyond where marriages were more for political alliance and station advancement than for love. I pulled upon my every resource from deep inside, from above and below me, to garner my composure.

My mother slipped her arm around my shoulder and I knew she felt my inner tremors. I flashed with a moment of irritation because she knew nothing of what I felt. Her marriage had not only been for love, but had been one she all but demanded. She was the first Lady of the Lake to marry in times memorable, all those before her having committed to their marriage to the Goddess alone and taking whatever lover they saw fit. Neither had my father, The Merlin of Britain, taken a wife in his incarnations, all but this one time when his love for my mother was so great. How could she know what I felt when in all her wealth of experience, from both this life and many others, she had never offered this one sacrifice?

After this day, unless Marcus put me aside or I lived as his widow, I would never give my heart in total love and marry for that reason alone lest I live in dishonor for abandoning a king. Yet he himself had a lover. He had someone who received his affections without conditions or expectations attached and I did not. Good Goddess, for what was I setting myself up? Was I truly to sacrifice my life, my maidenhead, my future, and my freedom for some bizarre quest invented by old men and women on an isolated island?

As the panic began to rise on me and I felt my constitution, usually so iron clad and certain, crumbling around me, my father entered the vestibule and smiled at me. His dark eyes were troubled, but his smile was sincere. He saw my mother comforting me and the stricken look on my face and his expression softened even more.

"Iris, my dear love," he said as he hurried to my side. The two of them encompassed me in a warm, parental embrace so that I could hardly tell where one of them ended and the other began. I wanted to weep, but it felt like such a fruitless waste of energy to do so.

"Breathe," my mother said. "Breathe in the Goddess and bring Her deep into your spirit. Put up your priestess countenance and show them who you are."

Despite feeling as if the walls of the vestibule were closing in on me, I pulled in air like a woman drowning. I felt helpless and inadequate for my bout of fear.

At last, I felt as though my feet were under me again and my legs could hold me up without dumping me in the floor.

"What troubles you, Father?" I asked, fearing the worst.

"Absolutely nothing that need concern you now, my Princess," he assured me. "You have one job and one singular focus in this moment and that is to walk with us down that aisle and wed King Marcus."

I nodded, unwilling to press further and confident that were it anything I needed to know, he would tell me. Never had I known my father to be unnecessarily coy or evasive and I trusted his assessment completely.

"Now," he continued, "We set aside all other concerns and take you into their sacred building to wed who I believe to be a good man and a just king. After meeting with him, I feel confident in trusting my daughter in his hands. He and I do not agree on all things in the realm of spirit, but I trust that a Priestess of Avalon is well up to that challenge and, if what I hear is correct, has already picked up that particular gauntlet."

I smiled despite the tension of the moment.

"Perhaps," I said, meeting his eyes in a meaningful gaze.

"Be careful of Francisco," He said, his tone turning grave. "I believe Marcus will honor you in all ways but that priest I trust not at all."

"Nor do I," I agreed. "I will be careful."

"Are you ready?" my mother asked.

I nodded.

"Then let us not keep the King waiting," my father said, tucking my hand into the crook of his elbow.

My mother was again dressed in finery accustomed the Lady of the Lake, blue robes over a fine, lighter blue tunic with matching blue veils over her head and running down her back. The Queen of Avalon never veiled her face, as so often did ladies of worth in the Britain Beyond. To hide her face was the hide the face of the Goddess.

My father also wore the robes of his station, the blue robes of a bard over a golden tunic and pale trousers. In a rare show of sovereignty, for my father was a paragon of modesty, he wore a narrow gold circlet on his brow and a golden torque about his neck. My mother wore thinner matching ones; her only nod to the grandeur of jewels. It was essential that all present understand that they were royalty in their own line as well as spiritual leaders. For all their back-stabbing and land-grabbing, the lesser kings and the High Court were nothing if not respectful in the public eye since one never knew what back room alliances were in place. A charge of treason could manifest in moments over the wrong king being insulted or maligned in some way.

Laoghaire slipped my golden veil back over my face and we made our way to the back of the abbey. As was Cornish tradition of the time, neither Marcus nor I had attendants. Our wedding was an opulent affair, but when it came to it, it was little more than a business contract.

CHAPTER 10

As music of harp and violin swelled, I walked down the aisle of Tintagel Abbey toward my future husband. My parents and I had to walk through a long line of people who congregated outside the building, unable to squeeze into the room that was filled. Footmen walked ahead of us clearing the way, pushing aside the lesser gentry and even some servants and other commoners who hoped for a glance at the new queen and her entourage, of which there was none save my parents. My father joined us at the door and I took his arm. My mother walked down the aisle with me on my opposite side and took a seat in the first chapel pew. Everyone in the church, which included no one I immediately recognized, rose as we entered.

Marcus stood at the altar with two of his advisers whose names I had heard and could not remember and Father Francisco. He wore his full royal regalia and the impact was stunning to me. I was marrying a true and actual king. His scarlet cloak was decorated with ermine over a tunic whiter than I have ever seen. He wore the formal crown of Cornwall, which was jewel encrusted inlaid into the finest gold. The sight of him caught my breath in my chest and my heart started to pound. He was so breathtakingly handsome. The grey of his hair swept against the gold of his crown and matched perfectly the color of his twinkling eyes. He smiled at me and the lines in the corners of those eyes deepened. My heart melted a bit until I remembered that he was mine in name only, in title only. His heart belonged to another.

But was it wrong for me to pretend, just for today, that he was my devoted husband and I his queen in all ways?

Good Goddess, I thought, *when did I turn into such a romantic sap?* Always I had been the practical, pragmatic one. Everyone knew that if any of us were to become dowager maids, I would be the one. My life was given in servitude to the Goddess and to the process of birth and healing. I, who had no use for men other than their progenitive capabilities even a month ago, now looked upon a man I barely knew like a love-struck, moony-eyed novice. Did it take no more than a couple of stolen kisses and some guarded sweet words to turn my heart to jelly?

Determined, I reached far into my inner priestess core and pulled up my power, letting it flow through me and from me in a torrential rush. My father stiffened beside me and I knew he felt the shift. I would engage my own wedding not as a simpering, besotted girl, but as the Goddess I was intended to be by birthright and training. I would reign as a queen before ever the crown was on my head.

So, damned be it.

My father turned to me and reached for my right hand, which he lifted toward Marcus, who took it graciously with a nod. Father then stepped back to my far left as my representative.

A thought occurred to me and I looked around as inconspicuously as I could.

Where was Princess Zelda?

I had barely seen the girl since my arrival, which I found strange given her notorious reputation. Would she create a scene as the wedding unfolded? Was she not included in the wedding party?

Father Francisco began to speak and I focused fully on what he said. The wedding was more of a legal agreement than any sort of romantic pledging. The two witnesses Marcus brought verified every royal stamp and signature, of which there were many. My father signed many documents on behalf of Avalon, verifying my dowry and what provisions would be for me in the instance of King Marcus's death. This included different allocations in the case of accidental death, of death in battle, death of old age, death after five years, ten years, twenty years… I was bound to an oath of fidelity for the purity of the royal line of Cornwall. I was bound to give my life for Cornwall if necessary. I was bound to an oath of Christian reverence that I would adhere to the religious practices of the court and no others. I looked at my father as this one came up, but he only nodded, so I pledged my troth.

All gods are one god, I heard him say in my head. *Fear not, daughter. The Goddess will not forsake you.*

After many oaths were pledged and many prayers were offered, there was a wedding mass filled with dire, ominous warnings and threats of any manner of wretched outcomes should I not be a perfect and pious wife to Marcus in all ways. No mention of his behavior toward me or the marriage was ever made, only my own.

We took the Holy Eucharist and I translated it in my mind to the ceremonialized cakes and ale from the holy regalia we shared at the end of each ritual on Avalon. At last, Father Francisco conveyed the final holy blessing upon us and declared us to be husband and wife, joined together for all eternity. Marcus lifted my veil and kissed me as chaste as a grandsire would have done. The audience stood and cheered.

Marcus's footmen then brought in an elaborate throne and placed it on the highest part of the altar, directly under the looming crucifix. I had not heard that anything in this respect that would occur, but I trusted someone would coach me if I had any involvement. Marcus took my hand and led me to the throne, then bid me to sit upon it.

Father Francisco came around behind me as one of the advisers approached with a box that looked for all the world like their holy Ark of the Covenant said to house the original commandments they so revered. Angels adorned the top of the golden box and seemed to herald what was inside. My mind went to the custom of human sacrifice if the harvest was in want for more than seven years and the pledge I had just made to give my life for Cornwall if need be. I stifled hysterical laughter over the idea that this had all been an elaborate hoax to sacrifice a daughter of the Goddess to the land that it might prosper.

The second adviser opened the box and inside it I saw a crown that was the smaller twin of the one Marcus wore and my heart nearly stopped.

Would my coronation happen now and not later as I imagined? Not in the throne room? Now?

And so it was that Father Francisco held the crown over my head and declared me to be Queen Iris of Cornwall, first of her name. From the same box came a large ruby ring with a filigree setting around it. The second adviser passed it to Marcus, who placed it on the first finger of my right hand.

Truly, it fit as though it had been made for me and apparently, my throat would not be cut to bless the land... at least not today. But then, the day was not yet finished. Father Francisco looked as if he tasted something truly bitter as he anointed me with sacred oils, blessing me as Queen.

"With this ring, this crowning, and her being duly anointed," Marcus said in a booming voice that could never be denied as royal, "I accept this woman as my *semper fidelis,* my *uxorem vero,* and my *vera illa,* from here forward."

To my surprise, after declaring me as his always faithful true wife and true queen, he knelt before me and kissed the ring on my finger.

"It is to she alone and to the Kingdom of Cornwall," he said, "that I pledge my troth and bend my knee. God save the Queen!"

"God save the Queen!" the audience repeated. "God save the Queen!" over and over again as the people outside joined in.

Never had I imagined such pageantry and to do over the crowning of a lesser queen. My eyes swept over the congregation and marveled that they all looked so happy. If never again in my life would I feel it, in this moment, my heart was full and happy.

~*~

I could certainly never have imagined a feast as elaborate and delicious as the wedding feast. I sat beside Marcus and shared his plate, thinking that this was the most time I had spent with him since my arrival. So many courses were served that I was full after only partway through the feast, yet Marcus kept encouraging me toward different sweetmeats, sips of soups, and other delicacies. Entertainers of all sorts kept the party lively with jugglers, dancers, harpers, singers, and a man who performed illusion magic, making birds and scarves appear out of nowhere.

My father and mother sat with us on the dais, as, to my complete shock, did Princess Zelda. I had not seen her during any part of the ceremony, and yet, here she was acting as a doting, loving daughter on the other side of Marcus from me. Before long, everyone was well into their cups as Herschel and Bersaba kept the wines and ales flowing freely. So long did the feast last that those, like myself, who did fill up early on eventually became hungry once again. Hours passed until I knew it was well past midnight.

At last, the orchestra sounded a brilliant fanfare and the herald stepped forward.

"And now the bride and groom, our King and Queen, shall be put to bed."

Marcus reached for my hand and escorted me off the raised stage as others followed behind us. Several servants with large baskets passed among the attendees and handed out noisemakers and rattles which they blew and shook with great revelry in time to the beat of the drummers that followed behind us. From the grand ballroom where the feast was held all the way up to the King's chambers, they followed us, making a ridiculous amount of noise.

At the large wooden double doors of his chambers, Marcus swept me up in his arms as the crowd cheered. He then carried me over the threshold and into his suite, kicking the door closed behind him. Outside, I could hear the cheers dying down as they no doubt made their way back to the ballroom to finish up the ale, wine, and food. I found myself grateful that at least they did not follow us into the room to personally witness the consummation.

I was at last alone with the King for the first time since our breakfast days before, discounting our stolen moment in the great hallway. Gently, he put me back on my feet and then removed his cloak.

"I was sweating like a bear in that thing. I cannot imagine I smell very pleasant right now. It feels like a winter breeze in here now with it off."

He sat on the end of the bed and removed his boots. After the flurry of the very long day, I suddenly felt uncomfortable, now alone with him in so familial a way. This was a man I hardly knew and now I was vowed to him for life, obligated to render my maidenhead unto him and honor bound to bear him children and secure his dynasty. A month prior, I had only known his name, his title, and a few wild rumors about his marriageability, all of which turned out to be true. In a breathless moment, the circumstances of my life became once again and quite suddenly clear and utterly terrifying.

Without considering what I was doing, I knelt before him and helped him remove his boots as I had seen my mother do for my father. He looked surprised, but pleased and as they came away, I gently rubbed each foot. He sighed with pleasure and leaned back onto the bed, supported by his elbows.

I was grateful for the task because it distracted me from the thoughts that pounded into my brain and threatened to bring panic up into my throat.

How was it that I, a holy priestess of Avalon, was thrown into this pack of ravenous Christian wolves who managed no modicum of respect for my beliefs nor my way of life? How would I find any joy in my life as such? I glanced around, painfully aware that I had never been in the King's quarters before. They were opulent; elegant in every way. I forced myself to breathe once, twice, and then smiled up at him and placed his boots near the bed.

Standing, I walked over to the mirror in the far corner of the sleeping area into which we had entered. I pulled the pins from my veil to occupy myself while I struggled to find the peaceful core within. I removed the veil and headdress from my head and laid it aside on a chair.

I startled as I felt his hands on my shoulders, soft and warm, then looked up to meet his gaze in the mirror.

"You are so young," he said, his voice soft against my neck. "I never imagined to have a bride whose father or even grandsire I might be. I can feel your discomfort, dear Iris. If the thought of being with me displeases you, there are ways to satisfy the appearance of consummation. Know now that I will never force myself upon your sacred and beautiful body. I will not take my pleasure with you if you also do not find your pleasure and desire in me. I have lived this long without a male heir and have found my peace with that loss. I will not discomfort you to have one, nor merely to take my own pleasure or meet some standard of royal tradition."

His words touched me deeply and I felt myself relaxing as he slipped his hands lower to surround my waist and pull me against him.

"Iris," he continued, "I have been with no woman since my wife died over fifteen years ago. I am accustomed to foregoing the act of physical pleasure and so if it is not your wish that we consummate our marriage, I will continue my time of abstinence for your comfort."

I saw my own puzzled expression in the mirror in front of us and knew when our eyes met that he did as well.

"Wait," I said, turning to face him. "What about this woman of which you spoke, the one who holds claim to your heart? Surely you must have…"

"No," he said, interrupting. "I am a Christian man as you know and our faith does not prescribe that I may lie with a woman to whom I am not wedded in the eyes of God. I have loved her and God knows I have desired her, but I have not shared my bed with her, nor shall I. My fidelity is now and will always be with you, Iris, my wife and my Queen."

"But you said…"

"I said that she had my affection and I said that if you became my wife, you would do so with the knowledge that I had a mistress before ever we came to the marriage altar. My sin that I confessed to you is that I love another woman who I can never wed and that I continue to carry affection for her while I am now married to another. I have not compounded that sin by taking her outside of wedlock. It would be sin as well if I allowed you to come to my wedding bed unknowing that I do carry love for another in my heart, as well as my affection for you. That is why I confessed it to you."

In that moment, I knew that above all other things, I could always depend on my husband to be truthful and honorable with me and of course, that caused me to love him more. I shall not lie and deny that I also felt a surge of relief and gratitude to know that only I would be in his bed and no other.

"And yet you allowed me the freedom to take a lover myself? Out of wedlock?"

He looked deeply into my eyes. "If you could so graciously afford this to me as my wife, then it was not my place to judge how you engage others you may love. That is at the peril of your own soul."

"I have no intention to love any but you, my husband," I said, meeting his gaze.

He smiled wanly. "And do you feel that in time, you might come to love an old man such as myself?" he asked, taking my fingers in his and bringing them to his lips to kiss.

"Your Majesty, My King, My husband, and my lover, I suspect that I already do."

"How so?" he asked, now playing with my fingers that he held, "When you barely know me? When you know so little of who I am as a man and as a King?"

"I know what I need to know," I said softly. "I never expected to love any for I did not stir in my younger years as my sisters in the House of Maidens did. I never giggled over boys or found myself looking at any in longing. I never even availed myself of the pleasures of the beds the other maidens in our house."

His eyebrows raised. "The young women on Avalon lie together with one another in such a way?"

I shrugged. "Certainly. The Goddess knows no rebuke for any form of pleasure and often the young women share it with one another."

"But you did not."

"No. I did not. I caught their babies after they found their own pleasure at the Beltane fires or with some young Druid they fancied, but I never knew of the passions that led them there. Not first hand, anyway."

"No?" he asked, lowering his mouth to my neck where he left a trail of the lightest, tiniest kisses that burned a fire trail directly into the core of my being. His voice was barely above a whisper, but the impact of hearing it made me shiver.

"No," I answered, daring to touch his soft, wavy hair at my neck. "Not until now."

"And now, my wife?" he breathed against my neck. "What do you feel now?"

I felt my knees weaken at his affections and my head reeled.

"Excited," I whispered. "Curious. A little breathless…"

His hands fell over my breasts and he cupped them tenderly, then with his thumbs, gently rubbed over each hardening nipple through the fabric of my clothing. The sensation was like lightning throughout my body and I gasped.

"…eager," I added.

In one movement, he gathered me up into his arms once again and carried me to his bed, our bed, in three great strides. He laid me down so that my head rested against the pillow and began to unfasten his own clothing.

"Let me," I said, raising up to meet him where he stood.

I was at once grateful for the lessons we received on Avalon concerning the acts of pleasure. Although I had never myself put them to use, the education I received years before flooded back to me. I unbuckled his outer tunic, the one encrusted with jewels and gold, and slipped it off of his shoulders. The equal cost of a large farm fell near his feet and he kicked it aside as if it were no more than a peasant's cloak. I eased my hands under his inner tunic and touched his skin beneath it ever so softly. He closed his eyes and sighed raggedly. I pushed the inner tunic over his head as one would undress a child and ran my fingers through the gray hair that curled on his strong chest, planting kisses across his upper body.

"You are going to drive me mad with wanting, Iris," he breathed.

I certainly hope so, I thought, but said nothing aloud.

Although I felt a wave of apprehension at what would come next, I unbuckled his fine trousers and pushed them downward. He stepped out of them and I remained kneeling before him, knowing that when I rose again, I would see his manhood in the light of the lamp. I had seen men naked many times, but never had I seen a naked man who was likely moments from deflowering me. That intention colored the moment madly.

I let my hands trail up his thighs, which were also quite hairy and sturdy, until I found the courage to confront what I so deeply wanted. His arousal jutted out stiffly from the rest of his body, big and hard. I wondered how I would manage to fit it all in, but then thought of the many babies I had seen take the opposite route out of a woman's body. Certainly, this was not so large as a full-term infant, so I was quite sure I could manage.

A tiny dewdrop glistened at the tip and I slipped my tongue out to catch it, wondering not only from a personal interest, but also from a medical perspective, how it would taste. His entire body shuddered convulsively as I did so, just the mere slip of my tongue over the end. My goodness. If that minuscule touch could give him such pleasure as that, what would he do when I showed him all that I had been taught?

I did know I would not do so in one bedding. Those were mysteries that would unfold over time, but to tantalize, I wet my lips and slipped them well over him, barely able to fit my mouth around him.

"Iris, no, I cannot…ahhhh," he gasped, snaking his fingers through my hair until I winced at the pulling against what pins remained. I clenched my thumb against the underside of his manhood to keep the climax from coming and stopped all other motion, holding him in my mouth while I gently milked against him with the muscles of my cheeks and tongue. It was exactly as was described to me before.

He continued to moan loudly, thrusting against my mouth so that he went even deeper into my throat. I made certain to keep my teeth back and not scrape against him as I began to gently run my fingers along the firm, rounded areas under his erection. They drew up tightly into a hard package under my hand and I let my fingers gently caress against the thin skin there. I felt him start to jerk under my light strokes and knew that there would soon be no way to hold back the flow. This was the moment.

I pulled away from him then, ceasing every touch, and then stood before him. His mouth was agape and his eyes wide and glazed. Certainly, he was close to finishing.

"My gown," I breathed, and turned my back to him.

I felt has hands shake as he unfastened each hook and let the layers fall away to the floor. At last, I was only in my under shift of soft linen, which I pulled over my head myself. I plucked the remaining pins from my hair and they too fell to the floor as my hair cascaded down my back and over my shoulders and I stood naked between him and the bed.

"Do you still wish to protect my virtue?" I asked.

"Iris," he said, as if tasting my name on his lips as I had tasted he drop of his passion on my own tongue. "You have taken me past the point of reason so that I could not guarantee your honor if I tried. To my shame, I am now forsworn of that promise."

"No room for shame," I said firmly. "Never shame between us in our bed. Come to me, Husband. Let me take you into me."

He eased me onto the bed on my back and his fingers found my wetness, the pleasure that threatened to take me over. As my breaths became jagged and irregular and my pulse pounded in my head, he pushed one finger inside and I clenched down onto it. Using his thumb, he lightly stroked the point of greatest sensation and the two feelings combined to nearly put me over the edge. Two fingers went inside, stretching me as he could, and I wildly thought of the massages we did to aid the baby's passage over the sacred threshold at the moment of birth. Must everything be relative to birth in some way for me always? I thought of the times when mothers claimed not pain, but overwhelming pleasure as their babies passed through that doorway to life and I could now see why.

Just before the overwhelming sensations completely swept me away on a tremendous current of pleasure beyond all other thought, he stopped and positioned himself between my legs, our now naked bodies coming together at last. Even the tip of him felt too big and he watched my face anxiously for signs of distress. As I moaned aloud, he pushed in deeper and my body, slick and wet, welcomed him as though he were already known to me. Briefly, his passage inward seemed blocked and he leaned forward to kiss me as he pushed hard into my body and I felt a part of me break way in a sharp surge of pain that made me gasp into his mouth.

Locking eyes with him, I began to move under him, pushing my hips upward until he was fully inside me and we were fitted together perfectly core to core. It felt as though I would split in half as my insides molded around him, but in a way that was pleasure and not pain. He gasped and moaned, calling out my name over and over and he began to move within me.

"Iris, my Iris," he said as his body moved with mine. "How I love you. I love you so. Iris. It is such madness, but already I can say that I love you." I believed him. Though maybe only words of the passion of the moment, I believed him with my whole spirit for my heart burst apart with the same feelings for him.

I felt the return of the previous sensations of pure bliss, now compounded by the movement of him in and out of my body. Wetness poured from me and I was unsure what was my passion and what was blood and I did not care. As my own climax overtook me, I was loud, but he was louder, and had I heard him and not known what it was we did, I would think him a man tortured. His body contorted into a hard spasm of release and as I descended from my own crest, the first I had ever in my life known, I felt his seed pour into me in wave after wave after comforting wave. He collapsed onto me with a final shudder and did not move. He did not even seem to breathe.

With my own breath heavy in my chest and his weight on me, I felt at once excited, alive, and oh so exhausted from the tension of the day and the headiness of the wine I had sipped through dinner. The scent of him was sweet against my nose and I turned so that my face was closer to his hair. I breathed in deeply, smelling the exotic oils and spices that his servants used to rinse it. In a state of complete joy and fulfillment, I let sleep claim me as surely as he had claimed my heart, as a collage of warm images of my future life paraded through my head and permeated my dreams. I was, unexpectedly and delightedly, a woman in love.

CHAPTER 11

I opened my eyes and blinked at the harsh sunlight as the King's Chamberlain, Herschel, husband to Bersaba, pushed open the shutters and a draught of cool air swept into the room. I had slept long and hard, not realizing how exhausted I was. As I came to full wakefulness, I realized I was in quite a state of undress and that Marcus still laid over me, his arm draped heavily across my chest and his face buried in my hair. I pulled a fine quilt over us and turned to kiss his cool cheek, which rested on my shoulder. Memories of the night before stirred in me and I found I had missed him even in sleep.

"Will you break your fast in here or in the formal dining area, Your Grace?" he asked. I was amused as I realized he was speaking to me and not to Marcus.

"In here, I believe," I said.

"Very well, Madam." He looked at me uncomfortably. "I will need…" He looked away and then back to me again. "I will need the sheets to present."

"The sheets?" I asked, attempting to move Marcus from off me.

"Yes, to present as proof of the consummation."

"Proof?"

"The blood, Your Grace."

"You are quite serious, aren't you?"

He nodded, clearly uneasy.

I sighed heavily. "Very well, then." I pushed at Marcus with little effect on his dead weight and felt fear creep in like a dark shadow.

"Marcus," I said, my voice intent. "Marcus, we have to get up."

"His Majesty has always been a heavy sleeper, even since he was a young child," Herschel offered with a smile. "Allow me, My Queen."

He went to the opposite of the bed and rolled Marcus off me. To my horror, the King fell onto the pillow, his eyes staring open and unseeing at the high ceiling of the room, his mouth open at an awkward angle.

"Marcus!" I screamed, the cold grip of fear turning quickly to outright panic.

"Good heavens!" Herschel shouted. "Sire!" He slapped at Marcus' cold, unmoving face and shook him fiercely while I screamed and screamed and screamed. No more words; not even the King's name. Just horrified screams.

~*~

Moving or functioning on any left were beyond me in the days that came after. Someone, I have no idea who but imagine it was Ursa or Bersaba, dressed me each morning and undressed me at night. The sheets showing the blood of my maidenhead and on which my groom had died were displayed over the castle wall for all to see and witness.

I could not bear to be in the bed where Marcus died, died on top of me, died while in me, so I slept in the chair by the window and, in fact, rarely moved from it. The pain within me was so extreme that my very skin hurt. I had a fleeting thought of going back to my own quarters, but could not find the energy to do so and did not wish to ask for help from the people around me who I barely knew.

Someone, I do not recall who it was, informed me that my mother and father were told that the Queen was indisposed and left the day after my wedding as they had initially planned. I felt nothing as they said Laoghaire had left with them, although when I reflect on that time, it is hard to imagine that I took the news so very placidly. I knew she had not enjoyed her few days in Cornwall, but I had not expected her to abandon me fully or my parents to endorse her doing so. The factoring of all that was so far beyond me in my state of grief and shock and fear that I had to let the thoughts roll away lest they puzzle me into even greater retreat. Something did not add up, but I was too bereft and detached to figure out what it was.

I saw only Herschel, Bersaba, Ursa, and Father Francisco, who ranted at me, calling me "Witch" and "Fiend," insisting I had poisoned my husband. He came into the King's quarters the day after the wedding and demanded that I leave Cornwall. I vaguely refused, my usually vibrant voice barely more than a whisper. I did not look at him. Could not look at him. I closed my eyes and pretended that it was he, not me, who was a vile demon conjured by the mages in Rome, the mages who disguised themselves in red Cardinals' robes. He hissed unveiled threats to me and I turned my face away from him and opened my eyes to continue gazing out the window that had already become my sole focus and indeed, my soul focus.

I did not care what he did to me. He threatened to have me drawn and quartered for regicide and treason, graphically describing how I would be hanged by my neck until dazed and then my internal organs cut away and held up to show to me while I still lived, then my hands, followed by my arms and legs, would be removed from my body. He doused me with their holy water and performed an exorcism on me as I refused still to look at him. No demons raged forth from within me. I did not rebuke him. I did not cry. I did not feel. His sacred rite did nothing.

On the third day after the wedding, it occurred to me to ask Herschel if anyone attended to the Princess Zelda. He knelt before me and gently explained that she was unaware that her father had died in his marriage bed… or at all. Her own ladies looked after her, oblivious to the tragedy and believing the King was merely immersed in getting to know his new queen. They saw one another rarely anyway and she would have little cause to wonder why he was absent.

It came to me then to wonder who did know the King had died. Obviously, Father Francisco knew. Did my parents know? Did Laoghaire presume I had no need of her now that I was married and only wanted her with me for the trip here? What was she told about me? About Marcus?

Had I been more in my right mind, I would have craved my father's guidance, but I felt only heartache and every minute, whether I woke or slept, hurt more than the one before it. In the bits of sleep I did get, nightmares plagued me, gruesome visions of corpses laid over me, wishing to violate my body in the ghastliest ways. In my waking times, I alternately wondered what would become of me and mourned for the future I would now never have. The brief glimpse of love and happiness Marcus had shown to me was now an ugly ruse. It was bait dangled in front of me to get me to act in a certain way, to do a certain thing.

My quest, my magic, my Goddess, were all far from my mind. I refused all food and drink. Bersaba tried to coax me with bread sopped in meat juices and cups of wine. What little I did eat just to stop her ministrations stuck in my throat like paste and caused me to gag.

Some days after the wedding, I could not say how many, Father Francisco came into the suite with the two witnesses to my marriage, who I learned were Sir Charles, the Duke of Sherborne, and Sir John, the Duke of Devon, both lifelong friends of Marcus. Some part of my mind recalled Marcus pointing them out to me at that first evening meal after I arrived. All three looked grim with Father Francisco including fury in his visage as well.

Bersaba and Ursa had already seen to me before they arrived, washing and dressing me like a doll. I hardly cared if I dressed, washed, or did more than stare out the windows from what I now thought of as my chair, which is where I was when they pushed into the room. I cared no way or the other, but I was at least covered in queenly attired when they arrived. My ladies may have known the men planned an audience with me, but I neither imagined nor cared if they did.

I am quite sure they knew that as well.

Father Francisco's sustained hatred for me permeated the room immediately, a tangible thing that entered the room before he did. It affected me not in the least. His opinion of me was sacrosanct only to him and certainly not to me. Sir John and Sir Charles were kind and efficient in their explanations to me whereas Father Francisco had only alternately cursed me and cleansed me in the days following Marcus's death.

"Madam," Sir Charles said, kneeling so that he was within my line of sight. "Your Majesty, can you hear me?"

I caught his gaze and nodded, trying to feign a smile and failing. He looked up at Sir John, who then also knelt in front of me in what I imagined must be a particularly uncomfortable position.

Sir John explained to me that they had no legal reason to believe that I was in any way responsible for the death of the King. The King always used a food taster and we had consumed no food nor drink in our marriage chamber, so poison was not suspected. The King's medical staff had undertaken a full medical examination of the King's body and found no sign of foul play. Merely, that he had died of a sudden apoplexy and given his age and the degree of exertion he extended on his wedding night, it was reasonable.

At this, Father Francisco scoffed loudly and was quickly silenced by the stares of the two dukes.

They then continued their explanation by saying that the King's death had not yet been announced to anyone other than the immediate staff that gave me daily care and the medical doctor who examined him. They would announce the death of the King and he would lie in state for a funeral once it was known whether I carried the King's child. With no small degree of discomfort, they pointed out that the sheets revealed the King had an "emission" on the wedding night and so conception was possible.

"Do you agree this is so, my Queen?" Sir Charles asked. Tears filled my eyes as I nodded mutely.

"Your Grace," Sir John said, touching my arm to make sure I heard him. "Are you well familiar with your cycles? Do you know when they should come?"

"The dark moon," I murmured. "I always bleed with the dark of the moon."

Sir John looked at Sir Charles and smiled, then back at me again.

"They were married at the Full Moon so the dignitaries could travel by the light the night before. It is possible."

"Yes," I said, suddenly coming into full realization of what they were saying. "It is possible. Is this the only reason I am still alive?"

I blinked back at their astonished gazes.

"My Lady?" Sir Charles asked.

"That is to say, are you going to kill me if I am not pregnant or after the baby comes if I am?"

"Why ever would we do that?" Sir John asked me. "You are the Queen of Cornwall. To put you to death would be regicide."

I slid a rage-filled look at Father Francisco, who stared right back at me. They followed my gaze to him.

"What have you been telling the Queen, Francisco?" Sir Charles asked him.

He sniffed piously. "Only that we take regicide seriously here and that she no doubt caused the King's death with her demon magic." He spat the last two words at me with tremendous venom.

"Oh, and so much more," I said, wearily, feeling my anger at last well up.

"Priest," Sir John said sternly. "There is much and more that you do not know about this situation. I realize that the King gave you power and leeway because of your connections to the High Court and to Rome. The King's advisers, including myself, honor that to an extent, but you need to know that things are different now that the King has died. You do not command this court and I will caution you to keep your tongue and your thoughts to yourself."

"Ah," Father Francisco said, his voice mocking and snide. "And how did all of this come about? Who then rules in the stead of the late King? Who comes to claim his throne?"

Sir Charles tilted his head in my direction. "She does."

Father Francisco and I both gasped.

"What?" I breathed.

"We have spent the past days in counsel with the other court advisers and ecclesiastics," Sir John said. "During his final days, when he saw that the wedding would indeed proceed, the King coordinated a will with the help of his lawyers and in it, he stipulates the Queen, Iris of Avalon, as *fiduciarius* to any male heir they may produce from their marriage, naming their child as *fideicommisarius*. If there is a child, she rules as regent for the child until the child is of age."

"And if there is no child?" the priest asked.

"Then per the rights of succession, she rules until Lady Zelda comes of age as he also issued full custodial and matriarchal rights of the Princess to the Queen."

"He *what*?" Father Francisco was agape and for once, the priest and I were in accordance.

"Her Majesty, Queen Iris of Cornwall, is, not only remains Queen of Cornwall, but is regent for Princess Eselde until Eselde is twenty-one-years-old. Even without issue from the marriage between them, Queen Iris is the Queen Mother. The document was witnessed and is binding. Of that we are certain. The King left a sizable donation from his personal fortune to the Church and the rest he bequeaths directly to the Queen, including full rights of succession and all governing parental rights of Princess Zelda. Certainly, it is understood that the King did not anticipate his own death so immediately and expected a much longer joint reign after his marriage; however, legal and binding the document remains unless and until the Queen remarries."

"But…" the fury in Father Francisco's face was tremendous, "…this cannot be."

"And yet," Sir John said softly, "so it is."

"Did he not speak to you of any of this, My Queen?" Sir Charles asked, ever so gently.

I went over our conversations in my mind so quickly that words blurred and melded into one another as my eyes brimmed with tears even after I thought I had cried all away all of them I would ever possess.

"He asked me if I could be comfortable mothering a girl closer to my age than his. I assured him I had overseen many young maidens on Avalon and that bringing them into reign was not a chore for me. I swore to love his daughter as my own and while I could certainly never take the place of her mother, I would gladly welcome her into my life and into my family. I am certain many women who marry a man with a child from a previous marriage would have a similar conversation."

Sir John nodded. "They would. Few, however, include the terms of royal succession in that conversation."

"I assure you all," I said, taking care to make eye contact with each man, "that I am as surprised by this as are any of you."

"You are, are you not," Sir Charles stood from his kneeling position as he spoke and nodded deferentially, "skilled in matter of a woman's health?"

"Yes," I said. "On Avalon, my specialty studies were birth and the health of women."

"We are not familiar with such things, my Queen. Can you tell us when we might know if you are with child? Not that it changes much in terms of your position, but it might soften the grief of Cornwall to know their King left behind a male heir."

I thought about this for a few minutes.

"My courses are always regular, but stress can throw off a woman's cycle and there has certainly been enough of that lately. I do not know what day it is. How long has it been since the wedding?" I could not bring myself to say, "...since the King died."

Sir John cleared his throat. "The wedding was a fortnight ago, Your Majesty."

A fortnight? It felt like only a handful of days.

"So, the Dark Moon is soon."

"Tonight," Sir Charles offered.

"We should know within a week," I said softly. "I may have other symptoms within a month's time."

The nodded in unison and a thought occurred to me.

"You said there would be a lying in after the announcement of the King's death. Where then, is the King?"

They exchanged glances.

"The King is..." Sir John began. Once again, they looked at one another. He continued. "The King is in chambers beneath the abbey. The area was devised as secure quarters should Tintagel ever come under attack. There are no windows and it is far below ground, so it is quite cool. Because of our proximity to the sea, the ground stays quite frigid year-round that far down."

"So, he is not... putrefied?" I had seen dead bodies before and the one longest dead, only a week past death, was in quite a state of decay.

"No, My Queen," Sir Charles said.

"A disgrace," Father Francisco seethed. "Keeping a holy King in what is little more than a root cellar as if he were a slab of boar."

They looked at him in unison and he crossed himself.

"Has his body been treated in any way?" I asked, hating to have to broach the subject at all.

"Treated?" Sir John asked.

"With herbs, spices, tinctures to delay the breaking down of his body?"

"No," Sir Charles said, "Only the cold keeps him… keeps him…"

"From rotting," I provided.

They nodded.

I closed my eyes, feeling the pulse of a headache pounding behind them.

"Send the court physician who examined him to me," I said.

"Yes, My Queen," Sir John said, bowing. "And send a serving woman up with eggs, salted meat, good milk, and a bowl of fruit. If I am pregnant, I have done poorly in nourishing the future King of Cornwall."

"Indeed," Sir Charles said, also bowing.

"Father Francisco?" I asked as the other two men turned to leave. They paused as if waiting to see if I would need protection, or perhaps he would. "Would you please remain so that I might get your thoughts on how to proceed with plans for the burial and lying in state?"

He looked at me, his shock clear in his expression as his mouth began to move without words coming forth.

"My beloved husband was, above all, a devoutly Christian man and he must be interred with every blessing of the Christian Church."

He stopped trying to speak and merely nodded.

"And will you also hear my confession, Father?"

He stopped short, now his mouth fully hanging open.

At last, he collected himself and spoke.

"If you will come to the abbey tomorrow after you break your fast, I will hear your confession and then I will instruct you as to the funereal and interment process."

I noted that he did not refer to me as "Your Majesty" or "My Queen," but I preferred to choose my battles.

"Thank you, Father," I said. I looked at all three men, who were blatantly staring at me. "Go," I said, making dismissive motions with my hands.

They scurried for the door, none of them turning their back to me as they exited.

After they left, I settled back into my chair and recommenced my process of staring out the window until my food arrived.

CHAPTER 12

"Bless me, Father, for I have sinned. I have never given confession."

"Receive the Holy Ghost; whose sins you shall forgive, they are forgiven them; and whose sins you shall retain, they are retained. You are a child of God. What are your sins?"

I leaned my head against the grated windows in the confessional and took a deep breath.

"I have borne hatred in my heart for you, Father. I have desired a man who was not yet my husband and felt for him what you would consider unclean thoughts. I have resisted God's plan for my life and avoided my responsibilities in my grief."

I tried to think of other sins I might have committed in my life.

"I was jealous of my sisters who were more beautiful and talented than I. I was cross and terse when my patience ran thin and I sometimes failed to demonstrate the kindness and charity that Christ taught us we should have."

"Unburden your heart and your spirit," he said, his frustration with me clearly apparent.

"I have judged others harshly."

"Have you followed false gods?"

I thought for a moment, choosing my words carefully. My fingers grasped the grating.

"I have followed the one true God in His many forms."

"Have you committed murder?"

"I have never taken a life, deliberately or accidentally."

"Are you a practitioner of the Dark Arts?"

"I am no Witch or sorceress."

"He that hideth his sins shall not prosper; but he that shall confess and forsake them shall obtain mercy.

"Proverbs 28:13. Indeed, I hide nothing and I confess all I know to confess."

"Do you wish to say an Act of Contrition for your sins?"

I thought for a moment, reaching into my teaching from long ago.

"O Holy God, I am heartily sorry for all ways I have offended you. I detest all my sins, because I dread the loss of Heaven and the pains of Hell. But most of all because I have offended you, my God, who are all good and deserving of all my love. I firmly resolve with the help of your grace, to confess my sins, to do penance and to amend my life. Amen."

He was silent for several minutes and as I waited, I wondered if he would find a way to kill me in the sanctuary. I knew it must chafe him to go through this ritual with me, of all people, and that it was likely he felt I made a mockery of his faith by doing so. My motives were nothing more than political. Already I was baptized into their Christian Church and now I had partaken of their holy rite of confession. Regardless of where my spirit rested, on Avalon's sacred tor or on the altar of this church, my outward actions would be fitting of a queen and beyond reproach. My father had said as much to me and I would honor my husband by a public show of his religious rites and by doing justice to the crown he saw fit to give to me. The condemnation of this horrible man who sat opposite me in judgment of my life and, in fact, all I represented as a priestess of the Holy Isle, would only complicate my mission. If I were to reign as sovereign and position myself to carry out my troth to Avalon, I would have to remove all doubt from his mind that I posed a threat to his position or to his Church.

In many ways, he was himself a guardian of the mysteries every much as the eldest druids and priestesses on Avalon. He too could walk between the worlds within his own faith and stood to potentially see or sense my underlying agenda if I did not guard it carefully enough.

At last, he spoke.

"Dominus noster Jesus Christus te absolvat; et ego auctoritate ipsius te absolvo ab omni vinculo excommunicationis et interdicti in quantum possum et tu indiges. Deinde, ego te absolvo a peccatis tuis in nomine Patris, et Filii, et Spiritus Sancti. Amen.

"Amen."

"Give thanks to the Lord for He is good."

"For His mercy endures forever."

I crossed myself and saw that he did as well. He had absolved me of my sins and there was no going back from that. I gave thanks to the old Druids who forced us to learn the most sacred rites of the world's many religions, including this one, insisting that we repeat over and over the verbal sacrament. I suddenly recalled a part of the ritual I had not heard from him.

"Father, how do you wish me to do penance for my sins?"

I heard him shift in the confessional, his robes brushing against the wood of the bench.

"God has offered absolution for your sins. You have already fasted for too long in your condition and have given a fortnight of mindful prayer as you sat in vigil for your husband's death. God demands no more."

"…and you?"

Again, he was silent and I felt he was choosing his words as carefully as I chose mine.

"As you said to me not so long ago, you stay on your side of the altar and I will stay on mine."

"Sic fiat"

"So be it," he replied.

I stood and pushed open the door to the confessional, praying he would wait inside until I left the abbey. Clearly from his final words of absolution, he wished no accord with me, either spoken or unspoken. However, would we work together in this unthinkable situation without any cooperation on his part? I had conceded to his religious rituals and extended the olive branch, to use the vernacular of his faith. Why would he give me no quarter at all?

As if in answer, his voice came from just behind me.

"Do not imagine that a few contrived acts of contrition engender any bond between us, Lady Iris. If you imagine anything otherwise, know now that you not are and will never be even one thing more than an affront to me, to my God, and to this court. I give my solemn vow that I will do all within my power to remove your influence from this Christian kingdom and keep it safe from you and your ilk."

I wanted not to turn, remembering how much easier it was for me to speak candidly with Marcus when we did not look one another eye-to-eye, and yet, I had to claim my power over the priest in this moment or lose it forever. I force myself to meet his gaze and pulled myself up in full strength. He swallowed hard, the only outward sign that he felt the shift. No more was I a grieving widow or loathsome sorceress that he could dominate. For a split second, I was the Goddess on earth. I was Queen. To leverage that moment could affect my entire future.

"For better or for worse," I said, keeping my voice firm and strong, "the crown of Cornwall sits upon my head. You put it there yourself. You anointed me to this position in your own God's holy name. I have done naught to rebuke you or your Church, but have honored it and its traditions out of respect for my husband and our king. I defy you to find any malfeasance for there is none. As Ruth said to Naomi in your holy book so did I say to King Marcus, 'Your people will be my people and your God my God.' I shall honor this promise and his faith in me with my every breath and my every action. Why is it that you, his trusted adviser, cannot accept and honor his wishes?"

"His wishes?" Father Francisco spat at me. "They were not *his wishes*. All that happened from the time you arrived was the influence of the dark arts woven by those people of that island of devils. Their intention of taking the thrown of Cornwall has borne fruit and the cost of that was a good and faithful Christian king."

"Your God is all powerful," I countered. "How then would He allow anything I do to go against His own plan? If I *did* contrive to steal the throne of Cornwall, *which I did not*, how would your God allow such a thing to happen? Tell me."

He blanched white with anger. "It is the work of the fiend, who poisons men to work against God's will. This is the undoing of all I have brought to this kingdom, of all that King Marcus wished for his land and his people. You are a mockery and it sickens me that someone such as yourself manipulated him into handing Cornwall over to you."

"I did nothing of the sort, Father Francisco. I left my home and my family to marry a man I did not know for the good of Avalon and Cornwall as well. You will recall that it was the High Court that contrived this marriage, not me. They wished to squelch any thought of a person from my lineage making claim to the High Throne or the sovereignty of Cornwall."

"And yet here you are now, sovereign of Cornwall."

I smiled, hearing his inadvertent admission.

"Regardless of how it came to be, yes, as you have said, I am sovereign of Cornwall and I expect to be treated as such, even by you. Were you any sort of man of God, you would be acting as your Christ did. There is a young woman who has lost her father, the only parent she had left. Sir John and Sir Charles have lost their lifelong friend. Within days, an entire kingdom will mourn the loss of their beloved king. My king, *your* king, lies in a dungeon below awaiting interment and yet you choose to stay here and malign me rather than honoring his wishes and praying for his very soul. Truly, Father, in this time of grief and sadness, do you have *nothing* better to do than to threaten your anointed queen?"

Red patches came into his cheeks in hot flush as he realized he had been led into a trap to admit I was, indeed, queen and that he was shirking his rightful duties as the spiritual leader of Cornwall. Tactical wisdom now required that I again throw him off kilter.

"I have no qualm with you or with your God," I said gently. "I honor the God my husband served and who has chosen you as His representative in my kingdom. You are the aggressor here. You are the one who seeks to undermine and destroy when you could work with me for the good of Cornwall. Could I do any more than what I have done to acquiesce to my position and accept the dictates of your faith? What fault do you find other than the place of my birth?"

"I will find it," he said, his own voice level and intent. "I will find your malfeasance, as you call it. I will find your offense. I will find your sin and I will leverage it. Wear that crown I placed on your head proudly while you can, for I assure you, it will not sit there for long. If you do carry an issue of this farce of a marriage in your womb, do not expect it to grow and thrive there, for my God will not allow it to be so. Enjoy no comfort in your position and expect no permanence, for I will not rest until you are vanquished."

"Then sir," I said, again meeting his eyes, "prepare yourself for a long life of little sleep for it is my husband's wishes I will follow and not yours. Already I have wasted for too much time and breath in attempting to reach any sort of understanding with you, who is to be my chief spiritual adviser. I have a husband to inter and a kingdom to manage. If you would send Father Damien to me to convey your suggestions for the funeral arrangements for the King, I would be most grateful."

Without waiting for him to respond, I turned and left. As I walked down the aisle of the abbey, I thought how different this exit was than the last time I had done so, on the arm of my husband surrounded by dignitaries and well-wishers. Now, I walked alone, followed out the door by hatred and rejection. I expected at any moment that his hand would land on my shoulder or worse yet, my throat. Never had I encountered so much sheer abhorrence directed at me and the impact caused me to begin shaking violently as soon as the door closed behind me. I leaned against the ebony wood, tears welling in my eyes and my throat locked in fear. I was surprised I could get out all the words I did and now without them inside me, I felt empty and hollow, gutted clean of any viscera at all. My breath left me completely and it took all the strength I had to walk back to Tintagel itself. By all that was holy to me or to him, I vowed at once that I would never again willingly be alone in the presence of Father Francisco, come what may.

~*~

It was mid-morning when I broke my fast and after eating so little for so long, my belly still fought with whatever I attempted to put into it. Of the wide variety of foods Ursa brought to me in my quarters, I only nibbled bits, sampling here and there to see what set best with me.

I was still sampling and picking when Father Damian arrived as I requested. He looked uncomfortable, so I suspected Father Francisco had more than a few words for him about our encounter. Still, he bowed and kissed my ring when I extended it and accepted the chair I offered.

"Thank you for coming to me in my quarters," I said, welcoming him. "I fear I am not my best self lately and my morning has left me tired and frustrated. I have much and more to do in the rest of the day, so if you do not mind, I would like to speak with you hear with my handmaiden present for the sake of decorum."

He nodded briefly and I noticed he sat close to the edge of the chair with his spine erect and tense.

"Father Damian," I said, hoping to defuse at least a small portion of the tension and pain inherent in my day, "I understand you are placed in an impossible position given Father Francisco's extreme abhorrence of me and I regret that you must endure such a task. Know that I have no interest in making the situation worse for you and in fact, have no interest in making anything difficult for Father Francisco. He is a man of tremendous faith and that is admirable above all else that flows between he and I. I tell you now, with Ursa and your God as my witness that I have no intention of creating discord in the spirituality of this court. I am of full mind that each person is free to worship as he or she choose and it is not my place as sovereign to interfere with that process."

He laughed nervously, and I wondered what I had said he found at all humorous and then resolved that it was likely but a release of his own tension.

"If what you say is true? And I have no reason other than the opinions of Father Francisco to believe otherwise? Then your position on religion is very like my own?"

I nodded, but I was unsure why I did so. Dear Goddess, but this was an awkward conversation.

"If I may be so bold as to speak candidly with Your Majesty? And in strictest confidence?"

"Please," I said, steeling myself for whatever it was he would say. "I value honest discourse above decorum, even if I do not agree with the position of my partner in conversation. Ursa?"

"I hear nothing," the girl said, purposely turning her head away.

"Father Francisco is my senior? But he is not my conscience? If that makes any sense at all? I honor his position within the Church, but I do not agree with him in all things?"

"I see," I said.

"In fact?" he continued, "There are very few religious theologies on which he and I see eye-to-eye? I find I must carefully sift to find those places where we do agree?"

"With him, I feel unsupported at best and threatened at worst."

"I believe that is an accurate assessment?" he said.

And I will ask you, given the clear animosity that emanates from him, if you will serve as my own spiritual adviser rather than Father Francisco? I do not wish to create awkwardness between the two of you, but I fail to see how he can act in concert with the organic needs of my soul when he harbors such hatred for me. I have extended myself more than once only to be attacked when I did so."

He nodded. "I am honored that you suggest such a thing? And I believe it is the best solution for all concerned? I will ask that you commit your wishes to writing and submit them to him and a copy to me, which I will forward further to the Church?"

"Indeed," I agreed. "Unfortunately, if I remove him from his position here at court, I not only dishonor my husband, but also validate his belief that I wish to eradicate Christianity from the court. Nothing is further from the truth. All I wish to remove is the persecution he seems so hell bent on pursuing."

"It is a difficult situation, My Queen? I was well blessed to receive this appointment? And of course, I wish to do nothing to jeopardize it? As a junior priest, my influence is truly negligible? Father Francisco guides the spiritual training of Princess Eselde and delivers mass in the abbey and my role is nothing more than his assistant? I am as little more than a glorified acolyte at best?"

"So, what you are saying then is that it would be a breach in convention for you to be adviser to the Queen."

He laughed, then covered his mouth as though embarrassed for doing so.

"That is putting it lightly? However, anyone can see that we are in an unconventional situation? While you do not wish to create further offense to Father Francisco, there is little denying that your very presence offends him?"

"You seem to have a strong hold on the situation, I must say."

"There is what seems to be an insurmountable breach between the two of you at present and I must believe that any Church official would agree that any spiritual counsel is better than no spiritual counsel? So, in that light, I accept your offer and ask only that the details be spelled out in writing in such a way that does not malign Father Francisco, yet achieves the desired result?"

"You should have been a diplomat, Father Damian," I smiled. "Your words are wise and your advice is sound. I will have my scribes draw up the necessary documents, but also stipulating that Father Francisco is to remain here as Priest of the Court to continue in the capacities in which he has served until now."

"As you wish, My Queen?"

"And did Father Francisco share with you any thoughts or plans concerning the King's state presentation and interment?"

He nodded. "He did and I have them here to discuss with you?"

As I expected, the plans were meticulous and specific, of such detail that he had clearly worked on them before I asked him to do so. Some of the points seemed overly ostentatious, but I reminded myself that Father Francisco, not I, was the expert on Cornish funereal customs as well as the rituals specific to the Christian Church. What I knew came only from second knowledge imparted by the druids.

In the end, the only thing I changed was to widen the distance between the mourners who filed past the body to pay their respect and the body itself, knowing well the indignity of death and the stench of a body even preserved. Even surrounded by flowers and spices, in the week it would take to arrange a funeral of the magnitude Father Francisco suggested, the body would continue to decay at a rapid rate. There was also the matter of determining my state of pregnancy or lack of it, which would take time.

My next two tasks, both of which were even more daunting than my encounter with Father Francisco, would take up the rest of my day and make me wish I had stayed in my chair staring out the windows of the room where my husband died.

CHAPTER 13

As I requested, Colin, the court physician met me just outside the abbey just past noon. After the customary bowing and ring kissing, he passed me one of the baskets he carried. Inside, I saw jars of herbs, spices, and tinctures, all carefully labeled. At first glance, I was encouraged as it looked as though my own basket contained much of what I requested he procure and if the remainder of the items were in his own basket, we might actually manage to complete our task, at least to the degree possible.

Once inside, I prayed I would not encounter Father Francisco. The combining of those two situations was too odious of a thought even to contemplate. The physician led me to down a long, narrow passage of stairs that wound upon itself over and again until I felt as though I descended into the Underworld itself. If I went into the Underworld, one could be sure I would bring my husband back with me, but where I ventured forth, my husband's soul would not be. Only his decaying body awaited me.

When at last we reached the lower floor, the physician lit torches in addition to the one he carried with him and the room was alight. I stifled a wave of nausea as the sweet smell of death wafted over me. The cold of the room, which caused me to draw the cloak I thought to bring around me, could not stop the decomposition of the King's dead body. It could only slow it. With luck and the contents of our baskets, perhaps we could slow it further. Still, we had another week or longer to go before he would be entombed and we must do what we could to slow his body's return to nature.

"Colin," I began, "Thank you for coming and for the care you paid to my husband's body, as well as for your complete discretion."

He nodded. "Of course, Your Majesty. The King was very dear to me, as he was to everyone who knew him."

He stepped toward the table that held Marcus's body.

"May I?" he asked.

I gestured my acquiescence and he pulled back the cloth that covered the body. I could see incisions from the examination performed after he died and the pooling of blood that darkened the lower portion of his supine body.

"I need a rack," I said, "strong enough to support his body. We have to drain away as much of the blood and body fluids as we can or the humors will speed the rot. Do you understand?"

"Of course, Your Grace." He looked uncomfortable. "As much as it pains me to say, the tunnels that lead from this place were once used as a dungeon and there is an area such as you describe several chambers in that will suffice."

"So, this was a place of torture."

"Yes, Your Grace."

"Well, we are in no position to be choosy." I felt my lips curl in distaste. "The breakdown of the cartilage of his body will make transporting him difficult."

"There is a wheeled device in the chamber that we may use," he said.

Of course, there was.

We brought in the wheeled table and together, shoved my husband's corpse onto it. Predictably, some of his skin remained behind on the heavier table.

"After we finish," Colin said gently, "I will clean the table."

"Thank you."

The wheels of the table, had likely not seen motion in decades and protested under his weight as we pushed it down the narrow passage, holding torches in our hands as we attempted to guide our cargo in the right direction.

The chamber was a quarter the size of the main room and as I held my torch aloft, I could see many other rooms of similar size that I presumed to be cells. I considered for a moment that my father had spent time chained in rooms such as these, perhaps even one of these given Cornwall's reputation for kowtowing to the High Throne. My cousin, Phillip, the rightful High King, was remanded to Tintagel after his dethroning. Had he stayed in one of those dark cells? My Aunt Ophelia? We had heard nothing from them in months and I had planned to ask Marcus what happened to them and had no opportunity to do so before he died. They could be anywhere, but it was unlikely they would be allowed to remain here in Cornwall once my betrothal to Marcus was announced. The opportunity for High Treason would be too great if two true claimants to both the High Throne and the Kingdom of Cornwall were within distance to conspire.

True to his word, the chamber contained a table with through-and-through slots down its length, deeply stained from years of use. Under it, the floor was uneven and tilted toward a sort of drain that led, presumably, into the moat. I shuddered to think of the acts that transpired here over the years.

"You boiled together the herbs I requested?" I asked.

"Yes," he said. "The jars are in the baskets."

"Do you have your surgical equipment?" He nodded, and slid a leather pack off his back. Together, we worked to cut the major veins in Marcus's body and then massaged the stiff flesh to move as much of the now putrefied blood as possible out of his body and down the drain. Rigor mortise had set in to the point that we could not reposition him well for maximum drainage, but we managed to relieve a good bit of the pressure and reduce the discoloration significantly. The blood was clotted as cheese and rank, hardly looking like what should come from anybody, living or dead. After what felt like hours of cutting key points in his veins and pushing out the contents, we began to stuff the incisions with the herbs and spices I asked him to bring and sewing up the flesh afterward. Surprisingly, he had indeed found everyone I requested. He was quick to learn and seemed fascinated by the process of body preservation. I assured him it would not hold out for long, but would slow the process of decay somewhat.

"Now, we bathe him in the brew you made from the herbs," I said.

Carefully, reverently, we washed him. The awareness that I was touching his naked body for the only second time and the last time nearly broke my composure, but I made the preparation of his body a holy sacrament and a testimony of the love I barely got a chance to feel for him, but would carry in my heart always. He had awakened within me a powerful force and even if no one ever loved me or desired me again, I would honor that gift. This process was part of the most powerful magic I would likely ever work.

"Did you find anything of import in your examination of the King's body?" I asked. "Was he known to suffer from any ailments that might have caused his death?"

"He was strong as a horse as nearly as we could tell. But when we examined his heart, it was clear there had been a rupture that bled out into the chest cavity."

"Were you aware that his father died at the same age?"

"Fascinating," he said, raising an eyebrow. "Each year since my arrival, I performed a physical examination on the King and the last one took place in early spring. He seemed the picture of health. I never imagined to determine a cause of death before the year was over."

"Are there still those who believe I murdered him?" I asked bluntly.

"Only the one," he said, still carefully sponging down the body with the herbal wash. "No one else gives the idea much credence."

"I did not kill him, you know. Well, not intentionally."

"Do I dare ask what you mean by that?"

"As I think about it, I believe he may have died…as our consummation culminated."

This time, he did stop wiping the body for a moment, then resumed.

"I was told that when Herschel came into your room the next morning, that the King was still…atop?"

By this time, I was well past any level of decorum.

"I thought he, like I, was simply exhausted and collapsed from the release. I have no experience with such things and I myself fell asleep almost immediately."

"Did you not feel him grow cold?"

"I felt nothing. I slept the sleep of the dead after such a long time."

"Apparently, so did he," he said. There was no jest to his tone, but I still shot him a striking glance.

"Forgive me," he looked at me aghast. "My humor tends more toward the dark in, well, difficult situations. I have never yet preserved a king's body with his queen while discussing their intimacies."

"Is it not exhausting?" I asked, sighing heavily and resting my elbows on Marcus's dead chest. "Having to always do and say the right thing? Forever worried at creating offense or breaking some rule you did not know existed? The whole thing just makes me tired. Tired to my very bones."

He laughed under his breath.

"It is rather tedious, is it not? The idea that one person deserves greater deference than other and must be spoken to only like this or that. Sometimes, it is a relief to be in a tavern and around only those of one's own station. I supposed your like never has that, do you?"

"Ha," I snorted. "I cannot even say what 'my like' is like. Up until a month ago, I was born and raised on an island where nearly all were treated as equals. This genuflecting is all new to me and I cannot say that it is growing on me."

"I suppose it is different when you are born to it as was the King."

"Maybe, but you would not know it from Princess Zelda."

"True, that," he smiled.

"Can we, perhaps, dispense with the formalities when we are alone, especially during the times when we prepare dead bodies for burial?"

He looked at me across the table as if to see if I was, in fact, serious or making fun of the situation.

"Come on," I said, "You are the closest thing I have to a colleague now that Laoghaire has abandoned me. Am I not at least entitled to one friend?"

"Do queens have friends?" he asked.

"Do queens cut up dead bodies?"

"Your point is taken…Iris."

I nodded my approval.

"You were very discreet in your examination, Colin. Many would not have even stitched him up again, yet your stitches are as fine as a handmaiden's."

He smiled. "My father was a tailor. He taught me well. But for so fine of a man and so high of a king, nothing less than returning the body to its best condition possible would suffice. Even this, the preparation of the King's corpse for burial, would normally be done only by the holiest men in the kingdom," Colin was saying. "But since only a handful of people know the King is dead, it falls to us."

"So it seems. So how is it that Father Francisco is not doing this since it falls to the holiest of holies?"

He rolled his eyes.

"Francisco is furious over the delay of the interment to see if you are with child. To illustrate his objections, he refused to do anything to preserve the body beyond 'what God Himself hath chosen.'"

"Brilliant," I smirked. "His malice overrides even his honoring of our royal dead."

"So it would seem. I am curious, however," he began.

I looked at him and raised one eyebrow.

"How is it that you know of such things, Iris? Is this part of your training as a healer?"

"Not exactly," I said. "It is more of my training as a priestess. All initiated priestesses are taught how to prepare the dying and the dead for their passage between the veils, as well as their loved ones for their passage through grief and release. My expertise was more invested in the arrival to life than the departure from it, but what puzzles me is how you are a physician and do *not* know about the preservation of bodies.

His tone was slightly indignant when he replied.

"As I said, it usually falls to the holy men to prepare the bodies for burial. My expertise, as you put it, is on the preservation of life, not the absence of it."

"Ah," I said, stitching together a small incision on the King's side that I had just packed. "I suppose tending to the dead is an uncomfortable acknowledgment of your limitations, then."

He laughed, I suspected despite himself. "I suppose it is. I apologize if that sounded arrogant."

I waved it off. "My experience is that male healers in the Britain Beyond are often quite full of themselves and that is the first time I have seen anything like it in you, so I consider myself lucky so far in our selection of a court physician."

"So far?"

I stood up and stretched my back, putting my hands onto my hips and arching back to stretch out the aches from leaning over for an extended time. I had worked for so long, seeing only the dead flesh up close, that I had lost sight of the fact that it was my husband's body. Now, I saw him again lying there on the hard wood table and felt the loss renewed that I would never get to explore his body and know his love as was my due. I felt as though fate had ripped my future out of my hands and left me with only this shell to remember the words he had said to me, the kisses, the feeling of him inside me. Such a moment of joy and excitement for my future, которая now looked dark and grim.

"How will no one miss him for a month?" I asked. "A month of not eating? Of not seeing his daughter?"

"It is not unusual for a royal couple to sequester for a fortnight or so, sometimes even going on a grand tour of the kingdom so everyone can see them and honor them. You are right, however. Since the two of you did not leave, we are well past the time when someone should have seen him. The Princess especially must be told soon," he said, holding the saturated cloth on Marcus's skin as I had shown him to do. "And yes, there will be talk. The sooner we know the realities of your condition, the better."

I thought for a moment.

"At the evening meal the third night I was here," I ventured, "I was served roasted herbed rabbit and there was plenty of it at the table. Does the court raise its own rabbits for meat or do the huntsmen bring them in from the forests?"

"Both. There are hutches within the courtyard and the hunters also bring rabbits to the kitchen."

"I need for you to bring me a female kit, living, one that has not yet birthed a litter. I need a cage and enough food to sustain it for two days."

"A rabbit?"

"Yes, to my quarters. I will also require the sharpest, most narrow reed you can find and a magnifying lens. Have you those things?"

"I do. I take it this is not going to go well for the rabbit?"

"Have you ever studied the effects of a pregnant woman's urine on female rabbits?"

"No?"

"Get me what I ask right away and with any luck, you will see something amazing."

He stared at me as I dried my hands on the front of my dress, which was now stained with body secretions and herbal brews. I wiped my brow with the back of my hand and took in a deep breath that stank of death, our own perspiration despite the cool temperatures, and pungent herbs and spices.

"Will you give me a moment alone with him?" I asked, meeting his gaze over the King's body.

He looked away and began gathering up his own medical instruments. "Yes, of course," he said. "I will clean the table while I wait for you. I suspect it is best to leave him here for now."

"Yes," I agreed. "I will not need long."

"Take your time," he said. He bowed to me and left the cell.

The bowing. All the bowing even after the dropping of formality. I did not imagine I would ever get used to it. I was left with only my torch, which dimmed the lighting significantly. Looking around the room, I saw for the first time that the walls were decked with locking cuffs and chains. Such an unseemly storage place for a just and fine king.

I took the final container of fluid from basket. This one I could not imagine he would manage to supply, but even in the low light, I could tell from the coloration and the smell that he had found every ingredient and brewed it for exactly the correct length of time.

I held the jar between my two hands, one on top and one on the bottom, and pulled up the power from within me, from below my feet, and from the sky above the structure where I stood. Somewhere, up there above the turrets, the watchtowers, and the guard walks, a late afternoon sun shone down on Tintagel just as it shined on Avalon. Below this rock floor, the Mother Earth rested and waited, pregnant with promise. I invoked them both into me and called the Goddess to my aid.

Breathing heavily from the flow of power, I took a drink of the tincture, which was bitter and harsh. I fought back my urge to wretch and forced more of it into me, clapping my hand over my mouth and tilting back my head to keep from vomiting it up.

I then forced back Marcus's tight lips and trickled some of the fluid into his mouth. Gases from the body tried to push it out again, but I managed to get some into him. Enough. The rest, I poured first over his genitals, quietly murmuring the words of magic, then over both of hands, both of feet, his chest just above his heart, and then over the remainder of his body parts. I placed my hands, palms down, over his body nearly touching the skin, and felt the herbs from the liquid begin to stir and move as though living. The liquid permeated into his skin and sank deep within his pores. As it did so, a faint glow formed over him and then it too sank into his body. I felt my own womb receive the herbal mixture as the connection between my living body and his dead one grew solid through the herbs and the magic that worked between us.

My womb seized into a cramp and I nearly doubled over from the pain. I did not cry out, knowing Colin would return if I did and there could be no witness to what I did here except for the Goddess. I braced myself against the table and slowly, the pain subsided.

It would now be as the Goddess willed it.

CHAPTER 14

After I washed myself and changed my clothes, Sir John and Sir Charles arrived in my receiving room within minutes of me summoning them. My legs ached from their lack of use over the past fortnight and my back still complained from the tedious work Colin and I had just done. My mind worked hard to remember my husband's face, beaming with love and desire as he looked down on me, but in a trick of transposition, kept substituting his dead stare and slack jaw instead. Forward movement was all that would distract me from those morbid thoughts. I prayed one day that I would have only the few good memories we shared and not the dark visage of death.

Sir John, Sir Charles, and Colin accompanied me to Princess Zelda's suite of room and immediately, the guards at the door stood aside to allow me to pass. I knocked tentatively, then harder.

A young, fresh-faced woman opened the door to me and immediately fell into a deep curtsy. Frustrated, I urged her to stand.

"Where is the Princess Zelda?" I asked abruptly.

"Why, she is in the dressing room with Nimien and Lady Charlotte changing for the evening meal," the girl said. "Shall I summon her, Your Majesty?"

"What is your name?"

"Beatrix, My Queen. I am Beatrix, the Princess Zelda's handmaiden."

"Very well, then, Beatrix, the Princess Zelda's handmaiden, please go assist the Princess Zelda in dressing sufficiently that she can receive us."

"Before the evening meal, even, Your Majesty?" Beatrix asked, with an expression that made me think she might be a bit slow.

"Now, Beatrix. Right now. And bring her ladies with her."

"Yes, Your Majesty." She turned to leave and then thought the better of leaving us standing in the corridor at the door. I had to give her at least that credit as she stood aside and gave me entry into the bed chamber. She curtsied again and hurried into the next room. From the adjoining room came voices that were agitated, angry, hurried, or all three.

Several long minutes later, when Princess Zelda finally emerged in a flurry of activity from her dressing room with two older women behind her, she made no effort to disguise her frustration at the imposition.

"Well," she said, declining curtsy, bow, or genuflect in any way. "If it is not the newest Queen Mum. To what do I owe this honor? Did you finally escape my father's voracious appetite long enough to come up for air?"

She smiled sweetly and leaned against the door between the two rooms. As much as I wanted to, I did not sit. I had no qualm about taking a chair uninvited, but knew as soon as I did, I must look up to speak to her and I was damned if I would give any illusion of deference, even in bringing her news of such great impact.

"Oh look!" she continued as she noticed the men who now filed into the room. "We have the entire royal entourage. No Father Francisco to keep us honest? Whatever shall we do? Without him, we could get into all manner of mischief."

"Zelda, we need to speak with you," I said, keeping my tone firm, but gentle. "It is important."

"It must be to warrant such a party in my quarters. Come. Invade my rooms like the Saxon raiders have claimed the Eastern shores." Her voice sounded bored and unaffected, but it was clear we were a tremendous inconvenience to her.

"And where is my father?" she asked, once we were inside with the door closed behind us. "Too tired from working out all those years of frustration to come say hello to his only child?"

"You should sit," I said. "We should all sit."

"And here I am without enough chairs for all of you," she said with mock disappointment. "If I had known I was entertaining tonight, I would have planned better. Such a shame."

My patience with her was thinning, but I knew that within minutes, I would give her news that would change her life forever, so I stilled my temper and smiled at her.

"Sit down, Zelda," I said sternly without room for argument. I decided to forgo her official title and treat her as my stepdaughter rather than a royal child of Cornwall.

"By all means," she said curtly and sat upon her bed corner.

"Zelda." I stepped closer her and she leaned back to maintain her distance. I had played this conversation over in my head and decided that it was best to get directly to the point. "I am quite sorry to tell you that your father has died. The court physician here examined him and determined that his heart failed." I looked at Colin for support and he nodded to her.

"There will be a formal interment within the week. I am so very grieved for your loss."

All the bravado, as well as all of the air, seemed to leave Zelda in a rush.

"Are you sure?" she asked, looking at the four of us in turns, clearly praying for some hope to grasp.

"It is certain," Colin said. "He is dead."

"When?" Her voice was soft and reedy now, barely a whisper.

"He was dead when I awoke the day after the wedding. Herschel was with me and we found he had died sometime in the night."

"But… but that was a fortnight ago, longer even…"

"Yes," Sir John said. "It was. There were legal matters to attend to before we told anyone. The Queen knew because she was there. Father Francisco had to say the Prayer for the Dead as soon as possible since he was unable to deliver last rites. Sir Charles and I had to clarify the rights of succession according to the King's wishes. Sir Colin knew because he performed the examination of the body to determine the cause of death."

"Who…who else knew this?"

"Bersaba and Ursa, who cared for the Queen as she mourned. No one else."

"And you thought not to tell his own daughter?" Her eyes reddened and I could see the fierce determination she used to fight back tears. To her credit, she would not show weakness in front of us.

"We knew you would have questions," Sir Charles said, his voice soft with emotion. "We wanted to wait until we had those answers before we told you."

"Did you kill him?" she asked me, seeking my eyes with her own dark ones.

"No," I said. "As I said, he died of heart failure. You likely know that his own father died at a similar age."

She breathed heavily, still fighting back tears as her breaths turned into heavy gasps.

"Are you here to crown me?" she asked. "Am I now Queen of Cornwall?"

"No," Sir John said. "Those are the questions we wanted settled before coming to you. You are still the Princess Zelda of Cornwall. Queen Iris is the sovereign and is your legal guardian."

"No," she said, simply. "No. I...I reject this. That...that is not possible."

"It is so," Sir Charles said gently. "Your father drew up papers in the final days before his death making the Queen your regent until you are of age. She rules absolutely and the King made certain the rules of succession were iron clad. If, by chance, your stepmother is carrying your father's child, the succession will shift to the male heir with the Queen as regent."

"Of course, it does," she said bitterly. "He trusts a stranger to rule in his stead, but not his daughter."

Sir John immediately cut off that line of rant for her. "With all due respect and deference, Princess Zelda," he said, his voice suddenly sharp, "You gave your father little evidence to support the idea that you are qualified to rule a kingdom. Your behavior has been less than regal."

"I am a Princess, John. I can do what I want."

"And as a princess, *Zelda*, yes you can. As a queen, you cannot and it is likely through that vision that your father made the choices he did."

"Your Highness," Sir Charles said, trying to defuse the tension that was thick within the room, "None of us expected this. Your father was, as far as we knew, in fine health and I am sure when he drew up the papers, he did not expect them to fall into use so quickly. And yet here we are. As much as it goes against your nature, I need, *we* need, for you to pay Queen Iris the respect that is fitting to her station and to honor her as your stepmother and your queen. Nothing else will suffice."

I waved him away and knelt in front of her. "Zelda," I said, "I cannot even imagine the pain of losing my father. He is the world to me, or at least was until I met your father and in the short time I knew him, came to love him. I know my grief is nowhere close to yours, I loved your father for less than a week, but you loved him your whole life. As I said, I do not pretend to know what you feel and what you *will* feel as this all sinks in. We are all doing our best to find our places in this tremendous change. I want you to know that I am here for you any time you want to talk or grieve or be angry or whatever it is you need to do."

"Will you do anything I ask?" she said quietly, looking at her hands in her lap.

I looked up at the three men and they all looked as though we faced imminent and complete disaster.

"I will try," I said, turning back to her. "I will absolutely do my best."

"Then get out of my rooms and leave me alone," she said, turning her head away from me and staring at the quilt that covered her bed. Beatrix hurried to her side and slipped a comforting arm around her, but Zelda stiffened and pulled away.

I pushed myself to standing. "You heard the Princess, gentlemen. Leave her be."

Sir John started to speak, but I help up my hand.

"That is an order," I clarified. "Make no mistake believing otherwise."

Before I left the room myself, I motioned to Lady Charlotte and Nimien to come to me, which they did without hesitation. In quiet tones, I told them that they were to do the impossible. They were to allow Princess

Zelda room to grieve in her own way, but to make certain she was safe at all times. They were to watch her carefully, but to also give her the opportunity to rage or to weep.

"You know her better than anyone," I said, "Give her what she needs but do not allow her to invite harm to herself in any form."

The women nodded and I added, "Do not hesitate to tell me, Sir John, or Sir Colin of anything the Princess might need and by all means, summon the physician if she requires a tincture to help her sleep."

They agreed and I closed the door behind me as I left.

Back in my receiving room, the three men and I fell into conference over how to proceed. As I had found the usual stride to be, Sir John was more given to forceful action and Sir Charles was the peacemaker. Colin interjected infrequently, but always with a strong observation we would otherwise have missed.

Despite the stress and admittedly grotesque tasks of the day, I was starving and asked a waiting servant to bring up a light meal for us. Once we left this room, news of the King's death would disseminate throughout the court and then through the kingdom. My absence at the formal evening meal would be quite understood by the time it would be served.

I presented the funereal arrangement set up by Father Francisco and agreed upon by myself and Father Damian.

"With all due deference, Your Majesty," Sir John asked, giving voice to what they all were thinking. "Have your courses come on? Is there hope of an heir?"

"Still hope," I said, "But again I caution you that stress can also delay a woman's courses and if you think I have not experienced stress in the past weeks, think again."

They all nodded and murmured in the most understanding way they knew how.

"The court physician and I will work together to provide a better answer for you. In the interim, it is essential that we release the news of the King's death and implement plans for the funeral straight away. I examined the King's body earlier today and cannot personally vouch for how much longer the integrity of it remains."

Very nearly as an afterthought, I sent all servants from the room and in private, advised them fully of the situation with Father Francisco. To my relief, they agreed with my decision to appoint Father Damian as my personal spiritual counsel as well as keeping Father Francisco on as the primary priest.

"Father Francisco's ambition within the Church is as dangerous as his fanaticism," Sir John said. "He will take any advantage to overthrow a sovereign he cannot control and put one in their place that he can, just as was done with the High Throne."

The others quietly agreed, even looking around as though they feared others might overhear.

"It is essential, My Queen," Sir Charles said, looking at me intently, "that you are never alone with him. You must, in fact, rarely be alone at all. The man is a danger and if he believes you are carrying the heir to the throne, he is an even greater danger. When you give birth to an heir, you solidify your long-term standing as a regent of the throne of Cornwall. He has had the teaching of Princess Zelda since she was a young child. Any child you bear will also have your teaching and your bloodline, so he will know his influence with the future sovereign in that case to be limited. He sees his power lessening with each day you are on the throne."

Sir John shifted uncomfortably in his chair as though the truths we were giving voice were pebbles under his bottom. "Sir Charles is absolutely correct, Your Highness. It is to Father Francisco's benefit that you, and if possible, your unborn child, do not survive. You must ensure your own safety always. There are plenty and enough trustworthy advisers and King's Guardsmen - I am sorry, *Queen's* Guardsmen - who can protect you. I cannot stress this enough."

The idea that Father Francisco truly might do me physical harm was a thought I believed existed only in my head until I heard them give it voice.

I all but scoffed at them. "Do you really believe he would kill me?" I looked at them with incredulity and they stared back, their eyes solemn.

"Madam," Colin said, "We would be remiss to not make every effort to fully advise of the danger. While the King lived, respect for the sovereign cowed Francisco. Since his death, however, we have seen him engaging in behaviors that are…" He looked at the other two for support.

"…concerning," Sir John finished for him. "The only overt threats he has made were the ones you reported to us that he made in private and we certainly believe your claim. He has, however, actively worked in maligning your claim and your credibility to the point that we have had to force his silence under threat of treason charges. He is grieving yes, for in his own way, he did love King Marcus. He is also, however, optimizing the moment of instability in the sovereignty to further his own ambitions. He is a real and present danger, however, as tempting as it is to bring him up on charges of treason, we do risk him becoming a martyr for the Church. The wisest course of action is to allow him some degree of power as he has had in the past, but to keep him out of your path and you out of his. That is why your plan is well suited to the situation."

"May I summon my father, who has extensive experience in court, to come advise me as I adjust to my new position."

"I wish I could say yes," Sir Charles said gently. "Unfortunately, although all of us personally revere your father and believe he would be a fine asset to the court, his presence would only serve to further inflame the fury of Father Francisco. We are told King Marcus had to take Father Francisco to task at the wedding for his treatment of your parents. Without the King present to intervene, we fear your father and you would be in even more danger than if he were not here."

I drew in a long breath, seeing the wisdom of what he said.

Oh Marcus, I thought. *How could you do this to me? Oh Goddess. How could you do this to me?*

"How is it that one man can hold an entire court hostage, threaten its sovereign Queen, and humble all of us into whispering our truths behind our hands?" I asked.

"It is not the one man," Colin said. "It is the new way of things with the Church in charge of the High Throne. There are ears everywhere and each kingdom save North Wales has its own Father Francisco to act as judge and jury."

"Oh really, and what is special about North Wales?" I asked thinking of Rose on her way there now.

"King Jacob Rowen is special. He has nothing but contempt for the Church, but is so remote that they have no interest in what he does. You, however, are in a financial stronghold. Cornwall supplies the tin and copper for most of the country and is a very wealthy kingdom. We pay our taxes well and our tributes are larger than any other kingdom. That is both a blessing and a curse in terms of the Church's attention on us."

"For a physician," Sir John noted, "You certainly know a great deal about the politics of the country."

Colin shrugged. "I trust in science," he said, "not in faith. I believe in knowing my enemy and I have never met a man of God yet that I trusted."

"Father Damian?" I asked.

"I cannot trust a man who only speaks in questions," he answered. "He seems a good enough fellow, but that lilt is unnerving as hell."

The other two men laughed.

"Our best move," Sir Charles said, "is to make this transition as quickly and as smoothly as possible, keeping the eyes of the Church off us. That means keeping Father Francisco quiet and busy. We do not engage him. We do not provoke him and we do not rebuke him in any way. If we imprison him, the Church immediately becomes involved in a major capacity, whether he is found guilty or innocent. If we kill him, and trust me, that idea has made its way to the table since the King died, the Church will miss him and become involved in a major capacity. We allow him to carry on his tasks. We protect you and the child, if there is one, and we carry on with your reign."

"But he is conducting the funeral and afterward, there is a daily funeral mass for a full month!"

"And you will be there every morning when mass is said for our king. Colin, Sir John, or I will be there with you. We give him no cause to believe that you mean any threat to the Christian Church and to this court being known as a Christian court. Now I must ask you in all honesty, do you have any intention otherwise?"

"Not at all," I said, meeting his gaze and I could say so truthfully because my quest was not to undermine the Christian Church, but to protect those who did not wish to serve it.

"Then we move forward with integrity. That is our only path."

CHAPTER 15

"So, you used the reed to inject your urine into the rabbit's bloodstream? For two days?"

Colin looked at me as if I had gone mad and I wondered if he had called to mind the rumors that I was a witch from the island of demons.

"Yes," I said.

"You have aggressively put your piss into a living rabbit?"

"Yes. And now we are going to examine the rabbit's lady parts to see how the urine affected them. If we see normal lady rabbit parts, there is no pregnancy. If we have engorged lady parts, I am indeed with child."

"I am guessing we turn the rabbit over and…"

"…not exactly. It is not the rabbit's outside lady parts we have to examine."

He sighed heavily. "Of course, it would not be, would it?"

I winced. "She will have paid the ultimate sacrifice for Cornwall."

"Long live the Queen."

"But not the rabbit," I said. With a deft twist of my wrist, I snapped the creature's neck and laid it out on the table in front of us.

He handed me a razor-sharp scalpel and I began to cut as he used a cup of water to sluice away the blood that flowed.

"Do you not have to know what unengorged rabbit lady bits look like to tell the difference?"

"Hand me the magnifying lens," I asked, though I hardly needed it. "There, do you see?"

He took the lens and looked where I pointed with the blade.

"Are you sure you pulled this rabbit from other than the breeding hutches?" I asked.

"It came directly from the baby hutches, one of the larger ones about to be moved to the breeding bins. The rabbit has never been bred."

"See how the ovaries are engorged?" I asked. "That is nearly conclusive that I am pregnant, along with the fact that I am now three days late on my courses."

"Stress?"

"Plenty of stress, but also the rabbit tells all."

"How do you KNOW these things?" he sat back in his chair with a perplexed look on his face. "I studied medicine long enough to become physician to the King of Cornwall and I have never heard of such a thing."

I wiped my hands on a cloth and began to clean up the mess.

"I have studied birth and the health of women since I was a young girl. On Avalon, we all have a calling and this was mine. Healers from all over the world came to Avalon to teach us and learn from us. A healer from the far eastern lands taught me about this."

"They have rabbits in the far eastern lands?"

"Apparently, they have rabbits pretty much everywhere," I shrugged and took in a deep breath and let it out. "So now my task is to carry this child to term, make certain it is a boy, and keep it alive long enough to become king."

"I would say that covers it," he wiped down the table after I picked up the cloth that contained most the rabbit leavings. "How do you feel?"

"Tired," I said, "but then, I rarely can sleep."

"It might help if you slept in a bed instead of the chair."

"Would you want to sleep in the same bed where your new spouse died?"

"There are other beds in Tintagel, Iris. I am quite sure the staff could round one up for you."

I sighed heavily. "I could go back to the Queen's quarters."

He nodded thoughtfully. "You could. Or you could rearrange in here. You do seem to like the view and there is not so much to look at on the other side of the castle."

"You are a clever man," I said. "Will you send some husky furniture finding and lifting people to me when we are done here?"

"I will aspire to find the best husky furniture finding and lifting people in all of Cornwall," he smiled. "Now what shall I do with the rabbit who gave all for Queen and kingdom?"

"I would say take her to the kitchen that she might be made well use of, but I have enough people here believing I am a witch and a spell caster. It would only add to the gossip if anyone knew I slaughtered livestock in my sleeping quarters."

"I take your point," he agreed. "Never fear. I shall secret her body out and bury her in the woods. No one shall be the wiser."

"And please tell Sir Charles and Sir John that I must see them immediately. I do realize that all of this fetching and finding is not in your usual purview, Doctor."

"I am afraid that as a lady in waiting, I am most inept, but I do try."

"Now that we have finished this bit of nasty work, I must get Bersaba up here with some food. I am positively famished."

"Shall I summon her as well, Your Majesty?" he asked. "Or would you care for some rabbit?"

"Ugh," my stomach rolled. "I was thinking more of quail eggs and cheese."

"Then I shall take my leave if I am pardoned to go."

"Colin," I said, realizing I had imposed greatly upon his easy nature. "What I meant by 'your usual purview' is that you do not have to do this…any of this. I realize the necessity of your work here and do not wish to encroach overly upon your day."

He smiled warmly. "It has been most enlightening, Iris. Never did I imagine the effect pregnant urine would have on a rabbit. If indeed your womb has quickened from the mighty seed of our king, I will gladly study at your dissecting table anytime."

"Thank you," I said. Although Sir John and Sir Charles had endeavored to assist me in matters of court and Bersaba was an attentive and motherly presence, Colin was the person in Tintagel with whom I most identified. I was grateful for his cheery company and willing spirit. When I was with him, I did not feel judged or pressured to produce an heir. It was a tremendous relief to share friendly banter with someone who seemed little invested in where I was raised and who treated me like a regular person.

After he left, I huddled in my chair with a wrap pulled around me. Since I left the underground torture cavern where my husband's body was stored, I could never seem to get warm enough even though the days outside were fair. Tintagel itself was a chilly fortress made of stone and held the lower temperatures brought in off the sea in an icy grip, even in the light of the year. I knew part of the chill was from the level of magic I had worked to ensure conception and to protect the tiny life inside of me if I did conceive. High magic always left me weak and faint, so it was hard to tell what was from magic, what was from fatigue and grief, and what was from the pregnancy. Or perhaps the damned castle was simply never warm.

I ate all through the day. Once Bersaba knew there was a chance I was with child, she forced food on me constantly. At last, my stomach had unclenched from the stress of the King's death and would allow me to eat more than a few bites at a time. I drank broth and goats milk and napped throughout the day as I could. Exhaustion claimed me often, but I found that if I napped midmorning and in the afternoon, I could spend the rest of the day out of bed.

The court staff appointed to the care of Princess Zelda reported that she ate very little and refused to leave her room. I sympathized with her completely because I felt the same. The entire court was deep in mourning. King Marcus was beloved to all and his absence weighed heavily on the people who served him.

Realizing the wisdom of Colin's point that I might sleep better in a bed than a chair, I requested new bedding and asked that the old ones be burned. The staff brought in all new bedding and had my belongings transferred from the Queen's chambers to the King's. I would honor him by staying in his bed where he wanted me, but I would not sleep on the very sheets where he died. If I could hide in my room and remain undisturbed as Zelda did, it would certainly be my choice to do so.

Father Francisco conducted the funereal arrangements with great haste once he received permission to proceed and the King's body lay in state in the main ballroom of Tintagel, surrounded by many fragrant flowers and spices with a wide berth roped off to keep mourners from getting too close.

Due to my "delicate condition," I was not required to stand vigil for the entire three days. I went to each mass said for Marcus and prayed for the soul of my Christian husband. I hoped he found his paradise, his Heaven, and I prayed that his beloved wife waited for him there.

Zelda did not appear either for mass or for any of the days of his lying in state. The morning that the King was to be interred, I went to her room and requested entry. Lady Charlotte admitted me into the room and it took several minutes for my eyes to adjust to the darkness, after which I could see the girl's shape huddled on the bed.

"Has she eaten at all?" I asked.

"Very little," Nimien, informed me. "A bit of bread, some wine, not nearly even enough to keep a bird alive."

"Zelda?" I said softly, sitting on the bed near her. Her back was turned to me and she did not move when I spoke.

"Zelda, can you please turn over? I need to speak with you."

"Go away," she said, her voice muffled. "Please, just…go away. You said you would."

"Zelda, dearest," I reached out and touched her shoulder and she jerked away from me.

"I SAID GO AWAY!" she said. "And do not mean merely to leave my room. Leave my home. Leave my kingdom. Please just…leave. Everything was fine before you came."

"Yes," I said, "I suppose it was. And it is true that nothing will ever be completely fine again without your father here. If you wish to say goodbye to him, you do not have much time to do so. We can do it in private if you want with no one else there. I will send them all away for whatever time you need with him."

"I don't want to see him dead," she said flatly. "If I see him dead, I will not ever be able to remember him any other way."

I sighed heavily because her reasoning made perfect sense. I was myself having trouble getting around the image of Marcus laid out on the stone table in the lower chamber of the chapel to reach the memory of his generous smile and twinkling eyes.

Tentatively, I reached out to place my hand on her back. When she did not pull away, I began to stroke it, tracing soft circles with my palm.

"You don't have to," I said.

I heard her sniffle and her body shuddered a bit. Still, I kept rubbing her back while she allowed it.

"Father Francisco and Uncle Charles and Uncle John will make me go," she said.

"No," I assured her. "No, they will not. If you do not wish to go to the funeral or to mass or see him at all, you do not have to. I will command it and they must do what I say. You saw that they left the room before when I demanded it, did you not? I will order them not to force you to do anything you do not wish to do."

She was still and silent for such a long time that I thought perhaps she had fallen asleep.

"Are…are you going to kill the woman in the tower?" she asked. Her voice came so low that I wondered if she spoke from a dream in her sleep.

"Zelda…what are you saying?"

"Are you going to kill the woman in the tower? The one that Daddy loved."

I am not sure if I was more stunned that she knew of her father's beloved or that the woman was here…at Tintagel.

"Zelda, I am not going to kill anyone. There is a woman in the tower?"

"She is ever so kind, when she is in her right mind, and very beautiful still even though she is old. I do not wish her to die."

"No one else is going to die, I promise you, and certainly not by my hand."

"Father Francisco says you are a witch from an island of demons and that you brought dark magic to our kingdom. He says that is why my father died."

"Father Francisco believes what he has been told by men who think they know about me and about Avalon, but do not. Someday, I will tell you about my home. It is very beautiful and a magical place, but there are no demons or witches there. There are only beautiful priestesses who live in peace and harm no one…ever. They are good people. They are healers and bards and artists and wise ones.

"I came here to marry your father because he needed a wife. Father Francisco says the things he does because he is afraid and because he cares about Tintagel, but he is wrong. I wish no harm to you or the lady or anyone else here."

"What is going to happen to me now?" she asked, sounding years younger than her age of ten and five.

"What will happen to you? Why, you will grieve your father, as will I and the entire court. You will continue to live here as you always have and when you are of age, you will become queen."

"Unless your baby is a boy."

"That was not my choice, but it is what your father commanded, yes."

"…and lives to be old enough to rule."

Her words were chilling and I slipped my hand over my belly protectively without even considering what I did.

"Yes."

When she did not reply, I continued.

"You will begin more aggressive training with your father's advisers to teach you how to rule as a queen. I would like it if you would sit in with me as I make decisions on behalf of the kingdom and give me your opinions of how things should be done in Cornwall since you know your kingdom better than do I. In six years when it is time for you to be crowned Queen, you will be ready. If I have a son, you will know much and more about ruling Cornwall and can help your brother when the time comes. Regardless, Cornwall needs you, but right now, as you grieve, you will do it your own way and no one will demand that you attend any part of the ceremonies if you do not wish to do so."

"When is the last of it?"

"The final ceremony is today and he will be interred afterward. Each morning at sunrise, Father Francisco says a mass for your father. That will be over in a little less than a month."

"I will think about it," she said, still speaking into the stone wall against which rested her bed. Never once did she turn to face me in the entire time I was there with her in her room.

"Is there anything I can do for you?" I asked, hoping to find some point of comfort I could offer.

"You can leave," she said simply.

And I did, because the rest of the day I would spend preparing to bury a husband I barely met but who I feared would carry my heart into the grave with him.

~*~

I slept restlessly that night, the events of the day playing through my head. Had Zelda actually threatened my unborn child or was it merely a child's question? Had Father Francisco intended to offend when he intoned that "we may never know exactly why or how our beloved king died, but God knows" or was he merely pontificating? Tears streamed down the priest's face throughout the funeral mass and if I doubted the love and devotion he had for Marcus before, I did not now. I felt then a million miles from Avalon and from the achievement of the goals of my quest. I did not know how to be a queen. I was supposed to have years to learn that at the side of my King, carefully guiding him toward inclusionary behavior toward those of other faiths.

I ate little at the funeral feast, my stomach pitching and boiling like a repulsive stew of acids. I felt alternately queasy and faint throughout most of the day and was grateful to have Sir John on one side of me and Sir Charles on the other, with Bersaba behind me. Twice, I nearly swooned, which irritated me beyond reason. *I do not swoon.* I prided myself of being made of much stronger stuff than that and fainting just before my wedding was less about my own constitution and more about suffocation by mechanical means. *I do not swoon.*

Zelda did come to the funeral mass wearing a simple black gown with her face veiled. I would not have known for certain it was she except that she removed her veil briefly as she stepped over the guiding ropes and went directly to her father's funeral bier without restriction. The King's Guard went to stop her, but I motioned then back. She bent to kiss his cheek, her tears flowing freely. The smell of his body as close as she was I knew to be unpleasant and she drew her handkerchief to her nose as she walked away and pulled her veil down over her face again. She actively avoided my gaze and stood across the room from me with her ladies in waiting, including Nimien, Lady Charlotte, and Beatrix.

His body was borne out of the main hall on an elegant horse drawn cart to the family tomb behind Tintagel's chapel once all of the guests had their moment of looking at the dead King for one last time. He was interred between his mother and his father, and above his first wife. She rested beside the marker for Edmund, their son who died when he was but tree weeks old. On her other side, an inscribed marker showed that there was a place for Princess Eselde when her time came. It seemed inevitable that there was no reasonable place for me among the dead royals of Cornwall and I straightened my spine and drew in a breath at the beauty of this design. Indeed.

Despite the height of summer, the day had a chill to it that cut me to my bones. The wind came in off the crashing waves and seemed to match the coldness I felt seeping into my heart. Despite the kindness of Bersaba and the guidance of Sir Charles and Sir John, I was utterly alone. Laoghaire had taken the first chance to abandon me. My mother and father were far beyond my reach. My sisters were scattered to the work of the Goddess. I had only my child to feel any kind of connection to me and even that seemed less than reality. I could neither feel nor sense any kind of life growing within me. My womb might well have been an empty fist, clenched up hard in my pelvis.

The one brief glimpse of happiness I had lasted only a few hours, just a quick night before I woke up to find my dead husband draped over my naked body. I had known love for a scant handful of moments. I had known desire for a few passionate minutes of lovemaking to which I had not even brought my best effort because of some ridiculous advice given to me by a mentor on Avalon who urged us to leave our lover wanting more. Now, I knew should I ever love again, which I doubted, I would treat every moment of lovemaking and intimacy as though it could be my last.

After the feast, which was punctuated by inane conversations murmured in a combined low roar throughout the formal dining hall, I plead exhaustion and went to my room, then sat curled in the chair and stared out at setting sun until the darkness came. Ursa lit the oil lamp by my bed and turned down the bedding, then quietly left the room after she made certain I needed nothing. On the contrary, I needed so very much and yet nothing that anyone within the walls of the castle could provide to me.

I dozed in the chair, but woke to my belly growling for food and after ignoring it for as long as I could, I sighed and swung my legs over the side of the bed. The angle of the moon shining into the window told me it was not long past midnight. The stone floor was cold under my feet, but I did not wish to light the lamp and search for wherever I had tossed my shoes, so I slipped out of my room in my sleeping shift and dressing robe with my feet bare. The halls were silent as I tried to orient myself in the darkness to find my way to the kitchen. Surely, there would be some sliced meats and hard bread left from the earlier feasting that would quell my hunger and let me sleep. Perhaps even a mug of beer to further entice a dreamless sleep and still my busy mind.

As I neared the wide staircase, I heard an odd noise that sounded like the slapping of reins against an unruly horse, over and over. Between the slapping sounds, I heard grunts and low moans. I pulled my dressing gown closer around me and followed the sounds to a bedroom just two doors down on the other side of the stairway from the direction of my own quarters.

The door was slightly ajar and a soft glow came from with. Was someone hurt inside? Gently, I pushed open the door and had to push the palm of my hand into my teeth to stifle my scream. My eyes widened with horror as I watched the man who knelt before a large crucifix in an otherwise sparse room. It was Father Francisco and he used a flail with barbs at the ends of leather straps to flog himself as blood streamed down from his back and pooled around him. Chunks of flesh torn from his skin where the hooks dug in were wrenched away as he pulled the flog free and beat himself over and over. He wept and moaned as the vicious strokes lashed at his back repeatedly while he prayed softly.

"For I have allowed sin and darkness to come into this place and take our King from us. For I have failed in my duties to keep this home sacred and a pure vessel to honor Your name. For I have allowed a witch to take control of this kingdom and to spawn a demon's child and call it the prince of my King. For I am a wretched, despoiled, horrible creature who is unworthy of Your love. For I have failed You and deserve not to enter the Kingdom of Heaven when I cannot protect the Kingdom of Cornwall from the reach of the Fiend who our Queen worships."

Repeatedly, he slammed the flog into his flesh, his baneful and self-deprecating prayers peppered with painful moans and some occasional whimpers, with only the array of lit candles and the dead stare of the wooden Christ to bear witness…and I as well. Gasping for air, I pulled the door nearly closed again and leaned against the wall of the hall, for once grateful that it was cool and damp to soothe the heat that had risen in my face. Had I walked in on someone pleasuring themselves or making love to another, it would have been no more of an intrusion to their intimacy. My head swam with vertigo and I was unsure if it was from the malnourishment of the day or from shock at what I had seen. My breath came in quick gasps and I forced myself to breathe in my nose and out my mouth, in my nose and out my mouth, until my heartbeat regulated.

    My appetite was now fully gone and I dragged my hand along the wall until I reached my quarters again. I barely made it to the wash basin before my traitor belly began to wretch up stomach juices and the dry heaves shook my body. Tears ran down my face and I felt as though surely the tiny blood vessels in my cheeks and eyes were bursting from the fury of my vomiting. I poured the cool water from the pitcher onto a linen cloth and wiped my face, still feeling faint and ill. Slowly, I made my way to the bed and curled into a ball, feeling every bit like an injured animal who waits for a huntsman to come put her at last out of her mortal misery.

CHAPTER 16

Meetings with the King's advisers…now the *Queen's* advisers, revealed that Cornwall was just as prosperous as our previous impromptu meeting indicated. The coffers were full and Cornish people paid their taxes without complaint. The council held the impression that the Cornish people were happy and held a better standard of living than did most of Britain, largely due to two factors. One was that the kingdom's remote location provided some protection from the Saxon raids, which tended to focus on the major townships that were more inland. The second reason for their prosperity was that the tin and copper mines of the area, which were the primary source of income for most people, were thriving.

The greatest challenge for all Britons were the new taxes the High Throne imposed upon all the lesser kingdoms to fund the advancement of the Christian Church throughout the country. Once Prince John took the High Throne, decisions regarding taxation fell primarily into the hands of his uncle and regent, Archbishop Gregory, whose sole ambition it was to convert Britain into a Christian land. Based on the significant and abrupt rise in taxes since Phillip was dethroned, conversion was a pricey endeavor and other kingdoms suffered far worse under the oppression than did Cornwall. My council believed the same as did the elders on Avalon, specifically that the new Prince had nothing to do with the running of the country and all executive decisions now lay in the hands of the Archbishop.

Each month at the time of the full moon, the King heard all petitions and dispensed judgment upon conflicts within the kingdom for those who could not find relief from their local lords and dukes. As the full moon approached, Tintagel was abuzz because my courses were still absent and the court physician confirmed that I was indeed carrying the King's child. Never had I imagined my personal body functions to be of such interest to total strangers.

Despite my stomach upheaval after witnessing Father Francisco's self-flagellation, I was surprised to find that I had no morning sickness as most pregnant women I knew did. I grew tired often through the day, but I otherwise felt as I always had. I took none of this for granted and knew that tide could turn at any time.

Bersaba continued to mother hen me, making certain I ate until I felt I would burst and drank gallons of milk. She tried to force the water on me, but my distaste for it grew and I could not bear to swallow it. Likewise, the fruit seemed tasteless to me because the fruits we grew on Avalon were so rich and sweet. She tempted me with exotic fruits like dates and dried foods from other countries and while I was happy to try them, they were less than satisfying.

I insisted that we keep the full moon hearings in place and sent word that I wished for Princess Zelda to sit with me as I passed the judgments. As the day dawned and Sir John and Sir Charles escorted me into the throne room, people were already assembled in a long line to test the mettle of the new Queen. I sat in Marcus's place and left what would traditionally be my throne open in case Zelda decided to make an appearance.

Sir John and Sir Charles took the list of petitioners from the heralds and read over the grievances before handing it to me. I scanned over the words and found no true surprises. Disputes over property, disobedient wives and children brought for judgment by the man of the house, business disagreements, one woman who claiming her husband was bewitched into betraying her by her neighbor, widows who begged clemency for their debts… all very mundane concerns.

"This list is far longer than usual," Sir John whispered to me. "It is likely that they just want a look at you and to see if you will rule as did the King."

I nodded, already suspecting as much.

"Shall we begin?" I asked, motioning to the Queen's Guardsman at the door to bring in the first petitioner. As the man entered, there was a commotion at the rear entrance to the throne room where I had entered and I was stunned to see Zelda, dressed properly for court and admonishing a steward who apparently did not receive word she might make an appearance and who made the error of suggesting she not interrupt.

I smiled and beckoned to her and he allowed her to pass. In truth, she was passing just fine on her own as she brushed him aside. Like a true queen, she marched to the throne and took her seat, folding her hands in her lap.

On Avalon, people often perceived me as authoritarian and I was sometimes even considered bossy. This knack of telling others what to do with ease, although some might call it a compulsion, occasionally got in the way of personal relationships, but it served me well as a queen. As each petitioner described to me their plight, my mind assembled the relevant facts like pieces to a puzzle, discarding the extraneous and targeting the missing pieces that were withheld or misrepresented. I asked the pointed questions that would lead to the truth of the matter and worked the matter around in my head until a clear path emerged.

In some cases, there was no truth or right answer and I had to go with my gut instinct and hope the verdict was fair. As the highest court in Cornwall, if not fair, it was at least absolute. Whether I found in their favor or not, each petitioner paid a tribute to the herald as they left.

Part way through the morning, after hearing several cases, two men presented with a sheep on a lead between them. The first man explained that his neighbor's prize winning ram had impregnated his own sheep and now insisted that he turn the three lambs birthed by the ewe over to him.

The second man interrupted, saying that the ewe was an ordinary sheep and it was his ram that had added tremendous value to the lambs and so they were his by right.

I looked at Zelda, who was sitting patiently at my side in the queen's throne, her boredom on full display, and I said, "Suppose you adjudicate this case, Your Grace."

She looked at me with stunned surprise.

"Me?" she asked, her eyes wide. "Not me. I am but…"

"…the future Queen of Cornwall," I finished, locking my gaze on hers with tremendous intention.

She sat up straighter on her throne and stared intently at the two men, as well as the sheep between them. After several moments, she spoke, her voice firm and strong without a single waver or break.

"A sheep is an animal of God. It is precious in that our savior is called the Lamb of God, but any further value is ascribed to the animal by men. To God, a sheep is a sheep, a ewe is a ewe, and a lamb is a lamb.

The laws of man do not address an issue such as this, which is why you have come to us with your dilemma. When the law of our kingdom has no authority to prevail, then we must turn to the laws of God, which say that these three lambs you claim," she motioned to the first complainant, are of no more worth than any other lambs. Each is precious in the eyes of God and they were birthed by the natural actions of animals, controlled by God and not man. Since these three lambs are, to God, naught but lambs, then we give one to each of you and the third to the throne as tribute for our adjudication."

"Your Majesty!" the first man argued to me. "Are we truly to take the ruling of this girl who does not know the ways of the world beyond these walls?"

I arched my eyebrow and stared him down.

"I found the Princess Zelda's ruling to be quite rational and wise. It stands."

The second man knelt at Zelda's feet.

"Thank you," he said. "Thank you for your wisdom and fairness."

The first man scoffed and turned to leave. I motioned the Queen's Guardsman to bring him back to me. I worked to disguise my rising contempt under a dispassionate mask.

"You will now apologize to your sovereign Princess," I said coolly, "and refrain from disrespecting her or any judgment she makes again."

Something in my tone connected with him and he bowed low before her.

"I beg mercy, Your Grace, for any offense" he said. Whether his solemn tone was forced or genuine, I cared not. All I knew was that his dismissal of her for her youth and her gender caused my gorge to rise.

"You are pardoned," she said with great sternness, then glanced at me and mugged a silly face before the man stood up and could see.

I coughed and quickly covered my mouth with my hand to hide my smile.

The day wore on into early evening with the line of petitioners seeming never to end. Zelda and I found our rhythm with me ruling on one case and her taking the next. Twice in the process, she deferred to me and although I presented the final ruling, I brought her into the deliberation of the case.

As the room darkened to the point that the servants lit torches along the wall, Sir John announced the final petitioner. Fortunately, it was a simple land case and Sir Charles pointed out that laws on the Cornwall books already set precedence governing the ruling, so we had merely to confirm to the petitioners what was already in place.

I did not realize how exhausted and weak I felt until I stood to go and very nearly fell over like a stone. No food and no nap for hours on end left me weak as a kitten. Both Sir John and Sir Charles rushed to my side and helped me down from the dais. Zelda had already made good her own escape by then without a word to me. I regained my bearings and asked that they have an evening meal sent to my quarters. Sir Charles hurried off to do so while Sir John allowed me to lean on him while he escorted me up the stairs to my quarters.

"May I have the court physician call on you, My Queen?" he asked as he pushed open the door to my bed chamber.

"No," I insisted. "I need only food and rest and I will be fine."

"With your permission, then, Your Highness, unless you require more?" he bowed briefly to me and turned to go.

"Sir John?" I asked, more on a whim than with any kind of strategic plan. "Why are you and Sir Charles so good to me? You barely know me and yet, you have been my strength through this. I do not know how I could have managed without you, the physician, and Bersaba."

"It is what he would have wanted," the man said as if it were the simplest thing on earth. "My best friend since childhood lies dead and entombed and he trusted you sufficiently that he would hand you the keys to our kingdom. He was a good king and a wise man. If he believed in you that much in such a short time, then so do Charles and I."

"Thank you," I said, truly humbled by his words and for the first time since Marcus's death, I understood the grievous loss they had all suffered. Although I had come to love him intensely during our days together, unreasonably so, in fact, they had loved him nearly their whole lives.

"Not to mention," he added with a smile, "that you are especially precious now that you carry the last gift he gave to us within you…his son."

I smiled and touched my belly without conscious thought to do so.

"Well," I said, "it could be a girl. There certainly are plenty of those through my family."

"But you do not think it so, do you Queen Iris?"

"No," I said, before I knew even I thought it. "No, it is a son."

He smiled and nodded.

"Good night to you, Your Highness."

I pushed the door closed behind me, only to hear a knock on it almost as soon as it settled into the latch. Bersaba was there with feast on two trays, one in her hands and one with Ursa behind her. I had only thought to take a little meat broth and some bread, but seeing my favorite, quail eggs, so late at night, along with the broth and bread for sops, a mug of warm, heady wine, and sweet fruits caused my belly to growl and insist on more. I had not eaten since I broke my fast in the morning and I knew that had any of my pregnant priestesses on Avalon eaten so little in a day, I would have admonished them soundly. I had to take better care of myself and my baby, even with the demands of running a kingdom.

The women stayed with me through the meal and carried on animated chatting about all that went on in the castle. Already, word of Princess Zelda's clever acumen in the receiving hall had spread like wildfire.

"So, you really tamed the little shrew for an entire day," Bersaba clucked. "That is a first."

"Watch out for that one," Ursa's dire warning drew my attention. "She is a rabid wolf in the guise of a lamb."

"Warning heard and remembered," I assured her.

"Truly, Your Majesty," she continued, her eyes wide and her tone something close to awe, "The girl has no limits, no boundaries. When she was a child, she was like a wild animal. She did what she wished, said what she wished, and never a thought to the feelings or needs of others. Now she leaves the castle on a whim and runs wild in the woods, cavorting with the commoners who live there in all manner of ways."

"Does she now?" I asked.

She nodded with stark surety. "Sometimes, she sleeps out there in the woods and does not return to the castle until the next midday, or so says Nimien. She nearly drove the castle mad with worry the first many times, but now they like as never expect her back no more. They's all afraid to tell the King for he would have the girl whipped."

"Pffft," Bersaba scoffed. "He would do no such thing. Had he ever once done that, she would not be as she is. If I had my way, the girl would have been thrashed a many time as a young'un to show her what 'tis and 'tisn't proper for a young lady, but the King forbade more than a scolding, so now she is more a wild thing than a princess. Havin' her whipped would be the last thing the King would do."

"Either way," Ursa said, "Now she next to never is even in th' castle and takes most of her time out in th' wild. I expect as most of the people here do that someday, she will just not come back at all."

"And should that happen," Bersaba smiled, "Is it not just fitting that we have a fine queen gifted to us by the good King Marcus to keep running things after he is gone. Can you imagine what would have happened had you not come to us when you did, as you did, or had the little monster run you off as she did all the others? Who would have taken the throne of Cornwall? Likely some many times removed cousin who never saw an inch of Cornish land in his time."

Your beloved king would be alive, I thought, *had I not come to him when I did and rutted him to death.*

Aloud, I said, "But I saw nary an inch of Cornwall when I came here. I cannot see that I am any better."

"But you listen and learn, child," Bersaba said, "Forgiving the familiarity, My Queen, but such a gift as to learn how to rule is one many people," she leaned in conspiratorially and whispered as though one might hear her, "especially *men,* cannot ever seem to manage."

Talking so comfortably with them caused a sudden rush of homesickness for my sisters, both of blood and of priestesshood. As if sensing the redirection of my attention, Bersaba stood and began gathering up the dishes and eating utensils, motioning to Ursa to help her. The girl took over the clean-up detail and Bersaba herself said, "Let's get you on to bed now, My Queen."

The sun was low on the horizon and it was not yet dark outside, but I felt the weariness of the day take me over. After I used the chamber pot, Bersaba took down my hair and brushed it out until it shown like obsidian and then twisted it into a loose braid down my back. Gently, she helped me disrobe, then held a sleeping shift for me to ease onto my body.

"Come on then," she said softly, turning down the bedclothes. "In with you."

Ursa had stacked the trays and dishes onto one tray for Bersaba to carry downstairs while she herself undressed, slipped into her nightdress, and covered herself at the end of my bed as she had done for the past few days.

"If you need ought in the night," she said from her position across the bottom of the wide bed, "You've but to ask and I will serve you." She looked at me with something close to worship, which was discomforting and I hearkened back to my conversation earlier in the evening with Sir John. *Why were these people so good to me?* Surely everyone in the Britain Beyond was not so kind. Father Francisco certainly had no love to spare for me.

I murmured my thanks, still perplexed by their behavior towards me. That was the last thought I had for many hours as the blackness of deep sleep claimed me.

CHAPTER 17

The next afternoon, a delivery arrived for me via courier from Avalon. When it arrived, I was in the atrium, meeting with the lord of a community in Cornwall who owned one of the largest tin and copper mines in the country. Sir John and Sir Charles hoped that he would employ some of the men from a neighboring mine that had suffered a recent cave in, leaving several dead, including the owner of the mine. The surviving members of his crew were temporarily unemployed, but the owner's widow was amiable to a quick sale of the mineral rights and mine itself at a reduced price if the lord would allow the local men to work doing clean up at his expense.

I found the man, Lord Arlington, to be a fair and thoughtful man and I appreciated the reasonable approach he took to the situation, using the perfect blend of good business acumen and kindness of the heart. We were at the end of formalizing negotiations on the widow's behalf when Herschel begged our pardon and presented me with a wooden trunk, small enough that a footman could carry it on his own, but clearly still under weight. I immediately recognized the seal of Avalon on its hasp and my breath quickened. What could they possibly send? As eager as I was to find out, I asked the footman to see that the trunk was placed in my rooms for further investigation. As the young man excitedly described the courier, it was clear to me that one of the odd little men who ferried the Avalon barge had delivered the precious cargo, whatever it might be. What a stir that must have created!

As soon as the final signatures and seals were affixed to the documents, I excused myself and hurried to my quarters where the trunk awaited me on my private dining table. Barely breathing, I used the small sickle priestess knife, which I still carried slipped into the cord that bound the waist of my dress, to pry open the hasp. As if made for the task, the curved end of the blade slipped behind the locking mechanism and released it. As it did so, a whisper of air released from the trunk and told me it was sealed with more than merely the lock. Gently, I lifted the lid and gasped at what I saw inside.

Packed ever so gently among layers of finely dyed Avalon wool were a dozen perfect Avalon apples. Firm, crisp, and sweet smelling, they lay in their padded litter, completely undisturbed by their long journey. To me, they were as valuable as all the royal jewels that came into my possession when I was crowned. I sighed, cooed even, and picked one up, feeling its substantial heft in my hand, then pressing the coolness of its fragrant skin against my face. The smell wafted over me and immediately transported my thoughts across the miles to Avalon…to home.

I bit into the apple with such relish that its sweet juice ran down my chin. My eyes rolled back with delight. I ate two of them with pausing, nibbling all the way down to the core, which my mother swore we should never eat because the seeds were of such magic that they would disturb the humors in a person's body. As was our way, I collected every seed and slipped them into a tiny velvet bag, which I then placed into my jewelry box.

As I went to close the little trunk, delirious with the blissful taste of Avalon on my lips, I noticed a rolled piece of parchment in the bottom of the case. I pulled it out, removed the tie that held it closed, and unrolled it. I heard a thunk on the floor at my feet and looked down to see a flat stone that must have fallen from the rolled paper. I picked it up and turned it over in my hand. It was a large fire stone, almost as big as my fist and like the opals in my mother's formal headdress. I looked at the open paper and read, written in High Latin which we were all taught to read, "Iris. Go to the mirror." The words were in my father's handwriting with his personal sigil pressed in wax on the bottom of the page.

My mother's mirror, like all the mirrors in the house, was covered with black cloth for the three moons of mourning. Father Francisco insisted it was so the sin of vanity did not distract us from honoring the memory of the King after he was laid to rest, but I was convinced he feared that he would see the spirits looking back at him through the mirrors when the veil was thin from one of our own passing over.

It still surprised me that I could think of Marcus as one of mine, or even feel kinship with those who mourned him. True that two months' past, he was only a name to me, but he had forever changed my heart and his life carried on within me in the form of our son. He was, indeed, mine. My King, my husband, my love.

I pulled the black cloth from the full length, freestanding mirror that was quite literally like no other in the world.

"Now, I want this back when you complete your quest and come home," my mother had quipped as we loaded it onto the barge the day I left Avalon for Cornwall. It crossed my mind that she seemed more concerned with the mirror leaving than with the departure of her daughters. The mirror was the most precious possession she owned. Given to her by Danu, one of

the oldest priestesses on the island, the mirror was one of the few remaining possessions of Evienne, the Lady of the Lake who my mother lived as in a previous life. It was her memories she carried with her, so throughout two lives, this mirror had been her own. As such, its value was incalculable, especially to my mother.

The mirror was an oddity in that the reflection was not milky like other looking glasses, but was clear and free from any green tint or cloudiness. The back was coated with a reflective substance and the glass onto which it was painted was pure beyond all reason. The oval mirror, which was easily as tall as she was, was mounted within an ornate wooden frame with odd carvings from the lands far to the East all around it. Precious stones lay within the carvings here and there, creating the eyes of beasts, the petals of flowers, or the berries of vines. At the top of the frame, two hands interlocked, palms up, with woven fingers creating a cradle to hold the largest stone in the frame, which I saw was missing. Odd that I had not noticed it gone before now.

Holding the fire stone in my hand, I slipped it into the chasm of the missing stone in the mirror's frame and it seated with no effort at all. As soon as the stone made solid contact with its place in the frame, the reflection in the mirror's surface began to shift. A mist rose that folded in upon itself much like the mists that surrounded Avalon. The edges of the mirror's surface darkened and churned around the gray mist that obscured my own reflection as it whirled and snaked across the surface.

I was never much for scrying, even though we all had certain tests of the skill that we had to master before we took our vows as priestesses. It was a chore for me and certainly not my Goddess-given gift like it was for my sister, Lily, who could get lost in her visions. The Sight was strong within my mother as well and all on the island revered her for her ability to look into both the past and the future, as well as gain insightful wisdom into the present that others could not see.

When we practiced scrying, we would polish a silver bowl until it was smooth and flawless, then fill it with water from the Sacred Well. Staring at the surface of the water, we would take our eyes out of focus and see with our Higher Self instead, sometimes waiting hours for the images that would flash across the water's reflective surface. The process always made me feel dizzy and nauseated, almost as though I would fall into the water and never did my visions come quickly.

I felt a similar lurch as the surface of the mirror seemed to pitch and swim before me. I touched the mirror with my hand, for a moment wishing it would act as a portal that would propel me back to Avalon. Instead, it was cool and solid under my hand, frustratingly corporeal while it went through its otherworldly dance.

After what could have been minutes or hours, the mist began to clear and in the middle, I saw my father.

"Iris?" he said, his line of vision extending beyond me. "Iris, is it you?"

"Father?" I said, tracing his mirror features with my fingers. I felt a sob threaten to choke me. "Father?" Tears then did stream down my face, hot and fast.

"Iris," he smiled locking my gaze with his. "You received the apples."

"I did," I said, feeling a grin stretch my face to such a point I thought I would never again stop smiling. "I ate two before I found the paper and the stone."

"I will send more each fortnight," he promised. "I do know how you love them."

"Is she saving the seeds?" I heard my mother ask, although I could not see her. "Ask if she is saving the seeds, Bran."

He glanced over his shoulder.

"Your mother wants to know if you are saving the seeds from the apples."

I nodded, unsure if he could see me or not.

"I have them" I said, feeling the nostalgia of familiar voices and ways wash over me. "I saved each one."

"They have stronger power in the Britain Beyond than they do here," he said. "Guard them well."

"I shall," I said.

"Your husband," he said, looking solemn. "Your King…"

"…is dead," I finished. "Dead and buried." I remembered how distracted and haunted he looked at my wedding. "Did you know this would happen?" I asked.

He looked askance as though he could not meet my eyes. "I knew some of it," he admitted. "Not until I met with Marcus and shook his hand. He was a good man, Iris."

"Yes," I said, with a wave of loss slipping through me. "He was."

"Just trust the process, Darling," he said. "I know you are going through challenges that we could not adequately prepare you to face."

"If I had known, I am not sure I would have found the courage to do it," I said.

"You are stronger than you know. We all are. And now you are Queen of Cornwall," he said. "And expecting a baby."

"News seems to travel quickly," I replied.

"It slides between the worlds." His tone was weary, almost as weary as I felt.

"What do I do, Father?" I asked. "I have no idea how to be a queen. This priest would slit my throat on an altar to his Christ as fast as he would look at me. My stepdaughter wants nothing to do with me and by all accounts, is running roughshod through the Cornish forests like a child raised by wolves, and during my time of grief, Laoghaire deserted me and left with you. Why? What did I do that was so horrible that she would leave? I need her! I need you! I am utterly alone and left to run a country when I am clearly unsuited to do so."

If ever I put my heart on my sleeve before, I did so now, allowing myself to voice the vulnerability of my fears to my parents when I could to no one else.

My father looked at my quizzically, "What do you mean Laoghaire deserted you? Is she not there?"

"They told me she left with you," I said, confusion warring with panic as they each raced through my brain. Angrily, I wiped the tears from my face. "Did she not? Is she not there with you?"

"She escorted us out of the courtyard and as far as the bridge, but there we bade her goodbye and she turned back. She has then been missing for over a month?"

I felt the color drain from my face.

"I will find out what happened immediately," I promised. "I was certain she was with you. I had no reason to believe otherwise."

"And we had no thought but that she was there with you."

Iris," he said, "Remember this. In your land, you are breaking the law to use the mirror to speak to us. Magic is forbidden and should anyone see you or know, your life will be in danger. Keep the mirror's fire stone with you always. Never risk it falling into the hands of another. You may contact me through the mirror when you know you must, but your safety is what is most important. I cannot be there with you in the flesh for so many reason, but I can speak with you and help you from afar."

"How can you always be there when I need you? You are the busiest man on Avalon! And how are you seeing me now, even? Where are you?"

"The Sacred Well," he said. "I can look into the Sacred Well and see through the mirror. Really, any scrying surface will connect to the mirror if I will it. Time is not the same through the mirror as it is for you or for me. Right now, I am likely on the Tor or sleeping beside your mother. The way that time bends between you and Avalon now, it bends even more between the mirror and the scrying surface I use. I am here and yet I am not here. Like a memory we can both control. If you call me, I will know and you will reach me whether or not my body is at the Sacred Well. I will find you."

There was so much about that explanation that eluded me, but I often had complex magical phenomenon fly outside of my level of understanding. I had learned to take it all in stride by now and subscribe to the belief that faith is good enough. I did not have to understand; I had only to believe it was so. Magic was magic and it was sometimes not for us to understand unless one was a supreme magical being like my father.

For now, however, what I wanted more than anything was to find out what happened to Laoghaire. Why had I so easily accepted that she left with my parents? Was it simply easier than worrying about another person in my grief?

"Did you tell her to keep the stone with her?" I heard my mother ask.

"Keep the stone with me. Save the apple seeds," I repeated.

"I told her about the stone," my father said over his shoulder. "She knows."

"And the apple seeds?"

"She knows about the apple seeds, Lilian."

"Can you not tell me where Laoghaire is?" I asked. "How do I find her?"

"She is outside of my reach for now," he said. "Not dead, but not reachable. It is up to you, Iris. You must find her. It will connect you to part of your destiny. That is the only reason I can imagine that would keep me from knowing where she is."

"Then I must go make inquiries," I said. "I cannot imagine... Father this is all too hard. I cannot..."

"Go," he said. "Remember, you are stronger than you know. You will find her. She lives still. I am certain of it."

I nodded, feeling the weight of the world on my shoulders. "Then I will find her. Goodbye, Father."

"Goodbye, Iris," he said. Then looked up and pointed from his perspective to the top of the mirror.

"Of course," I said, reaching for the fire stone. He smiled and I pulled the stone from its enclosure. Immediately, the darkness from the sides of the mirror's surface moved inward and the mirror became again reflective. I could only see myself in it and once more, I was utterly alone.

I put my hands on each side of the frame and leaned into it as though by sheer will I could bring him back. I could, of course. I could slip the stone into the crevice and call him and there he would be. Somehow, knowing I could do that felt more dangerous than thinking myself isolated. He was right. All it would take was for one person to see, one person to hear, one person to suspect their Queen talked to a mirror. They would think me a lunatic at best and a sorceress at worst. Both destroyed my credibility and one likely resulted in my death. This was fire and I was juggling it.

Already, in addition to the mirror work, I had performed the strongest magic I had ever in my life worked when I encouraged the conception. Technically, it was necromancy since Marcus's dead body was integral to the process and that came with an even greater prejudice than did common magics. Working quickly, I covered the mirror again and secreted the precious stone into a panel under the drawer in my vanity table, usually reserved for special jewels. I reminded myself to ask Ursa to bring me a strong sprig of rosemary from the herb garden. I could explain it away as a cure for morning sickness, but it would serve also as a protection token for my quarters.

And yet, how could I be so worried about myself when Laoghaire was most assuredly in harm's way. There was no other explanation for what could keep her away from both Tintagel and Avalon. I may not have been a friend of even adequate worth before now, but I was determined to be a better one in the future. For now, I just had to find her and bring her safely back.

CHAPTER 18

My first and most rational stop was to examine the quarters Laoghaire and I shared before my wedding. My own former room was tidied and looked much as it had on the day I arrived. The large wardrobes in the adjoining room were now cleared of any gowns and adornments that might fit me or be altered to fit me, which now hung in the royal suite of rooms. Bersaba was thrilled to hear of my lean toward thriftiness and that I saw no need to construct entirely new gowns when perfectly good ones hang here already. The room was clean, but empty of any personal effects.

The room that Laoghaire used was likewise undisturbed. In looking around, I found some of her possessions still there, but she and I had, in the interest of thrifty travel, brought little with us on the journey. I filtered through what was there and found nothing that indicated either a quick or a thoughtful departure. She was, quite simply, gone.

Bersaba also professed to seeing her ride out with my parents, but had not seen her since and admitted to being swept up in the shock and grief of the King's death. She claimed she had not seen the girl since my mother and father left and like everyone else, presumed she had left with them. Since Bersaba was the all-seeing, all-knowing eyes and heart of court, she would know about Laoghaire's whereabouts if anyone did, either directly or through Herschel, her husband. Between the two of them little that happened in the castle went unnoticed.

Sir Charles and Sir John arrived in my receiving room shortly after I did when I had only commissioned their presence while en route there. Their attention was quite admirable and in this case, helpful.

My blood was racing with rage and fear for my friend. If Laoghaire was now in trouble, there was no escaping the fact that it was because of me. But for my quest and for my husband having a heart attack on top of me, she would be happy and safe on Avalon. I had to find her and get her to where she wanted to be, whether that was here, on Avalon, or elsewhere. To do so, I needed the help of these men.

Someone, and I could not reach far enough into the darkness, told me during my grieving isolation that she had accompanied my parents from Cornwall. Who was it? The words had filtered into memory, but who said them?

"Your Majesty?" Sir John asked, breaking into my attempt to remember before it gave me an actual headache. "Is something wrong?"

"My traveling companion, Laoghaire, do you know where she is?"

They looked at one another in confusion. I scanned carefully for any sign of anxiety or alarm. Did they know more than they pretended? Marcus insisted I could trust these men, but he also put his trust in Francisco, which I could not.

"My Queen," Sir Charles said, stealing another look at Sir John. "Our understanding is that the Lady Laoghaire left Cornwall with your parents and is now on Avalon. Do you know otherwise?"

I realized that I was on shaky ground since in speaking to my father through the mirror, I had, in fact, worked magic, which was illegal in Cornwall and a direct violation of my promise to Marcus. Not to mention that the credibility of "My father sent me a message and a magic rock in a trunk of apples and I used the rock to talk to him through my mother's mirror and they told me she was not with them" was somewhat lacking.

"The delivery I received from Avalon yesterday included a letter from my parents and they believed her to be here with me." I prayed they would not ask to see the message. Deducing all of what I had said from a note that said, "Iris, go to the mirror," was a stretch at best. "This means she has now been missing for over a month. Who told you that she accompanied my parents back to the island?"

"We saw her with our own eyes," Sir John explained. "She had the pony you brought with you saddled and rode out past the causeway with them. I have not seen her since, have you?"

Sir Charles shook his head. "Not at all. Surely, she would have come to evening meals or presented herself in court somewhere if she were still within walls. Certainly, she would have heard of the King's death and sought you out."

"One would presume," I said. "So where is she if not on Avalon?"

When they did not speak up, I persisted. "Did anyone specifically *tell* you that she returned to Avalon? Or did you merely see her ride away and presume?"

"To our great shame," Sir John said, "we did not follow up on her departure. If you will be so generous of thought, My Queen, at the time your parents left, we had just learned of the King's passing and circumstances were quite frantic. I deeply regret that your friend was lost in the fray and I did only presume she left with them. I beg your forgiveness."

"And I, Your Highness," Sir Charles added. "Had I considered for one moment that she might be here or in trouble of some kind, of course I would have taken action."

They looked as though they thought I might beat them, so I drew in a breath and took a different approach with them.

"I do not know your kingdom," I said. "For that matter, I do not yet know your castle. Someone has to find out what happened to her. Is there anyone here who would hurt such a young girl?"

Again, they traded looks.

"She is but ten and *five*," I hissed, my temper and fear both boiling over together. "*Would anyone hurt her?*"

"Men in town, perhaps," Sir Charles said, quickly. "If she ventured to town or into the woods, it is possible she could meet misfortune. There are bands of highwaymen who rob the High King's coaches of tax money. There are drunkards at the inns who are too free with their hands. There are even wild animals in the forests. I cannot imagine anyone in the court would cause her harm."

Sir John shook his head, "No one in court comes to mind as dangerous. I will ask if anyone saw her return to the castle after your father and mother left."

"Do what you have to do, but find her," I ordered. "There are no other tasks before either of you until that is accomplished, do you understand? All matters of court are immediately suspended until I have definitive proof of what befell her."

"Yes, My Queen," they said in unison, bowing.

"Now, bring me the Princess Zelda. Whatever she is doing, I want to see her now."

"It will be done, Your Highness," Sir John assured me.

I waited much longer for Zelda than I did my two advisers, but after nearly an hour, she pushed open the door to the library and collapsed unceremoniously into her father's chair.

"You summoned me?" she asked, her tone acrid with disdain.

"I did," I said, taking the chair across from her. "I need your help."

Her eyebrows arched inquisitively. "You need me? How so? Do you have lambs to disburse or property lines to move? More queening to do that you are unable to manage on your own?"

"No, Zelda." For the time being, I ignored her barbs, knowing they were an attempt to draw a rise out of me. "I need your special expertise in an emergency."

"Oh really? Do tell, Mother Iris. What tragedy as befallen that would cause you to think, 'Oh, I must draw Zelda in on this? It is here area of special expertise.'"

Her sarcasm was grating my already frayed nerves. "When I arrived on Avalon, I brought with me a friend, a traveling companion who was to stay here with me in the castle. Her name is Laoghaire and she is your age. The day we discovered your father had died, she disappeared. No one has seen her since."

"A mystery indeed," she cooed. "And what do you think I can do about it? Or will?" She played with a stand of her hair that fell across her forehead, twisting it around her finger as though she had not a care in the world.

"You know every hiding place in this court and you know every footprint in the forest. I am sure of it. I want you to find my friend."

"Me?" she asked, acting for all the world as though butter would not melt in her mouth. "Why would I know anything about the forest?"

"Zelda, I have no time for games. My friend may be in danger…is likely in danger and I do not know the area well enough to even start to search for her. By all accounts, you spend most of your time out of castle in the village and the forests."

She looked aghast. "And you believed the servant's gossip about…"

"Zelda, stop it, please. If I waste even a minute arguing with you and something worse happens to Laoghaire in that minute, I could never forgive myself. Ask questions. Search. Snoop. Do whatever it takes, but please, for the love of all that is holy, *help me find my friend.*"

"Is this not a trap?" she asked. "Are you sharpening your mothering skills on me by getting me to confess to crimes you suspect I committed? If I say I know my way around the forests, am I taken to the tower and put under guard?"

I sighed. "No. This is not about *you*, at least not in that way. You have survived for years using the forest and the courtyard as your personal playground. I will neither condemn your nor try to stop you. I just need to find out what happened to Laoghaire."

She studied me intently for long minutes, then said, "Fine, what does she look like?"

"You would have seen her at the evening meals before the wedding. She is slightly built, fair-haired, rather plain, but pretty when she smiles."

She rolled her eyes. "You just described a third of the women in court. Tell me something unique about her."

I thought carefully, concerned because to my memory, there seemed to be nothing that *was* unique about Laoghaire."

"She is a midwife," I said. "And a healer. She has a sharp tongue and complains from time to time, but she is amiable enough. She fancies fine clothes, but wears men's britches when she rides. She was last seen riding a pony that would stand out because it is not as fine as those at court. It was more of a work horse."

"That would stand out here, but not in town or in the woods," she observed. "Most people who do not live in court have simple horses."

"But not everyone is a midwife."

"True," she agreed. "I can check with the healer in town and see if he knows of anyone plying the trade. But surely, if she were safe, she would have contacted you."

"I would hope so, yes."

"So, we must presume her either unsafe or heavily preoccupied."

"That is a fair assumption, yes."

"And she did not follow your parents to Avalon? You are certain?"

I nodded. "She rode with them to the bridge, but no further."

"Both she and the pony could have fallen over the side," she said, thoughtfully. "If that happened, we would never find either body. They would be swept out to sea. People fall off the bridge all of the time."

I shuddered inwardly and asked her the same question I had asked the men.

"Do you think anyone here would hurt her?"

She scoffed. "Father Francisco hates you both. For what it is worth, that merits you points with me, by the by. If he could not get to you to hurt you, he might take it upon himself to punish another witch instead."

I had considered neither this possibility, nor the idea that she might have fallen off the cliffs near the bridge. Zelda was positively brimming with depressing suggestions and offered them up with a tremendous absence of sensitivity.

"Do you think Father Francisco is capable of inflicting a physical attack on someone?" I asked.

"As capable as anyone," she shrugged. I imagine, and in case you have not been around him enough to know, he is certainly passionate about his quest to convert. 'The devil must be expunged from any crevice in which his foul stench lingers.' He is most assuredly convinced that the devil's foul stench lingers around you and likely any friend of yours." She adopted a haughty and intense intonation when she quoted him. I took her point.

"We must check the cells below the abbey," I said, "as well as his room, for any sign that he has her."

She looked at me quizzically. "You know about the cells under the abbey?"

I realized I could not tell her how I knew about the cells, that Colin and I had cut up her father's body in them and stuffed him full of tinctures and herbs to preserve his body. That I had enacted strong magic to make sure I conceived the child that would stand between her and any claim she might have to the throne of Cornwall.

"I know a great many things," I said, and decided to leave it at that.

"What else can you tell me?" she asked. I noticed that when she dropped the sheen of defensive disdain and spoke with authenticity, she was quite beautiful. I could almost believe that she looked forward to assisting with the search. "About your friend, I mean. Is there more I should know? Anything that could help me find her?"

I shook my head. "I fear I am not a good friend at all. I worked beside her for a few years, trained her in the healing arts, and slept with in the House of Maidens. I knew her to be a good person, if somewhat short tempered, but I cannot say I knew her well at all. I just knew her better than I know the people here and I found comfort in that."

"You are right," she said. "You are a terrible friend. Are you so inside your own head and circumstances that all you can tell me about the woman you chose to bring with you to Tintagel is that she is that she is ordinary looking, catches babies, and is short-tempered? That is how you help me find her? *Think, Iris*. What color are her eyes?"

"Green!" I said, "Green with bits of brown in them."

"Now we go through her quarters to see what of her clothing is missing. You did not see her after the wedding, correct?"

"I did not, but I already looked through her rooms."

"And what clothing was missing?"

I blinked at her.

"You do not know what clothing she *had*, do you?"

I shook my head and tears brimmed in my eyes.

"Who dressed her? Did any of the handmaidens help her?"

I stared at her.

"You do not even know whether she had someone to help her dress, do you? Blessed Jesus, Iris, you are hopeless. Did she just show up in your room every morning to eat, pre-dressed like a doll and you did not imagine how she got that way?"

She pushed up off the chair and leaned out the door, speaking in low tones to a servant.

"Does she fancy anyone here? Did she take up with any men? Women? Any friends other than you?"

"Zelda, we were here but five days before the wedding. She had little time to connect with people."

"You asked for me, Your Grace?" I had not heard Bersaba enter the room and I jumped when she spoke.

"Bersaba," Zelda turned to face her. "Who dressed the Lady Loaghaire while she was here?"

"Why, Damona did, Your Grace, each morning."

"Send Damona to me, then, please and thank you for coming so quickly."

"This is how you learn things here," she said, turning to me.

Within minutes, a plump woman with bright red hair tapped gently at the open door and Zelda motioned her inside.

"Close the door behind you, please, Damona," she said. When the woman had done so, Zelda said, "You dressed the Lady Loaghaire while she was with us, did you not?"

The woman nodded, "Yes, Your Grace, I did so."

"And did you dress her for the wedding?" Zelda continued.

"I did, and the Queen's mother as well, but I had Ursa and Pressie helping me that day."

"And did you dress her the day after the wedding?"

"The day after, Your Grace?"

Zelda closed her eyes and sighed.

"That is what I asked you, Damona. On the day after the wedding, the Queen's parents rode back to Avalon. The Lady Loaghaire rode with them to the bridge. Did you, in fact, dress her before she left?"

"I did, yes. That is to say, the Queen's mother dressed herself, but I dressed Lady Laoghaire, yes."

"And what did she wear?"

The woman blinked. "What did she wear, Your Grace?"

I saw Zelda swallow, the only indication of her growing lack of patience.

"Yes, Damona, what... did... Lady... Laoghaire... wear... that... day?" Zelda looked at her expectantly.

The woman's face lit up. "Oh, it was a warm day and she wore but a light shift and a gold colored gown. She took no cloak nor another wrap. Just the gown. She fussed about having to ride sidesaddle but the britches she brought with her that she wanted to wear for riding were unclean and I had already started to wash them for the day when she woke. So just the gold gown."

"And did she behave as though she would return after her ride?"

"Oh yes," Damona said. "She asked me when she might see the Queen again, and I told her as they was in their wedding confinement, she might not see them for a fortnight even. She said she was going for a ride and she would be back for the evening meal. She said she wished to explore the area a bit and find a decent pint of ale. I told her that we had kegs of ale right here in the castle, but she said she wanted a proper ale and that if it were made with the water here, it would not be proper, so she would look in the village. I directed her over to the Tin Cup and told her they had the best ale in town."

Zelda looked at me as if finding information was the easiest thing in the world to do.

"Damona," I asked, "Have you seen Sir Charles and Sir John today?"

"Oh yes," she said, "Just before you summoned me, I saw them."

"And did they ask you these same questions?"

"Oh no, Your Majesty, they only asked me if I had seen her since she left with your parents and I told them I had not. I answered them true." The woman smiled broadly, seeming quite proud of her accomplishment.

"Never expect men to know the right questions to ask," Zelda sighed, rolling her eyes at me. "I find them generally worthless."

"I did as well when I was your age," I agreed.

She tilted her head, "So when did all that change?" she asked. Her tone was impartial, but I felt as though she might have actual interest in my reply.

"When I met your father," I answered. "And not a moment before, although as I told you before, my own father is an extraordinary man. I suppose no one ever measured up to him before now."

She stared at me for an uncomfortable moment, then looked away.

"You really loved him," she said, her voice so low I barely heard her speak.

"I really loved him," I replied.

Damona cleared her throat and Zelda looked up.

"Go, go on, run along," Zelda said to the woman dismissively. "Thank you for the information." She made a "tsk tsk" sound and waved her hand.

Damona curtsied and backed out of the door.

"Well *done*, Zelda! You were *amazing!*"

She shrugged. "Most of it is knowing what to ask and who to ask. Sir Charles and Sir John are reliable in matters of court, but they could not find their own balls with both hands and barmaid. Now, we know she was riding to explore the area and to the tavern, so that is where the search begins. The weather was fair and the days still long, so it is unlikely any misfortune befell her at the bridge unless she tried riding back after dark."

"That is still a great deal of territory to cover and any number of misfortunes that could befall her."

"I will make inquiries and, as you so quaintly put it, I will 'snoop.' If I learn anything, I will let you know."

"Thank you," I said. "If I can help, please tell me."

"Oh," she said, her eyebrows arched, "Make no mistake, you will owe me a favor for certain, but we can settle that debt later. For now, you can best help by staying out of my way."

She turned to leave without waiting to be excused, then looked back over her shoulder at me.

"Also, I would keep this to yourself. If someone does have her, it is best they are not alerted. News travels like wildfire in the castle and if you take this beyond a few trusted people, everyone will know by nightfall."

"That is wise advice," I agreed. "I will trust your confidence in this as well then?"

With a curt nod of acquiescence, she left.

CHAPTER 19

It would be several anxious days before I or anyone else in Tintagel saw her again. She did not come to the evening meal and while some were accustomed to her frequent disappearances, others whispered that she had gone yet again into the forest to cavort with her unsavory friends therein.

I now saw in Marcus's chair at the evening meal with Sir John at my left and Sir Charles at my right. Next to Sir John was Colin and across from him was Father Damian. To Father Damian's right was the place for Princess Zelda and next to her was Lady Charlotte. Across from Princess Zelda and Lady Charlotte, were Marcus's three nieces to whom I was introduced at the wedding, but whose names never registered in my mind. The first two nieces were unmarried and the final niece sat opposite her husband, who sat next to Lady Charlotte. The rest of the table became a blend of faces I could not identify in a crowd, or even at my table, until the end of the table opposite me where Father Francisco now sat.

As it had been with Marcus, conversation with me during the evening meal was minimal. The table in front of me and the tables around me maintained a low hum of voices, but rarely did anyone speak directly to me.

Sir John and Sir Charles quietly informed me that they continued discreet inquiries, but had uncovered no information on what may have befallen Laoghaire. Sir John said that the scribes had completed the necessary court documents to name Father Damian as my spiritual adviser and they would present them to me the next morning to sign.

"Must he sit down there and glare at me for the entire evening meal?" I whispered intently to Sir Charles.

His eyes followed mine and he turned to me to answer so that no one else could hear or see his reply.

"We can have his seating order changed," he said quietly, "but he would see that as a slight, most assuredly."

"He never sat there when Marcus was alive," I pointed out. "Why must he now?"

"That is an excellent question, Your Majesty," Sir John interjected. "My impression is that it is his way of asserting power, of reminding you that he is also in a position of authority in the court."

"So, if I have him moved, I challenge him directly and…"

"…the Church becomes involved in a major capacity." Both he and Sir Charles finished my statement with me.

"Surely, I must not be expected to have him piss all over me for the duration of my sovereignty," I said, continuing to keep my voice low enough that Father Damian or others near him could not hear."

"No," Sir John said, "and I fear that the time is coming when you may have to firmly but respectfully put him in his place. If he thinks he has you cowed, he will push you as far as he can. If you show weakness, he will take great advantage. If you are aggressive with him, he will call in the Church dogs."

"Assertive," Sir Charles said. "Assertive, not aggressive. You must stand your ground, but from a position of authority, not of dominance. There is a subtle difference."

"How so?" I asked.

"What he is doing now with you is dominance. It is dominance that he, by letter of the law, has no authority to enact. Authority is enforceable by legal recourse. Dominance is not."

~*~

I stilled the urge to use the mirror to again contact my father and seek his guidance. It was easy to see how dependent I could become to leaning on my parents for support rather than delving into my own strengths. As I mentally reviewed our conversation from earlier, I searched for any hint, any sign of where to begin looking for Laoghaire. Truly, she could be anywhere from the castle to the shores of Avalon Lake, waiting for a barge to carry her home if she could not yet summon it herself. She was a newly initiated priestess and if she were in distress, it was fathomable that she would be unable to employ sufficient focus to call the barge herself. I wanted to look everyone at once for her. The thought of a young woman such as she, capable and stalwart as she may be, but still a maiden and naive to the world of the Britain Beyond, out there on her own was terrifying to me. She was here because of me and I must find her and ensure her safety.

By the third day, my concern escalated not only for Laoghaire, but also for Zelda, who no one had seen since our private conversation. Even Bersaba and Ursa, who were well accustomed to her regular disappearances, were showing signs of worry, as was Nimien, who knew her better than anyone. Frayed and anxious, they looked to me for answers that of course, I did not have.

On the fourth day, it was Father Francisco who stormed into my audience room without waiting to be announced.

"What have you done with her?" he barked, providing not even the courtesy of a preamble.

I looked at my constant companions, Sir John and Sir Charles, who were talking me step-by-step through an upcoming discourse with a new Lord within the kingdom who acquired his position through the death of his father, who served in that capacity for decades. With no legitimate heir, a search produced a bastard son who could provide witnesses to his lineage, as well as land afforded to him by his father and funds conveyed to his mother, a former cook of the deceased Lord, each month. After accepting the legitimacy of the claim, it was to me to convey the blessings of the crown upon his inheritance and welcome him into the royal fold. It was a simple and uncontested procedure, but also quite precise to ensure the legitimacy of his claim could not come under question after I condoned it.

All three of us looked up at the disturbance as the priest pushed his way into the room, past the guards who were half in awe of him and half confused as to whether or admit him or arrest him. At this point, my nerves were nattered from worry and my stomach had taken a mind to pitch and roll at all hours of the day, regardless of how much or how little food I gave it.

Admittedly, I had no patience for his insolence or his fervor.

"I asked you a question," he said, his voice gruff and demanding.

Ignoring his outburst, I looked to both Sir Charles and Sir John, calling to mind our conversation from the evening meal a few nights past. Dominance versus authority.

"Gentlemen," I asked, making no attempt to hide the frost in my voice. "Is there any legitimate protestation to or denial of my claim to the throne?"

They looked at one another and then back at me. Father Francisco grimaced and I suspected he knew the direction where my question would take him.

"No, My Queen," Sir John said. "His Majesty, King Marcus, was very clear in his instructions and there was absolutely no legal avenue for contesting his will."

"I see. And can you please tell me within the time of your memory, did Father Francisco ever challenge the authority of King Marcus or treat him with such disregard and rudeness as he just showed to me?"

"No, Madam," they said in tandem.

"For that matter," I continued, still not speaking directly to Francisco, "within the time of your memory, did *anyone* treat King Marcus with the blatant disrespect that Father Francisco just showed to me?"

They looked again at one another, as they were wont to do.

"No, Madam," they again answered together.

Father Francisco shifted uncomfortably and all but rolled his eyes.

"Then it seems to me," I said, considering my next move carefully, "that perhaps Father Francisco would do well with sometime in the cells to consider his behavior."

Now they all three men looked at one another and then at me, the shock of what I had said palpable in the room.

"Enough," I said with sufficient force that my voice echoed off the walls of the audience room. All three men startled as I spoke.

"I will have no more of your disrespect, Father. I have worked over much to show you kindness and respect for the esteem in which my late husband held you, but apparently, my good will was taken for weakness. Now, clearly, there is something on your mind, but unless and until you accept my sovereignty and treat me with the deference afforded to an anointed Queen of Cornwall, the guards will remove you from my sight. If after a time in the cells, you are unable to bring yourself to show the appropriate deference from within this court, you will leave Cornwall and not return and I am speaking of a royal banishment, not a matter of choice, do you understand me?"

He nodded without a word.

"I believe that if you do some investigating, you will find that except for Princess Zelda, aside and apart even from the provisions my husband made in his will, the rightful heir to King Marcus's throne is the closest kin of a previously legitimate Cornish sovereign, which is my father. Since he has no desire to rule both here and on Avalon, he will abdicate the throne to his own heir, which is none other I, the queen you have currently. This is all a matter of public record which I welcome you to examine, which means that by marriage or by lineage, take your pick, this throne is rightfully mine."

"That is preposterous," he blustered, unable to further contain himself. "The throne of Cornwall has passed to no female since Queen Morgan and…"

"…and she was my many greats grandmother. In the case of no male heir, and both my father and my husband have none, the sovereignty passes to the female heirs."

Sir John and Sir Charles each nodded their agreement.

"…and Queen Morgan was a witch as well," he spat. "Must Cornwall fall victim to the brides of the Fiend on such a regular basis?"

"The law exists outside of your ability to accept or appreciate it, Father," I said. "I have no further patience for your histrionics or your disrespect. You will find your peace with my reign or you will leave. In the interim, you will be jailed for treason."

"*Treason*?" he asked, his voice shaking with shock.

"Or sedition, or lèse-majesté, bringing offense to the sovereign, for you do offend me and that is, as my advisers just pointed out, against the laws of Cornwall. This hostility toward me will cease immediately. I care not what your private opinion is of me; however, in public, you will treat me with the respect due to my station."

He drew in a deep breath, clearly contemplating his position.

I motioned to the Queen's Guard, two of whom came to his side and took him each by an arm.

"No," he protested. "No."

"And why should I not?"

"My apologies, Your Highness. I was most remiss in my concern."

I waited a few moments for impact, and then nodded to the guardsmen, who released his arm. The Father readjusted his robes daintily and rubbed his left arm where the larger guardsman had grabbed him with considerably more enthusiasm than the younger one on his right.

"Now that we understand one another, Father. Please do tell me what that has you so concerned that you forgot your manners."

"Princess Zelda," he said. "She has not come for morning mass or for her lessons in several days."

"And you feel this must be because I have done something with her, as you put it?"

"I spoke out of turn." His eyes would not meet mine, but at least his words were now more respectful. "The Princess is missing and no one knows where she is. She was last seen more than three days' past. If any harm has come to her…"

I raised my hand for silence.

"The Princess is away from Tintagel tending to specific tasks at my request…tasks for which she is especially well suited. If there is need for concern or *for prayers for her safety*," I said deliberately, "I will personally send word to you. For now, you are to presume that she is undertaking a confidential mission at my own request. No more than this should be presumed or pursued. You are to insinuate yourself into this situation no further, do I make myself clear?"

"Yes, Your Majesty," he said, clearly unhappy with the lack of resolution and lack of power he found in the circumstances.

When he did not move, I tilted my head to one side and asked.

"Is there more, Father Francisco?"

"No," he said. "Nothing."

"Nothing… what? Father Francisco?"

"There is nothing more, *Your Majesty*."

I raised my eyebrows and made a dismissive gesture with my hand and without further ado, he turned and left.

There was silence in the room for several minutes after we watched him go, each of us looking at the place where he had stood filled with bluster and seething with righteous indignation.

At last, Sir John broke the silence.

"With all due respect, My Queen, you may have overplayed your hand ever so slightly."

I sighed. "What should I have done differently? He has rebuked me since first I arrived here and his behavior begged to be addressed. You just advised that I should be assertive."

"Agreed," Sir Charles said. "You had to take a stand and yet taking on the Church of the Christ is quite aggressive for a newly crowned sovereign."

"I am not taking on the Church," I clarified. "I am only taking on the man who outwardly and directly disrespect me."

Sir John shrugged. "It is the same. With these men of God, when you bring insult to one, you malign them all."

"Again, I ask you, what should I have done differently than what was done? How should I more appropriately make clear that his behavior is inappropriate?"

"There was naught you could do but what you did," Sir John said. "You are in an impossible situation with that one. It is unlikely he will ever submit to a female ruler and especially not one from Avalon. Particularly not a non-Christian."

"His own man baptized me into the Christian Church! I gave over to my husband's religion when I married him and took the throne. What more does he want?"

Sir Charles shook his head.

"He trusts it not at all. Accepting the will of the King and rites necessary to claim the throne is far different from conversion, which is all he will accept and even then, from you? I doubt he would ever believe."

"He does not have to believe, but he does have to submit, at least publicly. What precedence do I set by allowing him to openly display his insurrection, simply because he does not like who Marcus chose as his wife and successor? No. I must take a firm hand with him or face hundreds of others like him. Soon, everyone will believe they are entitled to treat the Queen with open disdain."

"As I said," Sir John concluded, "an impossible situation from which you can have little hope to emerge unscathed. Father Francisco has the ear of the High Throne, which is at the mercy of the Church. I fear a time will come when these Christians will force their way through every country on earth, converting and destroying all who stand in their way."

"Goddess forbid it," I mumbled, understanding more than ever the need for my personal quest.

"Do you truly know where Princess Zelda is, My Queen?" Sir Charles spoke the words, but their furrowed brows acted in unison.

"I know what she is doing, or rather, what I hope she is doing. I do not know where she is…exactly."

"Is there aught we can do to help?" he asked.

I thought for a moment, trying to imagine who would know the forests at least as well as Zelda.

"Send me the huntsman," I said. "The one who brings the boars and the venison."

They looked at me, puzzled.

"The huntsman, Your Majesty?" Sir John asked.

"The huntsman. Have him meet me here. Have we concluded all of the briefing I need to effectively seat Mr. Wilsley into his Lordship?"

"Yes, it seems so," Sir Charles said, rolling up the scrolls that represented the long hours of research that provided documentation to the man's claim, as well as the procedure for his installment into rank.

"Thank you, gentlemen. You are ever a strength and a blessing to me."

"We serve at your pleasure, My Queen," Sir Charles said, bowing as they left the room.

~*~

It was the better part of an hour later when a young man of indeterminable age was announced into my presence. I had asked Ursa to bring my midday meal into the receiving room so I could eat while waiting for the huntsman and I was just finishing the last bit of it when he arrived. He might have been sixteen or five and twenty for all I could tell. His skin was tanned and smooth like my father's and he wore his dark fair hair long and loose around his shoulders. His clothing was made of soft tanned leather and a quiver of arrows across his back informed me as to who he was even had the announcement not made it clear.

He removed his hat and bowed low as he entered the room.

"What is your name?" I asked as he kissed my ring.

"My name is Quinton," he replied. "Son of Quinley, Your Majesty."

"Rise," I said, since he was still on his knees all but kissing the floor. His genuflecting was the most aggressive I had seen since this madness of bowing first came into my life.

He stood and clasped his hands behind his back, waiting for my bidding.

"Am I to presume that you know the woods and lands around Tintagel well?"

"I do," he answered with a wry grin. "I was raised in those woods and know them as I know the back of my hand. There is little that happens there that I do not see myself or hear about from others."

"Very good," I smiled. "You would not mislead your queen or tell a falsehood, would you, Quinton?" I moved closer to him and tilted my head.

His face reflected his stunned fear. "No, never my Queen."

"Then tell me, Quinton, son of Quinley," I paused for effect and reached out to stroke his jawline with the nail of my index finger, "Where is the Princess Zelda?"

His cheeks reddened, whether from the question or from my proximity, and he drew in a breath.

"Quinton?" I purposely widened my smile and he began to fidget, absently rubbing the back of his neck and looking away from my gaze. He held his hat in one hand, but as the moments passed, he grasped it with both and began to twist it into new shapes.

"Beggin' your pardon, Your Majesty," he said, fumbling his words and shifting his weight from one foot to the other. "I…"

"Stop," I said. "Let me begin again. Quinton, do you know where the Princess Zelda is?"

He drew in a long breath and looked me in the eye at last.

"Yes, Madam, I do."

"And is it safe to say that when Princess Zelda is away from Tintagel, you generally know where she is?"

I thought his cheeks could go no deeper red than they were already, but when he went pale beneath his blush or flush, they were nearly scarlet.

He began to nod before he spoke, as though his muscles wanted to comply before his tongue.

"I am not going to punish you, Quinton. This is not about you. This is about Zelda. You have my word."

"Yes," he said. "That would be a reasonable assumption, yes, Ma'am."

"I see. And would it be an accurate one?"

He paused before answering.

"Yes, Ma'am."

"And since you seem uncomfortable telling me where she is, I ask that you please tell me why you are so distressed by the idea of telling me where she is?"

He continued to twist the hat in his hands until I thought it would tear in two.

"My Queen, to tell you where she is would be to betray a confidence entrusted to me by a person I feel is my friend."

"I see," I said. And I did. I had guessed correctly in who her inside help might be, but it took no genius to figure it out. The ladies who tended her were too obvious and clearly, their concern for the Princess was genuine, as was his friendship. As lonely as I perceived Zelda's life to be, I had no interest in forcing him to betray her trust. Perhaps there was another way.

"I have been behind walls since my arrival here at Tintagel," I began, choosing my words carefully as I circled behind him and came around to his opposite side. "As you may know, I am from Avalon and on the sacred isle, we revere nature and spend time out of doors every day, in work, leisure, and in worship. I do miss it and crave the feeling of the sun on my shoulders and the forest smells in my nose. I wonder, Quinton, if I were to fancy a stroll through the forest, would you consider accompanying me? I am unfamiliar with the area and would hate to get lost."

He looked puzzled for a moment, then took my meaning.

"I would happily escort my Queen on a walk through the woods," he said, relief falling off him like sweat.

"And while we are about, do you suppose you might show me some of the places that interest Princess Zelda?" I asked, every bit the innocent. "I am certain she knows all of the best and most interesting places."

He looked away, then back at me again, continuing to torture the hat he held.

"I could do that, I suppose. No harm in just looking around, is there?"

"None at all," I beamed at him with tremendous pride in both of us if the truth were to be told.

"'tis a beautiful day, Ma'am, if I may be so bold."

"Indeed," I agreed.

"Understanding that you are busy with all the duties of…queening and such, but would you care for a walk in the woods today, perhaps?"

I looked outside and saw that we still had hours before sunset.

"That would be lovely, Quinton. Thank you. Just give me a moment to let a few people know I will be away."

CHAPTER 20

"Letting people know I would be away" turned out to be far more daunting than I expected. Neither Sir Charles nor Sir John appreciated the idea of me out of walls with only Quinton to accompany me.

"Your Majesty," Sir John said, "we just advised you that you must never allow yourself to be without protection! That is why there is *always* a guard outside your door, why we walk you to your meals, to the atrium, to the dining hall…"

Sir Charles lowered his voice, "You know that Father Francisco is a danger to you. You cannot go traipsing off into the woods alone."

"I am not alone!" I persisted. "I have Quinton with me and he is armed."

"He is a huntsman!" Sir John argued. "He is not a warrior! He is ill-qualified to manage an orchestrated attack! Our kingdom is amidst a delicate transition and is vulnerable. We have to keep you safe and your baby as well."

"I could well have gone without telling you. This was a courtesy to let you know I would be out of pocket for a brief time. It is only for a few hours before the evening meal."

Sir Charles looked aghast. "A queen is not *out of pocket*. Your time is not your own as you seem to think it. Your *very person* is not your own."

"This is important," I said firmly. "Send who you want, but I am going and if they slow me down, may God have mercy on all of you for I will not."

"You will take one Queen's Guardsman," Sir John said, "as well as Quinton. You will return before the evening meal and if you do not, I will personally raise the alarm and send a search party into the woods and find you, do you understand?"

I narrowed my eyes at him. "Yes." I said, knowing that I was wasting time by arguing my good and valid points. "But he stays out of my way and allows me to go where I choose. A child minder when I go for a walk. For the love of all that is sacred and holy." This last bit I said under my breath.

Unaccustomed as I was to such scrutiny over my comings and goings, I felt irritated that I must ask permission and make concessions simply to go for a walk out of doors.

Eventually, Quinton and I were saddled up, as it was further of a distance than I could walk and return by my appointed time. My cloaked protector riding not far behind, but to his credit, he worked hard to avoid engaging me and kept a respectful distance from Quinton and I as we rode side by side.

It felt good to ride again and the sea breeze on my face was refreshing. I realized how closed and stale I felt from being inside for so many weeks. I enjoyed the outdoors and remaining confined for so long was completely against my nature. Excited, I nodded to Quinton and kneed my horse in the sides as we reached the causeway and left the populated portion of the courtyard ever further behind us. As if feeling and sharing my exhilaration, the horse happily broke into a run. Quinton kept pace and eventually pulled ahead with the Queen's Guard maintaining his distance behind us.

The bridge that led to the castle was not nearly as foreboding in fair weather and the horses stepped over it easily and without hesitation. Soon, we were on the other side and the landscape opened before us. It was the first time I had seen what my kingdom looked like since the fog and rain had obscured most of our trip toward the coast coming in. Even in the late summer as it was, the land was green and lush without sun burnt grass or browning trees. Quinton led us on a merry run down a trail that ran along the coastline and into the woods beyond, which were dense and richly fragrant.

As soon as we entered the forest, the horses became skittish and balked. I reached my hand down to the mare I had chosen to ride and patted her neck reassuringly as we continued to pick our way through the thick underbrush. Clearly, Quinton knew exactly where he was going, but I lost my sense of direction as soon as the trees and overgrowth closed around us. As my eyes adjusted to the dim light within the woods, I could see that a trail of sorts continued even into the forest floor. The rustle and chirping of birds through the treetops above us and occasional small animal fleeing into the bushes around us kept the forest alive with sound.

After the better part of an hour, during which I could not imagine how far we went since our pace quickened and slowed regularly, Quinton pulled his horse up short and dismounted. I did the same and we continued, walking the animals at what felt like a snail's pace comparatively.

We came to an open clearing, into which the horses flat out refused to enter. Quinton tied his horse's reins to a low tree branch and the pony began to rummage its nose through the underbrush as though he knew the area. My horse walked toward the other horse and did the same, even though only a rein held loosely in my hand guided it. I followed suit and tied the strap to a tree branch. Clearly, they had been here before, but had no love for what lay beyond the tree line.

"It is possible," Quinton said, keeping his voice low enough that the Queen's Guardsman could not hear, "that Princess Zelda sometimes enjoys coming here." He looked at me meaningfully.

"I see," I said.

"Being from Avalon," he spoke carefully as though picking his words for greatest significance, "perhaps you are familiar with… places in the world that are not quite what they appear?" He arched his eyebrows and moved his head in the direction of the clearing.

I stared at him for a moment and put together what he was saying with the shape of the area and the reluctance of the animals to enter within.

"Shit," I said softly, catching his meaning. I drew in a breath and looked back at the guard. Of all the possible answers to her frequent disappearances, this was not the most dreadful, but it was one of the most irritating.

I set my jaw and frowned, my head racing as I rapidly considered and rejected ideas for what to do next. At last, I stomped my way back to the guard, who was securing his horse in a similar fashion as we had done.

Using my sweetest, but firmest voice, I said, "Good sir, I understand that my advisers sent you out here with me with good intent. I can tell you that I do not intend to go further than this clearing today. I will rest within for a short time and then return. The huntsman knows his way quite well and will escort me back before dusk. Please do go back to your usual day's work within the castle and I will join you before long."

He ducked his head and said, "Your Majesty, I am under orders to…"

"…and those men are under orders from me. Now I am ordering you to leave me for now, having discharged your duties to the fullest. I am going to rest for a while, enjoying the air out of doors, and then return to Tintagel. Quinton is here should aught go wrong. If you feel you must stay, go to the edge of the woods and wait there."

"Yes Ma'am," he bowed slightly and took his leave with me grateful he did not protest more than he did. I would settle with Sir Charles and Sir John when I was finished if my hunch was correct.

After he left, I looked at Quinton with something that vacillated between resignation and frustration, knowing full well that I should not wish to kill the messenger simply because the news was not what I wanted to hear.

I drew in another breath and let it out slowly.

"I am going in to get her if she is still there. If you do not want her to know you told me, head on back to the castle and the horse will find our way back out again."

He stood up straighter. "I will not be a coward and leave you here," he said resolutely.

"How does leaving me here as I asked make you a coward?" I asked.

"People go in there and do not return," he said. "I am the only one who know where you intend to go, so I am the only one who can get you out if need be."

I sighed and put my hand on my hip.

"Your valor is appreciated, but misplaced," I assured him. "I have quite literally spent my life dealing with this sort of thing, so truly, I am in no danger of not coming back and if you do not wish to catch the sharp side of Princess Zelda's tongue, go now or prepare to accept the consequences. You did not wish to betray your friend and you have not done so. You simply led me to find the conclusion myself. If she comes out and finds you here, she will know."

His eyes twinkled. "Perhaps I will lead her to believe that your advisers sent me out to find you after you went off on a wild ride on your pony."

"Perhaps whatever you say, you had best remember the lies you tell so you can keep them straight," I said, narrowing my eyes at him. "Why compound the situation with falsehoods? I can take care of myself, truly. Now, get thee haste and I will see you at the castle."

He gave up far too easily and pulled his horse's rein from the tree branch.

"And stay available in case I have need of you again in the future," I said. He combined a nod with a bow and began to lead his horse away from the clearing.

Faeries. How I hated Faeries.

It seemed to be an even split among my sisters between those who loved Faeries and those who preferred not to go into their knee-buckling, mutable, time-bending world. It was easy to get lost in Faerie, which ran in a dimension parallel to our own. There were no cares or worries in Faerie and I could see how the allure would draw in a young girl like Zelda. The Faerie men were always fine to the eye and charming to a fault. The women were beautiful, sultry, and fun. In Faerie, life gave over to naught but pleasure. Wine flowed freely and strange incenses burned, the resins and herbs for which did not grow in our world, and caused me to feel dreamy and disconnected. The food was delicious and always there was a banquet laid for those who ventured into their kingdom.

Sensual pleasures of every kind were not only explored, but exploited in Faerie and even as a girl raised in a sexually uninhibited culture, the Faeries participated in acts of coupling that made me blush and look away. Faeries had no sense of obligation, restriction, or integrity. They appeared to serve no practical purpose other than to frolic in all hours of the day and night. In fact, there *was* no day and no night in Faerie. The sky was always a rosy, pink and purple color that could be dusk or dawn. Likewise, time passed differently there, even more so than between Avalon and the Britain Beyond. One might feel that they spent an evening in Faerie and return to find a week had passed. There were even stories on Avalon of a woman who thought she spent only weeks in Faerie, but returned to find the sun-bleached bones of her horse where the poor creature had long before starved to death tethered to a tree.

Thinking now of that story put a chill up my spine as I stood alone in the woods, despite the warm summer day.

"Here goes nothing," I muttered as I walked through the clearing's edge and into another world. To look at the area with mundane eyes, one would see a large open circle with sunlight spilling into it. On the far side was a dilapidated cottage that looked as though it would fall to the ground in a stiff wind. A keener eye would notice that the air was still and silent, too silent for a wooded area where one should hear insects, birds, and other forest creatures.

As I pushed through the magical barrier and into the portal to Faerie, the air around me wavered in such a way to tell those who had sight beyond sight that they were entering Faerie. Mundane people would walk right through the clearing and have naught but a sense of unease and even dread. They would likely even find a reason to walk around the portal. I, however, took a breath and pushed in.

Immediately, the familiar pink lighting was all around and I could hear laughter and music that grew louder as the veils between the worlds more fully parted and I stepped into an opulent room full of people in various stages of undress. The trees that circled the clearing in the mundane world were golden on this side and their branches held up a huge canopy with open flaps where rosy sky above peeked through. The air was rich with incense, the smell of decadent food, and body musk.

Soft, inviting lounge chairs and fainting couches were strewn about in what looked like a careless fashion, but strategically arranged in such a way that all areas of the room had pathways for access. Against one wall was a length of tables weighted down with foods both recognizable and foreign. Where the cottage had stood was a raised stage where musicians played music, sweet and melodic beyond compare.

"Iris!" came a female voice, clearly excited to welcome me.

She was ageless and small like all the Faerie people, and crowned with a circlet of small seashells and coral. Her gown was palest blue like the sky or perhaps more like sea foam and flowed around her sensually, sliding against her curves and accentuating the dip of her cleavage.

"We never thought to see you here. Presley," she called to someone across the room, "Look, it is the Queen of Cornwall, that little girl from Avalon!" The woman extended her small hand to me and I took it gingerly.

"I am Aphia," she said, "Queen of the Faeries. You know my sister, Minerva."

"Ah," I said, extracting my hand from hers after she held it for a few moments too long. "I know Minerva well, but does she not also claim to be Queen of the Faeries?"

She smiled broadly, "Of course, she does. There are seven of us, just as there are seven of you sisters on Avalon. We are all Queen of the Faeries, but we reign in different areas so as not to overstep one another. It works better that way, we have found. Funny that the seven of you did nearly the same thing. Ah… Presley, my mate. Meet Iris, the other Queen in Cornwall."

A svelte man, bare-chested and moving as smoothly as a shadow through the crowd of people, made his way to her side. He was slightly taller than I, which was unusually tall for a Faerie man, but he had the charismatic grace and dulcet voice customary to the race.

"All Hail Queen Iris," he purred, taking my hand and kissing it gently. I felt the tip of his tongue slip over my skin and gently pulled my hand away.

"Presley can keep you company while you visit us if you wish, Iris. Please," she gestured to the banquet table. "Have food and wine. Relax. Enjoy the music and escape from your responsibilities for a while."

My belly growled as my eyes returned to the banquet table and my midday meal felt hours away.

"Actually," I said, "It is my responsibilities that bring me here. I am looking for a young woman from my court who I was led to believe might spend some time on your side."

"Ah," she smiled. "I wondered when someone would come for her. I just did not expect it would be you." She took me by the hand. "Come with me. I believe there is little chance she would leave of her own volition, but if you have need of her, perhaps you can persuade her. Not that we mind her being here…"

She led me into another room within the tented canopy with Presley following close behind, seeming terrified of missing any moment of action that could ensue.

"We have a guest!" she announced with great fanfare in her voice. "Look who is here!"

A crowd of people moved aside and created an opening to reveal a couple locked in a passionate embrace on a bed festooned with roses and ivy up and down the bedposts. Both were half-dressed and kissing as though their very lives depended on their mouths creating a tight seal. Their hands moved roughly over one another as the crowd cheered and encouraged them. The woman draped over the man, her knees digging into his hips and her hair creating a veil that partially hid them while they kissed deeply. She ground her body into his, rolling her hips as he moaned into her mouth. I tilted my head to one side, wondering if they were copulating under there or if, as it appeared, their clothes were still on the lower halves of their bodies and they were only rubbing one another's genitals with their own.

I felt an unwanted and uncomfortable burn start in my own lower body and felt an urgency to get out of this world that was so different than the chilly air of Tintagel with its…

At Aphia's announcement, the couple broke their mouths apart and the woman swept her long, blond hair away from her face and turned her gaze toward me.

"Laoghaire!" I took no effort to disguise my stunned shock. "Laoghaire, what…what are you doing?"

She squinted and looked up at me, then her face broke into a smile.

"Iris!! You're here! That makes this place purrrrrrfect!" She opened her mouth into a happy smile and the dove back onto the face of the Faerie man under her.

I stepped over a few bodies and pushed my way through others who had gathered to watch.

"Come now, Laoghaire. It is time to go home. I have missed you."

She came up for air yet again.

"Oh," she said. "That is *so sweet*. I missed you too! I have been here for hours and hours, eating and kissing and listening to music. These Faeries throw such a fine party!"

"A month," I corrected. "You've been here for over a month, Laoghaire. Time to go."

I slipped my hand under her arm and pulled gently.

"Come on, then."

She came away easily, but the Faerie man she was with cast an exaggerated pout in her direction.

"Awww," she said, "I will be back, Sweetling. Save my place!"

She giggled as I half dragged her through the crowd and into the larger room.

"Have you seen Zelda?" I asked her.

She looked at me with drunken eyes filled with confusion.

"Zelda? Who is…? OH! The little girl. Yes, she is here somewhere…somewhere, I don't… I don't remember… somewhere."

Aphia and Presley caught up to us and I asked, "The Princess Zelda, where is she?" The music grew louder and I had to shout to be heard.

"Who?" Aphia asked.

"Zelda, my stepdaughter."

"Oh yes! She is here. I believe she is getting a massage over there." She fluttered a slim, graceful hand to the opposite side of the tent from where we stood.

"I am most grateful to you, Queen Aphia," I nodded, then grabbed Laoghaire's hand and pulled her with me. She came willingly, led like a child and stumbling like a tosspot. I myself could feel the uneasy haze of Faerie threatening to claim me and, shaking it off, forced myself to focus as we wove around revelers and bacchanalians. At last, I saw Zelda, stretched out on a chaise on her belly wearing nothing save a towel draped across her bottom. Two Faerie women and a Faerie man rubbed her body with scented oils. One woman massaged her legs, another, her back and the man stroked her arms and hands. I could hear her little moans of pleasure as they worked their hands deep into her muscled body.

I saw her clothes across a chair, picked them up and tossed them to her.

"Time to go," I said. "Thank the nice Faerie people and get dressed, Princess."

She looked up, startled.

"What are you doing here?" she barked.

"I could ask you the same," I said, "but there is not time. I want to get back to Tintagel before nightfall and I am taking you with me, so off you go! Put on your clothes and we are taking our leave."

I expected more of an argument, but she woefully stood and began to dress, careless of her bare body as the towel fell away. I felt a flash of appreciation that she did not subscribe to the parochial shaming of the body taught by the Christian church. At least here in Faerie, she did not.

Once she was clothed, I took her by one hand and Laoghaire by the other and began to make my way through the throng of people to where I knew I had entered. One thing about all places Faerie is that once you were in, it was a challenge to get out. There were no doors, only unseen portals in and out, and humans had to slip into the right niche between the worlds to get out again.

"Oh, *do* stay longer," Aphia cooed at my shoulder.

"I will visit again," I promised, knowing I would likely have to drag one or both of them out again now that I knew the portal was here. "But these ladies need to be home for a while."

An exaggerated frown pulled at her features and she drew Presley closer to her.

Still holding a hand of each girl, I smiled my thanks and nodded in her direction and pushed my way through. After a stomach-lurching wave of vertigo, we were all once more outside in the Cornish dusk.

It felt as if no more than a half hour had passed while I was in Faerie, but when we emerged, darkness was stealing into the woods. To my reckoning, I had lost two or perhaps three hours out here in what would be considered the "real" world.

Laoghaire's head began to clear as soon as she breathed in air from this side of the veil.

"Oh Iris," she said, "I am so sleepy."

"You are Faerie drunk," I said, feeling irritated. "Here, get onto my horse and we will be within walls soon."

She complied and I helped her to push her up into the saddle, where she leaned forward slightly.

"Ohhhh," she groaned. "I think I am going to vomit."

Zelda made a dismissive sound and took the horse's reins.

The horse, as I predicted, was as eager to lead us away from the clearing as I was to leave it. Zelda would surely know the way home since I suspected her frequent disappearances had been straight into Faerie and rarely were portals within a range of many miles from one another.

We had not gone far when a rustling in the bushes not far from us caused us to jump. I realized with painful alarm that we had no weapons at all with us. What if man or beast threatened us? I had my little sickle knife on my belt as always and moved my hand toward it, but otherwise, we were three women unguarded in the woods.

I let out a nervous breath that sounded like a laugh as Quinton stepped through the trees, a string of dead partridges slung over his shoulder and leading his horse by the reins.

"What are you doing out here?" he asked in feigned surprise.

"Yes," Zelda snapped at him, "What*ever* are we doing here? What a fucking surprise."

"Zelda!" I hissed. "Language!"

She rolled her eyes.

"Don't act as though you did not give me over, Quin," she sniffed.

"Me?" he gasped. "I was only out hunting for tomorrow's table! I never expected to come upon the likes of you. Your Majesty," he doffed his hat and bowed.

"Huntsman," I nodded.

"Would you care to use my horse?" he asked, offering me the reins.

We were surely almost out of the clearing, so I suggested instead that I ride with Laoghaire and he ride with Zelda so we could get home all the faster without subjecting to a walking pace. As I suspected would be the case, my guard waited just outside the clearing and silently joined our caravan back home to Tintagel. He did not question the addition of two others to our party and fell into silent vigilance behind us.

    The sun was low on the horizon and dusk was fully in command as we rode through the breezeway just in time to dress for the evening meal. Laoghaire declined, wishing only to crawl into her bed and sleep away the headache that had taken hold. She would feel better in the morning, I knew. Transition back from Faerie was not always pleasant.

CHAPTER 21

I thought perhaps Laoghaire would join me for the morning meal and I found myself eager to share with her all that had happened since she fell into Faerie. I also wanted to hear of how she came to be in that other world and what she did and did not remember about her time there. When she did not appear, I sent word to the kitchen to prepare a tray to serve in her room and promised myself that I would check in on her after she had time to rest and eat.

Ursa and Bersaba helped me to dress for the day. I knew that I still had weeks to go before my clothes grew tighter on me, but a part of me longed for my tummy to grow round and to finally feel the tiny movements inside of me that I had shared vicariously with so many other women. I knew it was possible this was the only time I would carry a child. I never planned to marry in the first place, much less quickening with a baby, and so this treasure within me felt more precious, aside and apart from the value it carried to the kingdom.

It was hard to believe not even two months had passed since I left Avalon. Already I was married, crowned, widowed, hated both by my stepdaughter and an irrational zealot of a priest, not to mention carrying the future King of Cornwall in my womb. It was far from the time when a firm shake of my shoulder would wake me from a deep slumber and tell me that this woman or that was at her time of delivery.

I missed midwifery and longed to get up to my elbows again in birth water and afterbirth. Supporting a woman while she labored and then pushed was my calling, not adjudicating where a fence line should be drawn or whether a vein of tin belonged to this mine owner or that one. As much as I was both a priestess and a princess of Avalon, daughter to the royal family, I had no designs on my mother's position of Lady of the Lake when she stepped down. Any one of my sisters could fill the role better than I and would love doing it. Reigning had never been in my blood the way birthing babies had been.

Laoghaire was every bit as invested in the birthing process as was I, which was part of what drew me to her as my favorite apprentice. She had an intuitive feel for the process and even as young as she was, automatically knew what herbs to give a pregnant woman for this ailment or that and what position to use to favor a better angle of the baby's head into the pelvis and get a baby who was stuck to move again. In that realm, she and I were a perfectly matched team. Rarely must we even speak when we managed a birth together. Our teamwork was flawless.

Would I ever return to midwifery? Marcus showed enthusiasm for the idea, but that was when I was a wife and a queen with a strong sovereign to do the royal heavy lifting. Had things gone as we planned, I would run the royal household, which pretty much ran itself after so long without a queen, host gatherings, and make babies. None of that would interfere with a midwifery practice. Acting as sole sovereign, however, was an entirely different prospect. Since Sir John and Sir Charles jerked me abruptly out of my grieving, I had done little but what Quinton referred to as "Queening."

Perhaps Laoghaire would want to start her own practice. She was certainly capable enough, especially considering what Bersaba had said when I first arrived about the court having no midwife. As her friend, I was again reminded of my own inadequacies in that position. I should know if her ambitions included such a thing and yet, I did not.

It never dawned on me when we were on Avalon to think about her needs as a young woman. I realized belatedly that in the past, I thought of her more as a tool than a person, as useful to me as the birthing rope women used to pull down on as they pushed or the precious oils we used to massage their birth openings as the baby emerged. I knew not whether she was virgin, if she favored any of the young druids on Avalon and perhaps missed a special paramour. I knew when we sat long hours with a laboring mother, she preferred dried venison and raisins for snacks and blackberry wine to drink. One of her legs was a half inch shorter than the other and if she stood for excessive lengths of time, her back would ache, so often she walked with the laboring mothers or sat on the bed behind them to rub their backs, their legs, or their shoulders rather than stand leaning over them. I did not know when she celebrated her name day or if she planned to take her vows to the Goddess when she finalized her training.

Having seen her in full abandon in the Faerie Kingdom, I realized how little I did know of her and that while I was a strong mentor to her, my conversation with Zelda showed me I was not a very good friend at all. I vowed to remedy that as soon as possible. She agreed to come with me on a quest that was not her own and sacrificed a peaceful life on Avalon to follow me into the unknown to the rocky, sea-beaten, end of the Earth or at least the end of Britain. She gave up everything for the promise of nothing. I at least owed it to her to make it worth her investment.

Since our arrival, all the fuss had been over me as a new bride, marrying a handsome king who was beloved by all. Why would she not feel abandoned and disregarded? Why would she not revel in the pleasures of the Faerie Kingdom and wish never to return?

For that matter, why would Zelda not wish to escape into such a joyful place when her own life was one of grief and responsibility? Would a young girl prefer to sit on a throne next to me, a stranger who stole her birthright? Or to succumb to the blissful touch of creatures who gave unconditionally with no demand of recompense?

Who was I to ask either of them to do otherwise?

What I did know is that I owed it to them to create a life here at Tintagel that did not force them to go into another realm to find joy and happiness. It would be a daunting task, but I would give it my best effort.

As I finished dressing and Ursa took my tray away, Zelda herself walked into my room without announcement or preamble and flopped unceremoniously onto a nearby couch.

"So," she said. "Remember when I said that you would owe me?"

"Good morning to you too, Zelda," I said, stifling a smile at her casual demeanor. "Yes, I do remember that I agreed I would owe you *if you helped me find Laoghaire.*"

"And I did. Is she not here now?"

"She is here now because of my efforts, not yours."

"Wrong," she said, raising one finger. "I knew when you said she rode out to the bridge and did not return that she had likely gone into Faerie. My actions were what led you there, so the debt stands. If not for me, you would not have found Faerie."

"No," I argued. "*My* actions are what led me there. I went there to look for you, not her."

"And you found me… with her. So, I found her first, not you."

"Had you gone to Faerie and brought her back, then we would have a deal."

She sighed, exasperated. "I knew you were going to find a way to talk yourself out of our arrangement."

"Truly, Zelda? Do you truly believe that I owe you when all you did was go play in Faerie as you have done dozens of times in the past?"

"Truly, *Iris*, should we not focus on the outcome, which is that your dear friend is back and the two of you can now braid each other's hair and play at rhyming games or whatever it is that ladies do where you come from?"

I stopped myself from going down this path with her, recalling to mind the thoughts I had just before she came to me.

"You know, you are right about one thing. I do owe you. You lost your father. Because of me, your claim to the throne went askew from what you were raised to believe it was. You have gotten little of what you wanted in the past few months except for that journey into Faerie. Since I am Queen and I am responsible for every soul in Cornwall, I am willing to take responsibility for your losses. Tell me, what can I do for you? When you imagined me owing you and came into my quarters to collect on that debt, what did you want from me?"

She blinked, but then collected herself and gave me the surprise of my life.

"I want you to find a way to let her go."

"Who?" I asked, stunned.

"The woman in the tower. Let her go and give her the means to support herself."

"The woman..." I tried to make sense of what she was asking. "Do you mean the woman your father loved, Zelda? The one you were afraid I would kill?" My stomach lurched and I feared I would lose my breakfast.

"Yes. She is a good person and she has been there a long time. I know now you do not have the stones to kill anyone, but she does deserve better than to die there all alone. You have all of this power," she waved her hand around my rooms, presumably illustrating my "power." "Use it to help her."

I nodded. "I will see what I can do, but Zelda, think about it. If this could be done, would not your father have done it long ago? He had far more power than I do and loved her well."

"Father was a puppet of the High Throne. As much as he was wise and kind, he still bowed to their every whim and to the dictates of the church. You, on the other hand," she flashed me a conniving grin, "are a demon worshiper from the island of devils at worst and a brand-new baby monarch at best. You are expected to bugger everything up in one way or another. It seems strategic to take advantage of that position and bugger things up in a way that helps people."

I considered what she said for a moment and found it concerning that I saw a degree of sense in her words.

"So, you are asking me to intentionally go against whatever dictate imprisoned this woman and then say, 'Oh my! What a mistake I have made. I am but a newcomer to the throne and must be expected to bugger things up.'"

She shrugged. "Whatever you do afterward is up to you, just so long as you make certain she is safe and cared for."

It seemed the least I could do, if not to win points with Zelda, then to honor Marcus by liberating the woman he loved. She did have a point. No one knew what to expect from me and likely anticipated some errors to fall. I could only hope none would lead to my own execution or imprisonment. But truly, what *was* the use in having executive power if you did not use it to help others?

I studied her for a moment as she chewed on her thumbnail and looked back at me through dark lashes. It was true. She did look like me and I assumed, therefore, looked like her mother. Her skin was like ivory, smooth and pale, with hair every bit as black as mine and my father's. Her eyes were deep and dark, wide and waiting, and defiantly locked onto my gaze, daring me to make the wrong choice and expecting me to shrink away from the challenge. She was a sharp girl and knew I owed her nothing other than the attention due to an errant stepdaughter.

"Shall you and I go visit her together?" I asked.

Now, it was her turn to look shocked.

"You want to see her?"

"Yes," I said, realizing that more than anything, I wanted to meet the second woman who had stolen my husband's heart before ever I got to him. Third, if you counted Zelda. "Yes, I do. Will you take me?"

"She is... different," Zelda said.

"I know. Your father told me that she had difficulty with her memory and her behavior and that at times, she did not seem to be in her right mind."

"He told you that?"

"Yes."

"She is better as of late, but the last time I visited her, she did not yet know he had died and did not know about you."

"Then we must be quite sensitive in how we speak to her, mustn't we?" I suggested.

"We must," she agreed.

I realized I was on thin ice, but ice that was thus far holding and looked as though it might lead to a shaky alliance, which was better than no alliance at all.

"It is obvious that she means a great deal to you, Zelda. I will honor that and do my best to help her."

"She is good to me," the girl ran her finger lightly over the stitching on the fabric that covered the couch. "She talks to me as if I am a real person and listens to what I say. She made my father smile and she spends time with me, working out puzzles and writing stories."

"I do not know if you knew this about me," I said, "but on Avalon, I was a midwife and a healer. I know that the court physician is a very good doctor. Perhaps together, he and I can develop a course of treatment that will help her to stay in her right mind. I am willing to try, at least."

"Dr. Colin never sees her," she explained. "Father Francisco forbids it. In fact, he will likely forbid you from seeing her as well."

"Then," I said, "We shan't ask him. Besides, I am Queen and he can *try* to forbid me, but he will greatly underestimate how stubborn I can be."

"When do you want to go?" I asked.

I smiled, "No time like the present. Shall we?"

She jumped up off the couch and nearly bolted for the door.

"Follow me," she whispered, even though we were alone in the room.

~*~

    The tower was in the very back of Tintagel. The corridors were winding and dark, but Zelda, of course, having explored the castle since she was a toddler, knew every nook and cranny. We walked until I thought that surely we must be in South Wales. She held a torch aloft and led the way expertly through the labyrinth of twists and turns.

    At last, we came to a winding staircase that led up and up, through hundreds of stairs, so far up that I could not see the top from where I stood on the castle floor. I looked up at the stairs winding into the darkness far above and groaned inwardly. She began skipping up the narrow steps like a cat and I held onto the rope that wound along the wall as a makeshift railing and began my slower ascent. The stairs were made of stone and were quite narrow. I stopped after it felt as though we were climbing forever and looked down, far down to the floor below. I had no fear of heights, but neither had I any interest in falling and the climb seemed treacherously steep. Even in the summer air, the cool stones were sweating, which made them quite slippery. My calves were aching and once I caught my breath, I hurried up the stairs faster to try and keep pace with Zelda.

    Finally, when I thought we must surely have passed the top of the castle, she stepped onto a landing and reached her hand down to help me up. There was a narrow wooden hallway with an iron railing of lattice work as its only wall between us and the deep chasm below that landed onto a stone floor. As had been the case when looking up, I could not see the floor below from where we stood. She dug into her pocket and pulled out a silver coin. I wondered what purpose it could have, but as we came to the end of the hallway, I saw that a single guardsman sat drowsing in a chair near an unadorned wooden door.

She kicked the man awake, shoving her booted foot against his outstretched one. He jumped to attention when he saw who it was. She handed him the silver coin and even though we were alone on the landing, he looked both ways before he opened the door. He eyed me suspiciously as I entered, but left the door ajar and reclaimed his position on the chair once we were inside.

The room was large and well furnished with bright sunlight streaming in from its only window. Plants of all kinds grew in pots throughout and expensive furniture of the finest caliber sat upon fine carpets. A tall woman stood, framed in the large window that dominated the west wall. From my perspective, she was but a shadow with the sun coming in around her. She braced her hands against each side of the window and stood there like a queen, her silhouette proud and regal.

"Guests," she said without turning around. Her voice was sweet and rang like a bell, cutting through the silence of the room. "How lovely. Have you at last come to kill me and free my spirit from this season in hell? Or do you bring me more scriptures to repeat so that my everlasting soul might be saved when at last I do shuffle off this mortal coil?"

"Just me," Zelda said, her voice sounding almost meek in contrast to the power that radiated as the woman spoke. "I have brought someone to see you."

As she turned, I realized there was something familiar about her and as realization dawned on me, I drew in a startled gasp.

"Iris!" the woman smiled, her hands flying to her face in delight.

"Aunt Ophelia?" I gasped.

CHAPTER 22

She looked as stunned as I felt.

"Iris? Little Iris? What on earth are you…? Truly, I have gone completely mad as they said I would. Now I am seeing what cannot be there."

"No, Auntie, it is me. I live here now." I ran to her and she swept me up in a warm embrace and held me as though she would never let me go.

She was my father's twin and had once been the High Queen of Britain. The familiarity of her scent, her strength, flowed through me like a tonic. I pulled back to study her and she looked at me with dancing eyes I remembered from my childhood. Her son, the true High King of Britain by birthright, had been deposed nearly a year before and while we knew that she and he had been imprisoned immediately afterward, we had heard nothing of their whereabouts or well-being since then. They were last known to be here, but I had not imagined they would still be within the walls of my only court.

"You live here?" she asked. "How can that be so? Why on earth would you ever leave Avalon for this wretched place?"

I laughed. "It is a long story," I said, dodging the obvious answer. "I will tell you all about it one day." A dark thought came into my mind.

"Aunt Ophelia, where is Phillip?"

Her expression darkened and it seemed that all the light left the room.

"They took him," she said, her voice cracking as she spoke. "I know not when. My memory plays tricks on me sometimes. I have not seen him in a long time. The priest here tells me that he is dead, but I always thought I would know," she touched her chest, "in here, if he died. I would feel it and I do not, so it is hard for me to believe it is so. I pretend he will burst in here one day and take me away from this place. I care not if he is ever King again, but I should like to see my son and know that he is safe and happy. It would please me to live with him again and see his wife and my grandchildren should he have any. Did you know he was High King?"

Her eyes searched mine as though I had the answers.

"I did know that," I smiled. "It is so good to see you, Auntie."

"And Zelda!" she beamed. "Why did you not tell me that you knew my niece? How wonderful that the two of you are friends!"

We looked at each other and then back at her.

"Yes," Zelda said. "Jusssst wonderful. I am glad it makes you happy."

"Did you know she has *six* beautiful sisters who are all priestesses on Avalon? They are my brother's girls. Have you met Bran? My brother? Such a fine man."

"How are you feeling today?" Zelda asked, taking Ophelia's hand as we all sat down at the formal table that took up one entire side of the room. How funny that a woman in a prison cell so elegant would have a formal dining table and chairs as if she would host a dinner party.

"I am having a good day," Aunt Ophelia smiled at Zelda. "I feel clearer and now you are here, and Iris, and that makes it a *fine* day indeed."

"Are you eating enough?" Zelda continued. As I watched her interact with the older woman, I realized it was the first time I had seen her show genuine concern for anyone other than herself.

"Oh," the older woman demurred. "I have not been very hungry. The food does not come up as often as it used to, so I make it last. The guard brought it up from the kitchen last time and not that priest as is usual. It tasted particularly good. There was soup. I have not had soup in a long time."

"Are they not yet bringing you food each day?"

"Oh no," she answered. "Maybe every two or three days, I lose count. They say it is too far from the kitchen to come every day, so I keep some there in the cupboard and dry the meat on the window sill so it will keep."

"Are they emptying the chamber pot?"

"Yes, mostly, the guards will. When they do not, I just fling it out the window." She giggled in a nearly juvenile fashion. "It is not like anyone is walking below."

My heart ached to hear my beautiful aunt, so full of integrity and grace, talk about portioning out her food to have enough and emptying her own chamber pot. She was markedly thinner than when I had last seen her several years back. Her hands shook slightly as she talked, but still, they fluttered around her when she spoke. My mother used to say that if Ophelia sat on her hands, she would be instantly rendered unable to speak because she so often used her hand movements to illustrate what she was saying.

"Is Marcus coming?" she asked Zelda, and I saw the flash of pain across the girl's face at this question. "I do miss him so and he has not been here for many days."

"Not today," she answered and the tenderness in her voice caused my eyes to sting with tears unshed. "Maybe another time, but not today."

Aunt Ophelia smiled.

"He is such a busy man. I do so enjoy his company and he has been so very good to me. I never thought to care for anyone again after my husband died, but your father's visits do cheer me so. And you, Iris," she continued. "Tell me everything that is happening on Avalon. How are your parents and sisters?"

I shared frivolous gossip with her and assured her that my parents were well, but for obvious reasons, left out anything about the quest, my marriage, or my pregnancy. She seemed satisfied and did not push beyond what I offered.

"I should go," I said at last to Zelda after a while. It was surreal to sit here visiting with my aunt, knowing she was the woman Marcus loved, knowing that she was a prisoner of the High Throne, and knowing that Zelda expected me to do something about it. The thought of going down all those stairs again caused my stomach to pitch and weave and I contemplated simply moving into the opulent cell with Aunt Ophelia.

"I will walk with you," Zelda smiled as if we were the best of friends. We both hugged my aunt and promised we would see her again soon as she walked us to the door of her prison, which I still must process lay within my castle walls.

"Eldon!" Aunt Ophelia snapped at the guard who was again sleeping at his post. "How are you going to watch over me if you are sleeping? I could escape right now and you would never know. Stay awake if you wish to keep your head, young man!"

He nodded curtly and sat up straighter in his chair as we began our descent back into the castle proper.

~*~

"Why did you not tell me it was my aunt?"

"How was I to know?" she shrugged. "I did not research your family lineage when I heard yet another insipid crown chaser was to marry my father."

I let out a sound of disgust. "Oh. Thank you, quite."

"You aren't so bad, I suppose," she conceded. "At least not like those others. They were unfit to groom my father's horse, much less wed him and birth a lineage of brats for him."

We were in my chambers, where she reluctantly agreed to have tea with me after our encounter with my aunt in the tower. Ostensibly, I lured her there under the premise of working together to find a plan to free my aunt, but my underlying motivation was to find out more about this enigmatic young girl who was in my care.

"What were they like?" I asked.

She lifted her nose as far into the air as she could and waved her palm toward the ceiling.

"They were ever so dignified," she said with an affected aristocratic edge to her voice. "With their fine silks and baubles and their strews of ladies in waiting barking orders at the servants... *my* servants." She mimicked a bitchy tone so perfectly I could hear the exchange in my head without trying, "Oh *no*, Princess Darrrrlington cannot posssssibly eat *currants* on her porridge. She must have only the finest cherries and cream mixed in."

I laughed at her mockery to the point that I very nearly snorted my tea out of my nose.

"Or else they were so vapid and young that the stupidity oozed like sweat out of their pores."

"Do tell!" I smiled.

"Your father will not like it if you are unkind to me, Zelda," she said in a exaggerated childish lilt, adding a *sniff* at the end for effect. "I am to be your mother. Is that not just the *finest* thing in the *world*? Are you not so *excited*? We will be like *sisters!*"

She made a gagging sound.

"Ugh," I said in agreement. "No wonder you ran them off."

She shrugged. "Father did not want to marry any of them any more than I wanted him to. He was doing it to please those old crows, Sir John and Sir Charles. I think he was grateful I got them to leave and let me tell you, it did not take much."

"Well," I ventured, "your father's advisers were right in a way. He did need to marry and create a down line, if you look at it from a royal point of view."

"Bah," she said. "Father and I always did just fine between the two of us. It was when people interfered about what I should wear and how a lady should act and dress that it all got so ugly. *Sit this way. Talk this way. Walk this way.* A princess does *this* and a princess never does *this*."

"So Zelda," I asked, wondering already if I had pushed the conversation too far, "why did you not try to run me off?"

She flung her legs up onto the arm of the chair and laid unceremoniously across it. She always wore men's riding britches and a tunic, so there were no skirts to arrange or modesty to conceal.

"You seemed harmless," she said. "Plus, I was interested in where you came from, so I decided to let you stay. I found Faerie a few weeks before you arrived, so I thought I could spend my time there if things got too complicated. By the time I came back, Father was already so besotted with you that there was no going back. Had I known…"

Her expression saddened.

"Known what?"

"That he was going to die. That I would have no more time with him… I would have stayed closer. I would not have left. I would have treasured my time with him more than I did."

"None of us could have known," I assured her. "He seemed so strong and healthy. I thought he would live forever. I thought I would get to love him all my days."

She looked at me without speaking for several minutes.

"You really loved him, did you not?" She had said this before, but seemed to need to hear it again for the words to sink in.

I nodded. "I really did. I did not expect to, especially so quickly. I hoped we might come to care for one another over time, but," I felt a smile steal across my face, "he was just so…"

She smiled back. "He was, was he not?"

"Yes. He was."

"I saw your father when they were here for the wedding. He is a handsome man. What are the marks on his body and his face?"

"They are magical sigils," I answered. "He draws them on in woad and changes them according to the magical work he is doing at the time. The ones he wore at our wedding were for the happiness and success of his daughter."

"Not for your marriage," she observed.

"Hmmm," I replied. "So, they were not. I had not considered this."

"Could it be he knew about my father."

"He well may have. He is a powerful and amazing man, but he said nothing to me of it if he did."

"What is Avalon like?" she asked.

A flash of inspiration hit me.

"Here, let me show you."

I picked up one of the apples my parents sent to me and tossed it to her.

"Do you like apples?"

"...yes?" she answered, wondering I am certain what this could possibly have to do with Avalon.

"Take a bite," I said.

She did and her eyes widened as the juice leaked down her chin.

"Oh my!" she smiled around the large bite in her mouth. "Oh my, that is amazing."

I nodded. "That is what Avalon is like. Everything, the water, the air, the fruit...is sweeter, richer, fuller...just...more."

"This is the best damned apple I have ever eaten."

"Oh yes," I agreed.

"Are these from Avalon?"

"My mother and father sent them to me. They knew I would get homesick for them."

She ate the entire apple with great enthusiasm, nearly moaning with pleasure from its sweetness.

"So, what are you going to do?" she asked as she wiped her mouth with her sleeve. "About Ophelia, I mean."

"I have an idea," I said, "but I will need a bit of time to work it out. She is weak from lack of adequate nourishment and it will likely be difficult to get her down the tower stairs."

"And where will you put her after you get her down the stairs? Wherever she is, they will come for her. She is convicted of High Treason."

"I know."

"Can perhaps your parents help? If they know she is in trouble?"

I shook my head. "It takes many days to ride from Avalon to Cornwall. I do not want to wait that long if we do not have to and there is no one here I trust well enough to escort her to Avalon. She would be safe there in my father's care, but getting her to the island is the problem. Can you imagine if I asked Sir Charles or Sir John to take her from the tower to Avalon?"

She winced. "We need a place to put her where no one will find her. We can then factor out the details of getting her to Avalon later. She is also quite incapable of taking care of herself in her current state, so she will need a capable companion."

"Zelda, if I can get transport her somewhere, can you be with her? You are right. She needs somebody she knows and trusts to keep her safe. I would do it, but people follow me everywhere. They are used to you leaving the castle for long stretches and we can use that to our advantage so long as you check back from time to time."

The girl nodded. "I can do it. Then as soon as we can, we will move her to Avalon and no one will ever find her? She can live out her days happy and safe?"

"You know, Zelda, I realize that my aunt looks ancient to you, but she is not yet even as old as your father. She may still live for many years."

She looked thoughtful.

"I had not considered that."

"But yes, if we can manage to get her to Avalon and into my father's care, they will make a home for her there and no one from Britain can touch her."

She let out an uneasy breath.

"So it is just a matter of keeping her safe once she leaves the tower and then getting her to Avalon."

"Yes. Do you know who takes her the trays of food? Who empties her chamber pots? Who sees her on a regular basis?"

"As she said, the guard empties the chamber pots and the kitchen staff cooks the food on her trays and send it up. Father Francisco is usually the one to take her food to her."

"Father Francisco? Why?"

"As a traitor, her soul is damned, so he tries to get her to confess. She refuses and the only good thing the High Throne did was forbid torture or execution orders for her, so he can say whatever he wishes, but cannot harm her."

"She said that the guard brought her the food recently."

"And the guard, as you saw, can be bought. This much we know."

"We need a distraction for Father Francisco for several days so that he does not take her food to her. We need a temporary place to keep her and we need a way to get her to Avalon."

"Piece of cake," she said, throwing her hands into the air almost as expressively as Aunt Ophelia.

"What about Phillip? Do you know what happened to him?" I asked.

She shook her head. "Never saw him. I am not even sure he was ever here."

"Does the High King know he is missing?"

She grinned.

"It was generally deemed best that no one at Cameliard know that we lost their prisoner."

"And now are about to lose the other one."

"So it seems."

"Let me think on this," I said. "There must be a way."

As she left, I tossed her another apple.

"Take one for the journey," I smiled.

~*~

Ursa slept with me, so I had to wait until I heard her soft snores before I crept out of bed and made my way to the mirror, praying the candle would not wake her and grateful that my dressing room where the mirror stood was separate from the sleeping area. On bare feet, I eased silently across the ever-cold stone floor and slipped the drape off of the mirror. Reaching into the pocket of my night dress, my fingers found the smooth stone I had placed there. Gently, I placed it in the crevice at the top of the mirror between the two hands and I waited.

I held my breath, imagining that the mirror would not come to life as it had before, but soon, the surface began to fold in upon itself and swirl in a spiral of mist. At last, the mist cleared and I could see my father looking back at me.

"Father," I whispered. "Father, I need you."

"Iris," he said, "Are you well? Whatever is wrong?"

"It is Aunt Ophelia," I said, "I found her in the tower. I must get her to Avalon. She is dying here."

"My daughter, you do realize that if you do that, you are committing high treason."

I paused, amazed that he would even question rescuing her. Moreover, he did not seem surprised at all that she was here.

"You knew?" I asked.

"Of course, I knew," he said softly. "It was no secret that the High Throne sent her to Tintagel."

My mind reeled.

"And you want to just leave her in that tower room to rot?" I asked. I heard Ursa shift in the bed in the next room and realized I had raised my voice.

"Iris, certainly, I do not, but my hands are tied in this."

"What about Phillip?" I asked. "Where is my cousin?"

This time, it was his turn for confusion.

"Is he not also there?" he asked.

"No!" I hissed, reminding myself to keep my voice low. "He has not been here the entire time. Only Aunt Ophelia? Did you not think to discuss such things with King Marcus during your all-night drinking session?"

I was more than slightly irritated.

"It did not seem prudent to discuss such things on the eve of your wedding," he said, gently. "I was going to bring it up on a return visit, but sadly, he did not live long enough for that to happen."

"How can you not do everything possible to rescue your sister? Your *twin* sister? She is not yet fifty and already her mind is slipping, likely from being locked away in that tower room on top of losing her son."

"Iris, please," he pleaded. "I love my sister. I will do anything I can to help, truly, but I am not willing to get you killed in the process. Do you not understand this?"

I sighed. "Of course, I do, but you need to understand that I cannot leave her there."

"Perhaps," he suggested, "You can arrange to have her in a more comfortable room, closer to you."

"No," I said. "If I ask for that, I have tilted my hand and the entire court will know I am aware she is here. This knowledge was kept from me deliberately and if I am to help her, I must do so without anyone knowing I am the one doing it."

"Then instead of reprimanding me, tell me how I can help."

"I need a place to keep her safe, away from the castle, where no one will see her, until I can get her to

Avalon. I need to move through the castle without anyone knowing who I am and I need a way to physically get her from the tower to the safe place."

"Ah," he smiled. "Is that all?"

CHAPTER 23

I did not see Laoghaire for the entire day after I brought her out of Faerie. I thought to look in on her, but did not want to disturb her if she was resting. Spending weeks in Faerie could wear down a person's reserves, even if it only felt like days to them.

She did join me in our room the next day for the morning meal looking far more human than she had when last I saw her. Well informed by the servants of the King's demise, she was the picture of sadness and contrition for her absence during my time of grief.

"Surely though," she said, "you did not grieve overmuch. You barely knew him."

Even though I knew what she said made perfect sense, still it stung my heart and I felt anew the loss of a love that lost a chance to blossom.

"Oh dear," seeing my expression, she read my thoughts accurately. "You did care for him. Iris, I am so very sorry."

"He was a good man and I admit, he roused up feelings in me I had never felt before. I miss…" I thought for a moment about what I did miss. "I miss what could have been. I miss each embrace, each kiss, each touch we never had."

"And now you are Queen."

I shrugged. "So it seems."

We heard a quiet knock on my door and when I bid the person to come in, I was surprised to see it was Zelda. Unlike her previous visit where she entered with great bravado and insolence, this time, she was far more deferential.

"I am interrupting," she said. "I will find you later."

"No! Do come in, Zelda," I smiled.

Laoghaire looked from me to Zelda and then back to me again, working hard to keep her mouth from falling open in shock.

"Zelda, this is my friend, Laoghaire. I doubt you were ever properly introduced in Faerie. She is also a Priestess of Avalon and a midwife. Laoghaire, this is my stepdaughter, Zelda."

"Hello," they both said at once, eying one another suspiciously.

"We are just about to have our morning meal," I said. "Will you join us, dear?"

She took the chair between us and I scooted my plate closer to her so that we could share. She served herself eggs, scones, and fruit.

"I was just about to share with Laoghaire the news of my aunt in the tower."

Zelda stopped eating and looked at me, seeming unsure of how to proceed.

"It is well, I promise," I assured her. "We need help when the time comes to move her and Laoghaire is one of the few people I can trust."

"You have an aunt here?" Laoghaire asked in amazement.

"My Aunt Ophelia, my father's twin sister."

I watched as realization flooded over her.

"The High Queen. I mean, the Queen Mother… she's here? Here in Tintagel?"

"Held prisoner," Zelda said, spreading jam onto her scone. "…in the tower."

"Oh my. So where is Phillip, the real High King?"

"No one knows. Father Francisco says he is dead, but no one has seen the body. And there is more," I said. "The King was, well, kindly disposed to my Aunt Ophelia." I arched my eyebrows meaningfully.

"He was good to her? Excellent."

"Yes, Laoghaire." I hoped she would catch my meaning without a great deal more detail. "They were *very* close."

Again, Laoghaire looked at me and then at Zelda.

"Oh for... They were *lovers*," Zelda said, "Did you not see her eyebrows going wild when she said 'kindly disposed?'"

Laoghaire gasped. "Ohhhh."

"They were not lovers in the sense of acts of pleasuring one another, but they loved one another deeply."

"How do you know that?" Zelda asked me.

"Your father told me and I believe him. He says he could not lie with her without marrying her and he could not marry her for what are now obvious reasons."

"And Ophelia does not know my father is dead," Zelda explained to Laoghaire, "and does not know that Iris married him and does not know that Iris is pregnant with his child. She is only sometimes in her right mind. Does that about sum it up, Iris?"

I let out a long exhale.

"That about does."

"So now we have to figure out how to get her out of the tower and somewhere safe. She is miserable up there." Laoghaire nodded her understanding to Zelda.

"How can I help?"

"We have to come up with a plan," I said. "We are three tremendously resourceful, capable women. I refuse to believe we cannot make this happen."

"You have claim to the throne of Cornwall by your own merit," Laoghaire observed. "Why not simply use that power for an executive order that she be released."

"Because she is a prisoner of the High Court," I explained. "Not of Cornwall although Tintagel is where she is remanded. This is simply where they sent her to serve out her sentence."

"Wait," Zelda interrupted. "How do you have a claim to the Cornish throne other than through my father and your child?"

"Oh," Laoghaire laughed. "Iris's lineage is a big, fat Gordian knot all tied up with Cornwall. Tell her, Iris."

"I will try," I said. "See if you can follow this. A man named Taliesin had a child with a Priestess of Avalon and the child's name was Ygraine. Ygraine married Gorlois the Boar, who was the King of Cornwall. They had a child named Morgan. Gorlois recanted his allegiance to Uther Pendragon, who defeated him in battle and came to Ygraine with a glamour over him to cause everyone to believe he was Lord Gorlois. The glamour was created by Taliesin, who came with him. Ygraine lay with Uther, believing he was her husband or knowing he was Uther or what have you and they conceived the child who would become King Arthur. Back then, when a man became king, he went to Dragon Island for a ritual in which he pledged himself to the land and consummated the ritual with a Priestess of Avalon. Without knowing she was the one who played the Virgin Huntress in the ritual, Arthur lay with Morgan, his older sister, at his own king making. Are you with me so far?"

She nodded mutely.

"In that coupling, they conceived a son, Mordred and Mordred had a son named Oswin, who fell in love with a priestess on Avalon named Marian. After Oswin was killed, Marian found herself pregnant and left Avalon to find him, thinking he still lived. She died giving birth to my father, Bran, and my Aunt Ophelia, who were separated at birth and did not know the other existed until they were adults."

"That is completely convoluted," Zelda said.

"Oh, it gets better," Laoghaire said. "Iris's father, Bran, is Taliesin, The Merlin of Britain reborn with all of his past life memories intact to preserve the continuity of wisdom, so in essence, the current King of Avalon is his own great great-great-grandfather…or something like that."

"So, since your father is a direct descendant of King Arthur, he has more of a claim to the High Throne than does even King Phillip."

"Correct," I said, and I felt a flash of pride in her ability to conceptualize what I myself could barely understand.

"I cannot believe you waded through all that mess to figure that out," I said. "Our family is apparently seen as a threat to the current regime, but my father has no aspirations to the High Throne. I carry a claim to the Cornish throne by way of the Lady Morgan through Gorlois, aside and apart from my marriage to your father."

"Will you pursue that claim?" she asked.

Now was the moment of truth or concealment. I chose both.

"I have no intention of remaining on the throne any longer than it takes to secure another person here who can uphold the same goals I have for Cornwall. Whether that is myself, or you, or a child of mine, or someone else altogether makes no difference to me at all. I want what is best for *all* the Cornish people, whatever form that takes, but aspirations to the throne, however, were never my motivating force. I would much prefer to be on Avalon catching babies."

"You could make the claim," Zelda said, her voice carefully neutral. "Cornwall is like Lothian. It has no qualm with a woman on the throne unless there is a male heir to preclude her."

"Yes," I agreed. "And the High Throne is well pleased to have me ensconced here, contentedly ruling at the end of the world, if it keeps me and my family from sniffing around Cameliard."

"So, to keep you happily enthroned here, perhaps they would be willing to overlook the sloppy escape of two convicted treasonists to whom they had already extended considerable gratuities."

"Perhaps," I said, seeing her thought process developing. "They would, of course, have to find out first and with Phillip's disappearance drawing no attention from our friends in the East, I have to believe that they would be far less interested in where his mother happened to be."

"Phillip is the threat," Laoghaire added. "So, either they have no idea of the whereabouts of a true heir to the throne or they do not know he is missing or…"

"…they know that he is in fact dead," Zelda finished.

My hope was that the Cornish preferred to keep their occasionally misplaced deposed monarchs to themselves. If Phillip *was* in fact alive out there somewhere, I would gather up that benefit as it presented itself to me. For now, my task was figuring out a way to keep his mother from wasting away in that tower prison cell. Ophelia was a barmaid who married the High King of England and became a shrewd companion to him after spinning straw into gold. She deserved better than this.

"Is that what I think it is?" Laoghaire asked unexpectedly, her attention focused on the bowl of apples on the small table under the window.

"Oh, the apples," Zelda cooed.

"Take one for you and one for Laoghaire," I encouraged Zelda, not that she needed much prompting.

"Wherever did you get them?" Laoghaire asked. She sighed as she bit into one.

I smiled, "My father sent them to me. His letter was how I knew you were missing. Everyone here thought you rode back to Avalon with my parents, but when he asked after you, I realized something happened when you escorted them to the bridge."

"I am grateful for that," she admitted, taking another bite. "You were there too, were you not?" she indicated Zelda. "It is all so fuzzy now, like a dream I had."

"I was there," Zelda answered. "I visit from time to time to escape from here."

Laoghaire looked surprised. "What is there to escape from? Do you not do pretty much whatever you want?"

"Hardly," she rolled her eyes. "When I am here, there is no one to talk to, really."

"You have Beatrix and Nimien, do you not?" I asked, surprised by her answer. "And Lady Charlotte? You have known them your whole life."

She shrugged. "It is not as though they are actual friends at all. Nimien is my lady in waiting and Lady Charlotte was my nanny. Now that I am no longer a child, they have little to do with me and mostly scowl and reprimand me. Beatrix is my servant. I am more of a chore to any of them than a person. It would not be proper for me to confide in them or treat them as a true friend. Look around you. How many people my age do you see here? Would you not wish to escape?"

"I take you point," I agreed. "But to Faerie? It hardly seems the place for a proper young woman."

"This coming from a Priestess of Avalon? I believe you have spent too much time with Father Francisco."

"Why do you come back, then, if it is so horrible for you here?" Laoghaire asked.

"My father," Zelda replied. "He was my whole life. Now that he is gone, it feels as though I have no life… and no reason to come back other than Ophelia."

My heart hurt for her.

"You are the next Queen of Cornwall," I said, firmly. "And before the weight of that crown hits your head, I intend for you to have some fun."

She smirked and I remembered the insolent child others described to me.

"Whether ever I see a crown depends on whether the bun on your oven is a girl baby or a boy."

I waved a dismissive hand.

"Do the counting, Zelda! I still have months until my baby is born and even then, he could not reign until he comes of age, which you do in less than six years. You will rule for a very long time until he is eligible to be King and by then, who knows if he will even want the crown? Not to mention, what if I carry a girl baby? You would be first in succession."

"Iris!" Laoghaire gasped. "You are pregnant? How?"

"Wedding night and my father's final act before he took his leave of this world," Zelda answered on my behalf. "As nearly as I can tell, he died on the down stroke. Came and went at the same time, as it were."

"ZELDA!" I hissed. "Respect!"

She batted her hand at me as if I were a pesky fly.

"The future of Cornwall is nestled right there in her holy baby basket." She wiggled a finger in the direction of my belly.

"Which means that more than ever, I need you here, not out reveling in the Faerie Kingdom."

She looked stunned. "Me? Why ever do you need me?"

Laoghaire eyed me carefully. "Because look at her. She is so exhausted, she can hardly sit up. I do not know why I failed to notice it before."

Nor did I and it was true. Already, my eyes were heavy and it was not yet midmorning.

"Women in their first few months of pregnancy have very little energy," she explained. "Their bodies have to adjust to carrying a new life inside and we three have a great deal to accomplish that cannot wait. We are limited in who we can ask for help with this, so she has to depend on the two of us to help her help Queen Ophelia."

"That about sums it up," I said, grateful for her understanding.

"Who does know that your aunt is here, imprisoned in the tower?" Laoghaire asked.

"A guard," I replied. "Father Francisco. Marcus knew, obviously. Who else, Zelda? Sir John? Sir Charles? They never once mentioned her to me."

"Hmmm, nor to me," she said, looking thoughtful. "But surely, they would know. They know everything about my father's court."

"Did they know he was in love with her?" I asked.

She shook her head. "No one knew that but me…and then you."

"So, they certainly do not know everything. And what about Father Francisco? His ties to the High Court and the Church in Rome are nearly fanatical. Does he think Phillip is dead? Or is he ashamed to admit to his superiors that Phillip slipped their grasp?"

"There has been no repercussion for his loss," Zelda observed, "and with great certainty, if he escaped and the High Court knew of it, someone's head would roll."

"If you had not told me, I would have no idea she was even here," I pointed out. "Something as critical as the care, feeding, and security of a prisoner accused of High Treason would come under my purview. Why would they not mention it?"

"But you must not ask or you reveal over much," Laoghaire added.

"No," Zelda said. "You… *we…* can speak of this to no one and especially not Sir John and Sir Charles."

"You do realize," I said, pointing out the obvious and the giant elephant in the room, "that it is a direct act of treason for us even to discuss this and that any of us could be hanged for it?"

Laoghaire's mouth dropped open, but Zelda dismissed my words outright.

"They'd not dare," she said. "Clearly, they care nothing about what happens to Ophelia or they would have checked on her by now."

"Do you not think that is what Francisco is doing? He is the puppet of the High Court and I am sure he makes certain she stays in check."

Her face fell and I realized this thought had not crossed her mind.

"So what do we do?" she asked, and my heart warmed that she trusted me enough to guide this rescue.

"We must contrive a way, some way, to get him away from Tintagel for a while. Now, think. Did you ever see Father Damian take food to Ophelia or check on her?

She shook her head, "I never saw him do so and Ophelia never mentioned seeing him or anyone other than two guards, my father, or Father Francisco. I am truly not certain if anyone else even knows she is here. Surely, they must, but I never heard a single word mentioned of her or saw the most modest reference to her in any of Father's documents."

"You know about your father's documents?" I asked, finding this highly unusual.

Her cheeks pinkened slightly.

"I may have searched through his desk once or twice."

"Once or twice?"

"Or many times. I also know how to open the safes in his study."

She could not hide her guilty grin at this.

"You are a bad, bad girl, Princess Zelda," I smiled.

She tilted her head and shrugged.

"So how do we get Francisco out of Tintagel or at least distracted long enough that we may move her?" Laoghaire asked, now fully invested in the adventure before us.

"And it must be done in such a way that he cannot narrow his suspicion to when *exactly* she left." Zelda pointed out.

"You are a clever girl and you are right. The less specific her departure is, the harder it will be to pin down who made it happen." I found I enjoyed the wily nature of my stepdaughter. She reminded me of who I wished I had been as a young girl rather than the stern, studious child devoted to babies and healing.

"This is where having so few eyes upon her is a blessing," she added. Her brow furrowed as each of us tried to imagine a scenario that would lure the priest away from the careful and judging eye that he cast on Tintagel's people.

Zelda clapped her hands excitedly, "Yes! Yes, I have it!"

"What?" I asked, the enthusiasm of her idea already contagious to me when I had not yet even heard it.

"It is not as close as I would want, but the Lughnasadh Fete is in but a fortnight. Cameliard will celebrate the beginning of the harvest. The day before the festival, the tax year ends for Cornwall and all the other lesser kingdoms, so they transport their year's worth of taxes to the High Court by carriage."

This was all news to me, but it seemed reasonable.

"And who accompanies this transport?" Laoghaire asked.

She smiled with tremendous satisfaction.

"The ruling monarch of the lesser kingdom and her advisers. There is a great feast at Cameliard and a grand ball afterwards and all of the lesser kings who are not out on campaign attend."

My face must have reflected the confusion I felt because she rolled her eyes and continued.

"…but since the sovereign of Cornwall is with child, she will be unable to travel, you see."

I did begin to see and appreciate where she was going with this.

"So," I said, continuing her thought, "if I appeal to the ego of Father Francisco and say that I trust him and only him to accompany the carriage to Cameliard in my stead because I am so very overcome with pregnancy…"

"…then he, Sir John, and Sir Charles, as well as half the King's Guard, I mean the *Queen's* Guard, are gone for a little over a fortnight."

I drew in a long breath and let it out.

"Zelda, it is perfect." In my excitement, I leaned over and kissed her forehead. "You are a bloody genius."

She looked stunned, but recovered quickly.

"You must not tell Ophelia of this," I said. "We cannot trust her not to tell Francisco in one of her weaker moments."

She waved her hand dismissively.

"He would not believe her anyway. There are times when she babbles completely out of her mind and he would presume it was one of those times."

I shook my head. "Do not take that for granted, Zelda, I am serious. This stays only between the three of us, understand? No one else must know." I forced her to hold her gaze to mine and reached out to take her hand for emphasis. "No one."

She squeezed my hand back. "No one," she agreed.

I looked at Laoghaire.

"No one," she promised.

"Now," I said, "We have to find a place to put her until we can move her to Avalon."

CHAPTER 24

    Within days, calculating the exact astrological moment that would lend the greatest energy to the act, my father worked high magic, stronger than any I have ever known him to do. Through it, the tumble-down cottage at the edge of the portal to the Faerie Kingdom became a lovely bungalow, fit for a former queen. Literally, one day I saw it and it looked as if it would come down if a strong coastal wind hit it just right. I planted the seeds of the apples from Avalon in front of the house and poured blessed water upon the soil around them. Instantly, a sprout shot up from the ground and through that, my father had an anchor for his magic. Only a handful of days later, the shambled cottage reformed into a cheery, solid, and welcoming home, clean as a pin and cozy as a mother's kitchen, complemented by a blossoming apple tree in the front garden.

    Once I knew the remote cottage was magically restored, I made good on my promise to visit Queen Aphia's realm again. Wanting no accompaniment on my journey this time, I plead out nausea in the early morning and said I would spend my day in bed and wished not to be disturbed. Laoghaire offered to care for me and under such orders no one, not even Bersaba or Ursa, would check on me for hours. Any person possessing an ounce of practical experience in the world would not dare to question a woman in the first half of her pregnancy who claimed to feel wretched. This also laid ground work for our story that would flatter Father Francisco into taking my place at Cameliard. My great fortune was that Sir Charles and Sir John brought the journey to my attention the day after Zelda told me about it. I feigned surprise and they looked worriedly from one another. I told them that I would return a decision to them within a week's time, which was mere days before they had to depart. My strategy was to avoid all conversation about the trip and head off any attempt at arguing that I should indeed go.

I slipped away from my room to return to Faerie, feeling as if miles of castle lay between me and the causeway. I made certain that my bedding was rolled in such a way that it appeared I was sleeping soundly and hurried down to the entry hall, careful to avoid anyone along the way. Laoghaire remained behind in my room to fend off anyone who dared come in while I was out of doors.

Once in the hall, I darted into an anteroom designed to hold the over boots and heavy coats of those attending formal functions within the castle walls. It had not been used since my wedding, so privacy was nearly guaranteed. Considering that my previous venture into the woods became a huge event requiring an escort and several rounds sung of *"Whatever shall we do with the Queen?"* I devised myself a plan.

Once I was secreted into the anteroom, I invoked a glamour onto myself that caused me to appear as an old beggar woman. Usually, a glamour is used to make oneself look lovelier or younger, but instead, I chose the visage that would least likely be stopped and questioned on the way. I thought again to Taliesin, employing a glamour onto Uther to let him take the woman he loved in the form of her husband. I hoped these residents of Tintagel were as easily fooled as those from the past. Once my disguise was complete, I left the castle and went into the courtyard.

I was concerned with what a glamour might do to the baby, but I knew from my training that a glamour is less about any change in the person themselves and more about how other people perceive them. This reduced my fear considerably, but still I infused my womb with a protection spell before I invoked the glamour onto myself.

My assumptions that I would be all but ignored in such a presentation proved correct. Courtiers trained themselves to look past anyone who might ask them for coins or food and my disguise assured that no one would pay me a mote of attention… save one. Earlier in the day, I met privately with Quinton and asked to meet an elderly lady at the end of the causeway and take her to the Faerie portal. I also advised him to tell no one of this, but to simply do it without question. Ever the obliging huntsman, he agreed, oblivious to the fact that I would be there to know if he failed to follow my command.

With my crone glamour knitted tightly around me, I waited at the edge of the courtyard until at last he appeared leading a second horse. He helped me onto it and soon we were riding toward the woods. If he knew the crone was truly the queen, he gave no indication and simply set about the task I asked him to perform. He must, I imagined, wonder why an old crone such as he saw want to go to the Faerie portal and yet, he did not question.

At the clearing's edge, I bade him to leave, telling him that he could find the horse tethered to the post outside the servants' quarters at dusk. I wanted plenty of room for the warped time I would spend in Faerie negotiating the arrangements I must make. When we reached the edge of the clearing, the dear man did exactly as I requested. He doffed his hat to the old woman who he had accompanied and then rode back in the direction of the castle with the horse she rode tied to the same tree we used before.

Too many people, I thought. *Too many people have seen too much too soon.* I prayed I was not being careless and that acting against my father's explicit warning would not be my undoing. He had willingly created the home in which she would live from a falling down shack, but I knew he did so only because he saw in my face that I was determined to follow through on saving her. I could only hope that I made the right choice. After this, however, *no more magic.* I would rule as the Queen and work to make Zelda and Laoghaire happy as I nested and awaited the birth of my baby. *No. More. Magic.*

As soon as Quinton was out of sight, I released the glamour and stepped through the portal, leaving my insecurities behind me.

Faerie was exactly as I had left it, in full fete that never ended. Again, Aphia and Presley greeted me with grand fanfare within moments of my arrival. When I told the Queen that I needed to negotiate a deal, her eyes narrowed and she licked her lips with obvious excitement. As much as Faeries loved good food, good sex, and good drink, they loved a good barter. I quickly explained to her exactly what I needed and what I had to offer in return. My mother taught me much about how to negotiate with Faeries: always look them in the eye, always offer far less than you plan to pay, be very specific about your terms, and always honor your debt. Faeries were notorious for finding angles the novice negotiator ill-considered in their agreement and exploiting them to the fullest.

I also knew that the one thing Faeries could never resist was gemstones. Fine jewels were not indigenous to Faerie and they had to obtained them from the outside world. Since opportunities to do so were few to none, they made fine bargaining tools and were quite valuable. That morning, I broached a conversation with Bersaba as she dressed me, asking about the history behind the jewels stored in the Queen's quarters upon my arrival. She gladly and proudly told me which ones were family heirlooms and which ones were left by the potential queens before me. Those, she dismissed with something akin to disdain. It was from that pile that I chose my stash.

My bargaining began with the three stones of least value, which I pulled from my pocket and laid onto the table in front of Queen Aphia. She smiled at me and picked one up, rubbing it against the shoulder of her gown and then holding it up to the torch light.

"Very nice," she said. "I suppose being a queen in the human world does have its advantages."

"And being queen here does as well," I countered.

"And so it does. Tell me, Iris, what does a queen from the human world want from us that she would bring such lovely barter our way? You care not for the food, for the men, for the women, for the drink. Your only interest before seemed to be taking the other women home just when they were starting to enjoy the party. What do I have that you want?"

"As it turns out, I *am* interested in your men. I need seven or so of them, but ones who are strong, protective, smart, and capable. Do you have such ones in your world of Faerie men?"

"Seven?" she asked, arching one perfect eyebrow. "Sounds like you want a very special party."

"Not for that," I smiled. "I need them as servants for a time."

"Have you so few servants in your castle? Why pay for Faerie men?"

A woman came up to the Queen and pressed her lithe body against her side as Aphia slipped an arm around her waist.

"Later, darling," the Queen whispered, kissing her delicately on the lips.

"Because I need their discretion and I may need their magic," I continued as the woman slipped away. "Court servants talk… a great deal… and they are accustomed to following instructions to the point that they are not the best problem solvers. I need servants for a very special task who can think on their feet and take care of any complications. They will be compensated beyond what I pay you. This," I gestured to the three stones, "is your own stipend. They will have additional pay."

"Indeed? How so?" she asked.

"There is a tin mine under the authority of the Cornish Crown directly toward the coast from the portal."

"The Tin Crown Mine."

"Yes. It was tendered to us as a tribute, but no one is working it. I can tell my advisers that I have hired workers to mine the tin in exchange for a half portion of the take. And you know what that means. You can do that thing that Faeries do."

"Turn the tin into diamonds."

"You can send as many to work the mine as you wish, but half goes back to the crown and have comes to you. I need seven men to work for me around the clock for me. It does not have to be the same seven, but I need to keep her familiar with who will be there."

"Her?"

"They are protecting an older woman who is very dear to me. They must cook for her, clean, be companions for her, read to her, massage her shoulders, hold her knitting wool, rub her feet whatever she needs."

"You know they will love that."

"Which is why I want men instead of women. No offense, but Faerie women are not…"

"None taken," she held her hand up to me. "We are not good at subservience and yes, we can get, well, *scrappy* at times."

I nodded. "I need servants who are devoted to her, who treat her like a goddess."

She smiled. "My men can do just that."

"The cottage at the edge of the Faerie Ring is now restored. They will live there with the woman."

"This I did see. How long are we considering this will go on?"

"That is the tricky part," I said. "It may be a month or it may be many months. I have no way of knowing."

"Then we shall negotiate as we go," she said, and I felt uneasy at her words.

"I prefer we make a pact now," I countered. "I do not like open ended arrangements any more than do you. I offer you these three to start, but will pay another three to you if it goes beyond three months."

"Five," she said. "Three now and two for each month that the arrangement continues beyond three months. Pay for the additional two months now and if you resolve your issues in time that you do not need the additional months, I will give the two back to you. Consider them a good faith deposit."

I pulled two more stones from my pocket and placed them on the table.

"To specify," I said, "I want seven men to watch over my Aunt Ophelia. They are to speak to no humans about her other than my stepdaughter, Zelda and my friend, Laoghaire. If her son, Phillip, is alive, they may speak to him as well, but no one else. They must maintain full discretion. They are to keep the cottage clean and act as her personal servants and companions. In return, they may work in the mine if they choose when they are not needed at the cottage, but their primary focus is to be my Aunt Ophelia and the needs of the cottage and all who live there. As many of your men as you wish may work the mine and you are to reserve half of what they harvest for the crown. Give it to Princess Zelda and she will bring it to the castle. I am paying you five stones now which covers five months. If I do not need the Faerie men for the additional two months, you will return the two stones to me. If the arrangements extend beyond five months, I will pay you a stone for each month. Is this agreeable to you?"

She spit in her hand and extended it to me. I spit in my own palm and shook her hand. Another thing about Faeries is that they never put anything into writing. Their word is their bond once you nail them down to specific, but nothing ever goes onto paper.

A few minutes later in Faerie time and likely hours later in my world, the deal was done. I did not use nearly as many of the gemstones as I expected and the remainder I would leave at the cottage for Laoghaire or Zelda to pay Aphia if needed. By my estimation, I had enough gemstones to barter nearly two years of Faerie man attention for Aunt Ophelia. I wanted no risk that should my pregnancy take an unfortunate turn, the Faerie support of the cottage would falter. When I returned to the castle, I would inform Laoghaire and Zelda of the arrangement and make certain they knew the location of the gemstone booty.

Refusing the Queen's offer to stay for the banquet, I pushed back through the portal, pulling the glamoury again around me and feeling satisfied with my accomplishment. We now had a place for Aunt Ophelia to go and a staff to care for her while she was there. All I needed was a way to get her to the cottage. As well as the rest of our plans were unfolding, I felt confident we would find a way to manage this as well. Optimism bloomed in me for the first time since my wedding night and it was a wonderful feeling.

I emerged to find the sun well against the horizon and my horse antsy to leave, so I pushed into the saddle and made my way back to Tintagel. Once the horse was secured and I was safely within castle walls, I released my disguise. A glamour is not complicated magic. Mostly, people see what they expect to see. Sustaining the glamour, however, is an ongoing investment of energy and can be quite draining. Even a practiced mage should not attempt to hold one for longer than a few hours.

With my head tucked low, I attempted to slip through the busy kitchen area unnoticed, but Ursa was there, helping to knead bread since I had dismissed her for the day from her duties as the Queen's handmaiden.

"Your Majesty!" she gasped, and everyone in the room immediately stopped what they were doing to curtsy or bow low. "If you had need of anything, you should have sent for me!"

"It was but an oat cake," I smiled. "I thought perhaps that would sit lightly upon my belly. It has pitched and rolled all day. I did not wish to trouble you for such a silly thing."

All aflutter, she said, "What you feed the bairn is *not* a silly thing! You go back to bed and I will be right up with a tray."

Genuinely exhausted from both the travel and the glamour, I thanked her and nodded to the rest of the staff, who returned to their tasks. That suited me fine. I was unbelievably hungry and it had been hours since I broke my fast in the early morning.

I eased myself into bed and Ursa arrived almost immediately with a tray of warm, rich bone broth, fresh fruit, and an oat cake. I thanked her and nibbled at the food rather than wolfing it down as I wished to do. When I was finished, I assured her that Laoghaire would summon her if I needed anything at all. She cast a stern look at Laoghaire, no doubt wondering if she would now be relegated to kitchen duties far more often than she desired.

Sensing the tension, Laoghaire said, "I do not think the Queen could make do without you, Ursa. Thank you for being so dedicated to my friend."

Ursa curtsied, her worries seeming resolved for the time, and took her leave.

Laoghaire crawled into the bed beside me and I told her the fine points of my trip into Faerie, but soon found myself drifting into sleep.

Well more than halfway through our plan, I knew that the next day I would have my first true obstacle: to speak with Father Francisco about his part in our strategy which he must undertake in total oblivion that he was an accomplice through his mere absence.

For now, I slept.

CHAPTER 25

Since the day he broke into my receiving room and was nearly arrested, Father Francisco had made genuine efforts to stay clear of me. When I attended mass, which I regularly did, the two priests carefully orchestrated for Father Damian to offer me the Eucharist. My petition to have Father Damian as my spiritual adviser with Father Damian managing the needs of the masses was dispatched to the High Court and would then travel to Rome for final approval. I made no further confessions and Francisco steered are wide berth around me. In fact, since the dressing down Sir John and Sir Charles gave him on that day, I saw the priest at mass and staring me down every night at the evening meal.

As such, it did not surprise me when I summoned Father Francisco to the library for a conference with me and the amiable Father Damian appeared instead.

I greeted him warmly, but was quite firm in my insistence that I must speak to Father Francisco personally.

The younger priest shifted uncomfortably and did not meet my eyes with his gaze.

"I wonder?" he asked with the questioning lilt his voice took in conversation, "If I might be of service to Your Majesty since Father Francisco is ill disposed?"

He looked at me hopefully and his face fell as I shook my head.

"No," I said. "I appreciate your offer and I regret the uncomfortable situation in which this places you, but I must speak with Father Francisco himself and straight away. I am certain you can arrange that for me?"

"Of course, Madam?" he said, bowing to me. "But are you certain…?"

"I am certain," I assured him. "Nothing whatsoever else will do and please inform him that this is a matter of the security of the kingdom."

"Very well?" he smiled. "I shall let him know?"

Servants and even advisers in the court mastered the art of leaving a room without turning their backs to me and still it amazed me. I could no more walk backwards than I could fly. It is likely why I was forever a terrible dancer.

Father Francisco looked around the room with obvious discomfort after he was announced to me quite some time later.

"Your Majesty," he greeted me with false cordiality. "No witnesses to either validate or police our conversation?"

"No," I said, offering him my ring to kiss, which he did, looking as if he fought down bile in the process. "It is only the two of us today."

"And what can I do for you?" he asked.

I motioned for him to sit and he declined, choosing instead to stand. It was unimportant to me whether the man sat or stood, but I did take note of the subtle defiance.

"I have been ill of late. I am not certain of word has reached you."

His expression became smug.

"I did take note that you were not at morning mass these three days."

"No," I said. "The pregnancy has caused exhaustion and illness that is beyond my ability to withstand," I said, intentionally keeping my voice low. "I am sure why you can see that this is not news I would like to take to all ears in the court."

"Of course not, Madam," he agreed, his face solemn and unreadable. "And you confide such a thing to me why?"

"I wish you to bless my child," I said. "My skills as a midwife have not served me in this case and I would like to know that a man of God has given blessing to my baby. It is what Marcus would want."

His face registered his surprise.

"Indeed," he said.

Much as a man would approach a wild animal, he ventured nearer to me, his hand extended.

Fortunately, I had Marcus's prayer book in my quarters and had correctly guessed and memorized the prayer I thought he would use.

"Our help is in the name of the Lord," he began.

"…who made heaven and earth," I replied. He looked stunned and then continued.

"Save your servant."

"…who trusts in you, my God."

"Let her find in you, Lord, a tower of strength."

"…in the face of the enemy." I looked directly at him as I said this and I suspected the next lines would ring harsh to his tongue.

"Let the enemy have no power over her."

"…and the son of iniquity be powerless to harm me."

"Lord, send her aid from your holy place," he continued.

"…and watch over me from Sion, I do pray."

"Lord, I do ask this on behalf of this woman."

"…and let my cry for mercy be heard by You, Oh God."

"The Lord be with you. Let us pray. Lord God, Creator of all things, mighty and awesome, just and forgiving, you alone are good and kind. You saved

Israel from all manner of plagues, making our forefathers your chosen people, and hallowing them by the touch of your Spirit. You, by the co-operation of the Holy Spirit, prepared the body and soul of the glorious Virgin Mary to be a worthy dwelling for your Son even as you put within this woman the deliverance of Cornwall. You filled John the Baptist with the Holy Spirit, causing him to leap with joy in his mother's womb. Hear our prayers, and grant the heartfelt desire of your servant, Our Queen, who pleads for the safety of the child you allowed her to conceive. Guard the life within her that is yours; defend it from all the craft and spite of the pitiless foe. May her child live to be reborn in holy baptism, and continuing always in your service, be found worthy of attaining everlasting life; through Christ our Lord."

He reached into a pocket in the folds of his robe and produced a vial of holy water, which he asperged over me.

"May God have pity on us and bless us and may He let His face shine upon us."

I knew this to be one of the psalms. I gave thanks for the Senior Druids who gave us careful instruction in the ceremonial genius of those words and forced their remembrance upon us as fledgling priestesses.

"...so may His way be known upon earth; among all nations, His salvation," I replied.

"May the peoples praise you, O God; may all the peoples praise you."

"May all the nations be glad and exult because you rule the peoples in equity; you guide the nations on earth."

"May the peoples praise you, O God; may all the peoples praise you."

"The earth has yielded its fruits; God, our God, has blessed us."

This verse was not included as part of the blessing of an unborn child, I knew, but was a reminder to me that in the Britain Beyond, the Christ prevailed over any of the Pagan Gods. I refused to grant him the satisfaction of seeing me falter on the words.

"May God bless us, may all the ends of the earth fear him. Glory be to the Father."

"As it was in the beginning," he intoned, "Let us give thanks to the Father, the Son, and the Holy Spirit."

"Let us praise and glorify Him forever."

"God has given His angels charge over you."

"To guard me in all my paths."

"Lord, heed my prayer for this woman and her child."

"And let my cry be heard by You, Oh Lord."

He drew the sign of the cross on my forehead with the water and he touched me so lightly, I suspected he feared my head would explode into flames when in contact with the sacred fluid. It did not, thankfully.

"The Lord be with you," he said.

"May He also be with you," I replied.

"Lord, we beg you to visit this dwelling, and to drive away from it and from this servant of yours, Our Queen, all the enemy's wiles. Let your holy angels be appointed here to keep her and her offspring in peace; and let your blessing ever rest upon her. Save them, almighty God, and grant them your everlasting light; through Christ our Lord." So rich were his words that I knew in my heart that he felt he could cast the evil out of both me and my child, which was my intention.

"Amen,"

"May the blessing of almighty God, Father, Son, and Holy Spirit, come on you and your child, and remain with you forever.

"So be it."

He stared at me for several minutes after we completed the calls and responses, not bothering to scutter away from me as I expected.

"Is that all, Your Majesty?"

"No," I said, and I drew in a breath as I prepared myself mentally and emotionally for the meat of this meal.

He waited with obvious impatience.

"Because I am ill and do not see an end to my weakness and stomach upset in time, I must ask you to accompany Sir John and Sir Charles to Cameliard to pay the kingdom's taxes."

"I?" he asked, his incredulous tone to that single sound temporarily revealing the insolence he felt toward me.

I nodded. "You are the only logical one to take my place. Zelda is yet too young to represent her father and with a change of sovereign, I do feel it is vital that we pay our respects to the High Throne in person and yet, I cannot. Even should I travel in a litter, I fear to slow down our passage at best and at worst, the potential for harm to the King's heir should misfortune fall."

"But of course," he said. I could see his mind reeling, attempting to find safe quarter in a conversation that truly disarmed him. It dawned on me that it was likely rare he found himself in such a position.

"You are clearly respected by the High Throne and Father Damian is well capable of shepherding our souls in your temporary absence. It seems only to make sense." I worked to weave a thread of desperation into my entreaty.

"Do Sir John and Sir Charles know of your request to me?" he asked.

"No," I admitted truthfully, knowing there was little love lost between the two men and the priest. "I thought it best to ask you first before I brought it to them as my wish and command."

"I see," he said, obviously pleased that I had left my advisers out of the decision.

"Father Francisco," I asked, willing tears to well in my eyes, "I formally ask that you serve in my stead for this diplomatic journey and convey my deepest regrets and reverence to our great High Court. I will not order you to do so if you wish otherwise, but it is my preference that you do as I ask."

For the first time since my arrival, his featured soften toward me and I felt a momentary stab of guilt at my overt manipulation of him.

He took his time in replying, obviously considering every aspect of my request, trying desperately to find the loophole that would hang him. My fear was that the guard who Zelda had paid off had gone to Francisco and informed him of our visit to Ophelia or that my aunt herself had babbled about my visit when she would have no way of knowing I was even in the kingdom. I watched him carefully for signs of any twinkle of knowledge he might possess of what we had done and saw none. At last, as I had hoped would happen, his ego won the race.

"I will do so, Your Majesty," he said. "I will begin preparations for my departure right away so that I am ready in time."

"Please understand," I said, "I would have asked you sooner had I known my illness would not abate. My late request is remiss to the extreme."

"No," he insisted. "No, it is good that you so carefully considered your condition and that you acknowledge the limitations it creates for you. Sir John, Sir Charles, and I will make certain that Cornwall is well represented to the High Court."

"You honor me and our kingdom," I said, "as well as our late King."

Again, I extended my ring and he kissed it, this time without quite so much hesitation.

"If you have no questions of me or guidance for my soul," I continued, "I offer you now your leave that you may make haste with your travel arrangements."

I suspected he would take the chance to enact further exorcisms of the Dark One from my spirit, but he merely bowed his way out of the room, even uttering a "Thank you, Your Majesty" to me as he left.

If our plan could continue forward motion until the men and their entourage were well on the way to Cameliard, the deed was as good as done. Thus far, the Goddess had blessed our goals with both concealment and opportunities and now, it was but a matter of days until our task was completed.

~*~

With all advisers preparing for travel, we forbore hearing petitioners that Full Moon. The representatives preferred to use the light of the Full Moon to increase the length of their traveling day, so two days before it reached full, they were on their way. The full assembly came to the throne room to ask formal permission to leave. Sir Charles and Sir John were not at all happy with my choice for their traveling companion, but did not try to dissuade me. Most on my side was the fact that it did make sense for Father Francisco to go. The three of them, the Master of Coin, a pinch-faced older man by the name of Percival, and half of the Queen's Guard marched out with tremendous aplomb, our banner raised high over the carriage and a fine array of red-cloaked knights around them. Paying our taxes and tributes without oppressing the people of Cornwall was a matter of tremendous pride both for the court and for the Cornish people, so the procession was more like a parade than a simple diplomatic departure.

The following morning, Laoghaire, Zelda, and I broke our fast together and finalized our plans, sending all servants on their way so that we could enjoy privacy for our scheming. Our biggest challenge was not that anyone would recognize Ophelia. Apparently, no one knew she was there, and thusly, no one would recognize her when we moved her through the castle. The devil, however, was in the details. Someone in the kitchen prepared the food that came up to her. Or did Francisco or the guard do it, bringing up whatever leftovers they could find from the evening meal? The latter was my most reasonable guess, but he must have made provisions for her care while he was away. Who would he choose to feed her in his stead?

I could not adequately sniff around and find out without risking others finding out that I knew. As to her absence once she was well and truly *absent*, we would play dumb. How were we to know what happened to her if we had not even known she was there? I had little opportunity for duplicity or outright deception while on Avalon. To be frank, lying around people who had The Sight was an exercise in futility and most children raised on the island learned early on it would avail them nothing but a swat on the bottom and some time in solitude to consider the disrespect in their actions. I wondered if I *could* lie when I had to for good cause or if my lack of experience would show through and I would be found out.

The guard at the door must be paid off in spectacular fashion and Zelda was quick to let me know which of the two was the easiest to manage. Fortunately, he was on duty that day and Zelda had established a grand rapport with him over the past several months. Laoghaire was little known among the servants and it would be best if she escorted my aunt to the clearing rather than me going with her. This plan allowed me plausible deniability should ever I be questioned. I would make certain that I was seen elsewhere in the castle at the time of the transfer.

As we ate our fruit, bannocks, and eggs, we tried to imagine any obstacle, any challenge at all that could present. At last, we felt we had covered every inch of planning territory and there was nothing more to do than to do it. We stared silently at one another for several minutes, each of us knowing the weight of what we were about to do and the trust involved on so many levels. If we failed, there was only ourselves to take accountability. If we had good fortune and succeeded, no one would ever know what a tremendous caper we pulled off between the three of us.

This was, there was no denying, High Treason against the High Throne of Britain. Anyone of us was as culpable as the other. My mind reeled with the many hundreds of ways we could fail and I knew theirs did as well. The route between the tower door and the cottage in the clearing seemed unimaginably long with witnesses at many points along the way.

    I thought again to the wisdom the elders on Avalon shared with me when teaching about the magic of glamoury. "People see what they expect to see." If we remained calm and acted as though what we were doing was the everyday business of life, surely no one would take a second glance. Four women walking together, chatting, sharing time, and visiting throughout the castle would certainly not raise anyone's attention… we hoped. In fact, we gambled on it. The Princess, The Queen, and her personal Lady in Waiting could entertain an elegant foreign dignitary that no one knew. They could even take the air with her out of doors.

    This was the work of the Goddess and was likely part of what I was sent here to do. I had to hold faith that She would lead me through the process and show me the way. With that thought in my mind, we set about our tasks, but *oh* what a hair-raising conflagration of events She had in store for us!

CHAPTER 26

If I were a great storyteller like my sister, Violet, I could go into detail here about how we did it, but since I am a simple midwife who happened by some twist of the fates to become the Queen of Cornwall and sole reigning sovereign there within a month of my arrival, I will simply say that we did it. It was neither easy nor safe, but we did it and I most certainly could not have managed such a thing without the two clever women who were my accomplices. Despite hell, high water, and Father Francisco, we did it.

We three made our way up the stairs which took the better part of an hour to climb in their entirety. I felt lightheaded as we ascended further and further, the floor disappearing beneath us as we climbed one narrow stair after another. The summer air was already muggy and my shift clung to me in a sweat under my gown before even we were halfway up.

I still could not breath well in the restrictive formal clothing and it came into my mind that if ever I again reached level gown, I would put on my priestess garb and refuse to take it off again. Now that my body was retaining fluid associated with a healthy pregnancy, my clothing felt tighter even than before.

"Are you unwell?" Laoghaire asked, looking back and down at me. I felt heat rise into my cheeks and steadied myself on the thin railing that ran along the stairs.

"A bit dizzy," I admitted.

"This is not the place to be dizzy," Zelda said, stopping to look back as Laoghaire had done. "Perhaps you should wait on the next landing."

I tried to draw in deeper breaths and realized all my body's strength seemed to have left me.

"Just to rest for a moment," I said, as I reached the small, square juncture that turned the stairs a quarter turn to move them further up the tower. I looked up and saw that we were a good three quarters of the way there and the way down was not nearly so challenging. The air in the tower was stale and dank and I felt my belly roll the morning meal around, threatening to eject it. I ran my hand along the back of my neck and drew it away soaked.

"We will go ahead of you and get started," Laoghaire offered. "Take your time."

They continued up the stairs as I perched on the landing, which was little more than a larger step in the staircase. After a while, I heard Zelda speaking with the guard. Sound carried well in the tower, but their voices were muffled. The conversation went on longer than I expected, but at last, I heard the door open and then a sudden burst of activity.

Drawing in a breath as deeply as I dared, I made my way up the rest of the stairs with the minimal haste I could demand of my body. I edged along the landing and was surprised to find that the guard was not at his post, but inside the room with Laoghaire and Zelda. Beyond them, I saw my aunt lying on the floor and Zelda and Loaghaire kneeling beside her with the guard standing anxiously over them.

"What happened?" I demanded.

"She's alive," Laoghaire said, "But barely."

"She was fine yesterday, Your Majesty" the guard stammered. "I went off my shift last night after Father Francisco brought up her food and when I left, she was her usual self."

"You did not check on her this morning?" I asked.

He shrugged. "Don't ever check on her. If she needs something, she tells me. Otherwise, she keeps to herself and does for herself."

Father Francisco knew he was leaving for no less than a fortnight. My mind reeled in ten, a hundred, a thousand directions and snagged onto one thought.

"Where is the food?" I asked. Laoghaire loosened Aunt Ophelia's clothing while Zelda poured water over a cloth and pressed it against the woman's face. My aunt was still as a corpse.

"Food?" the guard asked.

"The food that Father Francisco brought. What happened to it?"

"I...I don't know," he shrugged. "She ate it, I guess." He looked terrified, but what I needed was answers.

"No, she would not have done that. She rationed her food for the times when none came. Search the room. Look for any food you find, for the tray, for the drink...anything. Check the window sill where she dries the meat and the cupboard where she stores it."

I knelt with the other two beside Aunt Ophelia while Laoghaire tried to ease water between her lips.

At last, she made a sound, something like a groan and a sigh mixed together, and opened her eyes. Her gaze was unfocused and her eyes kept closing, but I could see her pupils were dilated.

"Lilian," she said, looking at me. "Lilian, I do not feel well."

Her voice was so weak I could hardly understand what she said.

"Has she hit her head?" I asked, hoping beyond hope to find a physical injury rather than what I suspected.

Laoghaire ran her fingers carefully over the skull area and shook her head.

"No swelling, no bleeding, no injury."

"Find that food!" I ordered to the guard.

"Here!" he shouted, pushing open a small wooden cabinet in the corner of the room. "This meat is no more than a day old and there is cheese here as well. Some wine as well."

"Zelda, I want you personally to pack up every morsel, every drop, and take it to my quarters, do you understand?"

I stared at her intently and at last, she read my thoughts and understood.

"Yes, Iris," she said. Unceremoniously, she poured out the contents of a wooden box onto a dressing table and slipped the bits of food inside of it, then tucked the wineskin the guard found into her belt.

"I likely do not have to say this," I made eye contact with the guard so that he saw that I was serious, "but I shall so there is no misinterpretation. You are not to breathe one word of this to anyone. Not a single word. If you do, you will be punished beyond your harshest nightmares and if you remain silent, you will be rewarded. Nod if you understand me."

He nodded.

"Now what I need is complicated, but it is essential that you do this."

Again, he nodded.

"You will pick up this woman very carefully and carry her down the tower stairs. You have climbed those stairs more than all of us put together and she hardly weighs anything, so you will have no problem doing this I presume."

"No problem. No, no problem at all, Your Majesty."

"Take her directly to my quarters. I stay where the King stayed. Do you know where that is?"

"Yes, Your Majesty."

"You are to make absolutely certain that no one, not one person, sees you do this. These ladies and I will be directly behind you. If there is anyone in my room, my ladies' maid or someone from the kitchen, you are to take this woman into the room next to it without being seen."

"Without being seen. No one is to see me."

"That is correct. What is your name?"

"Stephan, Your Majesty. My name is Stephan."

"Stephan, I cannot stress enough how important this is. Get her to my room and make sure no one sees her."

He nodded and stooped to hoist her limp body over his shoulder. As he did so, she choked and something dropped onto the floor.

Using my kerchief, I picked it up. A piece of food that was still in her mouth. Dear Goddess. It was true. It had to be.

He was strong, but he was swift. Stephan had her over his shoulder and was headed down the stairs before the three of us were in the narrow hallway yet again. We pulled the door closed and made our way down the stairs as quickly as we could, but even so, he was soon out of sight below us.

~*~

"Did anyone see you? Are you sure?" I asked.

"No one. I am certain. I encountered no one along the way and your room was empty when I arrived with her there." He nodded toward the bed where my aunt now lay. "Are you going to kill me?" he asked, his face going white beneath a layer of dirt that peppered it and his breath coming in nervous jags.

I blinked.

"Kill you? No, not if you do as I say."

"He will, though. He will kill me."

"Who?"

"Father Francisco. If he finds out I know about this. If he finds out that the Princess has been visiting or that you were in the room, he will surely kill me. He has done it before. I saw it myself."

I leaned in closer to him.

"Then we must make certain he does not know, mustn't we?"

He nodded.

"Stephan," I asked, "Do you have family here? A mother? A wife? A girlfriend?"

His eyes glazed over and I know he thought even more so that I would kill him for what he knew. He stood up straight and I could see him drawing up his courage.

"No, My Queen. I have no family," he said. "Just myself. All them that guards the cells have no family. They say it keeps us from doing the things we have to do if we have loved ones."

I put my hand on his shoulder.

"I ask only in case you wish to leave court. If you are truly frightened for your life, either from me or from Father Francisco, I invite you to take your leave of court, to get as far away from Cornwall as you wish. I bid you only to keep my confidence of what you have seen and heard within these castle walls. This will be enough and more to give you a new start elsewhere." I pulled a handful of coins from a nightstand drawer and made certain he could see them in my hand.

"I...I can go?"

"Of course," I said. "But do not linger in the villages. Go far away. And do not look for Father Francisco or anyone from this court again. Is that what you wish?"

"Yes," he said, "I have had enough of Father Francisco for this lifetime. Had I the means to go before, I would already have left. I will go to The Wall and fight with King Urien before I spend even another day in front of that door."

"And what of the other guard. Will he question when you are not there when he comes on shift?"

He shook his head. "It is not uncommon for the chair to be empty when either of us comes on shift."

"Will he check on the woman?"

Again, he shook his head. "No. We only enter the room if she or Father Francisco requests it."

I narrowed my eyes at him. "You two really are not very good guards, are you?"

"We are guards, Ma'am, not parents. When she asks for aught, we help her. Otherwise, we stay out of her way."

I moved the coins around in my hand and his greedy eyes followed them.

"Who else knows that the woman is there?" I asked. "Who comes to check on her? Who feeds her?"

"Just me, Eldon, and Father Francisco. Some of the royal uppity ups must know, but I only see Father Francisco come and go…and the Princess," he all but sneered. "She comes and goes as she whims to do so."

Zelda overheard and cut him a poisoned look.

I held out the coins to him and he took them with tremendous enthusiasm, disappearing them into his pocket.

"If you bring stories of this day anywhere in Britain," I threatened, "I may change my mind about killing you. You understand that, do you not?"

He nodded.

"Then off with you. And thank you for your silence."

"Thank you, Your Majesty."

"Take your leave and Godspeed."

He took his leave and wasted no time in doing so. As much as I hated having condemning information loose in the world, I could not tie the man into our web of treason against the High Throne. My sense was that he would do as he said and put quite some distance between himself and Tintagel. The Goddess loves irony and I condemned myself to resisting magic moments too soon. I knew I would break my vow before the night was over to do a binding spell on the guard and ensure his silence. By the time I was finished with him, he would barely remember what happened and imagine he won the coins in a game of dice, then decided to go fight at The Wall.

Zelda pushed a heavy chair against the door of my quarters while Laoghaire examined Aunt Ophelia.

"Her mouth is quite dry," she said. "Her breathing is slow and she is in a sweat, but it is hot as blazes today. She feels feverish."

"Nightshade," I said, pulling my handkerchief out of my bodice. "I believe she is poisoned."

"She needs to vomit," Laoghaire said, pulling Ophelia up into a sitting position and straddling her from behind, her legs reaching around the woman's thin hips.

"Zelda, bring me that case," I said, indicating a satchel next to one of the wardrobes.

Ophelia's head lolled limply against Laoghaire's chest.

Zelda brought the case and out of it, I pulled out a bottle containing a tincture that was guaranteed to cause anyone, even the nearly dead, to wretch.

"Hold her mouth open," I told my stepdaughter. She put her thumb under the woman's chin and pulled down with her fingers, causing her mouth to gape. I poured the tincture in and massaged her throat.

"Get out of the way," I told Zelda.

Quick as a cat she moved and just in time. My aunt began to heave mightily, going from lifeless to retching in moments. Bile and bits of food came up, telling me that it had been many hours since she ate. The dosage alone would determine the degree of damage the poison had done. Laoghaire held her up so that the woman vomited onto the floor beside the bed, repeatedly, even after she had nothing left to release.

Once she finished, I took another vial from my case, this one containing a powerful stimulant. I needed her awake, not sleeping.

"Again," I nodded to Zelda, who winced as she sidestepped the vomit to again open Ophelia's mouth.

This time, I metered out one dropper of the tincture and waited.

Ever so slowly, her eyes began to open. Laoghaire put her fingers against the frail neck and nodded.

"Stronger," she said.

"Get water," I ordered Zelda, who quickly moved off the bed and filled a glass from the pitcher next to my basin. "All the drinking water in the room."

She passed me a glass and I held it to Aunt Ophelia's lips.

"Drink," I said firmly, wasting no times on niceties. She did.

"I am so thirsty and my head... the pain...," she said, her voice weak.

~*~

"She was not addled, she was drugged, all this time?" Zelda asked.

"It is possible," I said. "One of the side effects of nightshade is hallucinations and disorientation. The fact that her spells would come and go seems to indicated that she was poisoned on an ongoing basis."

"But why did she not die before from the poisoning?"

"Dosage," Laoghaire explained. "The only true difference between medicine and poison is dosage. I suspect someone gave her just enough to keep her disoriented most of the time so that no one would ever take any of her claims seriously."

"Like that Phillip is alive?" Zelda offered.

Laoghaire and I exchanged glances.

"Perhaps," I said. "Or to keep her from trusting her own judgment. I remember she said that her memory played tricks on her, so she was aware something was wrong."

Zelda looked at Ophelia, who was now sitting propped up in bed looking absently at the wall.

"Will she recover?" she asked.

"She must have gotten quite a dose this time," I said. "It takes several hours for the poison to take effect. I suspect perhaps the person who poisoned her wanted to be well away from the castle before anyone discovered what happened. Zelda, if you had not befriended her, she would surely be dead."

"The person…" Laoghaire said, her voice dripping with sarcasm. "I think we all know who did this. He would not be here to watch her, so he tried to kill her."

"What do we do now?" Zelda asked. "We cannot keep her here."

"No," I agreed. "We move forward as planned and take her to the cottage. Zelda, I will need you to go back up to the tower room and pack up clothing and anything that might be personal to her and bring it to the cottage. Can you do that? Not a lot. Just enough for a few days. We will move other items as we can."

"Yes," she said. "I will meet you at the cottage then?"

Laoghaire nodded.

"Good, I will arrange for Ophelia and Laoghaire to get to the cottage while you pack. Are the two of you ready?"

"Ready," they answered together and I thanked the Goddess that I heard not one moment of hesitation in their voices.

~*~

While Laoghaire looked after Ophelia, I summoned Quinton, the Huntsman, to meet me in the library. Ophelia would have an exceptionally rough next few days as she recovered, but she would likely live. The quality of life she would have depended completely on how much damage her body had sustained from ingesting the nightshade, not just in a large dose as she had done recently, but likely over many months.

When Quinton arrived, I told him that I recently commissioned the cottage near the Faerie portal restored for my friend, Laoghaire, and her mother to use as their residence. Unfortunately, my story continued, her mother fell ill shortly after her arrival and would require special care in her transportation. We would need a litter arranged for her, as well as two horses that would remain at the cottage for their use.

He should also expect Zelda and I to visit our friends in the cottage from time to time as well. He looked confused, but accepted what I said in stride. I told him we wished to keep this arrangement quiet so that none knew that two women lived unattended in the woods.

He agreed and swore his silence. His job, as I informed him, was to provide them with the horses and litter and ensure their safe passage to the cottage, attracting as little attention as possible. He nodded his agreement and we arranged for him to meet them in the causeway. I reminded him that he was to tell no one of this and he nodded his understanding.

Ophelia had no strength at all, so we walked her between us, making sure to ease into the shadows during the few times that anyone passed us. With so many of the court members gone on the journey to Cameliard, there were fewer servants overall moving through the castle, so avoidance of servants and courtiers was not particularly difficult. In the causeway, Quinton helped Laoghaire into the litter, then we eased Ophelia into place beside her. Laoghaire wrapped her arms around the frail woman and Ophelia let out a breath of relief, relaxing into her unfamiliar embrace. Her extreme weakness offered her no choice but to submit to the care of those around her. As eager as I was to examine the food samples we retrieved from the tower cell and confirm my suspicions, my own weakness was wearing on me as well. I knew I would never again feel dismissive of women claiming exhaustion from early pregnancy. It was as though the life drained right out of me with every passing day.

I thanked Quinton and watched them ride off toward the bridge, praying the blessings of the Goddess upon them as they went. When they arrived at the Cottage, they would have food and assistance from the Faerie men who had arrived at dawn to prepare for their coming. My agreement with Aphia was that a few of the most trusted Faerie people would stay with the two women, protecting them, and providing them with food and any other needs they had. Zelda and Laoghaire would stay with Ophelia as she healed and then together, we would contrive some way for her to reach Avalon where my father could take her under his protection.

CHAPTER 27

When I returned to my quarters to rest, I found Ursa frowning over the vomit by my bed, believing it to be mine. I apologized to her for the mess and after she cleaned it up and washed her hands, she fetched broth, wine, and bread from the kitchen. My smile was weak as I thanked her and she looked at me with a scold in her eyes.

"My Queen, if I may speak freely, you cannot continue to deplete yourself in this way. The courtiers are gone. There is aught for you to do. Please, go to bed and rest."

I spent the remainder of the day in bed drowsing, moving toward and away from the edge of sleep. I must have slept at some point for I dreamt I was running through the halls of Tintagel, my feet bare and my heart pounding. No one else was in sight, but I knew I was not alone in the castle.

"Help!" I shouted as I ran. "Please help me! I must find my baby!"

I opened door after door looking frantically for my child. The hallways stretched in otherworldly ways so that I knew it would take hours for me to look in all the rooms. I could not hear him crying, but I knew he was there…somewhere…and that he needed me. I pounded on doors and then opened them, only to find empty rooms. There was no sound except for the slap of my feet against the stone floors, the pounding of my hands against the heavy wood of the doors, and my desperate voice, begging for help.

The scene shifted and I was outside, my bare feet slipping on icy stones and numbing to the freezing temperatures. I ran behind the castle and toward the abbey, slipping twice in the ice and snow, feeling the wind whip my clothes around me in an angry frenzy. Blood ran down my knee and I wondered vaguely if I needed to stitch it up. The wind intensified as I reached the door to the abbey and was so strong that I had to fight against it to pull open the door. At last, I wrenched it open, and there was Father Francisco with his back to me. He held my newborn son up to the macabre crucifixion sculpture, to the graven image of his Christ, and as he did so, his robes slipped down, revealing his bare back, which was wrought with deep scaring. As I watched, blood began to ooze from the scars and run down his flesh, drops staining his white robes that now hung off his waist.

My son wailed lustily, his lungs fully in command, and I could see even from the back of the chapel that his little fists were blue from the cold.

"Put my son down," I demanded, running down the aisle to where he stood. "Give him to me."

He ignored me, presenting my son as an offering to his murdered Christ on the cross while my son howled his righteous infant indignation. He was cold, frightened, and in the hands, literally, of my enemy.

As I ran toward them, the scene changed again and I was outside the chapel, still running so that I slammed hard into the closed wooden doors. My son bellowed from inside and I banged hard on the doors, demanding entrance, demanding my child, demanding to be heard. The crying stopped abruptly. Too abruptly. I banged hard on the door until blood ran down my forearms, dripping onto the snow below. The ebony door was unyielding. Oblivious to my pounding, it barely made a sound as my blood flowed harder from my damaged hands, the red standing in stark contrast against the pure white snow that now began to fall around me again, joining the hard-packed frost on the ground. The black ebony of the door, the immovable boundary between me and my child, was yet another contrast. Black…white…red… Like Zelda, like me, he would have had creamy white skin, red lips, and an aggressive shock of hair black as the ebony door. My mother's snow white skin and blood red lips, my father's ebony black hair. *Would have had… No… No… dear Goddess, no… no… no…*

I woke abruptly in a sheen of perspiration so heavy I could not tell tears from sweat, I had such an abundance of both. Still, I could hear the pounding, pounding on the door and as I came to my senses and wiped my face, I realized what I thought was pounding was only a light tapping and someone saying my name, "Iris? Iris, are you unwell?"

Without caring who it was, I said, "Come in" and Zelda pushed open the door, her face drawn with worry.

As soon as I saw her, I started to weep. The dream was horrible to the point that I even put my hands between my legs to check for blood. Had I, in fact, lost my baby already? Why would I think of him in the past tense in my dream when I could hear him crying? Until…I could not. The last part of the dream returning to focus. The silence from inside the chapel. I wept for Marcus and the life we would never had. I wept for my home and my family, so profoundly missed. I wept for Zelda who had no family anymore and who was so alone, she had to go to the Faerie Kingdom for comfort and acceptance. I wept for my child who would never know his strong, regal father. I wept for Marcus who would never know he had a son.

I felt Zelda slip a tentative arm around my shoulders and even my shock at her expression of affection could not break through my shroud of grief. After several minutes of my hysterical sobbing, Zelda poured water into the wash basin and dipped a linen cloth into it, wringing it out. She pushed it gingerly toward me as if she fed beef to a wolf and expected to lose a hand in doing so.

The cloth felt cool against my face and I took deep breaths, fighting to regain my composure. The last thing she needed was for the adults around her to lose control so that she had no hope of security.

"Thank you," I said when I could speak again. "I had a nightmare. I have not had many in my life and I am unaccustomed to how they can disarm a person."

"You… do not want to talk about it or anything, do you?" she asked, so obviously praying that I would decline that I had to smile through my sloppy, snotty tears.

"It was about my baby," I said, "But no, I do not need to talk about it."

"Oh," she said, without further elaboration.

"Tell me about Ophelia," I prompted, hoping to lose myself in the adventure of her day. The afternoon shadows played on the wall, telling me it was not yet night. How disoriented and disconcerted I felt from the dream!

"She is weak, of course," Zelda explained, "but she is awake and mostly lucid. She drank wine and ate a bit of food. The Faeries brought in enough for an army. Oh…" she reached into her pocket and pulled out a cloth wrapped bundle. "I brought you some sweet breads. Your friend said you liked them."

I stared, transfixed, at the bundle she put in my lap. It was no bigger than my two fists together, but for this moment, it meant the world to me.

"You brought this for me?" was all I could manage to say as tears threatened to erupt once again.

She shrugged.

"Well, it is only that you were so ambitious about helping my friend."

"And my aunt," I added.

"Ah," she said, "Yes, you did have a dog in that fight as well."

"I would have helped you anyway if I could," I said. "You are family."

She seemed to mull this for a moment. "Why do you say that? You barely know me."

"But I would like to get to know you better, as you feel ready. I know you care little for me, but your father entrusted you to my care and right now, you are the only part of him that I have left. He loved you and so I love you."

"Is it really that easy? For you to love someone?"

Something that was a short laugh and a scoff combined came out of me.

"If you only knew… I am probably the most practical and least loving of anyone in my family. Loving people does *not* come easily for me. Mostly, I have little use for people."

"Nor do I," she smiled.

"I love my parents, my sisters, my fellow priestesses on Avalon, but I always felt apart from them. They seemed to somehow appreciate one another to a greater level than I could. I felt as though I missed something that came easy for them."

"Was there anyone or anything that you really loved?" She sat down on the edge of the bed and looked at me intently, as though somehow, my response would hold answers for her as well.

I am not certain my wan smile provided any.

"I loved your father. Truly, I did. I loved the women who birthed under my care. Seeing them mighty and uncompromising as they pushed their babies into my hands moved me profoundly. I loved them for the feelings they created in me as we worked together to bring forth new life. I loved rubbing their backs, holding them up as they walked in labor, locking their gaze onto mine as we breathed together to work the magic of birth."

"You are not much older than I am," she observed, her face puzzled. "When did you begin learning about birth and know it was your calling?"

"When I was ten years old," I said, remembering, "my mother sent me to the birthing rooms to take Belen, our senior-most midwife, some herbs she needed for a particularly difficult birth. The herbs are often used to relax a mother enough that she can rest around the labor pains and regain her strength in a long labor for the pushing that is to come. Pushing is such tremendously hard work and if a mother is exhausted from a long and challenging labor, she may have trouble with the effort required for that stage of birth. I had never been around birth before and when I handed the herbs to Belen, she asked me to brew a tea with them to bring to the woman."

My heart warmed just thinking of that first encounter with birth and my hands itched with desire to massage a birth passage or lay warm towels on a woman's back or abdomen.

"While I made the tea, I watched as the woman rode the wave of her labor pains, how she gave over her power to the enormous task her body performed and in doing so, became more powerful. When the tea was ready, Belen helped her sip the brew and it soothed the woman's pain and helped her relax. I was mesmerized and from that moment on, whenever one of the priestesses was birthing, Belen and the other midwives invited me to be there."

"You have tended birthing women since you were ten years old?"

I nodded. "By extension, I learned a great deal about the use of herbs, tinctures, poultices, and other forms of healing. We only have a few babies a year on Avalon, so healing other conditions also was important."

She looked thoughtful.

"I cannot imagine knowing your calling from such a young age in life."

"But you were raised to be a princess and eventually, a queen!"

"I think that what one is expected to do because of their station and birth is often far different from what they are called to do, do you not?"

I thought about her words and felt the impact of what she said with tremendous alacrity.

"I do," I said. "Do you not wish to be Queen someday?"

She shrugged. "I do not think I have a choice unless you carry a baby boy. If I had my choice, no, I do not think I would choose to be Queen. Being inside these walls is a kind of torture for me. I feel most alive when I am out in the woods, not in Faerie, although that has its own appeal, but among the common people."

I felt an automatic flash of alarm go through me.

"You go among the common people? Into the villages?"

"And into the forests and to the shores where the fishermen work and to the mines."

It was clear that she was gauging my reaction, and I kept my face without expression so she would continue.

"I play with their children, talk with their wives, take them food from the kitchen sometimes when I can sneak it away."

"You are not afraid?"

She laughed. "I am more afraid here than I am out there."

"What are you afraid of here?" I asked.

"Afraid of becoming one of them," she picked at the finely stitched seam of her riding britches.

"One of whom, Zelda?"

"Those air-headed princesses who wanted to marry my father for his money and his station. The ones with no more to do than spin the neatest wool thread and gossip about who wore the finest gown to the last ball. I can never be that." She shook her head. "It would be a kind of death for me."

"Do you know Ophelia's story?" I asked.

She looked surprised. "No, do you?"

"Oh yes," I said. "She was raised in poverty by a drunken father and worked as a bar wench."

"How so?" Zelda's eyes widened in surprise. "She was High Queen of Britain!"

"Oh yes, she was," I said. "But she started life as common as any of your friends outside the castle walls. She won the heart of the High King and he married her. As it turned out, she was one of the wisest rulers our country has ever know and through her guidance, King Constantine became one of the greatest Kings of Britain."

"My father certainly thought not."

I laughed. "I remember. He thought him weak and ineffectual, a coward who shirked his duty for a personal vengeance, but that was before he married my aunt. After that, I suspect he took her guidance more often than not and as a result, Britain was moving toward tremendous prosperity and security during his reign and Phillip's."

"And now?"

I shrugged. "And now, the Church has taken over running the country and the taxation to support their efforts to convert every Briton to Christianity causes most of the country to live in poverty. We are protected here because of the revenue from the mines, but others, as you have seen, are destitute."

She nodded, "Not only in other areas. You believe what the courtiers tell you and they are not out there among the people. The miners in Cornwell are affluent, but anyone who does not mine is often taxed beyond their means. Mining helps those who work in the mine, the blacksmiths who forge the equipment, and the lords who own the mines." She laughed bitterly. "And the tavern owners."

I listened carefully to what she said to me and considered how keep her perspective on the situation seemed to be.

"Do your advisers tell you that the fishermen are in a seven-year downturn and struggle to fill their nets?" she continued. "Or that so many Cornish men and boys have gone to The Wall to fight the Saxons that the women, children, and old people who are left behind struggle to keep the farms and shops going?"

"No," I admitted. "To hear them tell the story, every person in Cornwall has a chicken in their pot and a bag of gold in their pocket."

She scoffed. "Far from it. Our people in Cornwall suffer just as those in the less prosperous kingdoms. The Queen's advisers, however, feed their egos with the delusion of abundance in our land."

"Do you not see, Zelda, how as queen, you can make choices for the kingdom that help those people? You can advise *me* on how to do so, then carry on the work when you become Queen. That is what Ophelia did. Because of how she lived until she was a young woman, she was uniquely positioned to guide King Constantine in making good changes for the people he ruled."

"But she was born common? I cannot seem to imagine that. She is so commanding and regal. When I met her, I knew that if ever I did become Queen, I wanted to be like her."

"The commonest common," I assured her. "Ask her some time when she is having a clear moment. She loves to tell that story of how she went from tavern wench to High Queen of Britain."

"Are you saying that you believe I can become a Queen and not be like the women here in court? That I can be myself and still rule?"

"Did your father not?" I countered.

"But he is a man," she pointed out. "And still, he was subject to the Church and often gave over his will to that of God. I do not know that I could bend the knee so easily."

"Would you have to?" I asked. "Kings and Queens throughout history have ruled in their own fashion. Besides, as you said before, who pays attention to what happens in Cornwall? We are in the far reaches of the country!"

Her mind was spinning, I could tell, processing this new way of thinking about her birthright.

"What would you do, Zelda?" I asked. "What would you change if you were Queen?"

The ambition contained in her instant response surprised me.

"I would find a way to help the workers in Cornwall and those who are unable to work and have no one to care for them. I would find a way to help the elderly people whose sons were lost in the war against the Saxons who now have no one to care for them, so that they live hand to mouth by what they find in the streets. No one should be reduced to stealing simply to eat. This should not happen in a thriving kingdom. I would tax the wealthy mine owners, but reserve a portion to create food dispensaries. I would provide incentives for farming families to work together to harvest their field so that no food lays waste into the winter."

I nodded. "I agree completely and Ophelia would agree with you as well. I tell you, she is a brilliant strategist and a wise counselor. That is why the High Court feared her and thought she would find a way to put Phillip back on the throne. When she is at herself, talk to her about your ideas. Tell her what you have seen and see what she feels you can do. I think there has never been a woman more in tune with how a country operates than my Aunt Ophelia. She will prove a tremendous resource and a wise mentor for you if she emerges from this latest disaster with her mind intact."

Zelda's eyes sparkled with possibilities, then her expression darkened.

"But do you not want your son to be King? To rule instead of me?"

I smiled. "If he wishes to, I support him, but he is not yet even born. I cannot feel him stir inside me and often, if I did not feel the need to vomit and were not so exhausted every minute, I would forget he is here. There are miles to go before he can even think of ruling. First, he must live to be born and then must live to be a young man. Then he must have an interest in being King and who knows what our land will be in nearly two decades' time? Meanwhile, you can rule in only six years if you choose to do so. In six years, he will barely have stopped shitting in his breechclouts. That is not who *I* want leading Cornwall. I would rather have the young woman who knows well all segments of society and considers the well-being of *all* Cornish people in her rulings. Not only the wealthy and affluent. I want a young woman closely advised by one of the greatest leaders our country has ever known, who also happens to be a woman."

She drew in a deep breath and let it out.

"Eat your sweet breads," she said, rising to leave. "You have given me much to think about, Stepmother."

"Can we," I asked, looking at her intently, "perhaps, have an accord, you and I? Zelda, I wish not to be enemies. I have no illusion that I can ever take your mother's place, but do you think that we could at least be friends?"

"I do not have friends," she said, her voice suddenly curt. "Not here, at least." She folded her arms over her chest.

"I understand," I said, opening the cloth surrounding the bread. Faerie bread was the most delicious luxury, nearly as good as the Avalon apples.

"But perhaps," she continued. "Perhaps we can be family. I do not have any of that either."

She held her hand out to me, then pulled it back slightly as though reconsidering, then extended it again. I took it and squeezed it.

"Thank you. For the bread and for saying that."

"I am going back to the cottage for the night to watch over Ophelia. I came only to bring you this and to tell you that all is well there."

"And again, I thank you for thinking of me thusly."

"Oh," she said, patting her tunic and reaching into a pocket. "I found this by the door of the cottage near the apple tree. For some reason, I felt it might be yours."

Curious, I held out my hand and she dropped a stone into it, the twin of the one my father sent. This one was veined with red lines and neatly faceted.

"I believe it may be," I said. "Your instinct was most accurate."

By the time she left, the sun had dipped below the horizon and the room was nearly dark. I lit a lamp on the bedside table and within minutes, Ursa appeared with a bowl of rich bone broth for me and sweet, dense bread. It stayed well on my stomach and I drifted off to sleep again full and comfortable. I did, however, leave the lamp lit to keep away any further bad dreams.

CHAPTER 28

The next morning after I broke my fast, I slipped the red stone into the crevice between the clasped hands at the top of my mother's mirror. Immediately, the mists began to swirl within the mirror and as they cleared, I saw the cabin where my aunt, Laoghaire, and Zelda now spent their time. I found that by tilting the mirror, I could see into the doors and windows, as well as around the outside of the area. Inside the cabin, which was larger than I first thought, several beds were lined up side by side. They were neatly straightened and I could see the women and four or maybe five Faerie men, short in stature, eating at a large table. They laughed and talked among themselves and it was a joyful scene to witness. Ophelia was sitting up and nibbling at the food in front of her, which was encouraging to see.

From my perspective, I saw them as though from across the room. At one point, Laoghaire stood up from the table and came directly toward me. I saw that she was talking over her shoulder to one of the Faerie men, then she reached just under my point of vision and picked up a comb and began running it through her golden locks. As she did so, she looked directly into my eyes.

My father had put a mirror in the cottage!

"Laoghaire," I said softly, completely unaware of how loud or startling my voice would be if what I suspected was so worked. "Laoghaire, can you hear me?"

Her hand froze in mid-comb and she looked stunned.

"Iris?" she whispered, looking over her shoulder and then back again. "Is it you?"

I could not stop my smile from spreading over my face. "Yes, it is me. Can you see me?"

She looked intently into the mirror, then smiled. "I can! Now I can see you. How are you doing this?"

"My father put a scrying mirror into the cottage and gave me a stone to connect to it from my mother's mirror. I can see you! I can see them! Is this not wonderful!"

"This is *amazing*," she said and let out a deep breath. "I felt so cut off here. Can I let you know this way if we have need of anything?"

"I am sure you can," I offered. "Or you can send Zelda."

Laoghaire leaned in closer to the mirror, "She will not stop talking about you, Iris. Whatever did you do to this girl?"

"What do you mean?" I asked, unsure if I should be happy or concerned.

"Everything is 'Iris this' and 'Iris that' and 'Iris says…' She acts as though you put the moon in the sky just for her and she is downright *animated*."

I let out a breath I did not realize I was holding.

"I am satisfied it should stay that way," I admitted. "I would much rather have her as friend than foe."

"You definitely have her as admirer!" she said.

I heard Ursa knock gently at the door and had only time to say, "I must go! I will find you later!" and to quickly pull the stone from its encasement.

Knowing I could contact both my father and my friends in the forest helped me to feel less alone and yet, I chastised myself that already, I had again used magic when I swore I would not.

~*~

"Your Grace," came the insistent, whispered voice in my ear. "Your Grace, you must wake."

I flew instantly up out of the dark depths of sleep to see Bersaba at my side holding a candle, her expression grave and drawn in its light.

"What is it?" I said, trying to discern the time with nothing but darkness around me. At this time of year, dawn came early, so it must be just after midnight. "What has happened?"

"They have returned," Bersaba whispered, even though to my knowledge, we were the only ones in the room. "The caravan to Cameliard is back. Herschel is helping them to dismount just now."

I pushed myself up in the bed, shaking off the last vestiges of sleep.

"Back? Why are they back? They would only now have made it to Cameliard."

"Best they explain," she said. "I will light the lamps and help you to dress."

With the speed and ease of one who has served for most of her life, Bersaba helped me into a shift and gown, foregoing the corset for now, and expertly brushed my hair and fastened it up on my head. Lastly, she chose one of the crowning circlets and nestled it into the folds of hair she created with the pins. In a matter of minutes, I went from dead asleep to fully regal and presentable. She helped me on with my shoes and we slipped in the main hallway.

Sir John and Sir Charles waited for me in the library where I conducted all of my smaller interviews and discussions. They looked haggard and worn. Sir John had dried blood on his face and new blood seeping from a wound on his temple. They both bowed as I entered.

"Forgive our appearance, Your Grace, and for waking you in the night," Sir Charles plead. His voice sounded tired and weak, although he had no outward appearance of injury.

"Tell me," I said. "What happened? Why are you not now at Cameliard?"

They glanced at one another and Sir Charles continued.

"Robbers," he said. "Our caravan was set upon by highwaymen not even halfway to Cameliard. They took everything. The taxes. All the tributes. Even the clothing but for what we had on our backs."

"Was anyone killed?" I asked, feeling the breath leave my body. I felt behind me for a chair and landed in it without ceremony.

"No one, not them and not us. They did not seem intent on harming, only on taking what was not theirs to take."

"How did they overpower you to the point of robbery without harming anyone?" I asked. "I do not mean to protract the obvious, but did none of the Queen's Guard fight for the treasure they carried? Are these knights not warriors skilled in combat and defensive arts?"

I could not help but think of how the Druid warriors on Avalon would have fought to defend such a bounty. Why had I never questioned the capabilities of the Guard? I merely presumed they were adept at defending the royal interests.

"These men," Sir John interjected. "They were like no warriors I have ever seen. They were fast and furious fighters. Their sword work was swifter and stronger than any I have seen. They came upon us as we crossed a creek bed that was swollen from the rain. The wagon could have made it across, but they had dug out the middle of the passage, so it sank down in the mud. They laid a trap and we fell into it."

He turned away from me, shame reddening his cheeks through the dirt that clung to him. I was used to seeing him immaculately turned out and it was odd to think of him muddy as a beggar and as smelly by half at least. I caught a wave of body odor from across the room and felt my stomach turn over.

"As soon as the wagon was mired, they were on us and they were like dancers across the wet rocks while we slipped and fell. They tied us to the wagon wheels in the swollen creek and took the trunks, the horses, and everything else on the wagon."

I looked at them warily.

"They tied all of you to the wagon wheels. They subdued every one of you with no injuries sustained."

They both nodded.

"Then why are you bleeding?" I asked Sir John.

"This happened after," he said. "I...I was assaulted in a village."

"He was in a tavern fight," Sir Charles all but sneered. "Like a common thug."

"I never!" Sir John insisted.

"He... He what?" As troubled as I was by the robbery, this story got better by the minute.

"We could not dislodge the wagon. To my mind, it likely sits in the middle of the creek even now. We walked back to the nearest village to attempt to commandeer horses to ride home."

"To that end," Sir John interrupted, "I went into a tavern to inquire as to a horse trader in the area."

"And the people there took him for a vagrant and bought him ale because it was a kindly town." Sir Charles shot him a look of disdain.

"And I was a bit too into my cups and fell as I was leaving."

"As you were being forcefully ejected, you mean."

Sir John shot him a fierce glance.

"There may have been a misunderstanding regarding a game of dice."

I bit back a laugh that threatened to shake my regality.

"I see," I said. A thought struck me.

"Wait. Where exactly is Father Francisco?"

"He went on to meet Prince John and explain what happened."

"On foot? That will take him weeks!"

"No, no, Your Grace," Sir Charles assured me. "The emissaries from the Summer Country came upon us while we were in the village and he rode with them. He will acquire a horse in Cameliard to return."

Sir John continued, "We warned the people from the Summer Country about the bandits and they made plans for an alternate route."

I nodded. "And so in the meantime, we are represented in Cameliard only by Father Francisco and without our taxes or tributes."

"That is correct, Madam," Sir Charles said softly. "My deepest apologies."

I thought for a moment. "There is naught we can do tonight. At sunrise, send me two of the finest and fittest members of the Queen's Guard and the huntsman. I will break my fast in here and wait."

"Madam?"

"You are excused. And bathe before I see you again. If that wound needs attention, please see the Court Physician."

"Madam, I must…" Sir John grappled with my assumption of authority in the situation, clearly terrified of whatever I planned. If he knew, he would be mortified beyond his current state.

I raised my hand to him.

"Do as I ask." My expression and tone invited neither negotiation nor challenging and I waved them off with my hand. Left with no recourse that other than insurrection or submission, they wisely chose the latter and left, bowing their way into the corridor.

~*~

I drowsed for a few hours, but felt no less irritated when I rose the next morning and Ursa helped me to dress for the day. I finished my morning meal, already missing Laoghaire's company for it. It would be easy for me to rely on the mirror to speak with her or with my father, but while I could excuse the use of magic for emergencies, I could not merely for my own amusement and reassurance, not after my blatant promise to Marcus that I would not do in his court. Granted, this was no longer his court, but that did little to assuage the essence of his influence, which was strongly against people who follow the Goddess and practiced magic of any kind. My narrow escape with Ursa the morning before left me uncomfortable, realizing that anyone could walk in on a mirror conversation and make my situation quite difficult.

No, whenever possible, I would follow traditional methods of problem solving and resort to the mirror only in times of emergency.

Quinton arrived as Ursa took away the tray of dishes and bowed accordingly. He kissed my hand when I extended it.

"Ever your obedient servant, Your Grace," he said. I noticed he held my hand for a few moments too long and looked deeply into my eyes with his golden-brown ones.

Oh dear.

"Obedience is exactly what I need right now, Quinton," I said. "This morning, please go directly to the cottage at the edge of the forest, you know the one, and inform the Princess Zelda that I have need of her presence immediately. Tell her she and I will ride out this afternoon on a very important task."

He did not try to hide the surprise in his expression.

"I will, Your Grace."

He bowed his head, but did not take his leave.

"You know her well, then, I suppose?" I asked.

"Since I was a young child," he said. "She is a few years younger than I am and often she and I spent time together in the past."

"In the past?" I arched an eyebrow.

"And sometimes in the not so distant past. I consider her to be my friend," he looked askance, "Well, as much of a friend as a royal girl can be with a commoner like myself."

"If you know her, you know she has little concern for such things as station."

"This is true," he said, "but I would never do anything to compromise her position. My family has hunted for the castle for many generations. There is no misunderstanding on my part about where the lines are drawn, if that is what concerns you."

I smiled. "That does not concern me. My point was that if you have known her for a long time, you likely are worried that she will refuse my summons."

He wiped away an errant smile with his hand.

"The thought did cross my mind, My Queen."

"You may tell her that I believe this is a task she will enjoy muchly. How about you? Do you feel up for an adventure, Quinton?"

His face brightened.

"With all due respect, My Queen, I would give about anything to see something different if that is what you had in mind."

"It is," I replied. "Prepare to ride out with us just past noon if you can get her here in time. We are going treasure hunting and we will not return until we have our reward."

"Yes, Madam," he bowed again. "I will bring her right away, kicking and screaming if I must."

I grinned at him again.

"I doubt it will come to that, but I do admire your tenacity greatly."

He bowed once more and left.

Immediately after he was on his way, two of the Queen's Guardsmen arrived.

"I asked for the finest and the best of you," I said as they dropped to the floor, each on one knee, with their swords out and grounded and their heads bowed. "Were either of you on the detail that arrived back in the night?"

"We both were," the tallest one said, "and we are prepared to accept whatever punishment you see fit to impose." This one was a great, muscular man, with flaming red hair like a northerner and powerful arms, bared in his summer tunic. His forearms were covered with the auburn colored hair and he looked like a magnificent beast kneeling before me.

"Punishment?" I asked.

"We failed in our task to protect the coffers of Cornwall," the other one, smaller and darker with more of a Roman look to him, said. "We stand before you in contrite humility to take the blame for the kingdom's loss and to shoulder the responsibility that falls onto the Queen's Guard for that loss."

"Stand," I said, extending my hand for yet more kisses. If I had to great many more, I would need salves to heal the chapping of the back of my hand.

They rose and stood at attention, looking as if they were a child's carved toy knights come to life. Their burgundy and gold robes flowed behind them, a stark contrast to their white linen tunics. My father once told me that many knights wore white tunics as a kind of arrogance, to display the blood of their enemies in prominence.

"There is no punishment," I said. "I have no time or patience for disciplinary action. I wish only to remedy the situation. We have, in fact, sufficient resources to send a second payment of the same value to Cameliard, but I have little desire to do so. I want our treasure back. If you are indeed the brightest and best of our Queen's Guard, then tell me what you noted of the men who stole from us."

"There was a dozen or so of them," the smaller, darker one offered. "They were dressed as hill folk, not as soldiers or knights. They were all ages, all sizes, all kinds of men. There was one woman among them who was just as good of a fighter as any of the men."

"Sir John and Sir Charles told me that they seemed not intent on harming anyone. Is that also your impression?"

"Indeed," the one who looked like a Northerner said. "They had swords, bows, knives, and other weapons, but they used them defensively, not to attack. They overpowered us by the element of surprise, by being so damnably fleet of foot, and by guile. Truly, Your Grace, nothing else."

"The leader of them ordered that they leave half of the food we had on the wagon to sustain us and they took the other half."

I considered this.

"They must be in need of food, otherwise, why take the food at all?"

The larger one grunted, "They were the most well organized bandits I have ever seen. I served three different kings in my life and fought the Saxons hand to hand and never did I see anything so well-planed and well-executed."

"I am sorry," I said, "What is your name?"

"I am called Sir Rory," he said, "I received a knighthood from your late husband and was honored to serve him for many years. And this is Sir Fergus. I would trust him with my very life and he has saved my skin on more than one occasion."

"Your servant, My Queen," Sir Fergus said.

"Knowing what you know about the men, or people, who took our coffers, would you think there could be any way of tracking them? Of getting back what they took from us?"

They looked at one another as though daring the other to speak.

"I know the direction they ran when they left us," Sir Rory said. "I was tied on that side of the wagon. If there has been no further rain in that area, we might see the tracks and find them again, provided they stay in one location. Many of the bands of highwaymen are nomadic."

"One has to consider, however, that in this case, we were targeted. This was no lucky score for the bandits. I suspect they know that the taxes are en route to the High Castle and are taking the treasure caravans destined for Prince John and the High Court." I looked at Fergus again and saw such a gleam of intelligence in his eyes that I was intrigued. The best of the Guard indeed.

"An interesting observation," I said. "You have thought of this. Tell me more."

"As Sir Rory said, they knew exactly what they were doing, what they were looking for in the wagon, and how to get in and get out. It would not surprise me at all if Father Francisco finds that other caravans were robbed on their way to pay taxes."

"Tell me about their leader."

Sir Rory said, "He was British, spoke with a fine accent, not rough like most bandits. He was masked, as were most of them, so I could tell nothing about his looks, but he was especially good with the quarterstaff."

"Truly?" I was intrigued.

"I am leaving today to find their camp," I said definitively. "I want my treasure back and I am not returning without it."

Sir Rory opened his mouth to speak, then promptly closed it again.

"Madam?" Sir Fergus said.

"Will the two of you accompany me, since you know the ways of this group of bandits? I am also taking Princess Zelda and Quinton, the Hunter, who is an excellent tracker and knows the woods well."

"Just the five of us are going after them?" Sir Rory at last found his voice.

"We are going after our treasure. I could not care less about them. Are you willing? For I will not force you to go when you only now have returned."

"Your Grace, I cannot advocate for both sitting monarchs to be in the same danger at the same time, away from the throne…"

"So noted, Sir Rory. Your concern implies danger, yet you have indicated that these bandits show no interest in harming anyone, so while I understand your concern, I do not share it. May I expect your assistance or not?"

"I am ever your devoted servant," he said, bowing his head.

"Sir Fergus?"

"At your service, My Queen."

"Prepare my finest wagon and fly our banners high. We will take on cargo, but from the kitchen, not the treasury. Tell *no one* where we are going under your blood oath to this court. This is a secret mission and I will decide upon our return whether to make the details public. Do you understand?"

"Yes, Your Grace," they both said together.

"I have work to do in preparation for our departure. Arrange our transportation and meet me and the others in the causeway for departure by midafternoon. Answer no questions."

"Yes, Your Grace."

I went to the kitchen myself and inspected our larders, including the root cellars and other layback areas. I ordered bags of barley, haunches of dried meat, oats, root vegetables, and other foods packed up and set aside for the departure.

"Queen Iris, what on earth are you doing?" The head cook, Elsie, looked at me as if I had gone quite mad.

"We are feeding the hungry, Elsie. In tribute and from our harvests, we are well blessed. This court will share its blessings with those in need."

She scoffed.

"With all due respect, you will be the one in need if you keep at it."

"And make certain that the servants here who take care of the court have sufficient to feed their families," I ordered. "No one goes hungry within my court walls." I remembered Zelda's concerns and thought that later, perhaps, we could extend our generosity beyond the walls of the courtyard, but this was indeed a start.

"Yes, Madam," she said.

"You know the food supplies better than anyone," I said, placing my hands on her shoulders. She stood all of maybe four feet tall and had to look up to speak to me. "Our harvest yields in what, a month? Two?"

"Something like that, yes," she agreed.

"And second harvest in three? Four months?"

"Indeed, yes, we get it all in before All Saints Day so as not to let it spoil in the fields."

"We have gold to buy more if it is needed and this is all from last year's harvest, is it not?"

"Yes, last year and the tributes paid."

"Keep back enough to run our household twice over, just in case worse should ever come to worst. The rest, I wish to see put aside. I am going on a diplomatic campaign and when I return, we shall distribute. For now, I need what I have set aside and whatever else you can spare into the causeway for transport. Rally up the men with strong backs and arms to help you move it."

"Yes, Madam."

"I am taking a wagon and a carriage with me. Bring out no more than will fit into our best wagon."

"Yes, Madam."

"What are you *doing*?" I turned to see Zelda gaping at me from the doorway into the kitchen area.

"It is what *we* are doing," I corrected.

CHAPTER 29

As I expected would be the case and in fact, counted on, Zelda was fired up and ready to ride as soon as I gave her the overview. Quinton joined us in the library and the prevailing attitude was less of "I am not sure we should" and more of "How soon can we leave?"

Zelda and Quinton would use their tracking abilities and their knowledge of how to negotiate wooded areas to get us to the exact location where the previous caravan was set upon. Sir Fergus and Sir Rory were our muscle and our strategists, given their experience with how our adversaries operated. Looking at how things happened with hindsight provided far greater perspective than when they were blindsided.

I needed air, wanted to be in the action, and refused to again send others out to do my duty, so despite the warnings of four knights, I was going. The royal carriage awaited. Quinton drove the carriage team from on top while Sir Fergus rode a fine steed ahead of us and carried our court banner, proudly displaying our mission. Sir Rory brought up the rear with a heavily laden wagon, its cargo covered, filled with food supplies, beer, and wine. Anyone seeing the wagon would presume it was our tribute and tax money, leaving late for Cameliard.

My fingers and neck I covered with the jewels of the jilting royals who sought to marry Marcus and abandoned their baubles to escape the wedding, leaving my own jewelry and that of Zelda's mother locked away in my quarters.

The weather was unseasonably fair and we made splendid time. I slept often and visited with Zelda when she remembered I was there. Mostly, she chose to ride on top of the carriage with Quinton. She was in fine spirits and excited for the adventure. Dressed in riding britches and a tunic with her hair tucked up into a hat, she looked more like a stable boy than the future Queen of Cornwall. She was within her comfort, however, and it showed. Inside the carriage, I could hear her laughing with him and relished in her happiness. Just as I came to care for her father quickly and intensely, this young woman, so dynamic and engaging, was creeping into my heart as well. There was a spirit in her that I admired and even craved.

As so many of the priestesses on Avalon, I was duty bound from the time I was quite young. We worked hard every day and although we took our fulfillment from the experiences and people around us and out of servitude to those same people, I never felt the unbridled joy I heard in her voice. I wondered how different I would be had I not been pledged to service to the Goddess from birth. We certainly had plenty to eat for the trip since our cargo was food. We traveled long hours, stopping for only a short while at night so the men could sleep. The moon was nearing full and coming into the Harvest Moon, it shown brightly and allowed us to continue traveling even after dark. I wondered at the stamina of the men who never complained and kept riding, on and on. I had the luxury of dozing in the carriage where the temperature was always pleasant. At night, the air was cooler and comfortable and in the day, a steady breeze kept away heat and stagnation within the carriage.

Zelda slept inside with me at times as well, but never for more than a handful of hours and then she would be back up on the carriage, speaking in hushed tones if she knew I was resting. That she could externalize to take someone else's wellbeing into consideration flew so in the face of how others described her to me that it gave me hope that she could come to care for me as well. I remembered her father's words to me before we married regarding her, that she was always biddable and well-behaved in his presence. I could see now that she likely was so without the contrived machinations I imagined.

We stopped for an afternoon meal with the sun high and bright on the second day of travel. The terrain had changed to open fields, nearly ready for harvesting, and as we ate, Sir Fergus leaned in and whispered, "Fear not, My Queen, but we are being watched."

"Aye," Sir Rory agreed, also keeping his voice low. "They have been with us for some time now and not far ahead is where our wagon mired in the creek."

"Was then the village we just passed through where Sir John met his misfortune?" I asked.

Their eyes widened and they exchanged glances.

"You know of that, then, Ma'am?" Sir Rory asked.

"Likely not all, but as much as I wanted to know," I said, biting into a tough piece of dried venison, and washing it down with a cup of beer.

"Yes, it was there," Sir Fergus confirmed, shaking his head. "I never saw a man so blighted as was he."

Quinton came back from a jaunt into the neighboring woods with three quail slung over his shoulder and laid them near where we sat.

"Thought you might enjoy a hot meal tonight, Your Grace," he said, his eyes twinkling merrily.

"That sounds lovely," I agreed, "I quite fancy quail."

"I love quail," Zelda said at the same moment I spoke and I realized we each thought we were the one to whom he referred. Zelda look at Quinton and I in turn and recognized her discomfort. She was sweet on Quinton, as if I had not suspected before.

"King Marcus also enjoyed quail as I recall, did he not, Zelda?"

"He did," she smiled at the mention of her father and the tension broke apart.

"You know we are being tracked, eh?" Quinton said.

The men nodded and Sir Rory said, "No doubt by them or others like them. This is near where they hit us. Like as not, we will be overcome before ever we get to cook those fine birds of yours."

"Stay to the plan," I advised. "If what you suspect is true, no one will harm us and if I can negotiate a trade, we can get back our coffers and pay our taxes without losing the esteem of the High Court."

"Will not Francisco already have told the High Court our plight?" Sir Fergus said quietly.

"That covers us if this is unsuccessful," I said. "I certainly cannot imagine the High Throne declining our taxes should I bring them forth. My ambition is to keep the eyes of the High Court off of Cornwall as much as we can. Failure to pay taxes under a new sovereign does not accomplish that goal at all."

"From your lips to God's ears," Sir Rory scoffed. "The last thing we want is those jackals breathing down our backs."

"Bad enough with Francisco poking his nose in everywhere and running that mouth of his. It is no wonder the bandits found their advantage. Could not hear a thing over his constant praying and prattling."

"Never imagined traveling with two women would be quieter than with that lot," Sir Fergus added.

"Ah, now watch yourself, Fergus," Zelda scolded. "Some of the best rulers Britain has known were women."

"True that," Sir Rory agreed, raising his cup of beer and draining it dry. "I got no compunction serving under a woman, especially one willing to go out and steal back her own treasure." He lived the empty cup in mock toast.

"Shall we get to it then?" I asked, standing to brush off the skirt of my dress, ridding it of dry grass, sticks, and underbrush stuck to it.

The creek was not as swollen as before when the first wagon became lodged. I could see the water marks on the banks where recently, the level was higher, but the warm, long days had dried it a bit. Our wagon was nowhere to be seen, no doubt salvaged by the same people who stalled it out in the first place. They were nothing if not resourceful.

Quinton drove the carriage easily across the creek at a crossing slightly further down than from the previous location. On my order, Sir Rory crossed with the wagon at exactly the same place where they had been stuck before. Sure enough, the wagon hit the same ditch as before and sank so far into the creek that the horses could no longer pull its weight out of the hole.

At that moment, men seemed to descend from everywhere, from the forests around us, from bushes on the creek banks on both sides, and even out of the canopy of trees above. They hooped and whooped as if they were at a festival. I felt a rush of instinctual fear, but then saw that, exactly as was described to me, they seemed not at all intent on harm. As I had ordered them to do, Sir Rory and Sir Fergus stepped back with hands up and visible as soon as they saw the men, moving away from the wagon. I stood on the far side of the creek with Quinton and Zelda, watching as the men flocked to the wagon like flies, pulling at the coverings.

"They certainly are efficient," Quinton said under his breath.

"I will need those baubles, Your Grace" said a voice behind me. None of us heard him approach, but there he was, nonetheless. He was taller than I was, and I carried my father's height, which was tall for a woman. Dark curls peeked out from under his roughly hewn mask which was little more than a burlap bag with holes in it.

"You need a better mask," I observed.

"And you need a better entourage," he countered.

"Do I?" I smiled

His voice was, indeed, smooth and cultured. He reached for my hand and removed the rings from it and then the other, then kissed each finger in the place now empty of its jewel.

"The ones around your neck as well, if you please. You may remove them yourself or I can share the intimacy of removing them for you. Either way, they are coming with me."

An eruption of shouting from the creek drew his attention.

"'tis only food!" a man yelled from atop the wagon. "All the way down, just food stuffs."

I smiled widely.

"Why do your men not resist?" the man beside me asked, his tone suddenly suspicious. "I understand this beautiful woman standing back, but do your men not have the courage nor the valor to defend you?"

"From what should they defend me?" I asked. "You taking jewelry that means nothing to me and the food I brought for you?"

His posture shifted immediately, rocking back on his heels with his fists on his hips, my jewelry still in his hands.

"Who *are* you?" he asked, staring hard at me, then he gasped audibly. "Iris?"

Now, it was my turn to be stunned. Who was this man to know my proper name and to use it in the familiar sense?

In a flash, the voice made sense to me, and the realization flooded over me like ice water. I fell to the ground, hard, on my bottom.

"Phillip?" I said, looking up at him.

"Iris!" Zelda shouted, kneeling beside me. "Iris, are you well? Is the baby…?"

"Baby?" my cousin said, absently pulling the bag from his head, revealing his face, which was far older than when I last saw him. Then, he had been a knobby kneed, annoying boy who asked too many questions and was more than slightly full of himself.

"Phillip?" I said again.

"What?" Zelda turned toward him. "Phillip? King Phillip?"

"Sssssshhhh," Phillip said, holding a finger to his lips.

"Your Grace," Quinton said, dropping to the ground in submission to Phillip.

"You are a loyalist?" I hissed to Quinton.

He stared at me hard and said, "It does not detract from my service to you, My Queen."

"Queen?" Phillip said, clearly astounded. "And you are pregnant? And here?"

"What do you want us doing with all this, Arthur?" the man on top of the wagon called out. "There is neither a jewel nor a piece of gold anywhere here."

"Shit," Phillip said under his breath, holding his hand out for me to grab onto as he hoisted me up to standing again. "What are you playing at here, Iris? What is going on?"

Zelda did little but stare at him as if he were a new breed of bird that landed in the courtyard.

"Leave it for now," he shouted to the man. "All is well."

The man waved a hand at him in outright dismissal, obviously frustrated by the turn of events.

"Tell me quickly why you are here and what you are doing for your story influences greatly how the rest of the afternoon unfolds."

As he spoke, Phillip clamped his hand onto my upper arm and only then did Quinton step forward.

"Sir, with all due deference to who you were before, I have to insist you unhand the Queen. I cannot allow her manhandled, even by you."

I smiled. "He will not harm me, Quinton, but thank you. Phillip was always a dramatic little thing."

"I am but a year younger than you are!" I heard the insolent child I remembered ring through his voice.

"Phillip was always a dramatic little thing," I repeated to Zelda and Quinton with an affected tone of confidentiality.

He did release his hold on me and asked again, "Iris, why are you here, dressed like this, hauling enough food for an army, protected only by two guards and these two miscreants?" He gestured to Quinton and Zelda. "You are a princess of Avalon. As such, why are you even *off* Avalon?"

"Shall I speak now?" I asked, raising my eyebrows.

He gestured a grand welcome that I do so.

"Less than a week past, you robbed my wagon and took my taxes and tributes and I want them back."

He laughed. "Oh you do, do you?"

"Yes," I said firmly. "I do and you are going to give them to me."

"Am I?"

"Yes, you are and I brought a wagon full of food to trade for them."

"And why exactly do you think that food is of any value to me?" he folded his arms across his chest. "If I did as you say and robbed your wagon, would that treasure not pay for much more food than is in this wagon?"

"You took half the food that was in the first wagon and left the other half. If you did not need food, you would have left it."

"And how is any of this, the food, the treasures I may or may not have commandeered, of any interest to you? Why do you claim it is yours?"

"Have you not listened to them?" I asked. "I am Iris, Sovereign Queen of Cornwall. I have been so for less than two moon cycles and I will not allow you to disadvantage me to those snakes who sit now upon your throne. If those taxes and tributes do not reach the High Court, I will have the whole of Christendom breathing down my neck."

"Cousin or not, I will hear no lies from you," he said, his voice not nearly as harsh as his words. "King Marcus rules in Cornwall and has for ages. I should know, I escaped from there barely with my life."

"King Marcus is dead," I said. "And he was my husband. By his order, I rule in his stead."

He looked to Zelda and Quinton, who both nodded.

"And I want back what you stole from me right now."

"You will need more than a wagon of food to convince that lot to not take the food and the treasure they took before as well."

"You are their leader," Zelda said, "Maybe you should convince them."

He eyed her so intently that she looked away.

"And why would I do that?" he asked her.

She boldly met his stare.

"Because we have your mother and can get you to her."

His eyes hardened.

"Now you really have crossed a line, son. My mother is dead." His tone could have cut into bone.

"Huh," I said, then realized I had done so aloud rather than just in my head. I was unsure whether I said it about the fact that he thought Zelda was a boy or that he thought his mother was dead.

"What happened to Aunt Ophelia, Phillip?" I asked, wanting more to see what he thought he knew than what he actually knew.

"They killed her," he said. "Your husband? That priest? They took her out of the cells where they held us captive and they tortured her until she died."

I blinked and slid my eyes to Zelda, who looked as confused as I did and shook her head.

"Did you see this happen?" I asked, choosing my words carefully.

"I saw them take her out," he answered, "and then the priest came back and told me that she had not survived his 'questioning.' That is when I knew I had to escape or I would be next. Without my mother, I had nothing left to live for except making those who took my throne pay in every way I could."

I reached for his hand. At first, he jerked it back, but then he let me take it and hold it. It was not the hand of a King. It was calloused, hard, and dirty. I tucked it between my two hands, which were thin and ivory colored around it.

"Phillip," I began, "Your mother is not dead. I saw her but two days' past. She lived in the tower at Tintagel and her cell was beautifully decorated. Mind you, a cell it was, but she was not tortured and she did not die. I took her out of the cell and now she lives in the forest near Tintagel with Laoghaire, a friend of mine."

He stared at me as if he wanted to believe, but could not.

"Father Francisco told her that you were dead, but she does not believe it. She says she would know if you died and now, she waits for you to come back to her."

The authenticity of my words struck him like a hammer blow.

"Truly. She is alive?"

Zelda and I nodded. Quinton looked confused and then I remembered that he thought Aunt Ophelia was Laoghaire's mother.

"Sorry," I mouthed silently to him. "It was a matter of Court security."

He narrowed his eyes at me, which I would take for insurrection if it were not utterly warranted.

I slipped my hands around the back of Phillip's neck and put my forehead against his. Now, he was the one who looked as though he might faint.

"Phillip," I said, tightening my grip on his neck. "Phillip, take the food, do whatever it is you do with the food you steal, and get me my damned treasure back here or I swear to the Goddess, I will find a way to destroy you. Get. Me. My. Treasure. Understand?"

I felt bullets of sweat begin to form under my hands and I knew he was processing all I had said, then processing it again and again. Shock would do that to a person. I had plenty of recent experience with true shock.

At last, he nodded and I let go of him.

As he looked up at me, his eyes were filled with tears.

"No one at Cornwall will hurt you now," I said. "They are my people, but I do recommend that you stay in the forests when you come to visit your mother. She will be thrilled to see you. Quinton, can you help him find his way when the time comes?"

"I can," the huntsman agreed.

"And I as well," Zelda hurriedly offered.

I smiled and nodded.

"She is alive, then?" Phillip asked. He looked like a lost child who finally found his way home. "It is true? You are sure?"

"She is alive. I swear to you, and we will take you to her."

He took a heavy breath in, out, and then another. And another.

"Arthur!" the man who shouted at him before was now off the wagon, standing ill at ease with the rest of his crew. The two Queen's Guardsmen still stood off to the side. The man made an exasperated gesture at Phillip.

"Come to the shore," Phillip yelled back. "I must speak with you all."

CHAPTER 30

We stayed that night at Phillip's encampment. He blindfolded us before leading us there, insisting that outsiders had never before seen how to get to it. It took some convincing to get Quinton and the two Queen's Guardsmen to accept their blindfolds, but Zelda was so eager to see it that she blindfolded herself. Admittedly, I did not yet fully trust my cousin to keep his end of the bargain, but could not ignore the fact that I was far better positioned than I might have been had my plan as failed miserably as it could have done. In fact, this was likely the best possible outcome I could hope for. As I rode in darkness, feeling oddly disoriented on the horse they had me mount without the benefit of sight, I realized how ragged my plan had been. No doubt, my companions, save perhaps Zelda who only wanted the adventure, would have disavowed themselves of it had I not all but ordered them to do it. And yet, here we were.

At last, the horse stopped and someone helped me off its back. I closed my eyes against the late afternoon sun as the blindfold came off and then eased them open again. Their campground was more like a child's playhouse with roughly built shanties scattered here and there, ropes hanging from trees with platforms here and there throughout.

A large, central fire pit was the focus of the area and several women and children gathered around it, the women cooking in large, heavy pots and the children playing. Three here kicking a huge ball made of old cloth, two throwing dice, four playing tag, running and laughing. As others arrived behind us, the women and children ran to greet them with great excitement, rewarded them with hugs and kisses.

The women saw the great delivery of food coming in and nearly danced with delight, one specific woman taking charge and dictating where it should go. One shed was used as a pantry of sorts and the dry goods were piled into it and the rashers of cured meat hung from the inside of the roof.

"Which is yours?" I asked Phillip, leaning my back against him so that only he could hear me.

"Which what?" he asked.

"Which woman?"

He scoffed. "I have no woman," he said. "Those are the wives of some of the men in my band. They take care of us, cook, sing, care for the children, and keep things happy around here."

"Have you a man, then?" I asked, hoping my jocular tone offset the offensiveness of what I asked. After our tense moments, I genuinely hoped for a bit of lightheartedness with him. I had all but grieved him as dead and now here he was, hale and hearty before me.

"I have many men," he said, "but none in the way you are suggesting. These are good people with no other home. Each lost their dwellings for their inability to pay the unreasonable taxes the High Throne demands. When they lose their homes, they come to me, with their families, and we make room for them. We feed them and keep them safe."

"And so you are still King," I smiled.

"Of sorts," he laughed. "Arthur…the once and future King. That one there," he indicated the man who had stood atop the wagon. "That is Angus. He was the first and is my right hand. He found me in the Summer Country and by accident of meeting, became my traveling companion. His wife and child died of exposure after their home was seized last winter, so he was on his own. He was on his way to meet a group of people who were likewise disenfranchised and invited me to come with him."

"And how did you become their leader?" I asked, knowing already his penchant for taking control of any situation in which he found himself.

"They had no leader. They settled on this land, which I knew from my time as King was near the major thoroughfare for Cornwall, South Wales, and the Summer Country to get to Cameliard. I came up with the idea to intercept the caravans at tax time and relieve them of their weighty burdens. Also, I could take any of the men in a fight, fair or unfair, so I became leader by the rules that have prevailed since we were all cave dwellers. I can fight better than they can and I came up with a plan to feed them when they were starving."

"Since the High Throne took from these people and took even more from you, you steal what is intended for the High Throne."

"That about sums it up," he says. "They, meaning the Church officials who collect the taxes, use that revenue to hurt people like you, Iris. People like your mother and your father. Trust me, they will not stop until they have wiped out every Goddess worshiping, Pagan person in this land. All must bend the knee to their Christ or suffer the consequences. My father would not rule that way. I would not rule that way. That is why they had to get rid of me."

"Does Father Francisco know you are alive?"

Phillip shook his head. "No, no one does but you and those two who were on the shore with you." He laughed again. "My own people here do not know who I am. They only know I have a white-hot hatred for the

High Throne just as they do. They do not ask my story and I offer it not."

"Father Francisco never mentioned you to me."

"He wouldn't," Phillip said. "To anyone who investigated my escape, it looked as though I went off the cliffs and into the sea. No one could survive such a fall and I will guarantee that leading the High Throne to believe that my mother and I were dead benefited both Father Francisco and your husband."

"But you were not. You are not dead."

"And I plan to get my revenge on that priest if it is the last thing on earth I do. Sometimes, being dead has its advantages."

We stood looking out onto the scene of happy domesticity below as the women set about cooking from the resources we brought with us while the men chopped wood for the fire and continued working to unload the wagon. Phillip placed his hand on my shoulder fondly and I covered it with my own.

"You can see her now. Easily. I meant that."

"I know you do, Iris. If I could rush to her now, I would."

"There is something I have to tell you," I said. "When she was in the tower, those who knew of her said she began to lose her mind. That she was not herself. When I spoke with her, she was mostly lucid, but said her memory failed her sometimes. As we were about to move her from the tower, we found that she had collapsed. She is recovering now in a secret place where I am confident no one will find her, but Phillip, I believe she was poisoned."

"Poisoned? Is she recovered?"

I nodded. "She is healing, but I do not believe this is the only time. I have some of her food to test when I return, but I am confident that deadly nightshade was added to it. It caused her to collapse, but it also causes disorientation and hallucinations. I believe someone poisoned her for months, maybe longer, and then recently gave her a larger dosage."

"Do you know who did this to her?" he asked.

"I know who most often took her food to her. I know she did not have enough food most of the time and that when I found her, she was not well nourished. I know that now, she has all the food she can ever eat and is on her way to recovery, growing stronger every day. I also know that she is growing more lucid every day and I know she is safe."

"Who took her food to her, Iris?"

I only stared at him.

"Francisco," he said.

I nodded. "He is in Cameliard now. I sent him with the taxes so that he would be gone from court when I moved her. My stepdaughter and I are the only other ones who know, and now my huntsman, who only learned today that Aunt Ophelia is not Laoghaire's mother as I told him. The only person I know of who is aware of what we did is the guard we bought off and he has fled in fear of Francisco."

"Forgive me for asking, and you have done so much for her already, but why are you not with her now if she is so fragile and ill?"

Although it was a reasonable question, his tone irritated me and I turned to look at him and snapped, "Why do you think I am not? I am pregnant with the child of my dead husband and I am frequently ill. I have little energy for excursions into my privy chamber to vomit, much less to chase halfway to Cameliard when I sent a delegation there on my behalf. Why do you think I am not with your mother, holding her hand and nursing her through the recovery of months of ingesting poison?"

He lowered his head in hard contrition.

"Because some arsehole stole your tax payment and tributes."

"Exactly," I bit back. "Believe you me, Cousin, I would much prefer to be tucked into my bed with warm bricks at my feet nursing on a cup of bone broth or tending your mother's bedside and seeing her improve with each day that passes."

"Thank you," he said, raising his face to look at me again. "I mean it and I am remiss for not saying it before, but thank you for saving her and for finding me."

The sincerity in his eyes forced away my moment of resentment.

"Well," I admitted, "I would never have found you had you not stolen my gold," I admitted, "So it is not all completely horrible."

He smiled. "This is true. But alas! It does still pain me deeply to see that treasure continue on to the High Throne."

"Both you and me," I said. "Had I a cup, I would raise it to that sentiment. The High Court never did a thing for me, but if I am to do what I need to do in Cornwall, I must keep their eyes off me and any misstep on my part draws their attention directly to my doorstep."

"You have their eyes right in your court through that priest," he said gravely.

"I know," I said. "I know."

"Be careful, Iris. It is a deadly game you are playing and now you with a babe to carry."

"I know that as well."

He suddenly stood bolt upright, nearly casting me aside.

"Who is that?" he asked, his voice at once breathy and low.

"Who?" I laughed. "You know everyone who is here."

I followed his line of vision and saw Zelda emerging from one of the shanties with two of the women close behind her, nudging one another and beaming broadly. She was dressed not as a princess nor as a stable boy, but as one of them. Her black hair was brushed straight and smooth and fell past her shoulders, at last free of the dusty ties she used to pull it roughly back onto her head, often stowed into a cap. A simple red ribbon ran behind her neck and to the crown of her head where it was tied in a bow that held her hair back from her face. The dress was a soft, white shift with a gold and blue tunic over it, the color of the sun with the color of the bright blue sky. It showed off her young body as it flowed around her, the summer breeze batting playfully at the hem of the shift.

She smiled and looked around her in an almost shy anticipation, the very picture of innocence and beauty.

"Remember the young man on the creek bank who you reprimanded for saying your mother was alive?" I asked, stifling a smile. "He was and that is my stepdaughter, Zelda."

From our perspective atop a small hill on the edge of the encampment, she stood out among the browns and grays other people wore like a lily on a pond. She was resplendent. I might well have not spoken or even have been there with him. Wordlessly, he left me and walked down the hill toward her. As I watched him go, energy caused the hair on my arms to rise, much like the crackles of power that hum through in the air after a lightning strike. This was important. This was history before ever it happened.

As the sun went down, the ale and wine we brought with us found its way into cups and the group around the fire thickened. People sat on benches, on hay bales, and on barrels, smoking, drinking, and digesting the feast of venison, root vegetables roasted deep in the coals of the fire, and the oat cakes we brought.

"We have not had cakes in ages," one of the women told me. "No place to bake out here in the woods. 'tis a blessing, Ma'am, it is."

Phillip and Zelda were not out of one another's sights for the evening, sitting with their heads together most of the time in animated conversation. Sir Rory, Sir Fergus, and Quinton were well immersed within the revelry, laughing and singing with the men as though those very hands hand not a few days prior tied them to a wagon wheel in a flowing creek.

I did not know how the men could stay up merrymaking after days of travel. The miles wore on me heavily and I felt sleepy not long after the sun went down. I asked a woman where I might sleep and she grinned and gestured to the ground around the fire. She disappeared into one of the huts and returned momentarily with two quilts, which she handed to me. I thanked her, then folded the first one in half to increase the cushion on the ground and covered myself with the other one. The night was fair and the warmth from the fire was a comfort. I did not see how I could sleep in the ribald laughter and talking that was all around me, but within minutes, I was drifting off into slumber, my last conscious thought being that I was still unsure whether Phillip intended on giving Cornwall's treasure back to me.

~*~

The next day, I recalled something my mother often said to my sisters and me as we struggled with the demands of priesthood, *"Demand more from yourself, girls."* She rarely forced us to do what we explicitly did not wish to do, but she made certain we knew that we were duty bound to certain specific obligations, often ones we did not appreciate. Her battle cry of "Demand more from yourself" was her way of telling us that we could do more than we believed we could and yes, through that, she did spur us on to greater heights of accomplishment.

I needed *that*, to demand more from myself, as Sir Fergus and Sir Rory helped me to prepare for my continued journey into Cameliard to deliver the taxes and tributes. We were still within the window of rendering them on time and if we made good progress for the rest of the trip, we would arrive well before the formal presentations.

The sound of clanging and men grunting orders to one another woke me from a deep sleep. The fire still blazed and I learned from one of the young girls near me that they never let it go out. There was always someone responsible for keeping it either banked or burning bright. I wondered what they did in the winter, in the snow, in the pervasive rain, to stay warm and to cook their food. I suspected the answer was grimmer than any experience in my own history.

The sun was just rising and the sounds I heard were men loading the trunks of money and treasure into and on top of the royal carriage. Phillip saw me sit up and came over to me smiling.

"I am not sure if we got everything packed that was taken from you, not the *exact* items, at least" he admitted, "because it was mixed with other items of value we have acquired over the past fortnight."

"Acquired?" I smirked.

"Stole," he said without blinking.

"I care not at all for the exact items," I said, "as long as it is of equal or sufficient worth."

He nodded, "Equal or better, I promise it. Oh, I am keeping your wagon."

"Fine," I said. "Consider it a hospitality gift."

"I know you judge me harshly for what I do, Iris. It is hard to know what it is like for these people when you do not live with them every day and see all they have lost because of the High Court."

"What you need to remember," I cautioned, "is that when you rob the caravans taking their payments to Cameliard, you making all of this," I gestured to the people around us, "as though it happened for nothing. There are people who lost their homes to pay the taxes the High Court demands. When you take the payment their sovereign makes on their behalf, they have lost their homes for nothing."

"Not if we give back to them," he insisted.

I winced. "Phillip, I know you think that is what you are doing, but you help some and not all. You take from some and give to others. There is no balance. There is no fair compensation to those who sacrifice. As sovereigns, we *must* pay our taxes to the throne, whether you rob us of them or not. Once they get to Cameliard, they matter not to me. Do not rob the caravans of people justly paying taxes for their kingdom. Rob the Church that persecutes us. Rob the church that taxes its people beyond their ability to bear. By taking my taxes and tributes, you gave Francisco a formidable weapon against me. He can now go to the High Throne and demonstrate that in all the year Marcus was King, the taxes were paid and now that I am Queen, they are not. He is already furious that a woman from Avalon now holds the throne in Cornwall and will take every advantage to have me removed."

"Yes, I understand. Zelda bent my ear considerably about that very thing long after you slept last night," his smile was bashful and precious all at the same time and I could not help but warm to him.

"Just consider what it is you do," I said, adjusting my clothing around me. He extended his hand to help me up off the ground and I then carefully folded the quilts. "There will be a way, some way, to balance the scales and reclaim what you have lost, but I am not convinced that causing others to lose is the answer."

"Your words are wise, Iris, and I will give them great thought. I also look forward to talking to my mother and hearing what plans she might have. She is nothing if not resourceful."

"Indeed, I look forward to her advice as well. But first, I must genuflect to the wolves in the High Court."

"I would love to be a fly on the wall for that," he smiled.

We broke our fast and prepared to depart quite early, despite several of my companions suffering from imbibing over much the night before as they reveled around the fire with "Arthur's" band of miscreants. By mid-morning, I was back in my royal carriage, now laden with its burden of tax payment and tributes, with Quinton on top driving. Sir Fergus and Sir Rory rode one in front and one behind me, each bearing the royal standards of Cornwall.

In the opposite direction rode Zelda and Arthur with two of his men, bound for the woods of Tintagel to reunite Ophelia and her son. I regretted missing that moment, however saving the integrity of the Cornish sovereignty took precedence. At least with Father Francisco still in Cameliard, any immediate threat to Ophelia was temporarily stifled and they could visit in peace. I prompted Phillip on dealing with the Faerie people who guarded and cared for Ophelia and Laoghaire and he swore his best behavior and greatest respect to them. He would not stay long. His band was still on the fervent lookout for the last, straggling caravans headed toward the High Court with their taxes ripe for the taking. Perhaps Zelda would hold greater sway than I in convincing him that he was robbing the wrong people. For now, I saved my battle for another day, grateful that I could at least go into the High Court with my head held high and my taxes and tributes in hand.

CHAPTER 31

The rest of the journey to Cameliard was uneventful. The people of the encampment, despite their own dire poverty, loaded us down with food for the next few days. I assured them we had our own huntsman who was perfectly able to provide for us, but they insisted and a stern look from Phillip ensured a smile of gratitude to my face as I accepted baskets of bannocks, fruit, dried meat, and cheese.

We rode through the royal gates still a day before the Lughnasadh Fete that represented the culmination of the convergence. On that day, before the festivities of the night, the seven kingdoms would bring their tax levies to the Master of Coin for the High Court and pay our tributes to Prince John in the Grand Throne Room...and ne'er the twain should meet. Although the rendering of year's taxes was the primary objective of the gathering, it happened nearly under cloak of secrecy whereas the payment of tribute was done with tremendous fanfare and pageantry. Business was on the quiet, but arse kissing was loud and in full public view.

Not knowing what or how much Father Francisco had said to the High Court by way of explanation of the robbery, I was truly flying by dark, on top of the fact that having never attended one of these fetes, I had no idea whatsoever how to proceed. I chastised myself for not bringing Sir John or Sir Charles with me, but my irritation with them upon my departure treaded heavily over my common sense at the time. Fortunately, Sir Fergus and Sir Rory had scant knowledge of the process, so I looked to them for guidance.

As we rode in, I saw many waving banners, flashing standards familiar to me from my wedding. The list of names of people to whom I was introduced had left my head as soon as it went it, so I was hopeless at recollecting who was whom from the crowds of people camped out in the courtyard. I had foolishly presumed there might be a bed where we could sleep, but many were housed in colorful tents on the massive grounds. I had no interest in socializing, although after my weeks of isolation, I should have been aching for a party such as the one that seemed well underway. We made our way through to the castle, my carriage stopping often to allow the revelers to pass or stumble in front of us. At last, we reached the entry and Sir Rory opened the door of the carriage to help me step down onto the cobbled stones, colored in such a way that they came together like a large puzzle to form the royal crest of the High Court in the walkway. Taught since birth of the power of symbolism, I had to wonder about the wisdom of creating such a work of art that involved others walking all over the symbol of a High Court's power.

The Chamberlain, a stern looking gentleman by the name of Wendell, and a groom met us as we approached. The groom took the horses and several footmen who appeared from nowhere as if invoked, to unload the carriage. The Chamberlain led me to a small room at the top of a large, stone staircase and apologized for the meager accommodations, saying they were informed I was not coming. I smiled my gratitude, thrilled I would have any place at all, and asked if my men might also be housed somewhere. Wendell assured me that the housing for servants and guardsmen was abundant since they did not require as much space for their needs. He asked about my women and was stunned when I said I had not brought any, but could dress myself. He insisted on sending a young maid of the court to me, Lucinda, who arrived within minutes of him leaving.

She chattered like a magpie, wide-eyed and excited about the festivities. I was exhausted from the journey and asked if she could fetch me a cup of broth from the kitchen and draw a bath for me. My motivation was not only that my belly was pitching and clenching from eating cold food in transit for days, but also so I could have a few moments to myself to collect my thoughts in silence. Even though Quinton and the Queen's Guard left me alone for the most part during the last part of our travel, I could always hear voices as they talked among themselves. Silence was a rare and precious thing to me.

I learned I was to share a dressing area with two other women, both wives of lesser royalty. Lucinda apologized profusely for this inconvenience, but I had no qualm about is so long as I could soak in a tub, find some scented oil for my body and hair, and then take a long nap. For all of the babbling she did, Lucinda turned out to be a far more attentive handmaiden than Ursa, helping me into the hot scented bath, massaging my shoulders after I sank so gratefully into the water, and helping me to wash my hair with scented soap. She dried my body with soft cloths, then helped me into a clean shift from the small selection of black clothing I brought with me. She asked me about the rest of my baggage and when I told her I had none, she blanched pale.

"But what will you wear when you are presented to the High Court?" she asked. "It is a time for your finest gown!"

I had not considered this. I left Tintagel only half expecting to retrieve the lost taxes and tributes and certainly not thinking I would present them myself. The gown I brought with me was not plain by any means, but neither was it any spectacular vision of loveliness.

"I must wear black," I explained, "as I am still within the mourning period for my husband, King Marcus."

"Of course," she said, dropping her head down. "But black need not be plain or dowdy. You just leave this to me. I will not have you meet Prince John looking like a nun of the Church."

I smiled a secret smile at her tenacity as she escorted me back into my room and helped me into bed. After giving me a warm cup of beef broth, she gently untangled my wet hair and combed it out while I gave in to the weariness that threatened to claim me. It was nearly dusk and outside the window, I could see torches springing up and hear the merriment increasing as the sun went down.

"Do you not wish for more than this to eat?" she asked me. "The evening meal will already have started, but I could ask cook for a tray for you if you wish."

I shook my head. "I need to sleep," I said. "I am with child and the journey has taken all my strength. If you could arrange for a larger meal for me to break my fast in the morning, I would be most appreciative. Heavier foods at the end of the day leave me restless in the night. It seems I live on broth these many days."

"Your guardsmen will arrange the paying of the taxes," she said, evidently noticing the fact that I had made no conscious plans for any of this. "Then you must present to the Grand Throne Room immediately after the morning meal. I fear there is much standing about and waiting until your court is called forward to pay tribute."

I smiled my thanks. "As you can see," I said, "I have not done this before and I have no one on hand to guide me. Your help is most appreciated."

"It is what any good handmaiden does," she said, shrugging. "We are meant to anticipate your needs before even you know them."

"Again, I thank you," I said, feeling sleep coming for me.

Lucinda pulled the covers over me and blew out the lamp beside my bed.

"I hope the fools outside do not spoil your sleep," she said. "They can get quite boisterous."

"I feel nothing will keep me from sleep this night," I answered.

As she slipped away, my assumptions quickly proved correct to the point that I barely stirred hours later when she returned to the room and laid across the bottom of the bed to sleep.

~*~

She woke me gently at sunrise, which came early that time of year, and proudly showed me a lovely all black gown she had scavenged from Goddess only knew where. I paused to wonder if all castles had armoires of abandoned fine clothing just sitting around for the pilfering. She helped me into the gown, which was quite snug around the waist and breast, but otherwise, fit perfectly. With a few strategic rips and a fine set of restitching with her needle and thread, she had the gown in a well presentable state in no time at all. She pinned my hair into an elaborate array, her deft fingers flying over the strands she pulled and tucked in among themselves. I shuddered to think of how I would have presented had I followed my original insistence that I could dress myself. Lastly, she slipped colorful summer flowers into the folds of my hair in such a way that it looked as though my hair itself were a headdress. Fortunately, I had the presence of mind to bring my tiara, half thinking at the time it could itself end up in the hands of a highwayman. It was not my finest, which was the one Father Francisco used to crown me at my coronation. This one was lovely in its own way, but smaller and easier to transport. This was the crowning touch, as it were, and it rested in the loops of hair and flowers, secured in place with even more pins.

 A kitchen servant arrived with a large tray of food and Lucinda set it on the small table in front of me. I lifted the lid to see steaming porridge, fresh fruit, and sweet breads, as well as cured meats and a flask of wine. My stomach growled with glee, but I nibbled my food carefully to keep from courting the nausea that was now my frequent and unwanted guest. Lucinda laid a wide bib of linen over my chest and skirt to avoid any soilage of the gown through dropped food.

 I was finishing my meal when Sir Rory and Sir Fergus knocked on my door and inquired after my well-being. I asked Lucinda to let them in and both bowed upon seeing me, but stared appreciatively and inappropriately at my appearance.

 "Your Grace," Sir Rory said, "We have come to escort you to the Grand Throne Room for the presentations of tribute."

 I smiled my widest and thanked them, taking each of them by the arm, much to their surprise, and walking between them rather than behind them. The castle was quite lavish and beautiful. I thought of my Aunt Ophelia ruling here. King Arthur's had ruled at Camelot, but no High King had ruled there since his death. Some even said his ghost haunted the great halls there. Feeling a goose walk over my grave, I gave an involuntary shiver.

The Grand Throne Room was shoulder to shoulder with people waiting their turn to pay tribute. Not only the lesser sovereigns, but also Dukes, Lords, and other royalty came to pay their tributes along with the higher-ranking nobles, their singular interest being to promote their own status, often with great hope of making a significant impression that would carve out an even grander positioning within the reach of the High Court or Lesser Courts.

The sovereigns presented first, so at least I need not wait for each viperous status climber to present their ostentatious display of wealth to the young man who sat on the High Throne. In fact, we stood in the room for less than an hour's time when we heard Cornwall announced by the herald.

"On behalf of Queen Iris of Cornwall, first of her name, appointed heir to the throne of the late King Marcus, regent for Her Royal Highness, Princess Eselde, the Venerable Father Francisco."

The herald's voice was loud and carried well through the room. Had no one told them, or more importantly, Father Francisco, of our arrival?

I looked to Sir Fergus and Sir Rory, who looked just as puzzled.

"Our tributes are registered on the roster," Sir Fergus assured me in low tones, "So they are to be brought forward."

We pushed our way through the crowd in time to see Father Francisco kneel before the throne where a young, lanky man sat uncomfortably, wearing what I knew to be my Uncle Constantine's crown. Prince John was dressed in elaborate formal attire, in an ermine trimmed robe and finely embroidered tunic over tight breeches. His hair was blond and fine, cut short in the Roman fashion and he with no facial hair. As fair and as young as he was, I wondered if he even yet *had* facial hair. Despite that thought, I noted that he did look older than I expected. From all description, I expected little more than a child to sit on the throne, his feet dangling in midair without hope of touching the floor. His face was angular with a strong, jutting jaw and a prominent brow over piercing blue eyes. He looked, I thought, like *a Saxon,* or someone from the far North. He was most assuredly handsome in his own right, but certainly a young man and not a boy as I thought.

Easily a dozen older men surrounded the throne itself, no doubt Prince John's advisers, as a telling reflection of the reality itself. One of them men wore a tall hat bedecked with elaborate jewels. This was the man himself, he who was the key that turned in the lock of oppression, Archbishop Gregory. He carried on the work of Patricius, the Archbishop who began the destruction of groves and sacred sanctuaries of the Goddess in Britain, as well as the active persecution of those unwilling to convert to the Christian faith.

Father Francisco began to explain his misfortune at being beset upon by robbers to Prince John, who listened intently to him. I drew in a breath and stepped forward from the crowd of people. As I did so, several in the room drew in gasped breaths, but as I was behind the priest, he did not realize they reacted to my presence and likely presumed it was in sympathy with his plight.

When he saw me, Prince John sat up straighter in his seat and held up one hand to stop the priest from continuing his explanation.

"Your Grace?" Father Francisco said, clearly confused.

"I wish to hear from her," Prince John said, pointing to me.

"From whom?" The priest said, turning to look at me. His curious gaze turned first to surprise and then to white-hot hatred.

I approached the throne and executed a perfect curtsy, despite my stomach attempting to reject in that moment what I had eaten and a sudden need to urinate. I prayed most sincerely that the Goddess would save me from vomiting and peeing during this most momentous occasion.

"Your Grace," I said. I made a point to stand beside Father Francisco, not in front of him, hoping to avoid further offense to him.

"With most humble respect, My King, Cornwall offers you tribute." As I said this, pages carried in our trunks of treasure and placed them before the throne. "We give greatest thanks to Father Francisco for representing us until we could arrive." I nodded in his direction. Fortunately, Sir Fergus informed me that one must always address Prince John as "My King" or "Your Grace" even though he would not legitimately become King until his twenty-first birthday.

"Queen Iris," Prince John said, smiling broadly. "I was told you were unable to be with us for the pageant."

My own smile could have melted butter from a mile away.

"I am honored to say that my circumstances changed and allowed me to attend your assembly."

"Father Francisco was just explaining that your tribute and taxes were stolen by bandits." He snapped his fingers to a scribe who stood nearby. The man handed over a scroll.

"And yet this says that your taxes were paid yesterday with an overage, in fact, and now you bring me this bounty of tribute. How so?"

I drew myself up into full glamoury, knowing that I was using magic for no reason other than to further my own ego and caring not one whit. "I am aggressive about reclaiming what is mine, Your Grace. I simply stole back what was taken from me."

There was muffled laughter from within the crowd and the Prince's grin broadened.

"This is a story I must hear for myself," he said, leaning forward.

"Ah, My King, a lady never tells," I returned his smile and hoped he would not push the issue. I had no wish to explain the details in public. "But your tribute I have presented and I give to you with the blessings and gratitude of the people of Cornwall."

He held out his hand and I came forward to kiss his ring, making certain to linger with my lips on his fingers for slightly longer than was proper. I knew I had to keep in this young man's good graces, even if he was no more than a puppet with little power.

Lively green eyes stared down at me, clearly entranced. *"All the better,"* I thought

"Always leave them wanting more of you," my mentor whispered in my ear through memories.

I curtsied again, then said, "I will ask no more of your time, My King, as so many here seek your attention." He nodded and I made my way back into the crowd where my Queen's Guard stood, still carrying myself tall and proud.

One thing I did not overlook as I left was the sight of Father Francisco, his fists clenched and his face contorted in mortal rage.

Inadvertently and with absolutely no malintent, I had made a fool of him in front of the High Court. While he mumbled explanations about the fearsome thieves who robbed the carriage, I came forward with a story that was not even a story about how I, a mere woman, had taken it back from them. Although the greater good was served and our dignity protected, any progress I had made with the priest was now surely lost.

Once I dissolved again into the crowd of people in the room, I felt a wave of panic come over me. What would Father Francisco do now, buoyed by the attention and support of his archdiocese? Would I even make it back to Cornwall alive? How easy would it be for him to arrange some misadventure to befall me on the way back home again?

Taking deep, long breaths, I pushed my way through the throng of people, eagerly seeking the door.

CHAPTER 32

By the time I reached the door, another lesser King was making a tribute of his own and I was grateful to have the spotlight off of me as I wove through what seemed like unending rows of people, both participants and observers. Making a grand spectacle of all of the tributes paid to him was one of the ways Prince John demonstrated his dominion and sovereignty. Finally, out of the room, I collapsed against the outer wall, feeling the cool stone against my palms behind me. Sweat was trickling down the back of my neck and between my breasts, sticking my inner clothing to me like a wet, second skin. I breathed deeply of the air in the corridor, which smelt of unwashed bodies, rich perfume oils, and incense.

"Come on then, Your Grace," Lucinda said, suddenly materializing next to me. "And make haste. 'tis not proper for me to be here with the gentry and royals, so I should be unseen before I am seen."

She slipped a cool, wet cloth into my hand and my fingers closed around it gratefully. I rubbed it against my neck at the nape and in the front.

"Queen Iris," I heard a man call behind me. With a reluctant turn, I saw Sir Rory approaching with Sir Fergus close behind.

"Please," I thought. *"Please do not need aught from me."*

"The Prince has asked his page to learn if you will attend the festivities tonight," Sir Rory asked with an anxious look. "What shall I tell him?"

I look at Lucinda, who was no less eager to leave.

"When do they begin?" I asked my trio of attendants. "Does anyone know?"

"There is a great fete in the courtyard for all in attendance after the presentation of tributes with games and ale and food and the like," Lucinda said, seeming the bastion of all information about the High Court. "Then tonight, there will be a private evening meal at the King's table for the High Court and the lesser sovereigns. After the evening meal, there is a grand ball in the Royal Ballroom and it is said that Prince John will choose a bride from the ladies who are presented there."

I sighed, my head woozy from the heat and the tension of the day, as well as the prospect of the celebrations extending well into the night.

"Tell him I am honored to attend the evening meal at the King's table. Beyond that, I do not yet know. For you and you," I pointed to my Queen's Guardsmen, "I want to ride out at daybreak, so do *not* go so far into your cups tonight that you lag tomorrow. I want to put this place behind me sooner rather than later. Extend our invitation for Father Francisco to join us or he may choose to ride back alone at his leisure. I know he wishes to visit with his associates here and I encourage him to take his time in doing so." Sir Fergus furrowed his brow. "And yes, you may convey my words to him exactly as I have said."

"Yes, Your Grace," they said in unison and bowed.

"Deliver your messages and then find your pleasure with the fete. Consider yourself relieved of duty until tomorrow morning, but I insist on having two capable escorts when we ride out. Find Quinton, wherever he has landed, and tell him the same."

They nodded and with a dismissive wave of my hand, began making their way back into the Grand Throne Room.

"I am starving," I said to Lucinda. "Do you suppose that once you have assisted me out of this dress you have sewn me into, you can fetch a tray from the kitchen? I have no care for what it is so long as it will fill my belly."

"Yes, Queen Iris," she said, bowing her head and dropping a curtsy.

As we walked, I marveled at how accustomed I had become in such a short time to the ways of being a queen. I now ordered people around as if I had done so all my life when up until two moons past, the only people I had commanded were those who helped me in the birthing hut. I would consider those thoughts more carefully when time allowed, but now, food and rest were all that gave my mind any sway.

Sure enough, Lucinda's fingers were just as quick to get me out of the dress as they were to get me into it. She hung it safely away and helped me into my shift. It was such a relief to feel the air once again upon my body and I sighed with gratitude. She was no older than I, but she tucked me into bed as if I were a child, fluffing the bedding around me and making certain I was as comfortable as I could be.

I began to drift into the place between sleeping and wakefulness almost immediately, rousing only when she returned what seemed like minutes later with a tray of food, but had to be longer given all that she brought.

I reminded myself that I had just eaten the morning meal not two hours before, but I felt hollow inside and needed to fill myself up. Lucinda brought a rich stew with venison and fresh vegetables in a delicious thick broth, as well as hard bread to dip into it and bits of cheese and fruit. The perfect food to nourish my lagging spirit. The ale was stout and promised to bring good sleep to me on top of how drowsy I felt. The food went down easy and I all but licked the bowl clean.

"I brought you this from the kitchen as well," she said, reaching into her pocket and pulling out a paper wrapped around springs of mint. "It will settle your stomach should the food be over much for it to handle."

It was such a sweet gesture and I thanked her warmly for her attention.

"Shall I find you another dress to wear to the King's table tonight?" she asked as she cleared away the dishes. "And what of the ball? It is ever so lavish and you will be wanting something elegant to wear."

"If you could do so for the evening meal," I said, considering carefully her offer, "that would be lovely. I believe it is likely best that I forego the ball. I have an early departure in the morning and the journey is exhausting for me as it is. I do not wish to court further weariness by staying up all night."

"Yes, Ma'am," she said with another curtsy. "And if I may be so bold, let me say that it has been a pleasure to care for you during this time. You are ever so kind and some of the ladies are not so."

I studied her carefully, remembering some of the stories carried to Avalon about the behavior of women of court, treating their ladies in waiting as something less than animals.

"You have been such a fine companion since I arrived, Lucinda. You have given beyond what I would expect."

She smiled with obvious pleasure, giving me a thought."

"You know, should ever you wish to live in Cornwall, I would happily add you to court's servants. They are treated well and seem happy there."

She froze for a moment and then resumed her task of placing dishes on the meal tray.

"Might that be a genuine offer, Ma'am?" she asked.

"It is," I nodded. "I have few people in my court and you have been so good to me. If you would like to come, I welcome you provided it creates no hardships here."

Her wan smile faltered a bit.

"No one here would miss me a bit," she admitted. "But you should know I have a wee bairn still at the breast. I nip back and give him a suckle now and then as a can, but otherwise, my mum sees to him. Since I caught a babe in me, my standing here is not so good as it was, but not for any lacking in my service, I promise you."

"I see," I said.

"I worked hard right up until my boy came and then went back to work right after."

"And the babe's father... will he object to you leaving?"

Her expression went grim and I detected a note of resignation.

"Oh no. It was... well, to say it was not a traditional way that I got with child."

"Not traditional? Is there another way?" My brain, still exhausted from travel, did not immediately catch what she was saying.

"I... I was taken by force, Ma'am, and he spilled in me and I got myself with child."

I closed my eyes against the image. These stories too had come to Avalon, horrible tales of women in service who were taken against their will and used as disposable rutting holes for men of power, then cast aside like garbage.

"More like he got you with child," I said, the foul taste of human wretchedness wafting into my mouth. "Is he in this court?"

"At times," she said, "He comes to some of the official functions, but he does not live here." She refused to meet my eyes as she explained. "He liked to pretend I like it knowing well that I do not. He catches me alone and…"

"He has done this more than once?"

"Near every time I see him," she said softly.

"Did you not tell anyone?" I asked.

"Does no good," she answered. "No one here cares about a maid. I am supposed to take care of myself and if I did have a husband or a father, they would not go up against the likes of him."

"What about your mother, then. Will she want to come as well?"

"Oh no," Lucinda answered. "She has a proper husband here and will be grateful to take care of him without tending the baby. I was a child born late in life and she is older, not really suited to caring for an infant."

"Can you be ready to leave tomorrow morning?" I wondered what I had gotten myself into, but was too far into the process to back out now without breaking her heart.

Her eyes lit up. "I can."

"Do you need to ask leave from the Housekeeper or the Chamberlain?" I was unsure of the protocols of such things within the High Court, but knew there would likely be some proper procedure. "I want not to offend anyone or create a scandal by you coming with me. I am far outside of the good graces of the High Court as it is."

"Permission is easy to get," she assured me. "I will take care of it and get travel documents signed tonight. Housekeeping will not mind turning me over to someone else. As it is, we are overrun with staff for the festival, so me going away will only make a permanent job for some of those who came in on the temporary. They will be glad of it. I swear I will do nothing to compromise your honor."

"Good then, we have a plan. You will leave with me tomorrow. For now, I need to rest."

"And you are sure I can bring my wee son?" she asked nervously.

"Of course," I said. "I would not dream of separating you."

She smiled broadly and nodded. "I will be ready... and I will have your dress for you when you wake."

She closed shutters on the windows, bringing darkness into the room and pushing out the midday sun. The food sat comfortably on my belly and I believed I might be able to sleep well.

My sleep was long, hard, and interrupted neither by dreams nor by Lucinda entering the room to hang a magnificent ball gown on the front of the wardrobe in my room. As though my body at last allowed itself to heal from the stress, strain, and changes of the past months, I lay in a womb of sleepy darkness, far away from concerns of any court or adjudication or priestly condemnation. For the first time in weeks, I allowed myself to not be Queen Iris of Cornwall, but merely an exhausted woman, her body depleted not only from ongoing tension and mental anguish, from grief and devastation, but also from the adjustment of growing a new life inside.

I awoke by natural means and from the orange glow on the horizon as I opened the shutters and the increased sounds of revelry that drifted in from outside, it was clearly late in the day. I had slept for many hours, it seemed. The room was stuffy from suffering closed shutters for so long and the breeze that wafted in when I pulled them open was like a breath of the Goddess herself. It was not cool by any means, but carried on it the sounds and smells of celebration. My mind instantly returned to the festivals on Avalon when the bonfires were lit and the sheep herded between them to purify them for the coming year. I smiled thinking of young druids and priestesses who leapt over the fires to bless themselves and the land with fertility and abundance.

At my home on Avalon, they would also celebrate tonight, the bringing in of the First Harvest and the sacrifice of part of that harvest in faith that the Goddess would provide an abundance. They would crown one of the young priestesses as Queen of the Harvest and she would dress all in white and the young druids would carry her to the altar on the Tor. There, she would bless the coming harvest and lose her virginity to the Stag King, who would call the beasts of the fields to the hunt that they might sacrifice themselves for the sustenance of the village. Together, they honored and drew in the food that would keep us alive for the year. So strong was the Church's hold on the outward expression of the seasons, so ingrained into the lives of the people of the earth and heath, I could imagine there would be none of those Pagan practices in tonight's celebration. At least, there would be none called as such or known as such except in the minds and hearts of those who still secretly believed.

It was that very freedom I was sworn to protect in Cornwall, not to trod down the Church for those who wished to place their faith thusly, but to protect the rights of the Goddess worshiping people who chose to celebrate in the old ways. How, I wondered, would such a thing manifest and why had the Goddess led me on such a merry chase down the rabbit hole of a dead King and husband, a stepdaughter who only now came to… well, hardly love me but at least not hate me, a furious priest who did in fact hate me with a fiery, righteous fury, and an aunt who hardly knew who I was… or who she herself was. Surely, She had a plan, but damned if I could see it.

Whether it was the sabbat celebration going on outside or feeling even further from home than I did in Cornwall, a wave of nostalgia and homesickness fell over me. I wished for all the world I could use my mother's mirror to talk to my parents and feel their love and support. Mother would know what to do now. She was the consummate Lady of the Lake, regal in all things and skilled in the art of diplomacy. I was a girl, a midwife, who knew no more about being a queen than what two advisers could shove into my head over a series of weeks and here I was to dine at the High King's table in representation of my kingdom.

"Are you ready to dress now, My Queen?"

I jumped as Lucinda spoke behind me, so lost in my thoughts and self-pity that I did not hear her knock or enter.

"Is it time?" I asked, my voice cracking from lack of use and lost emotion. I did not turn from the window, wishing her not to see my face and the feelings it reflected.

"Yes, Ma'am," she said. "Already the kings gather at the table, but you will have time to dress and prepare."

"Very well," I said. "The dress is lovely. Thank you."

"Then let us get you into it."

She helped me into my undergarments, then opened the hem of the dress that I might tunnel into it. This one fit perfectly, obviously cast off by a larger woman than the previous one. It fell to the floor on me, which was quite a task for a dress not tailored to my height. She hooked up the back with ease and then wrapped the restraining corset around my middle, lacing it up to a comfortable cinch and asking often if it was too tight. The gown was most assuredly black, the deepest ebony I had ever seen, encrusted with a fortune of black diamonds across matching corset. The gown had an accompanying cloak that added drama to the ensemble with a high collar that reached stiffly up to my crown. The back of the collar matched the dress, but the front was purest white, the only color visible other than the prevalent black.

I loved that the dress was black with the swatch of white. Even though it was not a traditional mourning garment, it reminded me of the women who held power in Cornwall. I, Zelda, and her mother both had creamy white skin and black hair. It was the perfect homage to Marcus, my husband, my briefest love, and my King, representing the three women he loved.

No, I thought, there was a fourth. There was one who ruled as High Queen within these very walls who he loved as well.

Lucinda slipped the tiara into my hair, which was still elaborately styled from her efforts earlier in the day. She repinned a few curls that fell out of position as I slept and produced a length of horse hair, dyed the exact color of my own black tresses. This she worked into the elaborate hair style she created until it was indistinguishable from my own hair. She was indeed a wizard in her own way. The gold of the tiara sparkled in the evening sunlight that came through my windows, reflecting on the tiny precious jewels that bedecked it on all sides.

Gold. I thought. Within some room of this castle, years ago, long before ever she knew my late husband, before she even knew her own husband well, Aunt Ophelia had spun straw into gold until her fingers bled and she lost consciousness from exhaustion. In doing so, she saved the kingdom and won her place as High Queen. The gold of my crown I would wear in honor of her and now, all four women Marcus had loved were with me in spirit.

"Just look at you," Lucinda said softly. "The finest queen I have ever seen."

"Have you seen my Queen's Guard?" I asked.

"They wait for you outside the door, Madam," she answered. "They will escort you into the Royal Dining Hall. When you arrive, there will be a card at your place setting to show you where to sit. You will be announced as you enter, but after that, you must find your own way to the table."

"How do you know so much about the formal procedures here?" I asked, curious.

She smiled. "I listen…and they never change much over time. Always the same."

"Thank you, Lucinda," I said.

"While you slept, I got these," she said, handing me two rolled scrolls.

One was a letter of recommendation, affirming her good standing as a housemaid in the High Court. The other was a right of passage that allowed her free movement through the kingdoms. Both were signed by the Chamberlain and affixed with the royal seal of the court. I could ask for no more, but I was surprised she could get such a favor on a day when the Chamberlain was in high demand.

"He has known me since I was a wee lass myself," she said. "My mother worked in this castle for many years and I grew up here. I have asked him for little over that time and I have worked hard since I was very young. As such, he does not deny me much when I do ask."

"Very well," I said. "You will be packed and ready to ride out tomorrow morning then?"

"I already am," she answered. "My mother packed the baby's bags and I have little of my own. Your huntsman has put the bags in the wagon and I will be here tonight to help you undress after dinner, then will sleep here to help you dress in the morning if that suits you."

"I will be fine," I said. "After you help me undress tonight, go be with your family. I will dress lightly for travel, so I need no help in the morning. Just meet us at the carriage ready to leave."

"If you are sure, Ma'am," she curtsied to me.

"I am sure. Thank you again for your help."

She nodded to me.

"Oh and Lucinda," I asked as I turned to go.

"Yes, Madam?"

"What is your son's name, may I ask?"

"Gideon," she said. "His name is Gideon."

"Gideon. A man who had seventy-one sons and who was a mighty and strategic warrior."

"Hmm...," she smiled. "I just liked the name. It sounded somehow bright and promising."

"A strong name. A good one," I agreed.

As she said, Sir Fergus and Sir Rory waited for me outside my door in their full Queen's Guard regalia. I drew in a deep breath and walked between them, this time with Sir Rory in front and Sir Fergus behind me.

CHAPTER 33

The Royal Dining Hall was on the opposite side of the castle as my quarters, appropriately positioned near the kitchen area. People spilled out into the hallway from its entrance and in talking to others, I learned that the hall had many large tables and would accommodate lesser royals as well as the seven sovereigns. Entry was by order of rank and the lesser royals, lords, dukes, and the like, could not enter until each of the seven sovereigns arrived and were seated at the table with their appropriate complement, in most cases, a queen.

Prince John, of course, would enter last with grand pageantry. Husbands sat across from wives at the table. If a king were unmarried, he could choose an adviser to sit at the table with the King's complements. Not all the seven were in attendance. King Urien in the North was at The Wall with his army fighting the Saxons. King Jacob Rowan of North Wales was a recluse who eschewed all contact with the outside world and sent his taxes and tributes via courier each year. All of this, of course, I learned from Lucinda as she dressed me.

I was the fifth and final sovereign announced into the dining hall. Everyone at the table stood as I entered and the room fell uncomfortably silent. Not even a click of crystal or scoot of a chair cut the tension. I smiled and nodded in what I hoped was a gracious fashion and the motion of the room resumed. I let out a deep breath and glanced around for my assigned seat, expecting it to be near the end furthest from Prince John as the most newly crowned sovereign. A footman took pity on me and arrived at my elbow, bowed elaborately, and indicated that I should come toward the head of the table.

Oh well, I thought. *Better than the other way around and presuming a position at the head of the table to be led to the foot.*

Sure enough, my name was carefully lettered on a card to the direct left of where Prince John would sit when he arrived. I pushed away a wave of sadness when I noticed my place was in the exact same position as I sat beside Marcus when I first arrived at Cornwall. Anxiously, I looked around for Father Francisco and saw him at a table in the far corner of the room, staring intently at me. Others around him wore clothing identifying them as men of the Church in varying ranks. I also took note of the empty chair across from me.

Drawing in a breath, I summoned the footman and asked him who would sit in the chair opposite me.

"We did not realize you were coming, Queen Iris, after Father Francisco explained what happened. Your men, Sir John and Sir Charles, would have sat across from one another further down the table.

"But who sits across from me now?" I asked.

"The King asked that you be seated at his right and the seat to his left is empty since you are unaccompanied."

"I see," my thoughts tumbled one on top of another, but I was eager to make peace in any way I could. "Would you please invite the holy man of my court, Father Francisco, to sit opposite me, but only if he wishes to do so?"

The footman bowed to me. "As you wish, Madam." He pulled out my chair and waited as I arranged my dress and sat down. I watched as he delivered my message to Father Francisco, who scowled and turned his face from me. I could not imagine a greater honor I could pay to him under the circumstances, but the footman returned and whispered discreetly in my ear.

"The father graciously declines your invitation."

I smiled and lifted my wine glass in the direction of Father Francisco, who had been unable to resist watching as his message returned to me.

"I am sure 'gracious' is a word you supplied and not the father," I said under my breath to the footman.

"Quite so, I am afraid, Madam."

"Then I apologize for putting you in the line of fire," I said.

"Frankly, Your Grace, it was my pleasure," he answered. "The man's behavior is deplorable. It is a tremendous honor you have extended to him and to decline it is the height of rudeness."

"Then look at me and laugh as though I just said the most enchanting thing ever," I smiled up at him.

He did, chuckling with great mirth that did not seem altogether feigned.

I thanked the footman for his time and looked across the table at the empty chair that gazed back accusingly at me. In a better world, I would have been seated in that chair, across from Marcus, the dignified Queen of Cornwall who arrived on the arm of the handsome King. Instead, I looked at a chair not even my priest would sit in on my behalf. The chair reminded me of how alone I was and quite frankly, all I had lost since coming to Avalon. I had no family, no friends, no calling, no lover, and at this point, no plan or direction. I was a leaf blowing aimlessly on the wind with no idea of how to fulfill any of the missions assigned to me. The empty chair spoke volumes and said nothing encouraging.

A fanfare sounded and everyone rose, so I followed along like a good little queen. Prince John entered the room from a back entrance along with his entourage. He smiled and waved, smiled and waved, as the assembled group applauded. The room was now filled with people, all assigned to their hierarchy of dining areas. As he approached, his smile looked exaggerated to the extreme. Being a midwife, I immediately equated it to a woman's birth opening stretched over the crowing head of a baby, causing me to want to slip my fingers into his lower lip and help it to move aside. I was quite certain this was not considered appropriate behavior in the High Court.

One of his men raised his hand into the air and said, "Long life Prince John" in a booming voice that seemed to shake the walls.

"Long live Prince John! Long live Prince John! Long live Prince John!" the crowd repeated.

As I wondered how it could do so, Prince John's smile broadened even further as he waved his hand to everyone and bid them to sit.

Servants quickly entered with large silver trays, laden with food for the first course. Most quickly and efficiently, food appeared before us with, I noticed, a significant disparity between what went onto our table and what went onto the tables of the lesser royals. Wine seemed to refill itself and as soon as one took a drink, the cup was full once more with a servant very nearly at every elbow to make sure it was so.

One man, elegantly uniformed, stood on the right of Prince John and his twin to the left, each sampling bits of food before the King ate and giving an approving nod. I wondered what would happen if one became full before the King did, but then supposed that was why there were two of them. A low roar of combined conversations filled the hall as we ate and more than once, I caught the glance of Prince John, who would then right away lower his gaze to the food on his plate that his tasters had approved.

The food was, to the credit of the High Court's kitchen, divine. The meat was juicy and tender, the bread soft and sweet, the fruits nearly as fine as those on Avalon, and the potatoes were perfectly roasted. After my large midday meal, I thought I would be unable to do such a meal justice, however buoyed by my ability to keep down what I ate earlier in the day, I sampled a bit of all that the servants put before me. As a final, elaborate stunt, the cook himself, resplendent in white uniform and hat and assisted by a kitchen boy, brought out a large pie and set it before the King, who looked at it as though it might bite him. Sensing he might know something I did not know, I leaned back in my seat and just in time. As he cut into the pie, a large flock of live and quite terrified birds flew out of it, swarmed around the top of the room and then, likely sensing a flow of air, exited the room as if with one mind. Applause again rang through the room at such a display, and then the individual conversations resumed. The cook and kitchen boy picked up the pie and took it away.

"Queen Iris," Prince John remarked with a wry grin, "You look as though someone has stolen your best toy. Whatever is wrong?"

"I thought there would be pie," I said. "The giant pie was delivered with great fanfare and the result was only a flock of half-cooked, angry birds and no pie."

"We do not eat *that* pie," he laughed. "It would be full of feathers and bird shit."

"Quite," I said drolly. "And yet the result is a moment of wizardry and we are left with no pie."

With two fingers, he beckoned to a nearby attendant and the doors from the kitchen opened. Servants with trays of pie slices filed into the room, placing an array of fruit pastries and pie around each person at the table.

"Is there no pie for the others here?" I asked.

"After we are quite through," he said, "and I shall not have you leaving here until you have had your fill of pie."

I smiled and helped myself to a cherry cobbler and a bit of apple torte.

"And I shall not allow you to leave here until you tell me the story of your adventure reclaiming your gold," he said, his voice slightly less jovial.

Fueled by several glasses of excellent wine, I gave him a vivid recollection of our adventures, leaving out, of course, the detail that the leader of the bandits was, in fact, the deposed and rightful King and also my cousin. In my tale, we simply outsmarted the bandits by offering them a wagon load of food in exchange for the return of our bounty. Sir Rory and Sir Fergus were even more valiant and protective in my story and the robbers gave over our taxes and tribute purely because they admired our moxie.

"And it happened like that, did it?" he asked, obviously skeptical.

"Mostly like that, Your Grace," I conceded, but smiled a secret smile that let him know I would tell no further.

His expression softened and I saw a young man no older than I was, possibly just as overwhelmed as I was, who had delighted in a fanciful story told, I hoped, with the fascinating aplomb my sister, Violet, would have employed. Now she was a storyteller and I was but a midwife.

"Might I implore upon you to join me for a dance at the ball tonight?" he asked, discretely taking my hand, which happened to rest on my knee under the table with a death grip on my napkin.

I know my eyes widened as I felt his hand slip over mine and I drew in an involuntary gasp.

"My King," I said, as gently and quietly as I could. "I regret I cannot join you for the ball tonight and must take my leave tomorrow morning. As Father Francisco may or may not have explained to you, my husband, King Marcus, died only two moons past and upon his death, I found myself blessed to be with child. This leaves me with little energy for social excursions and in fact, until I heard of the seizing of taxes and tributes, my plan was that the good father and my advisers would present to you on my behalf. I have been quite sickly."

"You look stunning," he said, "It must be the glow of pregnancy upon you for you are radiant. Anyone in the room pales in comparison."

I felt shy suddenly and my eyes dropped to my lap where he still held my hand.

"Your words are too kind, Your Grace, but I feel I could do no justice on the dance floor. The journey here, as well as the adrenalin of our experience with the bandits, has simply bled out all of my energy. I could not allow the indignity of allowing our taxes and tributes to go unpaid if there was aught I could do about it, but I admit the experience has taken its toll on me. I hope that when next we meet, I am of…" I paused meaningfully and looked at him from under my lashes, "…greater vigor."

I might be a widow and of lesser royal status than he considered himself to be, but I did take pride in how he blushed red and swallowed hard when I said what I did. I knew that of all diplomacy and politics, a woman's feminine wiles could move fleets of ships and send armies to march faster than the work of a man's sword or quill. I would take my power where I could find it and if I sprung up a lively hardness in this young man's tight pants, the chances were grander he would think of me and Cornwall fondly if ever I should stand in need of his assistance.

"I would be enchanted," he said, blatantly pulling my hand from under the table and kissing it in full view of everyone in the room. This time, it was his lips that lingered on skin. I cast a wary eye toward Father Francisco and saw that yes, he was taking in every moment of my time with Prince John.

"You flatter me, Prince John," I said, boldly using his actual name rather than his title.

"In other company, *or no company*, I would ask that you call me John."

"And I shall do so," I whispered to him, "should the situation ever present."

I extricated my hand, giving his fingers a squeeze as I did so.

"You must also consider," I said, "that I am still in my time of mourning for my husband, so a public display of frivolity, such as dancing at a ball, would be thought by many to be unseemly for a queen."

"And by that, you mean your Father Francisco?" he asked.

"If he is *my* Father Francisco," I said, going out on a limb, "then he is as an albatross around my neck. I inherited him from Marcus's court and he has no love for me, I can assure you."

"He has little love for anyone except his Christ," he said, surprising me.

"You know him well then?" Suddenly, I wanted to hear more.

"Oh, I know him," he said, his lips now pressed together in a grim line. "He bends the ear of my advisers every time he is here. The man can bleed all of the joy out of a room with a single word."

"Indeed," I agreed. "For I have never felt a moment's joy in his presence and expect it will always be so. I do not suppose you could elevate his status so that his service are required here at the High Court rather than at Tintagel?" I took a drink of wine and smiled prettily at him from around the rim of the glass.

He wagged an accusing finger at me. "You are an evil queen, Iris," he said, stepping further into the familiar than I had given him permission to do. Do you, in fact, have another holy man in your court?"

"I do. A fine man by the name of Father Damian who is much more amiable than the delightful Father Francisco."

"That is no great leap," he laughed. "I have hunting dogs that are more amiable than Father Francisco."

I chuckled along with him.

"Father Damian is a good man?" I said, imitating his lilt. "He is a younger man? And he speaks like this? As though all that comes from him is a question?"

Taking his own drink of wine, Prince John laughed unexpectedly and spewed wine onto the front of his bejeweled tunic. Right away, his food testers wiped up his spillage and looked at him anxiously as he waved them away.

"You are not accustomed to seeing me joyful," he chided them. "Be calm. I am not harmed. This is what we call 'laughing' in other worlds than these."

I attempted to hide my smile by pretending to wipe my mouth with my napkin, but he saw and his eyes sparkled.

"You really hate this, don't you?" I said in an unexpected moment of candor.

It was unexpected for him as well and I could see the mask fall as the smile left his face.

"I deplore it," he said, so softly I barely heard him. "I want nothing more than to have an ordinary life as the Lord of an estate or even a stable boy currying the horses. That is what I was meant to do, not this mummer's farce. People think I do not know what happens around me and in my court or what my true purpose is on the throne."

I was taking yet another drink and my glass stopped halfway to my lips. I looked around to see who else may have heard.

"Sire," I said. "Such things to say in private, of course, but here…"

"You are right," he said. "I forget myself. It is so rare that I can share open conversation with someone who seems to understand, well, *everything.* With great respect, Iris, you speak to me not as if I were King, but as a man and no one here will do that. I have no friends, no lover, no family here except for Uncle Gregory who is mad with power."

His words echoed my earlier thoughts so completely that I felt a lump rise in my throat.

"I do understand," I said.

"I believe you do and even that takes a weight off my shoulders."

"Do this if you wish," I said, more for my own interest than for his and yet, something in his frank admission tugged at my heart. "If you wish to continue the conversation, come to my room in the night after the ball and we will talk more. Dress plainly and slip away unnoticed if you can. Already, I have sent my waiting woman away for the night and will be alone. I offer you no more than companionship and conversation, but that I can gladly give."

    Gratitude flowed into his smile, a real smile this time and not the stretched facade of one I had seen before. Someday, perhaps, when many more seasons had passed and our stories were unfolded, I would tell him that when first we met, I wanted to put my fingers in his mouth and stretch his lips back to allow a baby to be born. By then, he would not think I was crazy, or maybe he would and we would laugh about it. For the second time in a handful of days, I felt the gooseflesh prickle on my arms and knew that this was a man whose fate was somehow interlocked with mine and that this friendship was, in fact, an intricate puzzle piece newly fallen into place.

CHAPTER 34

When the moans came again, I was sure they were the sounds of intense lovemaking in the next room, which would make perfect sense as the festivities outside in the courtyard met with the royal celebrants who reveled at the ball. Surely *someone* or many someones, would enjoy marvelous pleasures on a beautiful night such as it was with frivolity in the air and the excitement of a journey far from home.

As the moans intensified to the point that I could no longer sleep, I slipped into a heavy robe and eased out my door, realizing that the sounds were less like pleasure and more like pain. I could hear muffled voices in the room and was nearly knocked down when the door opened and two men rushed out, arguing intensely. Through the door, I saw a woman sitting on the floor leaning back against a chair, her face contorted in pain and a puddle of blood forming between her feet, which were flat against the floor. Sweat ran down her face, mixing with tears.

"What is going on in there?" I asked the men who stopped arguing long enough to notice me.

"It is none of your concern, My Lady," one of them said sternly. "Go on back to your room now. This is no business of yours."

I pulled myself up to full height. "It is indeed my business," I insisted. "That woman is in distress and needs medical attention now."

Exasperated, one of the men grabbed my upper arm and pulled me aside.

"I am the court physician," he said roughly. "She has medical attention, now get back into your room please, Madam."

"You will *not* speak to me in such a way, court physician or not," I said, now fully awake. "Who are you?" I asked the other man.

"I am her husband," he said. His irritation that he had to use valuable time to speak to me was apparent. "I am Lord Dustin of the Summerlands."

"Is she pregnant, Lord Dustin of the Summerlands?" I asked.

He looked at me blankly.

"Good God, man, is your wife with child?"

"Yes," he said. "She is still at least a moon cycle out from delivery and yet, the child seems to be coming now."

"And I have this well in hand, whoever you are, so please, back into your room and leave this to the professionals. We are sorry to have disturbed your sleep."

"I *am* the professional," I said sternly. "I am a midwife, fully trained."

"He wants to cut my wife open," Lord Dustin of the Summerlands said through clenched teeth.

"Cut her open? I am sorry, what is your name?" I turned my full attention on the court physician.

"Dr. Elliot," he said, "The baby is presenting feet first and the mother is bleeding from the placenta. She will die anyway. At least in cutting her open, I can save the child."

"And I can save them both," I said. "Are you going to help or are you going to start cutting?"

He stared at me, his mouth agape.

"I just said, she cannot be saved. The woman is going to die."

"Not on my watch," I said, taking off my robe as I entered the room. I stood there only in my sleeping shift and took in the sight. No wonder the woman was terrified with talk like that going on around her.

"Look at me," I said, kneeling so that I was in her line of vision. "Look at me and take deep breaths in and out, in and out. I need to get those breaths all the way down to your baby, do you hear me?"

She nodded and began breathing deeply and slowly.

"What is your name?" I asked, stroking her hair back from her face.

"Prr..Priscilla," she said as another contraction took her over. More blood trickled from between her legs and she bowed over her body, moaning in pain.

"Lady Priscilla," I said, "Look in my eyes and continue to breathe, in and out, nice and slow, like this." I breathed with her, in my nose and out my mouth, until she began to mimic me perfectly.

When the contraction ended, I said, "We are going to move you up onto the bed so I can examine you. I am a midwife and I am here to help you, do you understand?"

She nodded and continued the slow, deep breathing.

"Help me," I said to the two men.

They reluctantly fell under my orders and helped me to lift her onto the bed as another contraction came.

"Breathe," I said. "Breathe through this one and then we will get you comfortable."

"Madam, I am completely capable of delivering a baby with no assistance," Dr. Elliot said as he deposited Priscilla onto the bed without ceremony. At least her husband was a bit more considerate and gentle in handling her.

"Sir, have you no midwives here in court?"

"We do indeed," he said. "We have four and they are all completely drunk just now."

"Well, I am not," I said, "and you can either stay here and help me or you can get out of my way, but there will be no cutting anyone, do you understand?"

"I choose her," Lord Dustin of the Summerlands said. "I want her to take care of my wife and child."

"Then they will both die," the physician said between clenched teeth.

"Take it outside, gentlemen," I admonished. "I need black snakeroot and lots of it," I added to the doctor.

"Black snakeroot?" he sneered at me. "What kind of midwife are you?"

"And yarrow steeped in boiling water. Bring it now. The midwives will have those in their kits. GO, NOW!"

"GO!" Lord Dustin urged him. "And bring those things back or your King will hear from me!"

Another contraction came on and I breathed with Priscilla through it, then asked her to relax while I slipped my hand inside her.

As the physician described, the feet and not the head were positioned for delivery. Thankfully, her womb was fully opened, which explained why her contractions were coming so close together. The baby's feet were warm to the touch and moved when I stroked them. The child was still alive, but the doctor was correct that it would not be for long at this rate.

"Before your next pain begins," I said, getting her attention as she started to doze off, which was common at this stage, "I need you to help me get your baby into position. Do you hear me, Priscilla? We are going to turn your baby."

She nodded and would likely have agreed to anything I suggested at this point.

I urged her husband to put his hands under her bottom and lift, then to put bedding under her lower back and hips. This allowed the baby to move backward into the womb and remain warmer.

"Take a big breath," I coaxed. "The biggest you can, then when I say to, let it out hard."

She drew in a huge breath as I pushed my left hand inside her birth canal placed my right one on top of her rounded baby. I did not like how small her tightened belly felt.

"Now!" I said.

As she exhaled forcefully, I pushed down hard onto her upper belly with my right hand and shoved the baby's feet and butt upward with my left. She screamed loudly and for the first time, Lord Dustin of the Summerlands looked as if he lost faith in me.

The baby shifted, but I could not get good leverage on both ends.

I glanced at the door and saw Prince John, dressed in servant's clothing, looking at the scene with his mouth agape.

"Boy!" I shouted. "Get in here!"

In the excitement and wearing the dingy clothes he had on, no one would recognize him and I needed another set of hands. Lord Dustin was swaying on his feet and had gone white as a sheet, so he was not an option to help me.

"Put your hand on her belly, where my right hand is, and when I tell you too, push as hard as you can." He nodded and came to stand beside her.

I breathed with her through another contraction, this one her most painful yet since I did not remove my hand, which was now sharing space with her child. The baby felt bigger than I expected, now that my hand was fully on its rump.

"Big, big breath in, Priscilla," I said. I positioned my right hand below Prince John's on her left side where I knew the baby's head to be. John's hands were on the shoulders and my other hand was on the rump.

"Can you feel the shoulders?" I asked him. He nodded urgently.

"Blow out hard," I ordered her and again, she did.

Blood ran down my forearm to my elbow as we pushed hard, me shoving the baby's rump and feet up to John's hands while he pushed the shoulders and I attempted to guide the head downward from the outside.

Again, Priscilla let out an anguished howl and that was all it took for Lord Dustin of the Summerlands as he landed in a crumpled heap on the floor. I managed sufficient pressure from this angle and with the counter pressure John provided to disengage the baby's butt from her pelvis and guide the head directly downward. For a moment, Priscilla lost consciousness as well and I knew the procedure was unbearably painful for her, coupled with the loss of blood. The baby's pulse throbbed under my fingertips where the skull bones would soon overlap. It was slow, but strong.

"Slap her cheeks," I said to Prince John, who was holding her hand.

"What?" he asked, confused.

"Slap her cheeks. I need for her to wake up. Now."

He slapped at her cheeks gently while I called her name.

"Harder," I instructed. "I heed her awake."

He forced himself to slap her harder, wincing visibly as he did so.

"Priscilla!" I said sternly. "Priscilla, wake up now. I need you to birth your baby."

She stirred as another labor pain gripped her.

"Push!" I said. "Push down hard, now!"

She gave a mighty push and the baby slid down significantly, much to my relief. Often, when a midwife manually turns a baby, the birth cord twines in such a way that the child ultimately cannot descend.

"We have to get you up to push," I said as the contraction waned.

"Get behind her on the bed," I said to John, careful not to use his name. "Reach your forearms under her armpits and let her grab onto you as she squats. That will open up the birthing passage more and we can get this little one out."

Another pain came and I nodded to John, who heaved her into a squatting position, supporting her with his forearms while he knelt behind her. She was like a small rag doll in his arms, but she rallied when the contraction hit.

"Push!!" I yelled. "Push hard!"

She did and the baby shot out into my hands while she collapsed into the arms of her future king without even knowing she did so.

The court physician arrived with a tray and miracle of miracles! He had each herb I requested.

"Chew on this," I said to Priscilla, pushing a piece of the blacksnake root between her teeth. "Chew it until it gets pasty in your mouth."

Slowly, she began to work her teeth around the root.

"Give her sips of the yarrow tea," I told the doctor as I massaged the newborn child I held and tried to get it to breathe. At last, it gave out with a lusty cry and its blue-gray limbs and torso began to turn pink.

Seeing the living child in my hands, the doctor did not argue, but gave her sips of the tea around the snakeroot she chewed. The baby was tiny, but aggressive and reactive. There was certainly nothing wrong with its lungs, which was encouraging.

"I need her to give this baby suckle right away," I said. "We have to get the afterbirth out and stop the bleeding."

"What... what do I do?" the doctor said.

I looked at him in disbelief, then took the baby to her other side while John positioned her against the rolled-up bedding. She was in and out of wakefulness, so I placed the squirming infant in her arms and bared her breast. The doctor looked away, embarrassed by the sight of her bare breast, as the baby rooted around expertly. I pushed her nipple into its rosebud mouth and the child nursed as if trained in the womb to do so. At the sensation of the baby latching onto her breast, Priscilla startled awake and instinctively pulled it closer.

While she nursed the child, I turned my attention to her belly, where I began to massage her soft abdomen, feeling her womb boggy under my hands. There was blood on the bed linens. Too much blood and bright red, not the dark red of childbirth. I pushed harder and felt the womb tighten up, aggressing against my ministrations. More blood streamed out of her, but then she gave a groan and I saw the dark afterbirth showing at her birth opening.

I got between her legs again and encouraged her to give a little push. As she did, the placenta slipped out into my hands and I flipped it over to the side that had attached to the wall of her womb. The back was intact, much to my relief. Had any of the fleshy bits dislodged and remained attached to her womb, the complication would likely kill her under the circumstances. I nodded to the doctor, who sat down the cup of tea and handed me the wash basin that sat on a small table under the window. I tore off a thin strip of my now ruined sleeping shift and tied off the cord in two places. The doctor handed me a knife from his leather case and I cut the cord, then placed the afterbirth in the basin. I realized it was likely the knife he would have used to cut the baby from her body had I not heard her laboring and come awake enough to respond.

The snakeroot was starting to take effect and the flow of blood slowed as I continued massaging her womb to get it to clamp down on the wound left by the afterbirth. It was from there that the hemorrhage would kill her if the bleeding did not stop.

Her strength was gone, both from the harrowing experience and the blood loss. I tore off more of my shift's hem and used it to soak up the blood that pooled in the vault of her birth canal. Thankfully, on the third soaking, and I was starting to run out of shift I could modestly sacrifice, the bleeding seemed to have all but stopped.

Lord Dustin of the Summerlands was now once again conscious and was himself helping his wife to take sips of the yarrow tea.

"Keep massaging here," I instructed the doctor, placing his hands on her womb. "Make sure her womb stays hard under your hands. It should not feel spongy." He nodded and began to rub her tummy in earnest.

I stepped away, picking up a linen towel from the wash stand. Had I known it was there, more of my shift might have been spared and now it hung in tatters around my knees. To the three men in the room, I would look half naked standing before them. I wiped my bloody hands on the towel and slipped into my own room, picking up my robe from the corridor floor as I went. Once inside, I lit the lamp by my bed and washed the blood from my hands and forearms with water from the pitcher on my own wash stand, then washed the sweat off of my face and neck. I pulled off the shift and cast it aside, it now of no use to anyone, and slipped on the simple black dress from my traveling valise. Feeling more human, I went back to the room next door and saw that Priscilla was now fully awake and cooing to her baby, who was still hard at work on her breast.

"Is he too small?" she asked, looking up at me with worried eyes.

"It is a boy?" I asked. "I did not even see in the frenzy he created."

She nodded and looked at me hopefully.

"His lungs are good and he has excellent suckle," I answered. "I believe he will be just fine. What do you think, Doctor Elliot?"

He continued to faithfully massage her womb as he said, "Lady Priscilla, as nearly as I can tell, you have a healthy son."

Lord Dustin of the Summerlands let out a breath of relief and slipped an arm around his wife's shoulders. As he did so, Prince John quietly left the room with only me noticing his departure.

"Drink all of the tea," I told Priscilla, "and then two more cups after that. You have lost a great deal of blood and need fluids and the yarrow will slow the bleeding. Keep chewing the snakeroot as well."

I took over for Doctor Elliot, feeling her womb now small and firm. I checked between her legs and saw that there was no more blood than with any other childbirth.

"Have you moss and linens to staunch the blood?" I quietly asked the doctor.

He nodded and pulled some from his bag. "I found these when I picked up the herbs," he said.

I lined the strips of linen with moss and folded them into a pad to slip between her legs. "This will catch the blood, Priscilla." I said. "I am going to go next door and rest now, but I will be close by if you need me."

She nodded, beaming with joy.

"You did well," the doctor said as he joined me in the corridor. "I must apologize for my behavior before. You are right. You are a professional and you saved them both when I likely would have killed them both, it shames me to say."

"You are no doubt well skilled in battle wounds and broken bones," I observed. "My gift is in midwifery. We each have our place."

He nodded and turned to leave.

"Can you ask a servant to come and change out her bedding and clean up the blood?" I asked. "I do not even know who to ask or where to find them."

"I can," he said, and took his leave.

I was grateful for the deep sleep I enjoyed during the day and wondered if I could even sleep now. It was a challenge to come down after the rush of adrenalin took hold during a birth. I still felt it vibrating through me, but knew that morning would come soon and our departure was imminent. I was Queen, most assuredly, and the caravan would not leave without me, but I was eager to get home and after insisting that my men defer their revelry to be ready to leave in early morning, I was bane to take my own sleep while they waited.

I pushed open my door and crawled into my bed without undressing. As I leaned forward to blow out the lamp, I stopped cold.

"You were amazing in there," he said, so softly I could barely hear him. Unseen before, Prince John sat in the high-backed chair opposite the window and looked at me thoughtfully through the dim light of the full moon.

"Sire?" I said, pulling the bed clothes around me even though he had seen me in less when I was in my sleeping shift covered in blood.

He stood and came to me, looking down on me as if I were his own lost treasure that he came to recover.

"That was..." he let out a breath that was almost a whistle. "That was incredible. I have never felt so alive."

I smiled. "It is quite an experience," I agreed.

"I took you up on your offer," he explained. "I hope you do not mind. I did not expect..."

"I am sure you did not," I laughed. "Nor did I."

He looked awkward just standing there and on impulse, I pulled aside the bedclothes and scooted my body to the far side.

"Well don't just stand there looming about," I said. "Get in."

Grinning, he eased into the bed beside me.

"Now," I said, "tell me about the ball."

"I met the most beautiful, amazing woman," he said as I settled quite naturally into the crook of his arm.

"More beautiful and amazing than I?" I asked.

"Of course not," he said with mock sternness.

"Then you must tell me all about her," I said, patting his chest fondly.

We chatted through the night as if we had been friends forever, talking of matters of love, of politics, of faith, and of our upbringings. I marveled to myself that since I left Avalon, I had now lain in bed in the arms of two kings, one the High King of Britain by title. Not a single intimacy other than friendship passed between us, even though we now lay alone in the darkness and could do so if we chose to. For the first time since I left Avalon, I did not feel alone. Even during my time with Marcus, so much of our time was taken up by wedding plans and formalities that we hardly spent any time together. Now, as the hours took darkness away and dawn began to steal over the edge of the world, I felt safe and happy. We held hands and snuggled closely to one another, our voices no more than soft whispers and giggles in the night.

At some point while he spoke about the death of his own father and leaving his family home to come be the boy who would be king, I slipped into a peaceful slumber and did not stir until Lucinda gently shook me awake the next morning.

CHAPTER 35

"Apologies, My Queen," Lucinda bowed so low she nearly knelt on the ground. "I am remiss. I was to wake you early and my little one had such a difficult night that I slept well past when I should have been up and about. If you wish not to take me because of my weakness, I understand."

I looked at her groveling beside my bed and wondered at once when Prince John had so quietly taken his leave and left me undisturbed, how late in the morning it was, how long Quinton, and the dynamic duo of Sirs Fergus and Rory had been waiting, and where I might get a proper cup of tea. However long it had lasted, my sleep had been deep and dreamless and now I blinked at the sunlight coming into the room through the shutters.

"Please get up off the floor, Lucinda," I mumbled, rubbing my eyes. "Are the men saddled and ready?"

"Aye, Ma'am, they are ready to ride, as am I."

"And Gideon? Is he ill?"

"It is his teeth, My Lady. They pain him something fierce and he cries with them through the night. Hard for him to suckle for the pain, so he cries from them hurtin' him and he cries from bein' hungry."

"Bring me a hot tea kettle," I told her. "I want to make tea for myself, but I will also brew a soak to numb his gums a bit. You should also press on the swollen bits to help bring in the milk teeth."

"Press on the sore parts?" she asked, dropping decorum in a moment of disbelief.

I smiled. "It sounds counterproductive, but it actually helps alleviate the pain."

"How is it you know so much about the care of wee bairns when you've none of your own?"

"Where I come from, I am a healer and a midwife."

"You are a healer and a queen in Cornwall?" she asked, her eyes wide.

"No," I shook my head. "There I am only a queen. I am from Avalon, the Holy Island. I was trained in midwifery and healing there."

She gasped and crossed herself. "Are they not devils and witches there?"

"Do I look like a devil or a witch?" I asked her.

"The priests tell us that devils and witches never look as we think they will."

"I take your point," I said. "But no, I am neither a devil nor a witch. I am a priestess and a midwife. On Avalon, my father and mother are both of royal lines, so I am a princess as well. I became Queen of Cornwall when I married King Marcus."

"I am so sorry he died. I met him on two occasions before. He seemed a very kind man." She lowered her eyes as she remembered her deference.

"He was," I agreed. "He truly was. He was a good man and a good king. Now perhaps we can get that kettle hot and get on our way, shall we? Unless you are now afraid to travel with a priestess of Avalon?"

The morning was overcast and rain threatened to break at any moment as we loaded the final cargo onto the horses. There was not much. Lucinda had two trunks of belongings for herself and Gideon. I left with less than I came with, even considering the fine foods the kitchen provided for our journey back to Cornwall.

"Where is Father Francisco?" I asked Sir Rory as he helped me into the royal carriage.

"The good father has opted not to join us for the passage home, My Queen," he said. "My understanding is he will remain here for a few days yet, then ride out on his own."

"You inquired after him or your spoke with him directly?" I asked

"I spoke with a curate from the abbey here. I have not seen Father Francisco since the King's dinner."

"I see," I said, feeling an uncomfortable undercurrent. "This is not going to go well, is it?"

He sighed. "It is rare that anything goes well with Father Francisco. Rumor has it he feels he was made a fool of when the recovered taxes and tributes were offered. He seems to believe that you may have contrived events to humiliate him."

"Again the opinion of the curate?"

Sir Rory nodded.

"You know that is not true," I said.

"I know, Your Majesty, but he does not. He is one is looks for slights real and mostly those imagined. I fear you have made a powerful enemy in him and he is well-connected. Our best move is to get you home to Cornwall as soon as possible and find some way to assuage him once he returns."

"And hope that he is not in the process of doing irrevocable damage while he is here."

"Indeed," he said, "but what he can do is minimal. You made quite an impression on Prince John and while his influence is not as great as that of his regent, he does have sway. Your claim to the Cornish throne is ironclad. Remember that. To overthrow you as Queen, he would have to prove you are guilty of a crime or kill you."

"Either of which is likely within both his power and his desire."

He smiled, "Not on my watch, My Queen." He nodded to me and closed the half door to the carriage, which would allow airflow with the curtains pulled back.

I insisted that Lucinda and Gideon ride in the carriage with me and sleep as they were able. We soaked clean strips of cloth in the tea for him to bite down on with his sore gums and massaged the hard bumps where his teeth would soon erupt. He cried out in pain at first, then appeared much more comfortable. I washed the inside of his mouth with a mild sedative and gave a drink of it to Lucinda as well. Before even the morning was over, he had a fully belly, her breasts were no longer feverish and engorged, and both mother and son slept peacefully. My arms ached from the pressure I exerted to turn Lady Priscilla's baby and my belly threatened to eject the bread and jam I ate earlier to break my fast. Eventually, fatigue won out over those minor discomforts and soon I too dozed comfortably in the sway of the carriage, grateful I did not have to ride.

By mid-afternoon, rain beat down around us and forced us to close the upper doors of the carriage, making the inside unbearably humid and warm. As uncomfortable as I was, I could not help but think that the men outside likely felt as soaked and weary as I had when first I laid eyes on Tintagel from across the bridge. At least there was no fog as there was then, but mud mired the wheels of the carriage and slowed the horses. Twice, we had to stop as the wheels sank into mud too deep for passage and wait as the men pushed and pulled the carriage free. They knew of a longer but more stable route that wound further south and avoided the swollen rivers we would have to ford if we returned the way we came. It added an extra day onto our trip, but by the second day of travel, it was clear that the usual route would no doubt be flooded.

On the final day of travel, the sun came out and the moods of the men lightened. One could hardly blame them for being out of sorts. They did not bother to sleep as there was nowhere dry to lie down without veering far from the road. We passed several burned-out villages, one of which still smoldered, which brought home to me how fortunate we were in Cornwall to avoid most of the ravages of the Saxon war. By the time we reached Cornwall, they were exhausted, wet, and eager for hot food and a warm bed.

Every servant in the castle poured into the causeway to greet us upon our return, casting curious glances at Lucinda and baby Gideon. Bersaba fluttered around her, cooing over the baby and then hurrying off to prepare a room for them at my request. Ursa narrowed her eyes at the new ladies' maid as she ordered footmen to take our trunks to the appropriate rooms.

Sir Charles and Sir John themselves walked me to my room, pressing anxiously for news of the payment of tributes and taxes. I silenced them until we could convene in my receiving room and then called Sir Rory and Sir Fergus to meet with us as well. The three of us shared the details of our journey with the two advisers and warned them of the umbrage taken by Father Francisco over our retrieval and presentation of the stolen treasure. My companions and I on silent agreement left out the details that it was the deposed High King who had, in fact, robbed them and relayed to them the same story we told Prince John's court. I could see no value in burdening them with a truth that could place many in danger and create no positive outcome. Nor did it have any bearing on current circumstances.

"Is Princess Zelda in court?" I asked when our business was concluded.

As they seemed always to do, they looked at one another and then Sir John replied, "She has not been with us over much since her return. It is presumed she is safe and well."

I knew that to be their way of telling me that she was again lost to the woods, which I knew and they did not know meant that she was with Ophelia and Laoghaire. I was eager to see how Ophelia faired now that she was many days beyond her poisoning. By the grace of the Goddess, Francisco would pay for that if I had my way.

Since I knew Quinton to be exhausted from the journey and all eyes on me as the returning monarch, I summoned Ursa and the ladies to my rooms to put me to bed. It was only late afternoon, but I pleaded exhaustion and made it clear I did not wish to be disturbed until I had a hot meal and a good night's sleep in my own bed. I was fairly itching inside my skin as all of this played out. The women carefully undressed me and rubbed my body with scented oils, especially my belly which already felt dry and stretched, even though it would be another month before my pregnancy showed. As always, they took care with my hands and feet, massaging the oils carefully into my aching body.

Ursa herself slipped my sleeping shift onto me, holding it wide over my head so that it fell over my length as soft as a lover's caress. Although the day was warm and humid, I pulled the covers up around me and eased between the sheets, awaiting my meal which she would bring up once the other ladies took their leave.

After I excused her to go to the kitchen and collect broth and bread for me, I leapt from the bed, pushed my door closed, and quickly affixed the second stone into its correct position. Fog began to swirl in the mirror's surface and cleared to show me a lively scene.

Ophelia, Zelda, Laoghaire, and Phillip sat around a rough dining table, laughing and eating together. I watched for a few minutes, absorbed by their camaraderie and suddenly missing Avalon with profound grief. Phillip sat close to Zelda, his arm draped casually on the back of her chair. She glowed with happiness and frequently looked over her shoulder to smile up at him. Ophelia looked healthy and vibrant, much as I remembered her. I could not hear them, but I did not need to do so to know that they were a family.

"Laoghaire," I said, hating to interrupt, but eager to hear the report of how life went at the cottage. She stopped talking, cocked her head to one side as if listening, then excused herself from the table. Moments later, her face came into full view in the mirror with the others behind her, immersed in their own conversations.

"Iris!" she smiled. "You're back!"

"How is everything there?" I asked. "I see you met Phillip."

"He and Zelda arrived days ago," she said. "They are quite enamored of one another."

"So I see. How is Ophelia?"

Her brow furrowed. "It was a hard recovery. She was in and out of consciousness at first, but her wakeful times lengthened and gradually, she came more to herself. Seeing Phillip was the best medicine she could have. Now, she is mostly at herself, enough so that I could explain what happened to her."

"You told her she was poisoned?"

"I did. I thought she deserved to know what had been done her."

"What was her reaction?"

"She was not surprised. She took it all strangely in stride."

"She has had many horrible things happen to her," I said, more to myself than to her. "I am certain this is just one more."

"Mmm," she nodded. "Perhaps so, but it seems her life is redeemed with Phillip here, although he does plan to leave soon. Neither of my housemates are pleased by that prospect."

"If you may pry her away for a bit of time, will you please tell Zelda that I wish to see her tomorrow?"

"I will," she promised.

"And how are you faring? You have spoken of the others, but how are you?"

"I am well," she said. "The Faerie men take good care of us. I suspect I have a staff with even greater attentiveness than do you. They suss out our every need and make certain we want for nothing."

It brought me tremendous happiness to hear this, but I knew my agreement with Aphia was only temporary. It would take more of the jewels from the castle's holdings to sustain the arrangement beyond the five months we initially bartered for. I would take a more careful inventory of the various suites, drawers, wardrobes, and trunks in the coming days to know better my position. Certainly, no one other that perhaps Bersaba truly knew what baubles and trinkets were left here over the years. They served no earthly purpose sitting in jewelry boxes and vaults around the castle and if they could make the Faeries happy and improve life for Laoghaire and those with her, all the better.

"I have to go," I said, knowing Ursa would be back from the kitchen at any moment. "I will see you soon."

"I will get Zelda to you tomorrow." Laoghaire stared at me through the mirror and I felt she was trying to tell me something without saying it. "She is a good person, Iris. Not at all as we feared."

I nodded. "I know and I believe it even more so now that you have told me."

"Goodbye," she said.

I waved my hand in the sign of honor we were taught in our training as priestesses and pulled the stone from the mirror.

Mere minutes after I slipped back into the covers, Ursa arrived with honey cakes, which she knew I favored, rich bone broth, hard cheese, and a flask of wine. As she arranged the foods neatly on a tray resting comfortably on my lap, her discomfort was palpable to the point that I felt I must address it.

"Ursa, what troubles you? Clearly, you are upset."

She did not answer right away, but continued to obsessively arrange the plates on my tray.

"My Queen," she said at last. "May I beg to ask instead what I have done that has displeased you so?"

I paused with my cup of broth not yet to my mouth, searching my mind for what may have prompted this thought in her.

"I ask only that I might serve better in my next position," she continued. "Always Your Majesty's interests were foremost in my mind and if I have offended, I do wish to make amends if I may."

"Ursa, whatever are you talking about? You brought no offense and have displeased me in no way."

She stepped back from the bed and curtsied to me. "Thank you, My Queen."

"What caused you to say such things?" I asked.

"Only that you brought another waiting woman with you from the High Court. I did not imagine you would replace me lest I brought offense or failed in my duties to such that another pleased you so much more."

The Cornish were so, so very odd to me. How they leapt from one idea to the next without need of relation between the two forever baffled my mind.

"Ursa, I am not displeased with you. Lucinda had need of a rather rapid departure from the High Court. She served me well there and so I brought her here to join our court. It was no kind of reflection on you but more a way of helping a young woman in distress."

"I see," she said, lowering her eyes, but I could tell that clearly, she did not.

"We have few enough women in our court and I wished only to gladden our numbers. We are a court of abundance and have much in terms of resources in relation to the rest of the kingdoms. We can well afford magnanimity and charity. She is a hard worker and will prove naught but an asset if you will give her a chance to do so."

"Yes, Madam," she said, curtsying again.

"You are so attentive to me," I said, "and as my pregnancy continues, I will require much more care than you have given me so far. Surely you welcome a lightening of this odious load that is to come so that you may have a life of your own away from doting on my every whim."

"Bersaba and I take great joy in caring for you, My Queen," she said, staring down at her hands. "But I will make every effort that your new woman feels welcome here."

"Thank you," I said, with a fleeting thought that she might be less than committed to that idea. I made a mental note to ask Bersaba to keep her eye on the two of them. "There is no competition and no one has replaced you. If you would like, I will make certain that Lucinda knows that you are my senior woman in waiting."

"Thank you, My Queen. I will be outside if you wish for anything at all."

She slipped out of the door, quiet as a shadow.

These court dramas and dynamics I would never understand. It was a headache we did not endure on Avalon where everyone knew his or her place and where competition for status and power did not exist. From birth forward, our destinies stretched out before us. They were known and accepted by all…unless seven priestesses had to go out into the Britain Beyond to save the Goddess worshiping people from oppression. Then all bets were off.

CHAPTER 36

I spent the morning in my receiving suite with Sir John and Sir Charles, who briefed me on significant events that transpired while I was away. A kitchen servant sustained a burn so extreme that she was unable to work. The woman was widowed with children, so I instructed the men to have Colin continue treating her until she was healed and then allow her and her children to continue living in the servants' quarters, ultimately to find whatever work she could do in exchange for her boarding. Father Damian performed a wedding, the dispensation for which I had signed days before my departure. That couples must seek out permission from the monarchy to wed seemed ridiculous to me, but they took pride in receiving the coveted approval from the throne, so I happily doled it out.

"There is one other matter, Your Grace," Sir John said, looking grave. "A prisoner appears to have escaped from the tower."

"A prisoner?" I asked, suddenly on high alert and working hard to appear impassive. "We have a prisoner in the tower?"

"Not exactly at this time," Sir Charles answered.

Although these two were by far my most trusted advisers, every instinct in my body was screaming that I should not tilt my hand to them. I chose a one word response.

"Explain."

"Some time back, we were entrusted with the imprisonment of two treasonists," Sir John began. "They were prisoners of the High Court treated with diplomatic care. Their imprisonment was less of a punishment and more of a containment at the behest of the High Throne."

"Go on," I encouraged, with what I hoped was a dispassionate interest.

"Before you came to us, one of the prisoners died while in our care. A fall, from what we are told."

"And who told you this?" I asked.

"Father Francisco, who witnessed the accident," Sir Charles said.

"Did you see the prisoner's body?" I asked with feigned innocence.

They exchanged glances.

"No, not exactly," Sir John said. "Father Francis had the body buried in the unsanctified ground behind the abbey."

"And was the High Court informed of this death?"

Again with the shared looks.

"I believe Father Francisco did tell them, yes," Sir Charles said. "Yes, I am sure he did."

"You are certain?"

"We have reason to believe he did," Sir John replied.

I looked at both men sternly. "You do not absolutely know if he reported to the High Throne that their prisoner died in our care?" I snapped.

"Father Francisco assured us he had handled the matter," Sir Charles said. "We have his word."

I arched my eyebrow.

"And the second prisoner?"

They looked increasingly uncomfortable.

"At some point between the time we left for Cameliard and the time we returned, the second prisoner disappeared," Sir John said.

"Disappeared."

"She is no longer in the tower and there is no sign of her anywhere." This from Sir Charles.

"Is she not under guard?" I asked.

"She was," Sir John said, his words stilted and chosen with great care. "The guard is also missing. We suspect he was complicit in her escape."

"Why did not King Marcus or either of you inform me of this prisoner before now?" I asked.

"There seemed no need," Sir Charles offered. "The adjudication is from the High Throne. It is only the care and containment of the prisoners that falls to us."

"And we have failed at this," I observed.

"So it would seem," Sir John agreed.

"How often since their arrival has anyone from the High Court inquired after the prisoners?"

"Never of which I am aware," Sir John said.

"Unless it is through Father Francisco," Sir Charles suggested. "It is he who is in most frequent contact with the High Court and to him that that the primary care for the prisoners fell."

"Let us speak frankly, gentlemen," I said. "If the High Throne believed we lost one of the prisoners they commissioned to our care, it is reasonable to assume they would not be happy with us, yes?"

"That is likely a fair assumption, yes," Sir John said.

"And an escaped prisoner is of greater concern to them than a dead one, yes?"

"One would presume, yes," Sir Charles agreed.

I wondered if they did not know, had forgotten, or were choosing to omit the information that these two prisoners were of direct blood relations to me.

"Who knows of this?" I asked.

Sir John cleared his throat. "When no one came for the food for the prisoner, the kitchen staff alerted me and I, myself, went into the tower to take her food.

When I got there, I found she was missing. I questioned the guard who is still with us and he said he completed his shifts without incident."

"He failed to notice that the prisoner was gone?"

"The guard who is still in court is the night guard. Apparently, it is not uncommon for the prisoner to remain silent for the entire time he was there. He thought nothing of it and presumed she slept."

"To answer your question," he continued, "the guard, Sir Charles, and I are the only ones who know she is missing."

"And the kitchen staff?"

"They knew only that a prisoner received food every few days," Sir Charles said. "Not who it was or where they were. They raised the alarm only because no one came to deliver the food."

"And who usually came for the food?" I asked.

"Why, Father Francisco," Sir John said. "He always took the food up to the guard to give to the prisoner."

"Father Francisco made no arrangements *to feed a prisoner in our care* when he would be gone for a fortnight or longer?" I asked with incredulity.

"And so it seems to be, yes," Sir Charles said.

"And when he returns…"

"Yes, Father Francisco will know she is gone," Sir John finished.

"What was the state of the prisoner the last time she was seen?"

Sir Charles said, "She was an older woman, rumored to be in poor health."

"And now also starved."

I looked from Sir Charles to Sir John and back again to Sir Charles. Surely, they could see the obvious solution. I widened my eyes at them, hoping they would take my intention. Of course, I had the added knowledge that they did not possess. Father Francisco undoubtedly already thought their prisoner dead from the poison he gave to her before he left. Surely, he would not dare question her absence knowing he had caused her death. I had only to prove my suspicion by having Colin examine the meat strips I still had in my possession that I pulled from her tower window sill.

"Your Majesty," Sir John said, his voice lowered in a conspiratorial tone. "Are you suggesting...?"

I blinked at him without answering.

"Are you saying that we should perpetrate the fraud that this prisoner also died in our care?" Sir Charles whispered.

"I am suggesting that she was an older woman in poor health, exactly as you have told me. I am suggesting she was left unfed, by our carelessness. I am suggesting that we are a kingdom in a delicate state of balance after the death of a long-reigning monarch and the last thing we want is the High Throne insinuating themselves into the business of our court. I am suggesting that we are in Cornwall at the end of the bloody earth and *no one sees what happens here*. If the High Court believed Francisco when no one saw the body of the first prisoner, why would they not believe the same from us if ever we are asked?"

There, I had said it and I could not now take it back. I said again for emphasis, *"If ever we are even asked."*

"But what of Father Francisco?" Sir Charles asked. "What do we tell him?"

I thought for a moment. "We tell him nothing. The care of the prisoner was in the hands of Father Francisco. Clearly, he neglected to make provisions for her care before he left. Had the kitchen said nothing to you, Sir John, we would have no way of knowing she was unsafe. My thought is that this is on him. He managed the disappearance or death of the first prisoner. He can manage the disappearance or death of this one as well."

"Your Majesty..." Sir John repeated. "First you all but single-handedly reclaim the tributes and taxes stolen from the royal caravan and get it to the High Court in time for the ceremonies. Now, you recommend that we conceal our culpability in the escape of a prisoner of the High Throne and lay the responsibility with Father Francisco?"

I again stared hard at him, defying him to find my fault. Instead, he surprised me as he shook his head and chuckled.

"I can well see why King Marcus appointed you his successor, despite the age ruling. We are honored and blessed to have you as our sovereign."

"Indeed," Sir Charles said. "This is a wise and judicious decision, but I feel our words should not leave this room. This remains between the three of us for it is said that three people may only keep a secret if two of them are dead and I am quite certain there are no two of us here who wish to die."

"Between us, then," I agreed.

"Between us," Sir John nodded.

"Wait," I said. "What age ruling?"

"A male heir may take a lesser throne without a regent when he is eighteen years of age and the High Throne at twenty-one years," Sir Charles said.

"A female heir," Sir John continued, "May take the throne at twenty-one years of age. Your Grace is not yet twenty-one years, however, King Marcus included an exclusion in the event of his death that you ascend to the throne as regent regardless of your age."

"He planned to die within three years?" I asked. "How could he know?"

"He did not plan to die," Sir Charles corrected. "But King Marcus was meticulous about seeing every possible outcome and planning accordingly."

"Need I say that it is patently outrageous to believe that a man is fit to be King at eighteen but a woman is not fit to be Queen until she is twenty-one?"

"Some do say it is so, yes," said Sir Charles. "It is, however, the law."

"What is the law?" Zelda asked as she pushed open the door without ceremony. With similar nonchalance, she plopped down onto the chaise and caught the Avalon apple I tossed to her from the bowl near me. She jerked her head in thanks and took a big bite, then smiled.

"That you cannot take the throne until you are twenty-one years old. It is ridiculous."

She shrugged. "It is not as though I *wish* to take the throne," she pointed out. "The longer I can put off being chained to that ugly chair, the better in my opinion."

"Zelda!" Sir Charles scolded. "It is an honor and a privilege to sit on your father's throne to rule Cornwall."

I held up my hand. "She is entitled to speak freely, Sir Charles. Not everyone loves to reign. I certainly never aspired to it. I expected to be embroidering baby gowns and gossiping with my ladies in waiting by now and here I am."

"God forbid," Zelda rolled her eyes. "That is a fresh kind of hell in my opinion."

She was dressed in men's britches and a light tunic with the smell of dirt and sweat coming from her. It was certainly hot and humid, the sun beating down on the wet that still lingered in the air from the days of rain before. The men looked at her with disdain, obviously forgetting they were addressing their future monarch.

"Are we finished here, gentlemen?" I asked, catching their eyes with a meaningful glance to solidify our vow of silence and procedure. "If so, I have an appointment to speak with my stepdaughter."

"Indeed," Sir John said.

"Then close the door behind you, please," I asked, smiling. They nodded and took their exit.

I sat down on the couch by Zelda. "So tell me about the cottage," I began. "How is Ophelia? Are you getting along well with Loaghaire?"

"She is bossy," Zelda said, "but not horrible. She does a good job of running the cottage and keeps the Faerie men on their toes. They want to relax like they do in Faerie and she makes them work. The cottage garden is the best I have seen now and already they have vegetables growing in the back. Ophelia is nearly healed. I have never seen her so clear-headed and strong. Phillip rode back with us, but you knew that." She narrowed her eyes. "Suppose you tell me about your little mirror trick, Stepmother Dear."

I saw no need to lie to her or else conceal myself.

"Come with me," I said. I took her to my room and was pleased to find no one there. Between Lucinda and Ursa, I was in full attendance most of the time. I pushed the door closed and motioned for her to come to the mirror with me.

"This is my mother's mirror," I said, "I brought it with me from Avalon. Do you remember this?"

I slipped the stone from out of my pocket.

"The rock I picked up by the cottage," she said, looking puzzled.

I nodded and slipped it into the opening on the mirror frame. The fog began to move on the mirror's surface.

"Oh!" she said, "Oh my!"

"You see it?" I asked, unsure if perhaps only those trained in scrying could see the change.

"It is like fog, swirling."

"Yes," I said. "Now watch."

Gradually, the fog cleared and we could see clearly into the cottage where Phillip and Ophelia embraced.

"I can see them," Zelda said. "Right in there as if they were in the room with us."

"Yes," I said, "The mirror is a portal. If I put a different stone in the top of the mirror," I showed her the opening, "I can see Avalon and my parents."

"And you can talk to them?" she said.

"I can, but I only do so when absolutely necessary because…"

"…because it is witchcraft," she finished.

"No," I corrected. "Not witchcraft, but definitely magic and not in favor in this court."

"Can I talk to them?" she asked.

"I imagine so, but I think it would only confuse them."

"Where does this…?" she looked confused herself.

"The mirror that hangs on the east wall. That is where it connects."

I nodded. "I imagine so, yes. For my parents, it is through a surface of still water, so I suspect that would work as well. But you must tell no one. I took a great risk in showing you."

She ran her fingers around the surface of the mirror, tracing the outline of the people she saw in it. "Does anyone else know?"

"No one," I said. "Only Laoghaire."

"Father Francisco would..."

"Yes, he would," I finished, cutting her off, not wishing to think of all that Father Francisco would do if he knew I had a magic portal in my quarters.

"Phillip is leaving," she said, her voice carefully guarded against showing emotion. "He is going back to his encampment."

"When?" I asked.

"Tonight," she said. "He rides at night to avoid anyone seeing him. He promises to visit often...to see his mother."

"And you?"

She returned my smile briefly and then was immediately stoic once more. "And me."

"Then you mustn't waste time with me," I said. "Go back to him. See him while you can."

This time, she did not try to hide her beaming smile. "Are you sure?"

"Absolutely," I said. "And give him my love and best wishes."

"Oh," she said, "I was to retrieve something from the tower for Ophelia. She left a bundle of letters there, some from my father and some from her first husband."

"I will get them for her," I said. "You go. See your young man and give him a proper goodbye. Where can I find the letters?"

"There is a cavity under the window seat," she said, "They are in a box in there. You will know them when you find them."

"You may count on it. Now go! Come back and see me soon and you can pick up the letters for her. I will hide them in my room until you come."

To my surprise, she leaned forward and gave me a warm hug, then pulled back shyly.

"You really aren't so bad, you know," she said, a warm flush creeping into her creamy cheeks.

"You are not quite the monster they made you out to be either," I laughed.

She pushed herself to standing.

"Tell no one," she warned with mock sternness. "I have a reputation to uphold and I shall not have it tarnished with tales of softness and do-goodery."

~*~

Oh, how I had forgotten how brutal were the stairs going up to the tower. The good news was no prisoner equaled no guard to bribe. The tower was empty and the court thought I napped in my bed, safe and sound. I held tight to the rope that ran along the wall beside the winding, narrow stairs. Up and up and up, I went, feeling the sweat bead on my brow, between my breasts, and run in rivers down my back. My head swam with the height and the heat and I felt my stomach heave and pitch like a ship at sea. My calves ached, my hips hurt, and still the stairs went ever upward.

When I reached the landing, I leaned against the wall and let the stones, always cool in any weather, press against my cheek. Gradually, I got my bearings until I looked over the edge, down to a floor I could barely see even though the light was as good as it would get in the tower. My vision swam and I felt vertigo threaten to take me. Pulling back, I walked to the end of the landing and pushed open the door.

There were four towers, one at each corner of Tintagel, each with a lookout window and rampart to guard the castle. This one looked out onto the sea, far below. Someone had put a window seat in front of the entrance to the rampart, so one could either sit and look out onto the crests or step up onto the rampart and stand outside. I imagined how many times Ophelia sat looking at the waves crashing against the shore. I glanced at the tiny sill made into the rock wall where she dried her meat, the very food that likely had poisoned her into near madness and near death.

Opening the window seat, I quickly found a carved box and in it were the letters Ophelia requested. I looked around the small room, wondering if there were any other personal effects she might want to keep, but remembered that I would have to carry down and further explain anything I salvaged from the room. I took a breath and slipped the bundle of letters into the bodice of my gown and pulled the door closed behind me, hoping I never saw the tower room again. I had the letters. There would be no reason ever to return. If I had my way, I would burn the damned thing out for good.

I remembered that the way down was easier than the way up and that gave me some degree of relief merely to consider it. I would tell Ursa to inform the cook that I wished to eat well and hearty tonight. The day had not been strenuous, but seemed long and daunting. Only two days before, I had promised Zelda I would get the letters and it had taken me this long to arrange enough time alone to slip away to the tower. I considered using the glamor again, but did not feel I had the strength to maintain it, so in the end, I simple used my usual excuse of a nap and then hurried to the tower when no one was looking and started climbing.

The heat at the top of the tower was far worse than it was at the bottom and I drew in a deep breath that felt sticky and hot in my lungs and let it out. I put one foot on the stair below the landing and the next thing I knew, I felt a hard push on my back and was flying, arse over teacup, hitting stair, then wall, then stair again.

Then, I knew nothing at all but blackness.

CHAPTER 37

"Your mother sent it. It is water from the Sacred Well. Drink it."

The pain was exquisite and ran through my entire body. Quite literally, there was not one single place on me that was not alive with pain beyond measure. I nearly gagged as water went into my throat and my windpipe at the same time, but just the act of choking caused me to cry out piteously. I drank what I could, feeling the cool, clean water flow through me. Greedily, I took a bit more, still coughing and spluttering as I did. I could not raise my head, which complicated drinking considerably.

The night was so dark I could barely see. Only make out shapes of people around me, speaking in low tones. Someone was weeping quietly over my right shoulder. I knew if I could go back into the darkness, there would be no more pain, so into it I went.

I opened my eyes and it was still night, so I knew not much time had passed. The shapes were still there, milling about, speaking quietly, as omnipresent as the pain that wracked through me in waves. Why did they not put light to a lamp?

"The Queen is awake," someone whispered.

"No," I mumbled. "No, she is not."

And in fact, I was not.

Still dark, dark as the newest sliver of moon on the Winter Solstice. A warm glow slid over my vision so the blackness became gray instead. Black again. Then gray.

"Your Majesty, can you hear me? Your Majesty?"

I opened my mouth to speak, but the effort was more than I could bear. My lips felt dry and cracked. My tongue felt too big for my mouth.

Again with the water.

"Drink it." It was Laoghaire. "Drink, Iris."

I took small sips, letting the water cool my parched throat. The pain was not as bad as it had been before. I wiggled my toes and felt a stab go up my legs to my hips and winced with a gasp. The pain slowly let go of me and subsided. I wiggled the fingers of my right hand and felt a streak of pain run up to my elbow. I wiggled the fingers of my left hand and nearly wept as I felt no pain at all.

"Turn on the light," I said, hearing my voice barely croak out the words. "Turn on the light," I repeated.

"My Queen?"

It took me a moment to place the voice. "Colin? Turn on the light, Colin. I am weary of darkness."

There was a pause and in it, I could again hear people whispering to one another.

"It is full daylight, Your Majesty," he said, using the same voice I used to deliver information a patient did not wish to hear.

My thoughts were a confused muddle of which I could make no sense at all. Daylight?

"Can you see this, Your Grace?"

I saw nothing but the darkness.

"No," I said. "I see nothing."

"Do not despair," he said. "You had a terrible fall and hit your head… among other things. It is a wonder you live at all. There is swelling inside your head that is likely causing some blindness. You are safe now and you have aught to do but heal."

A fall?

"The baby?" I asked. I could hear the weariness of the world in my voice and felt I already knew the answer to my question.

A hand slid into mine, smooth and warm, but firmly gripping my own. Laoghaire. I could smell her scent near me. Her closeness left me feeling vulnerable and tears began to slide down my cheeks in hot streams.

"We know not," she said. "You did not lose the baby outright. You had no bleeding from the birth outlet, but I cannot imagine a baby could survive the fall you took. And yet…"

She carefully took my left hand and placed it on my abdomen, where I could feel the swell of my belly protruding through the fabric of my shift.

My belly? I felt simultaneously elated and horrified. My child somehow lived and continued to grow, but how long had I been unconscious?

"How long?" I asked, squeezing her hand, terrified of letting her go. "How long?"

Her other hand pressed against my forehead, both holding me down as I tried to rise and giving me strength.

"It is nearly Mabon," she said softly into my ear. "You have been abed for nearly two moons."

My breath began to come in ragged gasps as I processed what she was saying.

"Do not let her move," came Colin's voice. "Keep her still."

All around me, hands held me down, pressing me firmly to the bed. A wave of panic swept over me at the restraint and I felt as though I could not breathe.

"Ssssssh," came Bersaba's voice in my right ear. "Quiet now, My Queen. You must be still or you will harm yourself further. Deep breaths. Breathe in and out, in and out, as if you were giving birth. In and out. In and out."

Her tone was calm and reassuring and I found myself doing as she said, taking long, deep breaths. Slowly, the anxiety abated and the hands released me.

"If the swelling reduced enough that you could wake up," Colin said gently, "then it will soon reduce enough that you can likely see again. Once you can see, you will not feel the panic so much. When you are ready, I can examine you with your involvement, which is much better than when you were unconscious. We know your right leg is badly broken and your right arm took quite a hit. I set them to the best of my ability. I suspect your pelvis is fractured, as well as several ribs and likely your collarbone as well. The facial contusions have mostly healed, but you were quite horrid looking there for a while."

"Marvelous," I said.

"You suffered multiple bruises on your left leg, arm, and side and possibly some hairline fractures. Your right side took the worst of the fall. Worse than any battlefield injury I have ever seen."

He placed his hands on each of my hip bones.

"Take in as deep a breath as you can and let it out," he said.

As I exhaled, he pushed in on my hips and I nearly screamed in pain.

"Most definitely a pelvic fracture," he said. "You have good circulation in your right arm, but I had to reset the shoulder joint back into place and I suspect a break right here…"

He pressed in on my upper shoulder and again, I shouted in pain.

"At least you can breathe now," he laughed. "You would not scream if you could not breathe. You are lucky the fractured ribs did not pierce the lung. You have had no bleeding from the mouth since your teeth tightened up again, but at first, had some from the ears and nose that slowed after the first day."

I appreciated him giving me details, healer to healer, for it allowed me to objectify my own condition and assess as I would any other patient. A severe head injury with bleeding from the ears and nose was concerning and now that they knew about the subsequent blindness, even more so.

But my baby. How did the baby survive? Did the baby survive? Had my womb filled with unreleased blood? Had that caused the protrusion? I moved my left hand over my belly and pushed in slightly. No pain, not from my abdomen at any rate.

My eyes widened as I felt my belly rise and fall on one side.

"My baby," I said. "He moved. I felt it."

Laoghaire clapped her hands and smiled. "Brilliant," she said. "He is well within there. I knew it."

Colin poked, prodded, asked questions, and generally moved my body about here and there as he thoroughly examined me. By the time he was finished, I was utterly exhausted and I hurt far more than I had when first I opened my eyes. Without intending to, I slipped again into a doze.

~*~

"I put your letters away for you."

The whisper in my ear caused my eyes to fly open. Letters. Not mine. Ophelia's letter.

"They were in your gown when you feel. I helped to undress you when they brought you in and I found them. Worry not, My Queen. Your treasures are safe."

"Lucinda?" I said, vaguely recalling the sound of her soft voice.

"Ursa brought some bone broth for you and I told her I would sit with you. Do you want some? It is still warm."

Bone broth sounded wonderful, but what I desperately wanted was to sit up in bed. My bones ached from lying still, likely for months. Laoghaire would know to turn me to avoid the bed lesions that sometimes happened with long-term illness, but to my mind, I had slept in one position for far too long.

Mindful of my pelvic injury, I began to ease myself up in bed. Apparently noticing my intention, Lucinda adjusted my pillows and gently tugged me into a more proper sitting position in such a way that my shoulders were elevated, but my hips remained flat. The pressure against my right shoulder caused a dull ache, but nothing more.

"Is it still daytime?" I asked.

"No, My Queen," she replied. "It is dead of night."

"Is a lamp lit?" I asked.

"No, it is quite dark. Would you like me to light it now?"

I felt I would. Even if I could not see it, it felt better knowing that there was light somewhere in the world.

To my surprise, I saw the tinder flicker and a warm glow come over the room. I could make out more than shadows, although my vision was fuzzy and dim.

"I can see," I said simply. "Not well, but I can see."

"I will get the physician," Lucinda said. "He will want to know."

"He just examined me earlier today," I said for no discernible reason.

"Oh no, Your Grace, it was two days ago that you woke up and he examined you. You have been sleeping again."

My heart fell. "In a coma? Again?"

"No, no, Ma'am. He said you were only sleeping and healing. This was different. I will return in a moment."

I closed my eyes and she was back, along with Colin who passed the lamp in front of my eyes.

"Your pupils react," he said. "Now tell me, what can you see?"

"Shapes," I said. "Colors now, but fuzzy. I can tell I am not in my quarters. Where am I?"

"You are in a room near the tower. We wanted to move you as little as possible."

That made perfect sense. I had been in the tower to retrieve the letters. Ophelia's letters. I had fallen. Little wonder with those hellish stairs. But I had not gone down the stairs. I had…

"…suspected, the swelling must be going down and…"

"Get me Sir John and Sir Charles. Now," I said. "Bring them to me."

I saw that his shape set back a bit as though stunned.

"Very well," he said. "I take it this is a case of royal emergency?"

"It is," I said, urgency making my tone brusquer than I wished. "I need them now."

I heard him open the door and say something to a person outside in the corridor, then he was back.

"They will be here momentarily," he assured me as he sat down on the edge of the bed. "Is there anything I can do for you?"

I thought for a moment. "I want meat," I said. "I have a tremendous craving for meat, cooked rare."

"Meat...cooked rare," he repeated. "What kind of meat?"

"Any kind. Organ meat if you have it. Bird. Beast. Fish. I care not what kind. Just rare meat. Make it bleed."

"I will see what I can do," he said, standing again.

There was a brief commotion at the door as the two men entered. I could see their outlines in the dim light and knew I must have driven them from their beds and yet, they were here so quickly.

"Your Majesty," they said bowing. I was pleased that I could now see well enough even to tell them apart.

"Make certain we are alone," I said, not trusting my newly returned vision.

Sir John motioned with his hand and I heard people leave the room.

"We are alone now, My Queen," he said, taking my hand.

"Can I trust you?" I asked, feeling a sudden flash of vulnerability. Oddly, within castle walls that were unfamiliar to me, and yet I had not seen even a third of Tintagel myself despite living here for months, I had rarely felt frightened or in danger. Now, it felt as though danger lurked behind every face and every door. I had heard of some warriors who returned from particularly vicious and bloody battles who were never again the same, waking with night terrors and reliving their battle horrors during even their waking hours. Could I have a similar condition? Fear was not common to me, after all.

"Of course, you can," Sir Charles said, kneeling beside me. "We treasure you not only on behalf of Marcus, but on behalf of Cornwall."

I drew in a breath, remembering our most recent conversation and my feeling that what was said could never be retracted. As my father used to say, "You cannot unring a bell."

"I did not fall by accident or misadventure. I was pushed. I remember it clearly. I was at the top of the tower steps and someone deliberately pushed me from behind hard enough that I fell."

This time, the looks they exchanged were grim.

"Why did you go to the tower room?" Sir John asked.

I organized my thoughts before answering.

"You had just told me about the prisoner," I said. "I wanted to see where she was kept… how she lived."

"And you told no one you were going. In fact, you said you were going to rest in your quarters."

"Yes, that is true," I said. "I wanted to go alone and knew otherwise I could never do so."

"Your Majesty," Sir Charles said gently. "We cannot keep you safe if you do not let us do so. As you can see…"

I nodded. "It will not happen again," I said, hoping I spoke the truth.

"Did you see anyone?" Sir John asked. "Anyone at all before or after you fell?"

"No one. I would have sworn I was alone, but I definitely felt hands on my back and a push."

"This means we have to look at who wants revenge or who would benefit from your death or the loss of the baby," Sir Charles said.

"And how is Father Francisco?" I asked dryly.

"He is not here," Sir John said. "He returned briefly after you fall, then left again almost immediately, saying he had business with the High Court. He has been gone for over a month."

"He returned *after* my fall?" I asked. "How long after?"

"Two days, maybe?" he answered.

"Did anyone actually see him ride in?"

"Well, no," Sir Charles said. "There was a rush of madness after Zelda found you and our attention was fully on you, My Queen, and of course, the baby. Your friend, Laoghaire, and Sir Colin were certain the baby would be lost. I suppose he could have come in at any time in all of that, but we did not see him until you had been abed for at least two days and he appeared to have only arrived shortly before we saw him."

"He was furious, you know," I said. "In Cameliard, he would not sit at the King's table with me nor would he accompany us home."

"We know," Sir John took my hand in his. "Sir Fergus told us. It was high honor that you invited him to accompany you at the King's table. I am without words that he declined your offer."

"Who but he would be angry enough to want to kill me or would benefit from my death?" I asked.

"Who indeed?" Sir Charles said with grim antipathy. "Who drove away all of the other potential queens until she met one such as yourself that she could not best? Who loses her right to succession if the child you carry is a son? Who knew exactly where to look to find you and who disappeared as soon as you were in our care?"

"No," I said, my voice resolute. "Absolutely not. I refuse to believe Zelda did this."

"Your Majesty, I light of your memory of being pushed, we must examine all possibilities. We know that Zelda knew about the prisoner in the tower and, in fact, visited with her on occasion. It is very likely she aided in the woman's escape the moment we were gone and she saw her way clear to do so, then when she saw her chance to rid herself of not one, but two rivals to the throne, she did so."

Sir John tried to silence Sir Charles, but he continued.

"It only makes sense."

She did not want the throne. She likely found me when she returned to collect the letters from me. She left to get Laoghaire to come to me and then stayed to care for Ophelia. It all made sense, but I could not tell them any of it without revealing all.

"I will tell you now, Zelda did not do this. I cannot reveal how I know without breaking a confidence, but you must believe me when I say that I know. Turn your suspicions elsewhere."

"Yes, My Queen," they said together.

"As far as Francisco goes, quietly search his quarters. See if anything at all turns up that is suspect. I want to know when he left Cameliard and when he arrived back here. Talk to the stable hands. They will have taken in his horse. He may have paid them for their silence, so do not stop at asking one. Talk with Father Damian. See if he knows what business Francisco has with the High Court."

"Consider it done, Madam," Sir John said.

There was a knock at the door and a kitchen servant arrived with a tray of food for me. I did not know how much I could eat, but I knew my body craved the vitality of meat. I lifted the lid off of the dish.

"What is this?" I asked, poking at the unfamiliar food. It was a gray tinged, textured mass with pink shot throughout it.

"Sheep's liver," the young boy answered. "Cooked rare."

"Excellent," I said, waving away the bowls of fruit and loaves of bread away. I had what I wanted. "Leave the wine," I said around a mouthful of liver, and reached for it, washing down my food with a long drag from the neck of the flask. It went down as smoothly as silk flows between the fingers.

CHAPTER 38

Over the coming days, my vision refined until it was almost as good as it had been before the fall. My close vision remained unfocused, but I could function well and felt no bother from it since I never had to thread a needle for stitching up skin anymore. Should ever I take up my role as an active healer again, I knew that limitation would be a challenge. I found I could manage both reading and writing with some head tilting and arm stretching. Colin assured me that my eyesight could improve even more over time.

Within a few days of regaining consciousness, several burley male servants carried me on a litter back up to my own bed. I ached more from my extended time in bed than from my broken bones. By the time I came out of the coma, the primary bone knitting had completed and once I began to move and shift in the bed, the pain lessened considerably. Colin commissioned the woodworkers to fashion a walking stick for me and slowly we worked at rehabilitating my leg and pelvis where the most damage was done. My shoulder ached if I over extended my right arm or carried anything with heft to it, but my pelvis was what gave me the greatest pain. Sitting for any length of time was torture.

The first time I walked it was more like assisted stumbling. I had Colin on one side of me and Sir Jory on the other, each taking the bulk of my weight as I stood, then easing me onto my feet. I nearly buckled not from the pain, which was certainly there, but from the atrophy of my muscles from being in bed for so long. Colin took care to move my legs for me and have me press my feet against the palms of his hands before I tried to walk. Still, my legs gave way and they men caught me with ease, then let me try again and again. At last, I was able to put pressure on my legs and walk, albeit wobbly and unstable and only a few steps, with my stick. Thankfully, with help from my ladies, I could dress, still in my black mourning clothes for the traditional year after Marcus's death, but in clothing beyond my shifts, which helped me to feel more alive.

Each day, I forced myself to walk further until at last, I could hobble my way down to the dining room with someone on each side of me in case I fell. Walking further than that was an impossibility and it took a very long time for me to make the trek. I felt more human with each passing day and by November's full moon, with the customary chill in the air, I could receive petitions and hear cases for a few hours in the receiving hall. By then, the court had heard no petitions since summer, so many were eager to plead their case. I begged Zelda to come assist and she begrudgingly did so, again demonstrating natural wisdom and discernment, despite her disdain for every moment she spent on the throne. By the time the last claimant was satisfied, my entire body ached and I chewed on some willow bark to ease the pain.

Sir John and Sir Charles found nothing of interest in the sparse room Father Francisco used, not that I expected them to. They did, however, find a stable boy who remembered Father Francisco arriving "the day before the Queen fell," despite the stable master's adamant assurance that the Father had not arrived until two days after. The stable master's story was suspect, but not completely disavowed. There was certainly not enough evidence to form a case of any kind that it was the priest who had pushed me down the tower stairs.

A new cask of Avalon apples arrived from my mother, reminding me that I had not used the mirror to communicate with my parents since before I went to Cameliard. The apples held little interest for me and I asked Quinton to take them to Zelda, knowing how she and Laoghaire loved them. The tree that grew tall and strong outside of the cottage would not bear fruit for another year.

After trying several different types of organ meat, I found my cravings were best satisfied with venison heart and Quinton teased me, saying that there would be no deer left in the forests at all by the time the baby was born. My body needed the nutrition of the undercooked organ meat. This I knew. Whether it was to heal myself or nourish the life growing within me, I was unsure, but the craving was strong and would not be denied.

Every movement of the baby reassured me he was still fighting to survive, despite the fall and my inadequate nutrition over the many weeks of my recovery. My belly was rounded and full by the end of November, jutting out on my body that had lost far too much weight when I lay abed. Laoghaire visited often and kept a careful eye on me, as did Ursa, Bersaba, and Lucinda, my ever-present watch dogs. Ursa adjusted my gowns to accommodate my growing belly and deepened the seams around the bodice so my clothing did not hang loose on me.

I did not feel melancholic as much as defeated with a sense that impending doom hung over me. My faith feel flat, failing to see how a broken, exhausted person like myself could rescue the Goddess worshiping people of Cornwall from tyranny. I could not even rescue myself. Days dissolved into more days, but my heart no longer knew how to be joyful or hopeful. I went through the motions of sovereignty. I slept. I ate deer hearts. The chronic pain overwhelmed me at times and was easier at other times. Colin offered me tonics for it, but I declined, knowing it was impossible to predict the effect they would have on the baby.

Just before the Winter Solstice when my belly was growing so big I could barely wobble down the stairs with my stick, Laoghaire came rushing into the main dining room as we ate the evening meal. She did not wait to be announced and fell hard against he heavy oak door, panting.

"Send the doctor," she said. "Something is wrong with Zelda."

Colin immediately stood, wiping his mouth as he did so, and rushed to the door. "I will get my bag and be right back," he said.

As we waited for him to return, Laoghaire told us that Zelda had taken a bite of one of the Avalon apples I sent to her and then collapsed onto the floor of the cottage. Nothing would revive her.

Colin returned and they rode away together, promising to keep us informed.

"Poison," I said to Sir John. "Someone poisoned the apples trying to get to me. Where is Francisco?"

"Still in Cameliard, My Queen," Sir Charles whispered to us.

"Find out for sure," I said in equally low tones. "We know he has been up to something. I want to know exactly where he is and what he is doing."

"Yes, Your Majesty," Sir John said, bowing.

"And get me a litter," I ordered. "Send for Quinton and have him put the litter between two horses. I am going to her."

"Madam, you cannot!" Sir Charles protested, but my look cut him short and he realized this was not a negotiation.

The light was dim in the sky as we left Tintagel and it was full dark when Quinton brought the litter to a stop outside the cottage door. Aching from the ride, I disembarked with his assistance and went into the cottage without knocking.

Zelda lay on the settee with her head in Ophelia's lap, her face deathly pale and her body unmoving. Colin was close by and he shook his head at me and motioned me outside.

"I cannot tell precisely what is wrong with her," he said. "She is dying. Her pulse is slowing, her breathing is so shallow I can barely detect it, and there is no sign of trauma."

"Was the apple poisoned?" I asked.

"I cannot tell," he said. "If it was, it was a poison without color, smell, or other symptoms. She has not vomited and her bowels did not release. She showed no sign of abdominal pain or seizures before she collapsed. They say she took a bite and immediately fell down unresponsive."

I pushed open the door again and looked inside. She looked so small lying there, like a child, really. Ophelia wept openly and the Faerie men gathered around her, stroking her arms and legs, her brow, trying to call her back into herself. I knew they were using their own Faerie magic to try and save her. She lay so deathly still.

How had things gone so very wrong?

Suddenly, the energy in the cottage shifted with the palpable absence of something that had been there a moment before. Ophelia began to sob even harder than before and the Faerie men stepped back from Zelda.

Just like that, she was gone. Gone from us. Her sarcastic smile. Her devil may care attitude. Her wounded spirit. Gone. Colin went to her and felt for a pulse, then crossed her hands over her chest. Tears began to flow from my own eyes and my breath came in choked sobs. Someone pushed a chair behind me and carefully lowered me into it. Try as I might, I could not stop crying.

The Faerie men left, quietly moving out the door in single file. Ophelia stroked Zelda's hair, easing the trendils behind her ear with a mother's touch. Laoghaire sniffed into her handkerchief and I sat in the chair and wept.

Marcus had trusted her to me and I had failed to keep her safe. Had I insisted she remain within castle walls, would she now be alive? One moment, she was laughing with her new family, taking a bite of the fruit she loved sent from the magical island of Avalon. The next, she lay dying and then dead. What greater or more bitter testimony was needed that Avalon was an evil place? What was more damning than the very fruit I sent to her taking her life?

When I managed to somewhat compose myself, Quinton gently asked to take me back to Tintagel and I refused. My child kicked hard in protest, no doubt wanting whatever he got from his regular infusion of deer heart and blood. I felt bereft beyond measure and grief deeper than any I had known before, even with the death of Marcus. Marcus had lived a long and full life and even though he and I did not have our chance at love and life, he died with a life well lived. Zelda had barely gotten started, had only just found love, had only just tasted life. She never had a chance to feel joy and to rule her own life without having to wrestle others for it.

When the dawn came, the Faerie men returned and wordlessly lifted her body between them and carried it outside. Curious, we followed and saw a glass coffin sitting atop a flower covered hill. They laid her inside it with the utmost of care and closed the lid, sealing it tightly on all sides. I did not have to ask about her body lying in state for all of Cornwall to see. Her family was here and this was where she would want to rest. Within castle walls, the people she loved most, the fishermen and their families, the village folk, and the Faeries, could not easily come to pay their respects. She hated being in Tintagel while she lived. I could not condemn her to that fate in death.

I looked across the garden and caught Ophelia's gaze. "We have to get word to Phillip," I said. She nodded, but did not move.

Quinton, his eyes red and brimming with unshed tears, took my arm and guided me to the litter, this time without asking permission. I did not resist and allowed him to help me inside without protest, then collapsed against the padding within.

If I was without joy before, I was now devastated beyond all measure. The feeling of my child moving inside me brought me no modicum of pleasure. Going back to Tintagel burned a hole in my aching heart and reminded me of all that Zelda hated there. All I wanted was to go to Avalon and heal after over half a year of pain and loss and to abandon this horrible place that brought me such devastation. I wanted to go home and weep in my mother's arms while my father stroked my hair. I wanted to have my baby around my priestess sisters and no longer care about whether Cornish people were safe to worship as they chose or even if someone's fence encroached on someone else's land.

We were at the edge of the forest closest to Tintagel when I felt the litter stop and opened the curtains to look out. Nine men on horseback stood around the litter and Quinton spoke with them in heated tones. I noticed that one of the men was Father Francisco and he looked more satisfied than ever I had seen him before. In fact, he looked happy, which I had certainly never seen.

After a time, two of the men grasped Quinton firmly between them and held him aside while two others dismounted and came to my litter.

My head spun as one of them said in a loud voice, "Lady Iris of Cornwall, in the name of Prince John, High King of Britain, I hereby place you under arrest on charges of regicide and of witchcraft. You are to be remanded in the tower under guard until a judicial body from the High Court arrives to hear your defense and pass judgment against you."

John? I thought. John was having me arrested?

I pulled back the curtains of the litter more fully and leaned outward, wincing at the pressure the position placed upon my right hip. One look at Francisco told me that John knew nothing of this. His name was used and not his permission or likely even his knowledge. He was as much as pawn as I was. Quinton wrestled against the hold the two knights had on him to no avail and looked at me with helpless grief spelled out all over his face.

Not bothering to reseat me into tighter custody, the arresting official climbed onto the horse Quinton had ridden while the other mounted riders flanked the litter on all sides.

One leaned into the litter and said, "If you run, I will not hesitate to kill you. Do you understand?"

I laughed, thinking that I could barely walk, much less run. I did not answer him, but instead, leaned my head against the frame of the litter. Was this just not perfect?

The murmur of voices told me that we had reached the causeway of Tintagel and would soon enter the courtyard where all would see the Queen's litter surrounded by soldiers of the High Court. As quickly as news traveled through the court, surely someone would come to speak for me.

As if on cue, I heard Sir John's voice ring out in protest, the stop suddenly after a soft thud I could not see silenced him. When the horses could go no further into the castle, the caravan stopped and I felt the litter unfastened and hoisted onto shoulders. They carried me through the castle as such with the litter shifting awkwardly between them. I dared not look out, wishing not to incur further wrath almost as much as I wished to not look into the eyes of any of my people, be they courtiers or servants.

The pain in my leg and my hip blinded me as they half-drug me up the tower stairs. I passed out twice that I know of and perhaps more. I woke up on the narrow bed in the cell that had housed my aunt for so long, looking up at Father Francisco who stood over me with his arms folded over his chest and a serene expression on his face.

"I knew I would eventually see you here again," he said, his voice placid and calm without a single flicker of the resentment I knew he felt. "This time when you go flying, My Queen, there will be a rope at your neck," he whispered to me. "God is good. God is faithful. Praise Him in all things."

"Praise Him in all things," I repeated, turning my face to the wall.

The sun rose and fell twice before I saw anyone again. At last, a guard I did not recognize came into the room without knocking. I had used the chamber pot, but he did not bother to empty it. I remembered my aunt's trick of the contents out of the window, but did not care enough to do so. The guard dropped a tray down onto the table and left. As much as I wanted to resist, I tore into the hard bread and cheese like a woman possessed. The only drink was a cloudy glass of water, but I downed it thankfully. When I ate the last bite, I remembered Aunt Ophelia waiting so long between meals and wondered if I had done wrong by eating it all. My body craved the meat I did not have and I began to shake from the adrenalin of simply eating. I had not taken food or drink since the evening meal two nights before, which had been interrupted with Laoghaire's arrival.

From the highest point in the castle, I could hear no sounds of daily activity. No voices calling out to one another as they went about their chores, no music drifting in from the conservatory where occasionally the courtiers would play instruments and sing. No gentle encouragement from my ladies as they combed my hair and eased me into my clothing. There was only the crash of waves against the shore below.

The room was cold with an icy wind coming off the sea. I found a lamp that had little oil in it and I marveled that I had never considered that my aunt had little or no light available to her other than what the sun provided. Living in the cottage must now be a luxury for her. I did not light the lamp, saving it instead for any emergency that might present in the night. So deep into the fall, the days were short and the nights very long. I spent a great deal of time in darkness.

My aunt's books remained in the room and when I did not sleep away the long, hungry hours of night, I read, holding the book an arm's length from my eyes to focus on the letters. I marked off the days on the wall. No one visited. I saw only the guard who brought food once a day and always the same: hard cheese, hard bread, and water. Like my aunt before me, I learned to ration it out to eat through the day. I longed for the pieces of cured meat she received and considered that at least Francisco had been kinder to her through her captivity than he was to me.

I thought he would come at least to gloat and to see me fallen to such a low place by his own hand. Yet he did not. I wondered with Zelda there, who ruled in our stead, who missed us, who worked on my behalf unseen. Cut off as I was from the rest of the castle and, in fact, the rest of the world, I could only speculate and become lost in my own thoughts as the days blended one into the next.

CHAPTER 39

On the twelfth day by my calculations, four men came into the room and pulled me down the stairs. It would not have taken four. I am not sure why they thought I was a warrior with the power to resist. One could easily have pulled me away from the cell since I had no will to resist.

I had not changed my clothing, brushed my hair, or bathed since my arrest, so I was, I am sure, a sight. I could no longer smell myself, which was a blessing. They took me directly into the royal ballroom where sat a dozen or so authoritative men, none of whom I recognized. Was I not even to be tried by my own people?

The room was crowded with people, many of whom I recognized and many I did not. Sir John and Sir Charles stood grimly on either side of the door, their faces lined with grief so that they looked easily twenty years older than when last I saw them. Colin was next to Sir Charles, also looking grim and sad and Father Damien stood by Sir John, looking just as bereft. I wondered what questions his lilting voice would ask today.

Even my kitchen staff was present, pushed into the room alongside the gentry of court to see what fate befell the Queen. Did they love me? Did they fear me? My sin was that in all the time I had stayed at Tintagel, I had never sought to learn how they felt about me. Zelda could tell me. If Zelda lived, she would know the pulse of every beating heart in the castle. Belatedly, I considered what a fine queen she would have been, so in tune as she was with the hearts and minds of the lesser of her subjects rather than only the greatest. If only she were here to take the Cornish crown from my head and to rule as the strong monarch she accidentally raised herself to be.

One by one, witnesses came forward to testify on behalf of the Crown. Not *my* crown, mind you, but *the* Crown from much higher up. Presumably on behalf of John, who was not present. John, in whose arms I had lain and with whom I had smiled and whispered a night away not now so long past and yet a million years before by how it felt. John, with whom I had spent one of my last peaceful and happy moments.

A scullery maid in the kitchen said she witnessed me change into the form of an old woman and go forth into the woods.

A livery stable boy claimed he saw me turn into a wolf and kill a child, ripping it apart before his terrified eyes.

Quinton was forced to admit that I had myself asked him take the apples to Zelda, that I ate the raw hearts of deer, and that I ordered he take me to the forest on multiple occasions and that he witnessed me reveling with the very bandits who robbed our caravan. The prosecutor speculated I was in league with the highwaymen in effort to malign Father Francisco and Quinton looked at me pitifully as his words turned into accusations. I smiled at him, willing him not to worry for me.

Laoghaire described how Zelda dropped to the ground like a stone after taking a bite of the apple I sent to her, but she was silenced as she attempted to speak on my behalf.

Ursa confessed to coming into the room unnoticed and seeing me talking to people in a magic mirror. When asked how I came by the talking mirror, she had to admit that it arrived with me from Avalon and belonged to my mother.

Father Francisco testified that I had bewitched King Marcus into marrying me, then making me regent, all before I murdered him on our wedding night. He swore that within the sanctified walls of Tintagel Abbey that I had blasphemed and argued the word of God.

By the time they finished, I was myself fairly certain that I had done all they said.

My right to defense was overruled out of fear that I would cast a spell upon them all and force them to release me. Had I the power to do that, I could have assured them, I would already be free and on Avalon's shores awaiting the barge.

Oh Father, I thought. *If only you, with your gift of words and of arbitration, if only you could have offered my defense. If only you and mother knew of this. Father, Mother, I am sorry. I have failed. I have failed mightily. Dear Marcus, I have become exactly what you begged me not to be through my own ego and hardheadedness. Marcus, beloved, I have dishonored you and the faith you placed in me.*

The fact that there was no deliberation confirmed what I suspected. The verdict was decided before ever I was dragged into the "courtroom" where I had danced with Marcus on our wedding day. The hearing was a mere formality, a ruse to convince the assembled that I was guilty of the sins the Church wanted to lay upon me. Admittedly, of some I was guilty, so how could I sort what fate I should and should not endure?

I was sentenced to hanging for regicide, for the willful murder of Princess Eselde of Cornwall, and I was sentenced to be burned alive at the stake for practicing Witchcraft, according to the laws of Britain. I wondered how they would manage both, but one of the judges explained to the crowd in the simplest of terms that I would be hanged until *nearly dead* and then bound to a stake and burned alive. *Nearly* dead. Would it be Colin who pronounced me *nearly dead* and fit for further execution?

Good times.

Because of my ability to shape shift, I was not allowed the luxury of the tower cell, but was instead sentenced to finish my pregnancy in one of the dungeon cells. They could not, after all, execute me while I carried inside me the future Sovereign of Cornwall. As soon as I gave birth, the sentence would be carried out and my child would become the Sovereign under the regency of Father Francisco. If my son emerged from me a monster, as they knew happened on occasion with witches, he would be immediately put to death, even before my own execution. With the physical trauma and lack of adequate nourishment I had endured during my pregnancy, I had long since lost hope that my child would be normal in any case.

During my confinement, it was ordered, I would have no visitors due to the risk of collusion and my ability to influence others with my keen sorceress powers. If I felt alone before, I was now truly and utterly alone.

As I knew they would, they took me to the very cell where we had stored Marcus's body and tossed me in with neither ceremony nor food. Unable even to care anymore, I carefully crawled up onto the wooden table where he had last lain and pressed myself against the wood still stained with his body fluids. Here, I had worked the magic to make certain my conception. Here, Colin and I cut into the precious flesh of my husband to let the clotted blood drain and stuffed him with sacred herbs and spices so he would not stink quite so much. Here, I had last touched him, his body cold and stiff as now my heart felt.

The dungeon cell was absent of any sunlight so that I could not judge night from day, leaving me with no idea of how long I was there. The same guard who was with me in the tower cell now brought me food once a day in the dungeon cell. I had no chamber pot, so I was forced to use the corner of the cell. Why should anyone clean for a condemned woman? Absently, I imagined that my urine was dense and brown from so little water to drink, but I could not see it to tell, not that it even mattered. They fed me only to keep the baby alive and barely enough for that. Certainly not the wide range of colorful, healthful foods he needed to grow.

Without Aunt Ophelia's books, and certainly not the light to read them even if I did have them, I was left only to sleep. I remember waking at some time, night or day I could not tell, wondering how they would know when I went into labor since I spent all of my time alone. After wallowing with the question for many hours, I deduced at last that they were relying on a long labor and that the guard would see and tell them. I lay in the darkness and the filth and could not even cry. Although I knew no passage of time, my body was under no such illusion and my belly continued to grow.

"Congratulations," the guard said on one visit, speaking to me for the first time since I had laid eyes on him in the tower and the only time during my confinement. He put the plate of food on the table beside me. I blinked at him, not caring about the food, but wanting to eat it for the baby's sake alone. I was no longer hungry, but my thirst was such that I thought it would never slake.

"You are no longer a murderer," he said. "Princess Eselde arrived at the castle yesterday very much alive, so those charges are now dropped."

"Zelda is alive?" I croaked, my voice harsh and raspy from lack of use. I raised up onto one elbow from where I lay on the table and looked at him in the dim light. "You saw her? You know it was truly the Princess and you know this to be true for a fact?"

"I did see her," he said. "She came to demand entry to see you, but even she cannot overturn the will of the High Court. She gave me this," he flashed a gold coin. "Pity I could not help her." His laugh was cruel and I hated him for it.

I had a sudden thought. "Does this mean I can leave?"

"Oh no," he said. "You are still a witch if not a murderer. It is just that now you will only be burned and not hanged as soon as you squeeze out that baby."

Zelda was alive? I saw her die and yet…she lived? How so? I laughed, knowing that madness had at last taken hold and I had not even needed Father Francisco's poison to get there. Or was he poisoning my food as he had with Aunt Ophelia? Who could know? Had the guard really said this to me or did I imagined it? Yet, why would Father Francisco poison me if I were already condemned to die? Helping me to lose my mind in the dungeon's darkness would be a blessing he would not afford to me.

My time was coming. I could have been in the dungeon for a week or a year. There was no way to tell. Time ceased to exist except for my growing belly and equally growing discomfort. At least in the tower cell, there was light. I could mark the days and breathe in fresh air. The bigger the baby got, the more my damaged pelvis ached. Partway through, I could no longer walk at all without excruciating pain and limited my trips to the corner as a result, holding in my waste for as long as I could stand to do so. The time came when I could no longer get myself onto the table and was forced to lie in the filth and stench of the cell floor. If the pelvis had healed poorly and could not shift properly during birth, the baby and I would both die and a part of me knew that was for the best. Better for me to die in childbirth than to die in an inferno. Better for my child to die before drawing breath than to be Francisco's pawn from his first day forward. Death was my friend and should the Death Crone come to crook Her bony finger at me and my babe, I would embrace Her with gratitude.

My back ached. My pelvis hurt. I vomited my last meal and I heard rats come to pick through the mess to find what they could salvage for themselves. Something sticky was on my leg, but I could not see well enough to tell what it was. Was I having labor pains or was this just the pain of wounds badly healed? I could not think, could not focus, but my bile rose again and my damaged ribs ached as I dry heaved into a corner where the smell of my own wastes urged me to even greater depths of retching.

The pain intensified and I breathed through it as if by rote. As if it mattered. My training took hold of me and I could do no differently, forcing my body to relax around the pain and take leave of my senses when it peaked, which was not at all that far of a trip. I imagined I was in the birthing hut with my priestess sisters rubbing my back and my legs, putting cool clothes on my forehead and the back of my neck, walking with me, stroking me, cooing encouraging words, singing to me... I smiled, feeling them as if they were there.

Something popped and warm fluid pulsed down my thighs. I laughed thinking how clean they must be now. Beautiful clean patches on my thighs where the hot urine or body fluid or whatever it was washed the filth away. In my mind, my sisters laughed with me and ran their fine fingers through my hair, which was silky clean and brushed to a high shine in my unreal world.

"Let me in," I heard a man say. "Let me in there now! Are you daft, man? Do you know who I am? By the word of God, I will have you killed if you do not open this door!"

There was a thud and a groan and a scream, then some part of me realized the scream was my own as pain again washed over me. I had given into distraction and lost my focus, allowing the pain to rip me away from my separate place where there was peace and love. In a moment of dismal clarity, I was back in the dungeon cell, feeling the intense pressure push my damaged pelvis apart in pain unfathomable. A ruckus of some kind happened across the room as carefully, deliberately, I went back to the birthing hut in my mind, back to the happy place. Priestess sisters, stroking, loving, singing… Whatever befell me in the room meant nothing. Was nothing.

"Iris," a voice forced through my vision, an unwanted intruder into my awayness. "Iris, with the next pain, I want you to push as hard as you can, do you hear me? Push!"

In my mind, Laoghaire said the words to me but she sounded like a man, which made me laugh again. It felt so good to laugh, but there was a madness to it that would trouble me if I paused to care. Before I could consider this fully, the pain came over me, taking me completely.

"Push," Loaghaire said in the man's voice. "You can do it. Push him out to me."

I pushed hard and felt a burning sensation, then a pain through my pelvis like no other, followed by a rush of relief. The pain stopped, all but a dull cramping deep in my belly. I felt at once empty and elated, nearly missing the pain that had become so much a part of me. After a few minutes, I heard the shrill cry of a baby, just as I had heard in my dreams. He lived. Whether he was anything close to normal or a beast in the Man-Laoghaire's hands, he lived and *he was furious*. I laughed again at his indignation, so like his sister.

"The afterbirth is coming, now bear down a bit, love" I said calmly, just as I had said it for so many laboring women before, then I reached my hands down to catch it. It slipped out of me with a flow of sticky fluid that could only be blood. I prayed my life would bleed away with it. Someone put the baby to my breast and it latched on immediately. I gasped at the sensation, never realizing how tightly the suckle would be on my tender nipple.

"You have a son," a voice said in my ear. The man voice, but not Laoghaire. My mind was returning as the pain became a dull memory. Laoghaire was not here. I had only imagined her being so because in my dreams, it was always she who helped me birth my baby.

"No," I said, not trying to disguise the bitterness in my voice. "Francisco has a son. And now I will die."

"Not while I am King, Lady."

I forced my eyes to adjust and saw John there, Prince John, not Sir John.

"Prince John?" I said, holding my baby as close to me as I could. "What a welcome hallucination you are, my friend. If I am to go into true madness, I am grateful you are there with me. Prince John... my friend..."

"That is King John to you, Queen Iris. I turned twenty-one on my name day three days ago. I am going to push in on your belly now as you did with Lady Priscilla to keep you from bleeding."

"Oh," I said. "That is so very kind of you. Thank you, Dear One."

He pushed hard on my abdomen and an immense cramp ran through me as I felt a rush of blood leave my body. My tortured pelvis screamed in protest to the pressure. I wanted to tell him to stop, to let my life leave as the blood flowed, but still he pushed and massaged. Between the urgent suckling at my breast and the aching in my pelvis, I could not form words in that moment.

Then I let my other friend, the darkness, take me and I knew nothing anymore.

CHAPTER 40

Someday, I thought to myself, I would tell Marcus, Little Marcus, my son, all that befell us during those dark times that surrounded his birth. Or at least most of it. Marcus, with his strong little body and his fierce sense of determination. Perfect Little Marcus with his piercing gray eyes and quick smile.

I would tell him how his Uncle John ran out of his own coronation dinner when he heard that I was about to be executed for witchcraft and rode his horse near to death to get to Tintagel to save me. I would tell him about the King's Guard who rode after him, thinking the High King had gone quite mad. He rode without rest or sleep, then used what he had learned assisting with Lady Priscilla's complicated birth on my relatively simple one. I would tell him how King John had issued an executive pardon, even though I had been rightly convicted of witchcraft, releasing me from my sentence, sparing me from death and returning my status as regent Queen until the Princess Zelda came of age. She would then hold the throne until he himself turned eighteen and could reign… if he chose to do so.

I would tell him how his brother-in-law Arthur had, before they married, thought Zelda to be dead and rushed to the cottage in the forest to grieve his beloved. I would tell him that so profound was Arthur's agony that he wrenched open her coffin and kissed her dead lips deeply and in doing so, knocked away the piece of poisoned apple that Colin had somehow missed and that had kept her in a sleep so deep it was like death as it continued to feed poison into her system. I would tell him how when the apple fell away, she gasped and woke, smiling up at her sweetheart as if she had been only napping.

I would tell him of the party the Faerie people hosted when they knew Zelda lived, a party that went on for three nights and three days with food and wine that seemed never to end. He will laugh with disbelief when I tell him that his Great-Aunt Ophelia danced like a dervish and held court of her own as the people of Cornwall came to pay their respects to their Princess who had cheated death and found life again. Some of those people of Cornwall may or may not have been on the Queen's Guard.

I would tell him about the years of peace in Cornwall where we lived until he was nearly six-years-old. I would tell him about his valiant, handsome father and the brave knights, Sir Rory, Sir Fergus, Sir John, and Sir Charles, who kept us safe after he died. I would tell him about sweet Bersaba, who would pull him onto her lap and sing to him in her strange, foreign tongue and feed him honey cakes and then wipe his sticky hands as he giggled at her false scolding.

I would tell him how he and his best friend, Gideon, nursed side-by-side on Lucinda's lap and how I had not even known I needed a wet nurse when I brought his with me from Cameliard and how I did not know that the baby whose gums I massaged so he could sleep would become my own son's lifelong companion.

There were, of course, things I would not tell him. Some things are not meant for children to hear.

I would not tell him of the terror that haunted Lucinda when she realized that the man who serially raped her and fathered her son was now in the very court where he had fled to escape him. That man was Father Francisco, who took his release through violence and dominance. He found Lucinda, despite the pains she took to avoid him after seeing him testify at my trial, and on a stormy night, such as we so rarely have in Cornwall, he raped her for the final time. She fought him off like a wildcat, but such behavior only aroused him further and so great was his passion for her by the time he entered her, that he did not notice Zelda, who flung herself onto him in such a fury that the table over which he had forced Lucinda broke in half. Zelda lifted the priest up by the back of his robe and hurled him into the wall. She pummeled him fiercely and in doing so, pushed him out the window of the servant's room and onto the flagstones of the courtyard below.

Those who saw it happened swear that at the very moment he fell, a thunderhead erupted above him and a lightning bolt stabbed into his body. Whether the priest was dead when he hit the ground, he certainly was after his God finished with him. He fell on his back and still his robe was wrenched up to display his nakedness and shame for all to see.

I would never tell him that his sister had killed his father. She had not intended to. She meant only to stop the crime he committed and yes, perhaps to punish him a bit in the process. But still, he died. How Zelda managed to come upon them at the time to save Lucinda is a mystery of the Goddess, but as she passed by the door and heard Lucinda's screams, she pushed it open and flew into action.

No charges came against Zelda and like the "deaths" of the two prisoners who once housed in Tintagel's cells, it was never spoken of again. Father Francisco would have been mortified that no one from the High Court asked after him or questioned his absence. He was simply gone. Only I, Father Damian, Sir John, and

Sir Charles knew the truth of the matter beyond those directly involved.

I would not tell him why his mother limps so and must always walk with a stick. Only that she fell down stairs and sustained an injury.

I would not tell him of the sidewise looks I suffered after I could at last leave my bed and walk through the castle, months after he was born. The weakness of starvation, dehydration, and badly healed broken bones took their toll and he was a toddler, racing through the castle corridors, before I could walk fully upright again and sit long enough to receive petitioners.

Once my body was clean and I lay in my own bed, I would gladly have forgiven anyone anything. I was little more than a skeleton with skin stretched tightly over my prominent bones. Sunlight seared my eyes for weeks after my confinement and it would be months before I could again walk in the sunlight without tremendous eye and head pain. I no longer craved raw organ meat, but my stomach was so sensitive from months of starvation that I again could only take in bone broth and a bit of bread. Bersaba fussed over me mightily and encouraged mushed food of all kinds into me. I ate to please her and not from any joy of it and slowly my strength returned.

From what I was told, while my court sat huddled in fear and mourning for me, the High King of Britain rode his horse into Tintagel and demanded admission to the dungeon cells. He emerged sometime later carrying both me and Marcus, who I clutched tightly in my arms, and took us all the way to my bedchamber. He did not leave my side until I woke and he was confident those around me would care for me as he intended.

When my senses fully returned to me weeks later, I called Sir John and Sir Charles to me and asked that they locate the man who guarded me while I was held prisoner. It was no easy task since he was employed not as a part of our court, but by the High Court, and was gone from Tintagel as soon as King John rescued me. Once I knew that, my spirit rested a bit easier. He would not return to Cornwall. I would not have to see his face again. From here forward, there was only healing and that was a very long road.

Not all the servants and courtiers believed in my innocence, but gradually, gossip turned to other things and the accusing looks faded away.

For two years, Zelda ruled in my stead through what was called a "Special Circumstances Degree" signed by me and witnessed by Sir John and Sir Charles. She took frequent trips to the cottage to confer with Ophelia and to revel with the Faerie men because, as she still insisted, one cannot *always* be Queen and, as she reminded the court often, *"These are special circumstances."*

Quinton came to me and wept like a child, devastated that his words helped sentence me to death. I assured him that with or without his testimony, my fate was sealed. He told naught but the truth and that was as it should be. Likewise, Sir John and Sir Charles begged my forgiveness for their inability to sufficiently argue for my release and I wondered how they could imagine anyone could stand against the focused power of the Church.

In fact, I pondered that same depressing thought in relation to my own quest. I had nothing left to give to it. My husband was dead, my body was broken, my mind clung to sanity by a thin thread, and my faith was desperately compromised. Had I done enough?

Sacrificed enough? What more could I possibly do to promote freedom *from* the Church as well as freedom *of* the Church within Cornwall?

When Zelda and Phillip married the summer that Gideon was three and Marcus was nearly two, Marcus toddled on one side of the bride and I walked on the other side, holding her arm to present her to her new husband in one hand and my walking stick in the other.

Father Damian ventured with us into the clearing, now decorated by Faerie hands under the direction of Ophelia. The wide-open area was now a wonderland and the priest and I gaped openly at it. So different from my own wedding in the abbey, the bride was barefoot and wore a long, thin white dress with Cornish wildflowers twined in her dark hair.

The wedding was just beginning when my gut tightened to see a throng of royal knights of the High Throne ride to the edge of the clearing, flashing back to the day of my arrest. Looking quickly to Quinton, who stood beside Phillip as his witness, I saw he had the same reaction. I let out a long sigh as from their midst rode in King John, fair and splendid on his horse. Taking quick dismount without waiting for his page to assist him, he came to me with a warm embrace and kissed me fondly on the forehead.

"It is good to see you well and safe, Iris," he smiled.

I hugged him tightly to me.

"Because of you," I said. "I can never thank you enough for having the balls to defy the church and rescue me."

"In a way, you rescued me," he replied.

He turned to Phillip who eyed him warily, looking for all the world like a mouse about to shake hands with a cat.

Before I could make introductions, John pulled a rolled scroll from inside his tunic and tapped Phillip on the shoulder with it with unwarranted familiarity. I thought Phillip would faint straight away.

"Sorry to interrupt, but I thought you might like to marry your bride without a price on your head," John handed Phillip the royal parchment. Phillip unrolled it and his eyes grew wide.

"This is a full pardon," he gasped. "Truly? I am a free man?"

"As free as any," John answered. "Will you be coming from my throne now?"

"Are you hoping I will?" Phillip laughed, half with joy and half with nervous release.

"I believe either of us can do well for the people of Britain and I can certainly see benefits to being overthrown," John said. His tone grew more serious as he added, "I will acquiesce to your claim for truly, you were done wrong and done so in my name before ever I knew."

"I have no claim now," John answered, shaking his head. "As much as you have angered the Church with your recent escapades, can you imagine the outcomes if they had to deal with me again? No, I would say you are well on your way to doing anything I would do sitting in your chair."

"We are finding our way, the Church and I," John admitted. "They did not expect me to have a mind of my own once I no longer had a regent standing between me and the law. If you do not wish my throne, will you at least act as my adviser? I have few I can trust and could use another reasonable voice by my side."

"Let me think on that," Phillip smiled. "I may have my hands full in Cornwall in a few years. I have to plan wisely for the time in between."

"The offer stands," John said, his eyes reflecting the authenticity of his words.

"Already you have pardoned two of the most hardened and wicked criminals to the High Court," Phillip said, "A witch and a treasonist who is also a highwayman. How do you justify this to your overseers? Would you truly want one of them on your council?"

John shrugged, "I justify nothing. Your experience showed that we are all expendable. Any of us may be pushed aside if our oppressors gain the proper leverage. All we can do is make wise choices while we are here and help all those we can."

The wedding party seemed unruffled that the High King interrupted the proceedings. John quietly took his place in the crowd as the ceremony proceeded. Afterward, the Faeries provided a feast, well, fit for a king, and we ate and drank well into the night in joyful celebration.

There were many hurts and fears, nightmares and dreams, of which I would not tell Marcus when he was older. It took time before the sun began to shine in my life again as I saw that not all years would be like that first horrible year of loss and devastation. I had a family of my own in Zelda, Marcus, Laoghaire, Ophelia, and Phillip. I had wise and loving support from Sir Rory, Sir Fergus, Sir John, Sir Charles, Ursa, Bersaba, Lucinda, and Colin, not to mention Father Damian who oversaw the Christian communities of Cornwall with a far more open mind and loving heart than had Father Francisco. There were many blessings, but I had many demons within myself still to wrestle.

As time passed, the joys gradually stood out more than the fears and the pain.

I told Marcus of the Goddess, sharing stories from my childhood and crafting a presence of Her in his life that would be as real as She was in mine. I had promised his father that any child we had would be raised in the Christian Church and I made certain Father Damian taught him those theologies as well. He would know both and would honor both.

I was certain Father Francisco would have my mother's mirror destroyed, but Lucinda insisted he was too frightened to go near it, much less try to break it. It and the stones were exactly where and as I left them when I returned from my confinement. I reached out to my parents now and then and while they were tremendously sympathetic to what I had endured, I felt no comfort from my interactions with them.

I struggled with my own feelings regarding the almighty quest and what they willingly sacrificed on our behalf as means to an end. In my heart, I knew they could not know what I and my sisters would encounter as we worked toward achieving the goals they set for us. My father had suffered in his own determination to keep peace between what had now become two factions: The Church and The Goddess. He had been imprisoned. He had plead for the lost causes, but he also had slowed the rampant stampede of conversion for a time. My mother could intellectualize what we experienced, but could not directly relate to our challenges. Her position as Lady of the Lake was and had always been to hold the field in Avalon, to oversee the training of competent priestesses, and to govern the island. She was born on Avalon, she grew up on Avalon, she actualized on

Avalon, and she would likely die on Avalon without knowing firsthand the persecution the rest of us faced.

The truth was, a part of me was angry, very angry, that my sisters and I had to leave our safe home in Avalon and fight wars of different kinds out here in the Britain Beyond, wars for which we were painfully and profoundly ill-prepared. We were ill-prepared because of the very thing that protected us most on Avalon: its separateness. If the elders knew the levels of challenges we would face and prepared us so little for them, they were cruel. If they did not know and sent us anyway, they were reckless. My mother represented the one side of the argument – those who were naïve to what we would encounter. My father represented the other side – those who knew and sent us anyway. The more I thought of it, the more it troubled me.

Slowly, I realized I was not angry at or estranged from the Goddess. I was angry at my parents. I was angry at the elders for throwing us into such an unbelievable and unworkable situation.

The Goddess had not done this nor had She commanded this. My parents and their council of elders chose this path for us in the hope that we could keep things as they had been before. The Goddess was not about preservation, however. She was the very essence of change and reform. When She spoke to us through nature, it was through death and rebirth, the survival of the fittest, and about adapting to the environment.

Of course, I did not believe it was right that the Church persecuted those who chose to revere The Goddess. Likewise, I did not believe that any of us were entitled to encroach upon the beliefs of another. Here in the Britain Beyond, it was easier to see clearly how things *are* rather than how we believe them to be while sitting comfortably on Avalon. Here, the reality is that we must make different choices and that danger lurks behind many corners. Not all, but many.

John said it best when he said that we are all expendable. We are all temporary. The best we can do is to make wise choices while we are here and help all the people we can, Christian or Pagan, courtier or servant.

I would not tell Marcus what a long time it took for me to stop being angry and to open my heart again. I had to forgive my parents for being magical humans, but humans, nonetheless. I had to look back and see that I *had* made a difference, despite feeling thwarted at every turn. I believe I had a hand in Zelda finding her place in her sovereignty and making peace with the Queen she could be rather than the Queen everyone expected her to be. To me, Zelda represented this entire situation. She was the struggle of progress under the mantle of tradition and exemplified the process of creating the future while honoring the past. She became Queen on her own terms, in her own fashion.

I believe John saw things differently because of my influence and that of the people around me. Aunt Ophelia was now safe, healthy, and happy and a source of tremendous support to Zelda and eventually, to John as well.

Zelda's dedication and attentiveness to the less prosperous of her subjects raised her own sensitivity to their needs, which included the spiritual. Many of them still held to the old ways and she would protect their interests in every way.

Marcus worshiped his sister, Zelda, who he was quite certain was the true queen of his world. Against the will of my advisers, she took the boy exploring in the villages and woods beyond the walls of Tintagel and I insisted that it be so. Not through my line would there ever again be a sovereign of Cornwall out of touch with the people in his kingdom. Zelda created that very change and it would persist through her reign and those who came after her.

I would tell Marcus about how ultimately, his beloved sister was crowned Queen of Cornwall, releasing me from my regency and freeing me to return home again, home to Avalon. I would tell him how the wise and kind Queen he knew so well had once been a devilish rogue who sparked fear in the heart of the servants of Tintagel, but eventually embraced the changes she could make as She Who Wears the Crown. I would tell him how the love of an outlaw soothed her broken heart and gave her purpose and direction to make certain Cornwall was ruled justly and well, far from the tyranny the Church wished to inflict upon the people of Britain. I would tell him how his sister made Cornwall safe for all its people to worship as their spirit called them to do.

I would tell him how Laoghaire took him to Avalon, along with returning my mother's treasured mirror to her, while his Uncle Phillip escorted me to Sherwood Forest to see the new lands King John gave to his people. I would tell him how those who once lived in a rough encampment, robbing from the kingdoms to seek revenge, now inhabited a vast and fertile area where they could build permanent homes and farm the fields. I would tell them how King John made every effort to put right the wrongs against each family and helped them to finance the building of homes and shops on their land to create a thriving village.

I would tell Marcus how Phillip made certain his merry men and women were settled and thriving before returning to Cornwall to be with his mother, who decided to remain in the little forest cottage at the edge of Faerie, and with the queen of his heart who became the Queen of Cornwall as well.

Ophelia no longer required the care and protection of the Faerie men, but they gladly provided it anyway. So aggressive were the Faeries in their mining efforts and so meticulous were they about honoring the terms of our agreement, that the Crown of Cornwall soon saw the Tin Crown as one of their most prosperous resources and extended my agreement with the Faerie people into perpetuity.

I would tell Marcus how I came upon my sister, Aster, broken and weeping on a mound in Sherwood Forest, far from The Wall where she began her own quest and how together, we rode home to the shores of Avalon. I would not tell him the grief she and I shared or the way our faith was shaken to the core by our experiences.

I would tell him how I came to the shores Avalon with nothing more than a horse and saddle bags, leaving behind the gowns, the jewels, and the riches behind and wearing only my priestess garb once more. We even left the horses with the farrier who first supplied them to us before we returned to the shore and found the Avalon barge waiting for us, the odd little men who propelled it across the lake ready to take us home. I returned with my little sickle knife, my robes, and no more expect for the son I sent ahead with my apprentice.

I would tell him how Aster, who of all of us most could not wait to leave the Holy Isle, stood straight and tall and summoned the barge to Avalon for us, then parted the mists so that we could return home. I could not have done it. I did not have it in me. I was too world weary and too confused about my own faith and my place in the process of the Goddess. I still had to heal and find my peace with all that had happened.

Aster, however, was filled with the power of the Goddess as she worked those magical acts and parted the way for us to return home to Avalon rather than continuing to the shores of Glastonbury. Glastonbury... that place to where Laoghaire and I had been erroneously credited when first we entered the royal dining room at Tintagel.

Someday, I would tell him all of this, but as Aster lowered her arms and the mists rolled away, our home came into view and all I could think of was how very glad I was to be home and to share the magic of Avalon with my beautiful, magical boy. A small ember still burned in my spirit for the routines and rituals of the Goddess... of home. Soon, I would catch babies again, heal illness and injury, and hobble my way up the Tor to celebrate the changing moons and seasons.

One day, Marcus would be King, if he chose to be, but for now, he was my son and someday, I would tell him all those things. Perhaps he would even take up the old practice of having a kingmaking on Dragon Island to cement his balance of the two faiths of his parents. At least he knew well and good that whatever masked maiden came to him as the Virgin Huntress would not be his sister. Progress. The Goddess embraces the death of the old and the birth of the new. She *is* the death of the old and the birth of the new.

There was so much to tell him one day.

But today was not that day.

THE END

About the Author

Katrina Rasbold has provided insightful guidance to countless individuals over the past three decades through both her life path consultations and her informative classes and workshops. She has worked with teachers all over the world, including three years of training in England and two years of practice in the Marianas Islands. Katrina is a professional life coach who holds a Ph.D in Religion. She is married and she and her husband, Eric, co-authored the Bio-Universal Energy book series.

In addition to writing, lecturing, and life coaching, Katrina works as a professional conjure woman and owns Two Sisters Botánica in Roseville, California.

Katrina lives in the forested Eden of the High Sierras of Northern California near Tahoe. Katrina is a hermit who lives inside her beautiful mountain home, pecking away at her computer keyboard. She frequently teaches workshops on different aspects of Bio-Universal energy usage in the El Dorado, Sacramento, and Placer counties of California. She has six children, one teenager at home and five others who are grown up and out there loose in the world.

Other Books by the Author (Available on Amazon.com)

How to Be a Queen

Where the Daffodils Grow

The Daughters of Avalon

Rose of Avalon

Aster of Avalon

The Dance Card

Energy Magic

Energy Magic Compleat

Beyond Energy Magic

CUSP

Properties of Magical Energy

Reuniting the Two Selves

Magical Ethics and Protection

The Art of Ritual Crafting

The Magic and Making of Candles and Soaps

Days and Times of Power

Crossing the Third Threshold

How to Create a Magical Working Group

An Insider's Guide to the General Hospital Fan Club Weekend

Leaving Kentucky in the Broad Daylight

The Real Magic

Get Your Book Published

Goddess in the Kitchen: The Magic and Making of Food

Spiritual Childbirth

Tarot for Real People

Weather or Not

Weather Witchery

Printed in Great Britain
by Amazon